GIANT DAYS

VOLUME ELEVEN

BOOM! BOX

BOOM! BOX

GIANT DAYS Volume Eleven, October 2019. Published by BOOM! Box, a division of Boom Entertainment, Inc. Giant Days is ™ & © 2019 John Allison. Originally published in single magazine form as GIANT DAYS No. 41-44. and GIANT DAYS: WHERE WOMEN GLOW AND MEN PLUNDER No. 1. ™ & © 2018 John Allison. All rights reserved. BOOM! Box™ and the BOOM! Box logo are trademarks of Boom Entertainment, Inc., registered in various countries and categories. All characters, events, and institutions depicted herein are fictional. Any similarity between any of the names, characters, persons, events, and/or institutions in this publication to actual names, characters, and persons, whether living or dead, events, and/or institutions is unintended and purely coincidental. BOOM! Box does not read or accept unsolicited submissions of ideas, stories, or artwork.

BOOM! Studios, 5670 Wilshire Boulevard, Suite 400, Los Angeles, CA 90036-5679. Printed in China. First Printing.

ISBN: 978-1-68415-437-1, eISBN: 978-1-64144-554-2

GIANT DAYS

CREATED + WRITTEN BY
JOHN ALLISON

ART BY
MAX SARIN

"WHERE WOMEN GLOW AND MEN PLUNDER" ART AND STORY BY
JOHN ALLISON

COLORS BY
WHITNEY COGAR

LETTERS BY
JIM CAMPBELL

COVER BY
MAX SARIN

SERIES DESIGNER
GRACE PARK

COLLECTION DESIGNER
MARIE KRUPINA

EDITOR
SOPHIE PHILIPS-ROBERTS

SENIOR EDITOR
SHANNON WATTERS

CHAPTER
FORTY-ONE

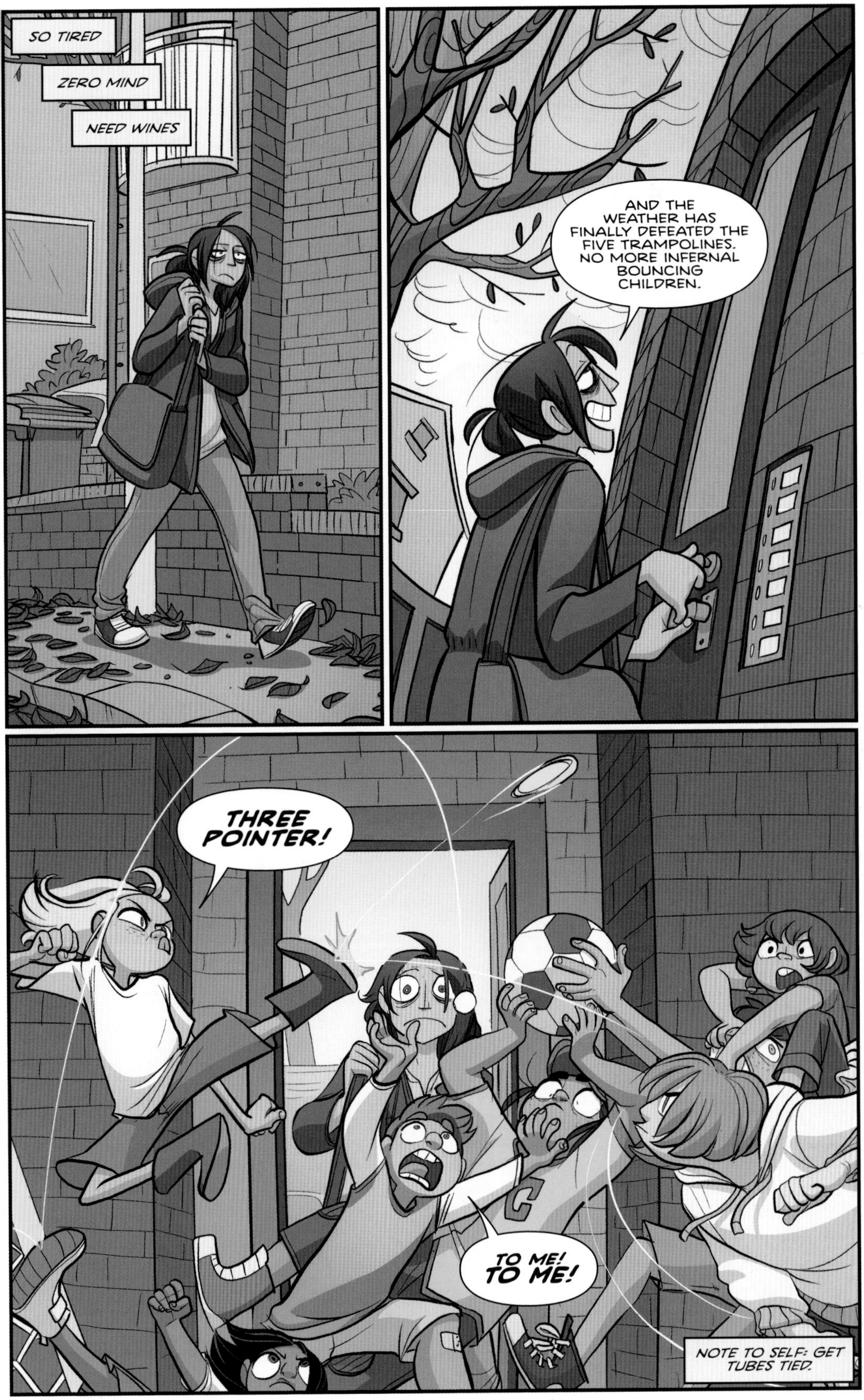
SO TIRED
ZERO MIND
NEED WINES
AND THE WEATHER HAS FINALLY DEFEATED THE FIVE TRAMPOLINES. NO MORE INFERNAL BOUNCING CHILDREN.
THREE POINTER!
TO ME! TO ME!
NOTE TO SELF: GET TUBES TIED.

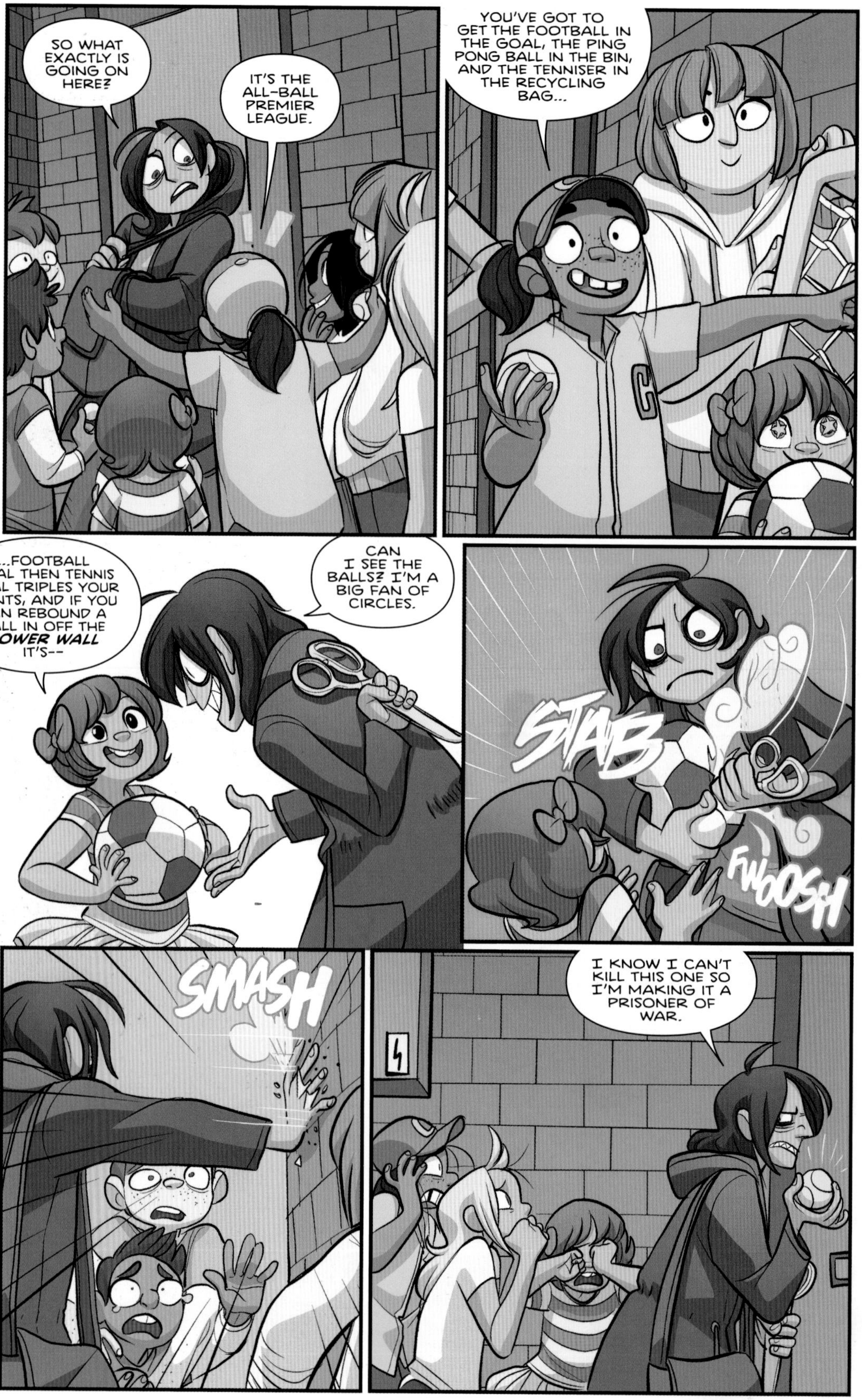
SO WHAT EXACTLY IS GOING ON HERE?
IT'S THE ALL-BALL PREMIER LEAGUE.
YOU'VE GOT TO GET THE FOOTBALL IN THE GOAL, THE PING PONG BALL IN THE BIN, AND THE TENNISER IN THE RECYCLING BAG...
...FOOTBALL GOAL THEN TENNIS GOAL TRIPLES YOUR POINTS, AND IF YOU CAN REBOUND A BALL IN OFF THE POWER WALL IT'S--
CAN I SEE THE BALLS? I'M A BIG FAN OF CIRCLES.
STAB
FWOOSH
SMASH
I KNOW I CAN'T KILL THIS ONE SO I'M MAKING IT A PRISONER OF WAR.

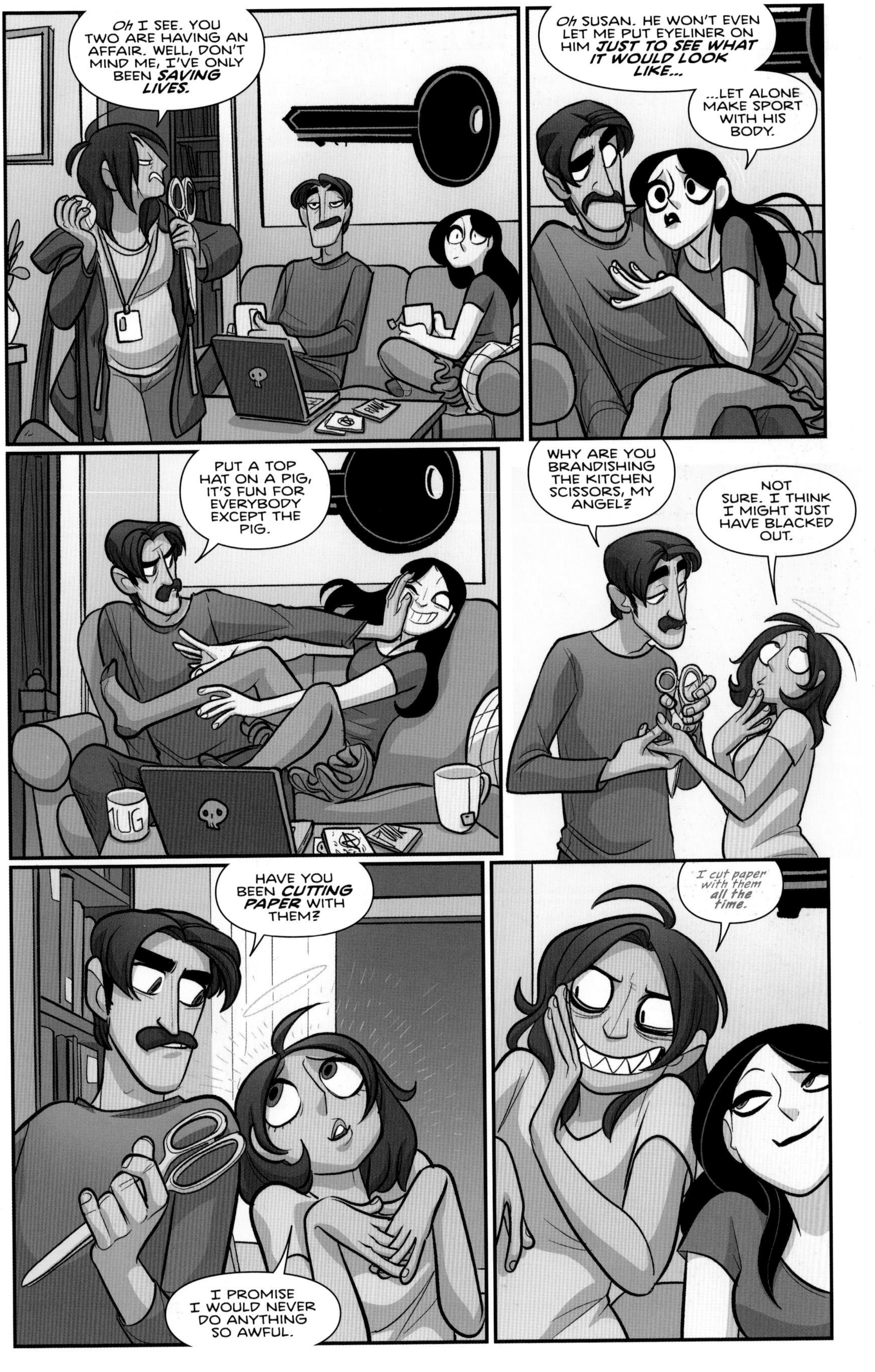
Oh I SEE. YOU TWO ARE HAVING AN AFFAIR. WELL, DON'T MIND ME, I'VE ONLY BEEN ***SAVING LIVES.***
Oh SUSAN. HE WON'T EVEN LET ME PUT EYELINER ON HIM ***JUST TO SEE WHAT IT WOULD LOOK LIKE...***
...LET ALONE MAKE SPORT WITH HIS BODY.
PUT A TOP HAT ON A PIG, IT'S FUN FOR EVERYBODY EXCEPT THE PIG.
WHY ARE YOU BRANDISHING THE KITCHEN SCISSORS, MY ANGEL?
NOT SURE. I THINK I MIGHT JUST HAVE BLACKED OUT.
HAVE YOU BEEN ***CUTTING PAPER*** WITH THEM?
I PROMISE I WOULD NEVER DO ANYTHING SO AWFUL.
*I cut paper with them **all the time.***

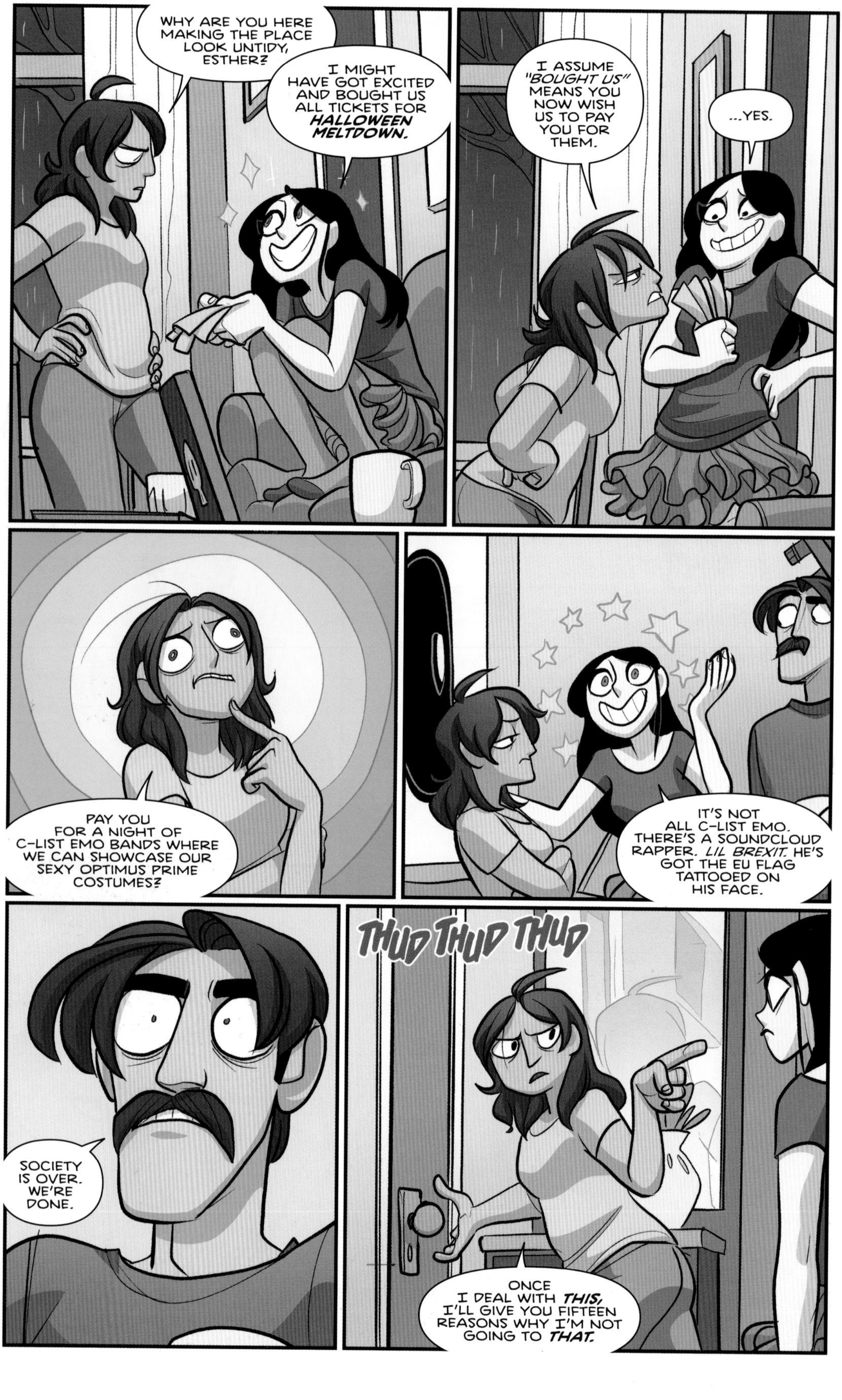
WHY ARE YOU HERE MAKING THE PLACE LOOK UNTIDY, ESTHER?
I MIGHT HAVE GOT EXCITED AND BOUGHT US ALL TICKETS FOR *HALLOWEEN MELTDOWN.*
I ASSUME *"BOUGHT US"* MEANS YOU NOW WISH US TO PAY YOU FOR THEM.
...YES.
PAY YOU FOR A NIGHT OF C-LIST EMO BANDS WHERE WE CAN SHOWCASE OUR SEXY OPTIMUS PRIME COSTUMES?
IT'S NOT ALL C-LIST EMO. THERE'S A SOUNDCLOUD RAPPER. *LIL BREXIT.* HE'S GOT THE EU FLAG TATTOOED ON HIS FACE.
SOCIETY IS OVER. WE'RE DONE.
THUD THUD THUD
ONCE I DEAL WITH *THIS,* I'LL GIVE YOU FIFTEEN REASONS WHY I'M NOT GOING TO *THAT.*

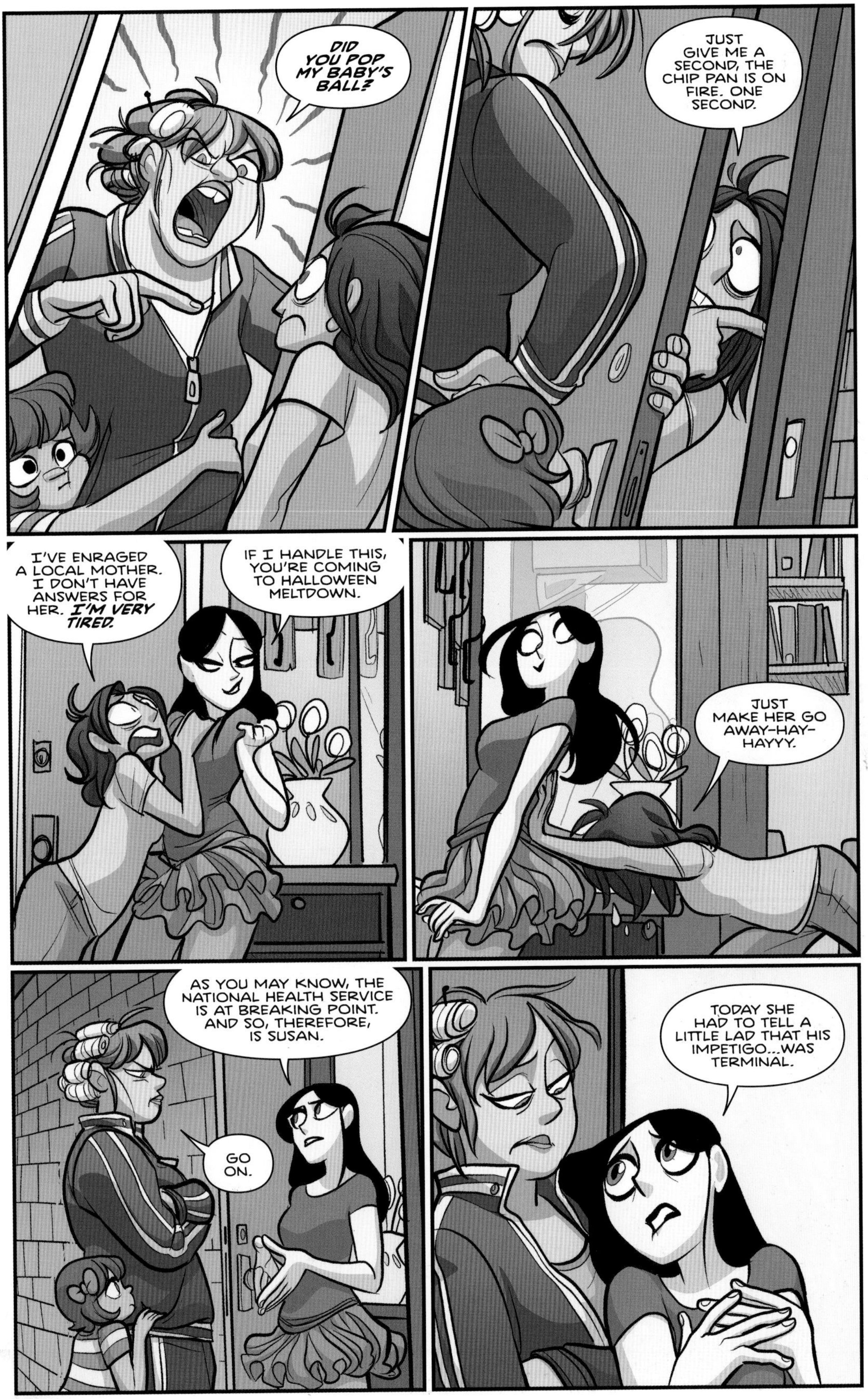
DID YOU POP MY BABY'S BALL?
JUST GIVE ME A SECOND, THE CHIP PAN IS ON FIRE. ONE SECOND.
I'VE ENRAGED A LOCAL MOTHER. I DON'T HAVE ANSWERS FOR HER. *I'M VERY TIRED.*
IF I HANDLE THIS, YOU'RE COMING TO HALLOWEEN MELTDOWN.
JUST MAKE HER GO AWAY-HAY-HAYYY.
AS YOU MAY KNOW, THE NATIONAL HEALTH SERVICE IS AT BREAKING POINT. AND SO, THEREFORE, IS SUSAN.
GO ON.
TODAY SHE HAD TO TELL A LITTLE LAD THAT HIS IMPETIGO...WAS TERMINAL.

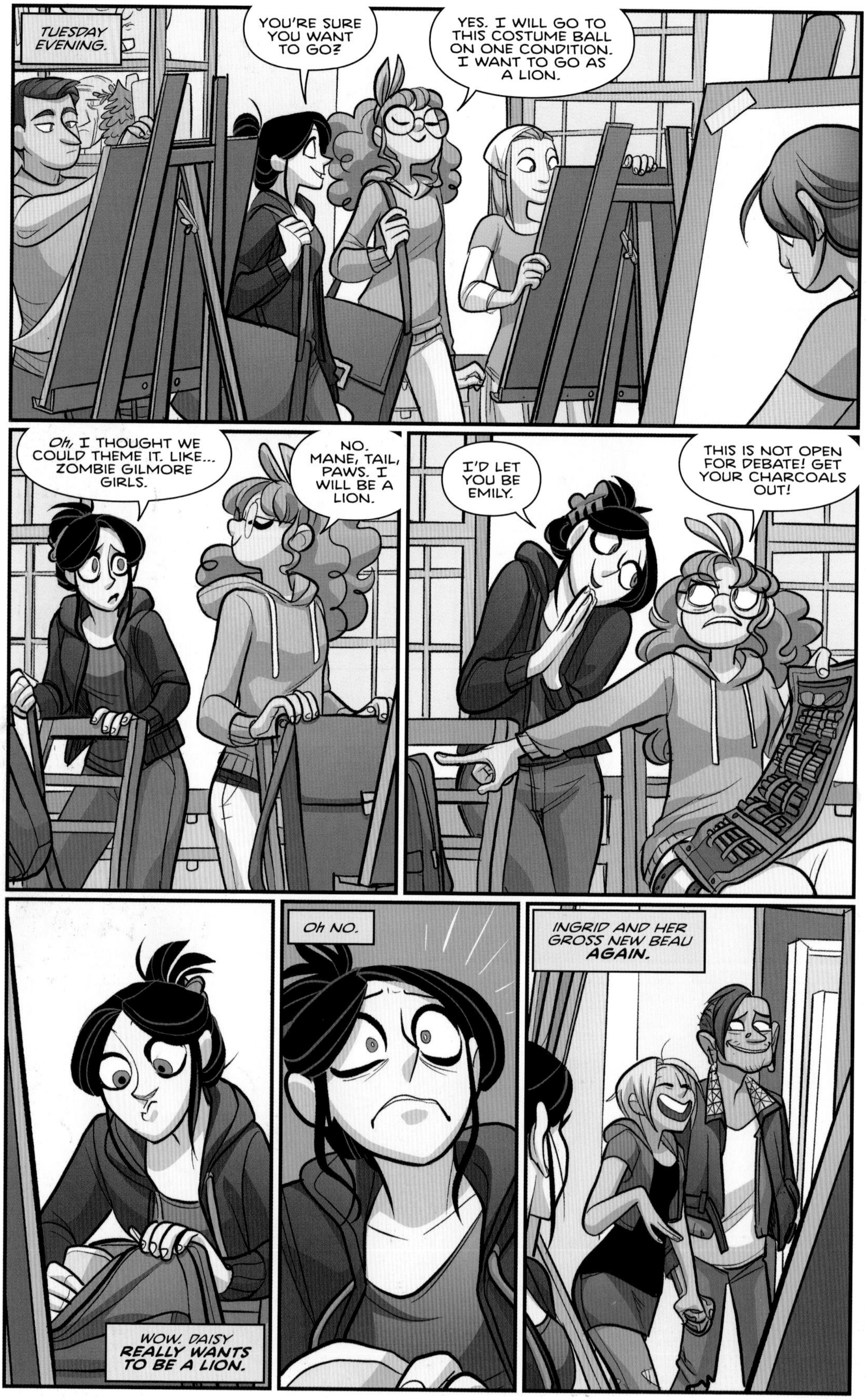
TUESDAY EVENING.
YOU'RE SURE YOU WANT TO GO?
YES. I WILL GO TO THIS COSTUME BALL ON ONE CONDITION. I WANT TO GO AS A LION.
Oh, I THOUGHT WE COULD THEME IT. LIKE... ZOMBIE GILMORE GIRLS.
NO. MANE, TAIL, PAWS. I WILL BE A LION.
I'D LET YOU BE EMILY.
THIS IS NOT OPEN FOR DEBATE! GET YOUR CHARCOALS OUT!
WOW. DAISY REALLY WANTS TO BE A LION.
Oh NO.
INGRID AND HER GROSS NEW BEAU AGAIN.

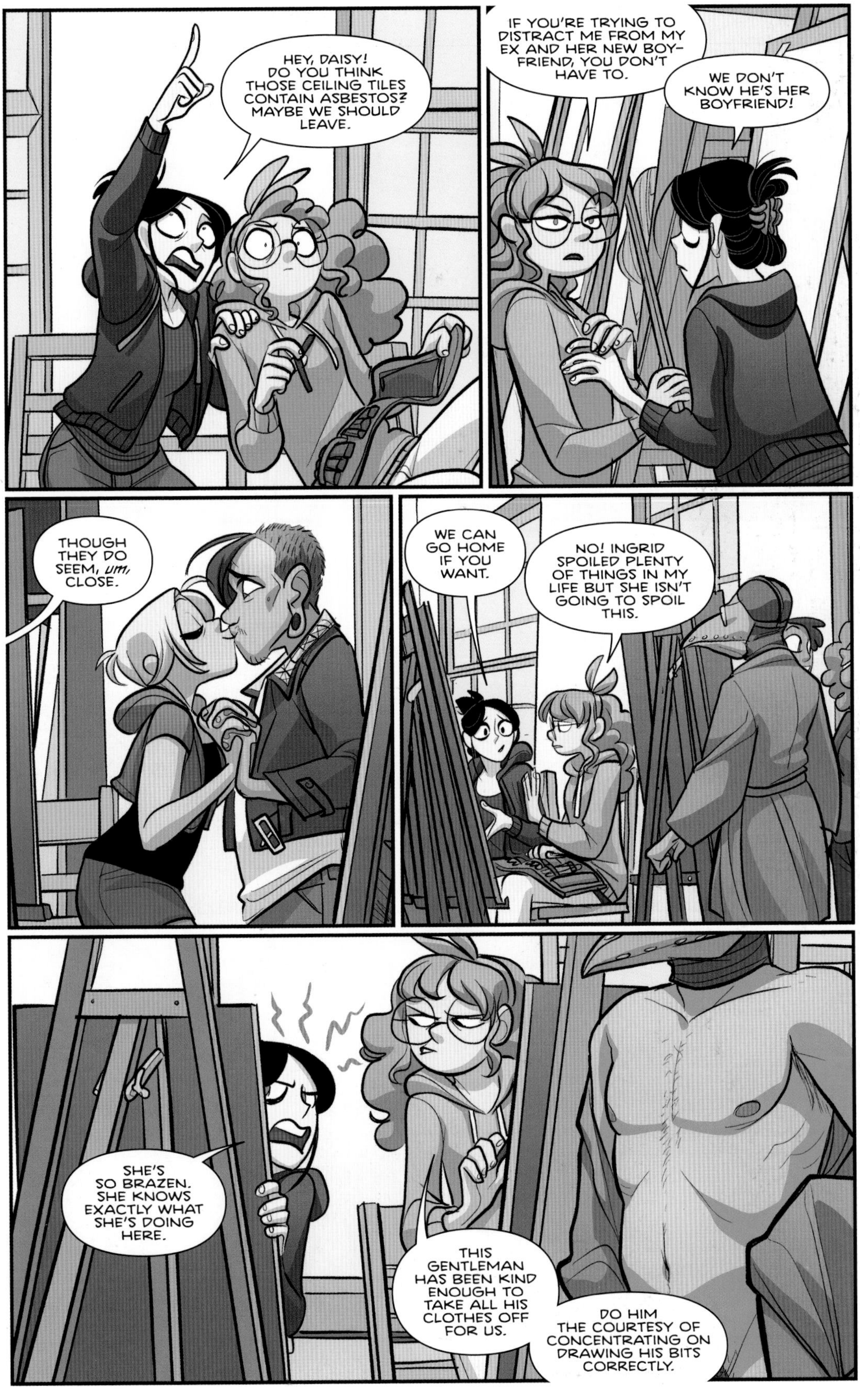
HEY, DAISY! DO YOU THINK THOSE CEILING TILES CONTAIN ASBESTOS? MAYBE WE SHOULD LEAVE.
IF YOU'RE TRYING TO DISTRACT ME FROM MY EX AND HER NEW BOY-FRIEND, YOU DON'T HAVE TO.
WE DON'T KNOW HE'S HER BOYFRIEND!
THOUGH THEY DO SEEM, *UM*, CLOSE.
WE CAN GO HOME IF YOU WANT.
NO! INGRID SPOILED PLENTY OF THINGS IN MY LIFE BUT SHE ISN'T GOING TO SPOIL THIS.
SHE'S SO BRAZEN. SHE KNOWS EXACTLY WHAT SHE'S DOING HERE.
THIS GENTLEMAN HAS BEEN KIND ENOUGH TO TAKE ALL HIS CLOTHES OFF FOR US.
DO HIM THE COURTESY OF CONCENTRATING ON DRAWING HIS BITS CORRECTLY.

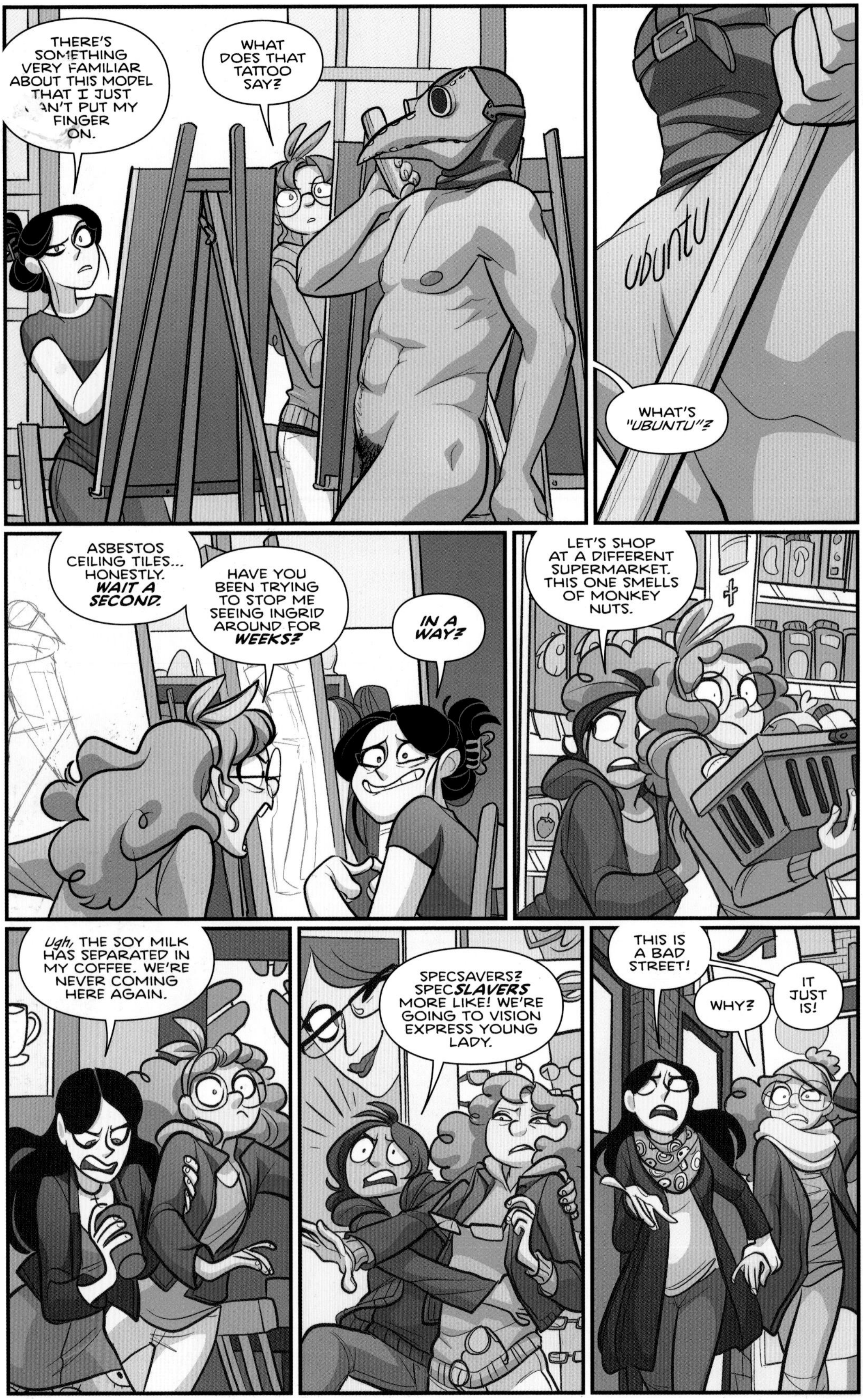
THERE'S SOMETHING VERY FAMILIAR ABOUT THIS MODEL THAT I JUST CAN'T PUT MY FINGER ON.
WHAT DOES THAT TATTOO SAY?
UBUNTU
WHAT'S "UBUNTU"?
ASBESTOS CEILING TILES... HONESTLY. WAIT A SECOND.
HAVE YOU BEEN TRYING TO STOP ME SEEING INGRID AROUND FOR WEEKS?
IN A WAY?
LET'S SHOP AT A DIFFERENT SUPERMARKET. THIS ONE SMELLS OF MONKEY NUTS.
Ugh, THE SOY MILK HAS SEPARATED IN MY COFFEE. WE'RE NEVER COMING HERE AGAIN.
SPECSAVERS? SPECSLAVERS MORE LIKE! WE'RE GOING TO VISION EXPRESS YOUNG LADY.
THIS IS A BAD STREET!
WHY?
IT JUST IS!

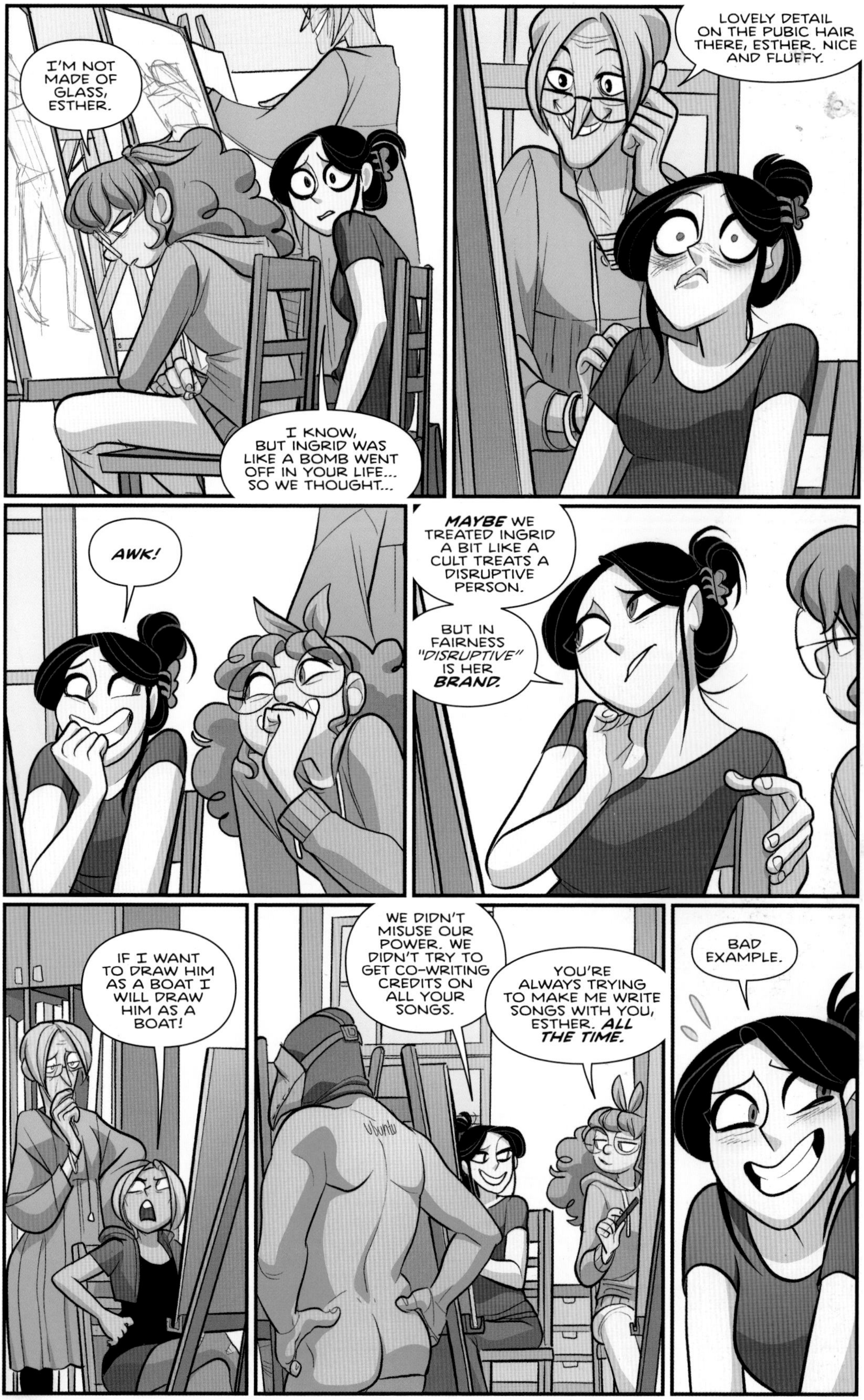
I'M NOT MADE OF GLASS, ESTHER.
I KNOW, BUT INGRID WAS LIKE A BOMB WENT OFF IN YOUR LIFE... SO WE THOUGHT...
LOVELY DETAIL ON THE PUBIC HAIR THERE, ESTHER. NICE AND FLUFFY.
AWK!
MAYBE WE TREATED INGRID A BIT LIKE A CULT TREATS A DISRUPTIVE PERSON.
BUT IN FAIRNESS "DISRUPTIVE" IS HER BRAND.
IF I WANT TO DRAW HIM AS A BOAT I WILL DRAW HIM AS A BOAT!
WE DIDN'T MISUSE OUR POWER. WE DIDN'T TRY TO GET CO-WRITING CREDITS ON ALL YOUR SONGS.
YOU'RE ALWAYS TRYING TO MAKE ME WRITE SONGS WITH YOU, ESTHER. ALL THE TIME.
BAD EXAMPLE.

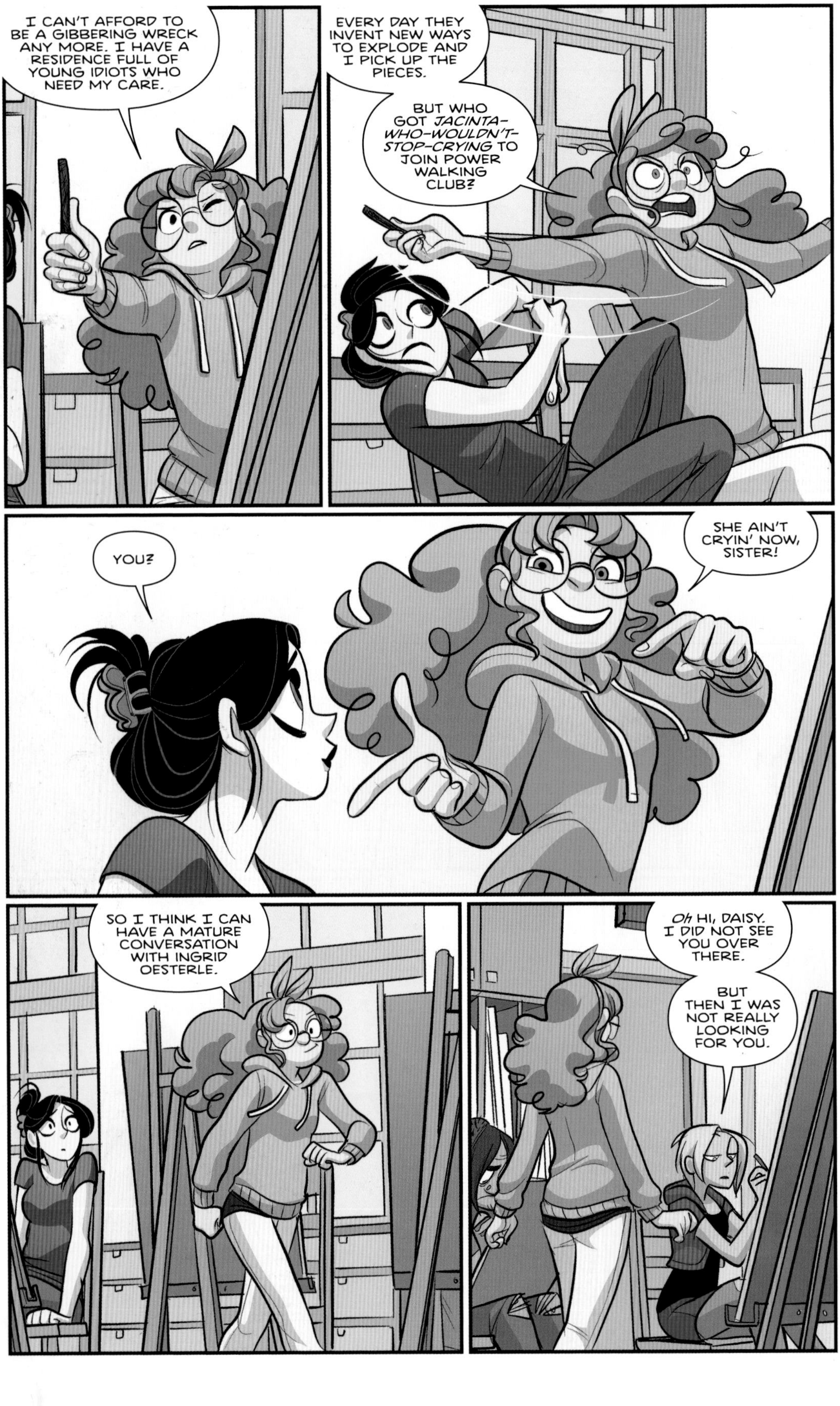
I CAN'T AFFORD TO BE A GIBBERING WRECK ANY MORE. I HAVE A RESIDENCE FULL OF YOUNG IDIOTS WHO NEED MY CARE.
EVERY DAY THEY INVENT NEW WAYS TO EXPLODE AND I PICK UP THE PIECES.
BUT WHO GOT *JACINTA-WHO-WOULDN'T-STOP-CRYING* TO JOIN POWER WALKING CLUB?
YOU?
SHE AIN'T CRYIN' NOW, SISTER!
SO I THINK I CAN HAVE A MATURE CONVERSATION WITH INGRID OESTERLE.
Oh HI, DAISY. I DID NOT SEE YOU OVER THERE.
BUT THEN I WAS NOT REALLY LOOKING FOR YOU.

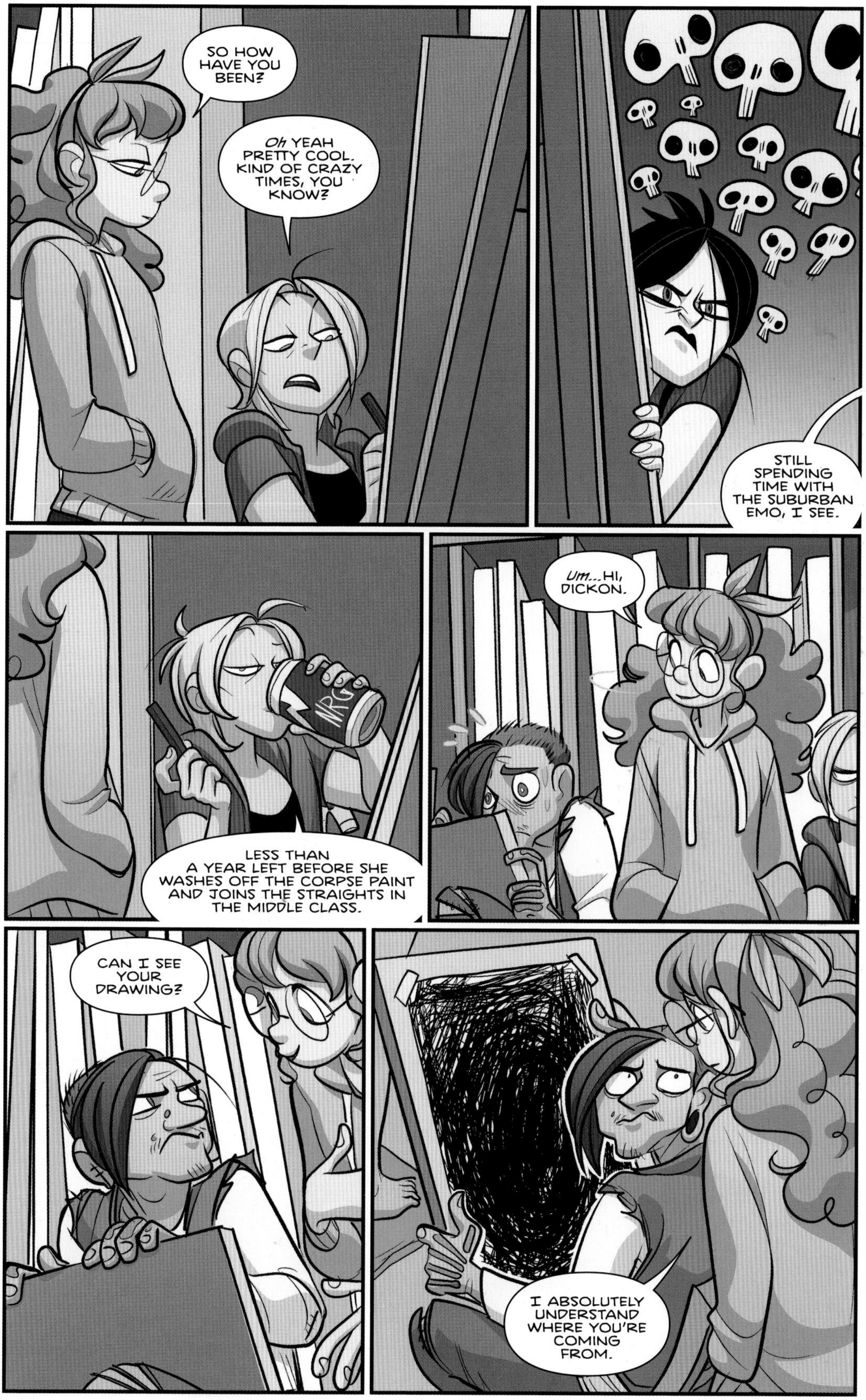
SO HOW HAVE YOU BEEN?
Oh YEAH PRETTY COOL. KIND OF CRAZY TIMES, YOU KNOW?
STILL SPENDING TIME WITH THE SUBURBAN EMO, I SEE.
NRG
LESS THAN A YEAR LEFT BEFORE SHE WASHES OFF THE CORPSE PAINT AND JOINS THE STRAIGHTS IN THE MIDDLE CLASS.
Um... HI, DICKON.
CAN I SEE YOUR DRAWING?
I ABSOLUTELY UNDERSTAND WHERE YOU'RE COMING FROM.

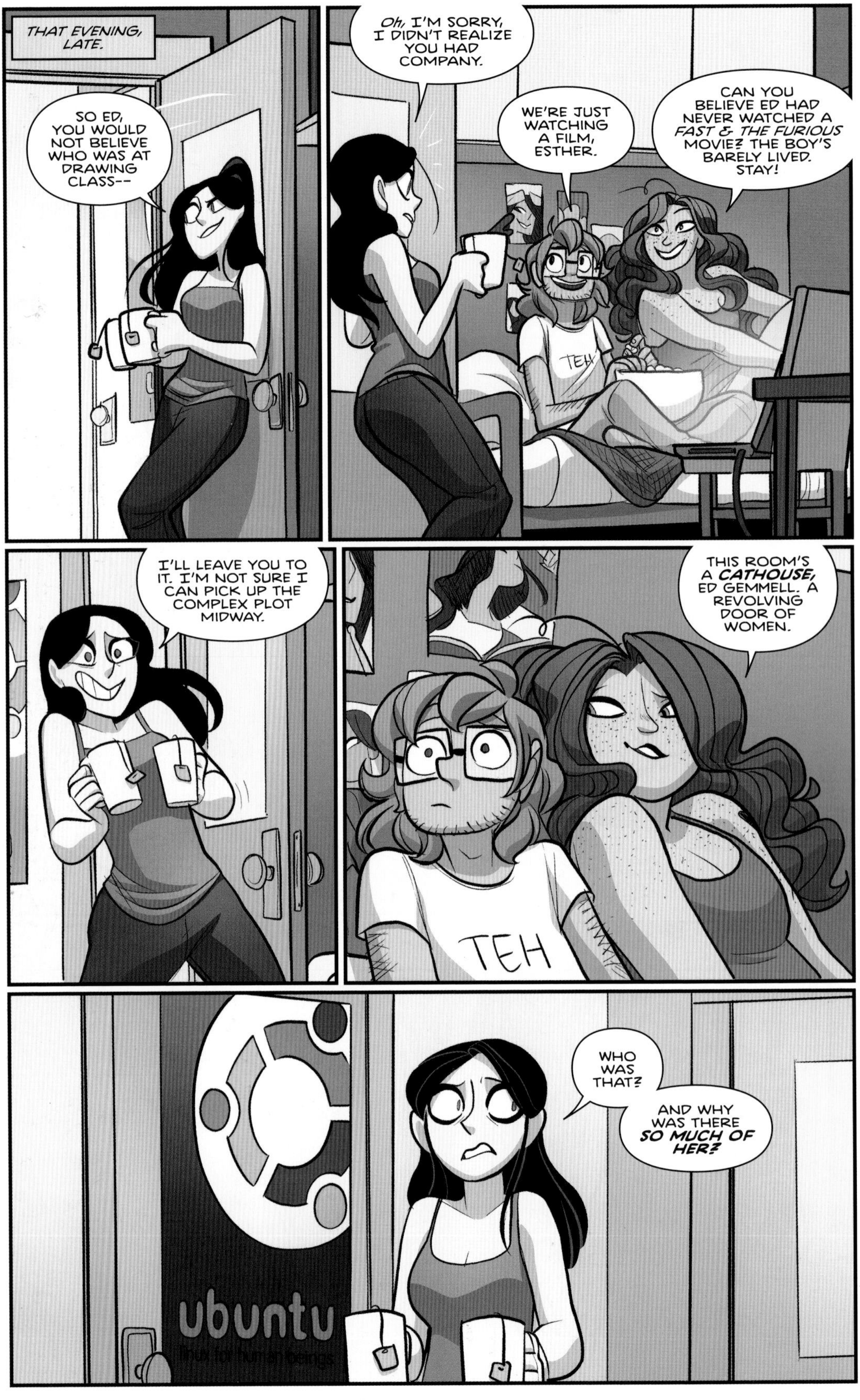
THAT EVENING, LATE.
SO ED, YOU WOULD NOT BELIEVE WHO WAS AT DRAWING CLASS--
Oh, I'M SORRY, I DIDN'T REALIZE YOU HAD COMPANY.
WE'RE JUST WATCHING A FILM, ESTHER.
CAN YOU BELIEVE ED HAD NEVER WATCHED A *FAST & THE FURIOUS* MOVIE? THE BOY'S BARELY LIVED. STAY!
TEH
I'LL LEAVE YOU TO IT. I'M NOT SURE I CAN PICK UP THE COMPLEX PLOT MIDWAY.
THIS ROOM'S A ***CATHOUSE,*** ED GEMMELL. A REVOLVING DOOR OF WOMEN.
TEH
WHO WAS THAT?
AND WHY WAS THERE ***SO MUCH OF HER?***
ubuntu
linux for human beings

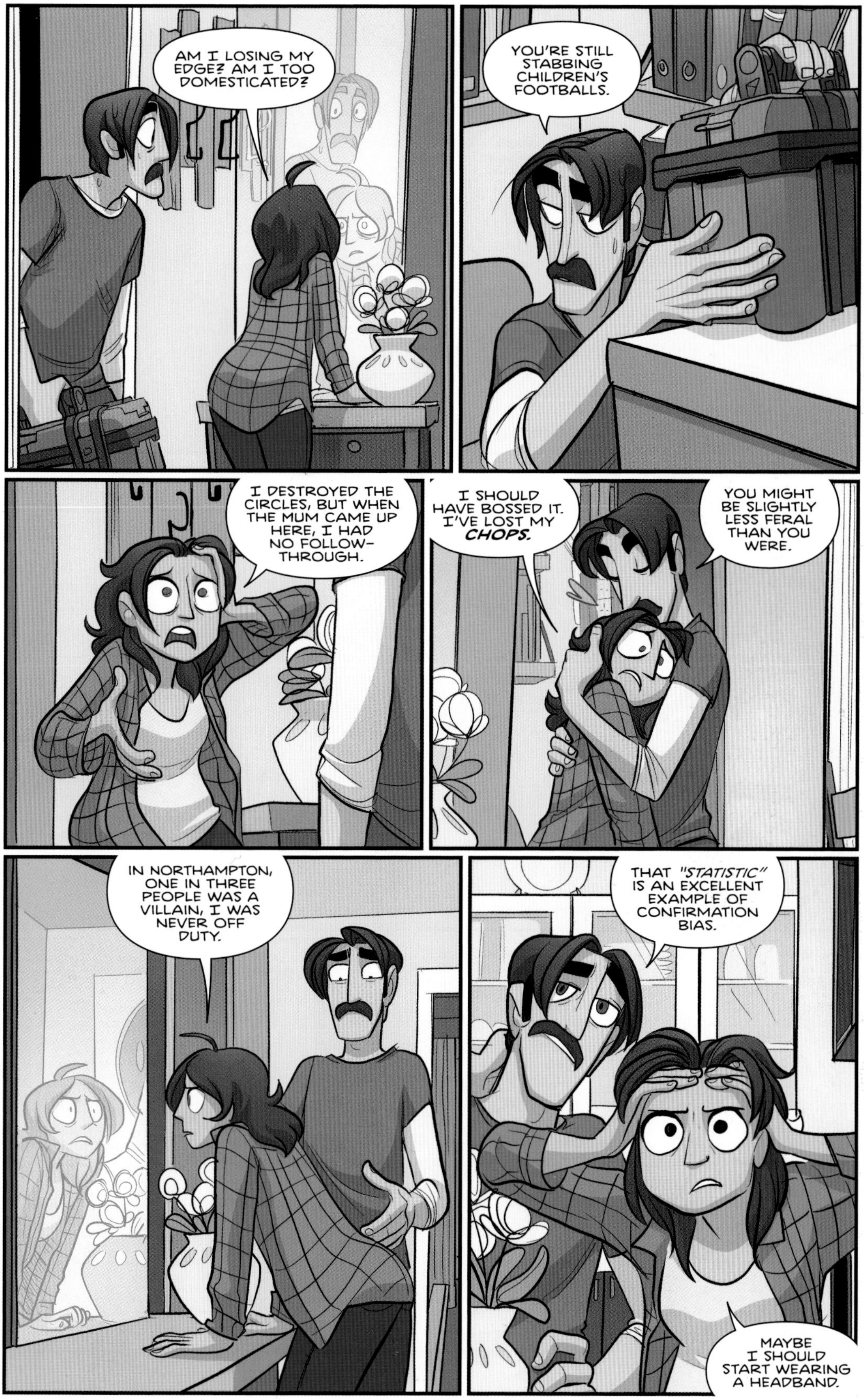
AM I LOSING MY EDGE? AM I TOO DOMESTICATED?
YOU'RE STILL STABBING CHILDREN'S FOOTBALLS.
I DESTROYED THE CIRCLES, BUT WHEN THE MUM CAME UP HERE, I HAD NO FOLLOW-THROUGH.
I SHOULD HAVE BOSSED IT. I'VE LOST MY *CHOPS.*
YOU MIGHT BE SLIGHTLY LESS FERAL THAN YOU WERE.
IN NORTHAMPTON, ONE IN THREE PEOPLE WAS A VILLAIN, I WAS NEVER OFF DUTY.
THAT *"STATISTIC"* IS AN EXCELLENT EXAMPLE OF CONFIRMATION BIAS.
MAYBE I SHOULD START WEARING A HEADBAND.

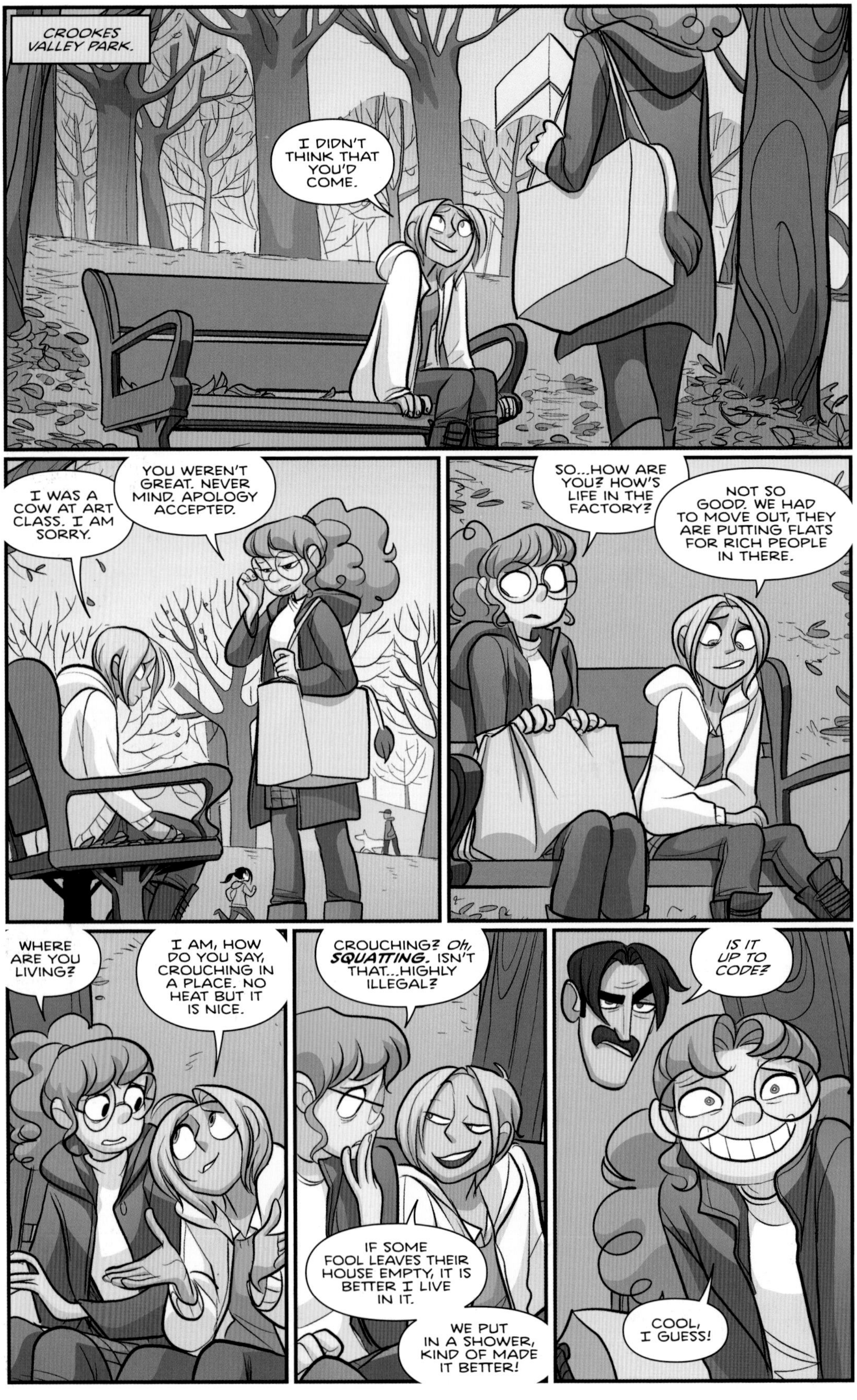
CROOKES VALLEY PARK.
I DIDN'T THINK THAT YOU'D COME.
I WAS A COW AT ART CLASS. I AM SORRY.
YOU WEREN'T GREAT. NEVER MIND. APOLOGY ACCEPTED.
SO...HOW ARE YOU? HOW'S LIFE IN THE FACTORY?
NOT SO GOOD. WE HAD TO MOVE OUT, THEY ARE PUTTING FLATS FOR RICH PEOPLE IN THERE.
WHERE ARE YOU LIVING?
I AM, HOW DO YOU SAY, CROUCHING IN A PLACE. NO HEAT BUT IT IS NICE.
CROUCHING? Oh, SQUATTING. ISN'T THAT...HIGHLY ILLEGAL?
IF SOME FOOL LEAVES THEIR HOUSE EMPTY, IT IS BETTER I LIVE IN IT.
WE PUT IN A SHOWER, KIND OF MADE IT BETTER!
IS IT UP TO CODE?
COOL, I GUESS!

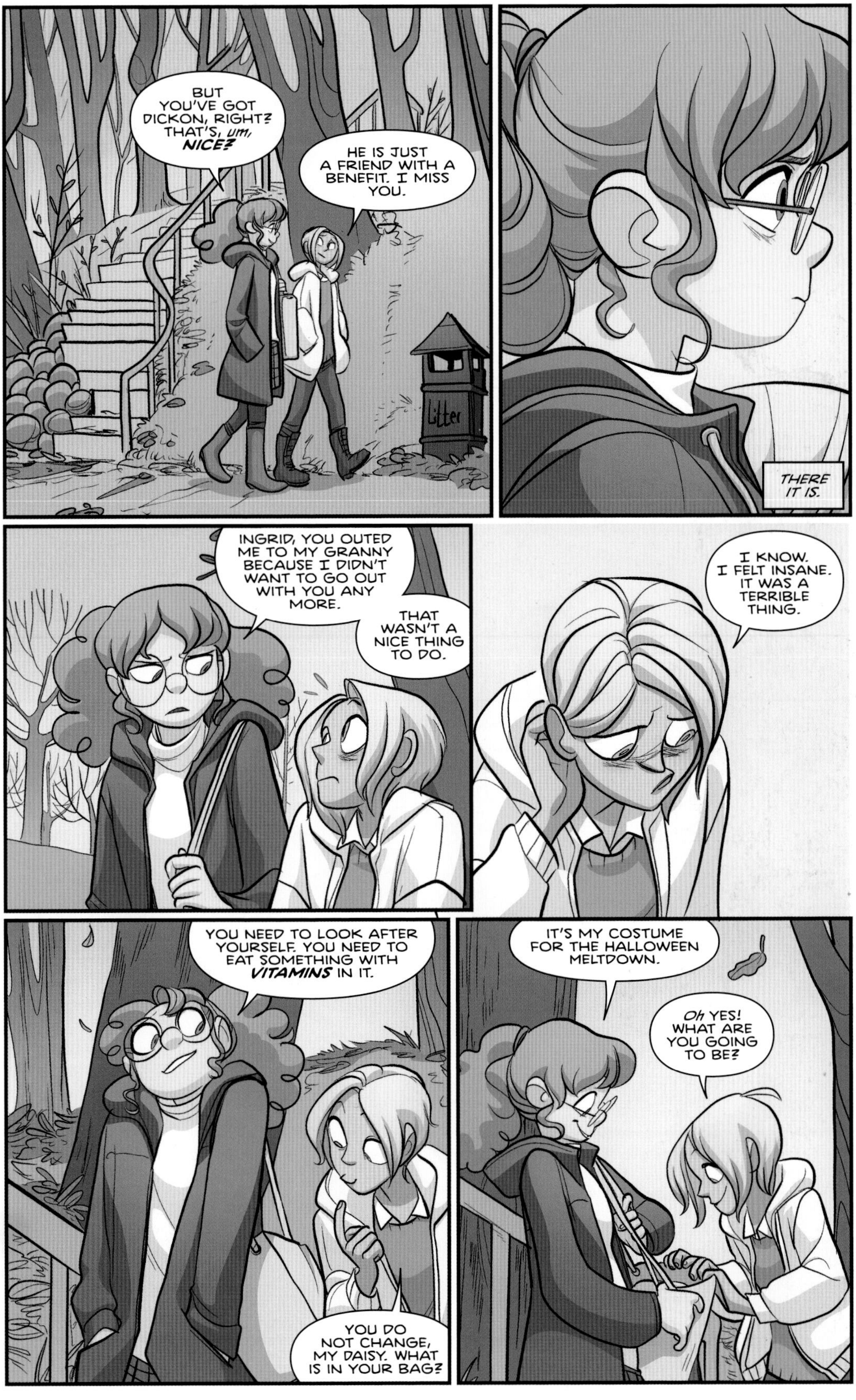

BUT YOU'VE GOT DICKON, RIGHT? THAT'S, *um,* ***NICE?***
HE IS JUST A FRIEND WITH A BENEFIT. I MISS YOU.
Litter
THERE IT IS.
INGRID, YOU OUTED ME TO MY GRANNY BECAUSE I DIDN'T WANT TO GO OUT WITH YOU ANY MORE.
THAT WASN'T A NICE THING TO DO.
I KNOW. I FELT INSANE. IT WAS A TERRIBLE THING.
YOU NEED TO LOOK AFTER YOURSELF. YOU NEED TO EAT SOMETHING WITH ***VITAMINS*** IN IT.
YOU DO NOT CHANGE, MY DAISY. WHAT IS IN YOUR BAG?
IT'S MY COSTUME FOR THE HALLOWEEN MELTDOWN.
Oh YES! WHAT ARE YOU GOING TO BE?

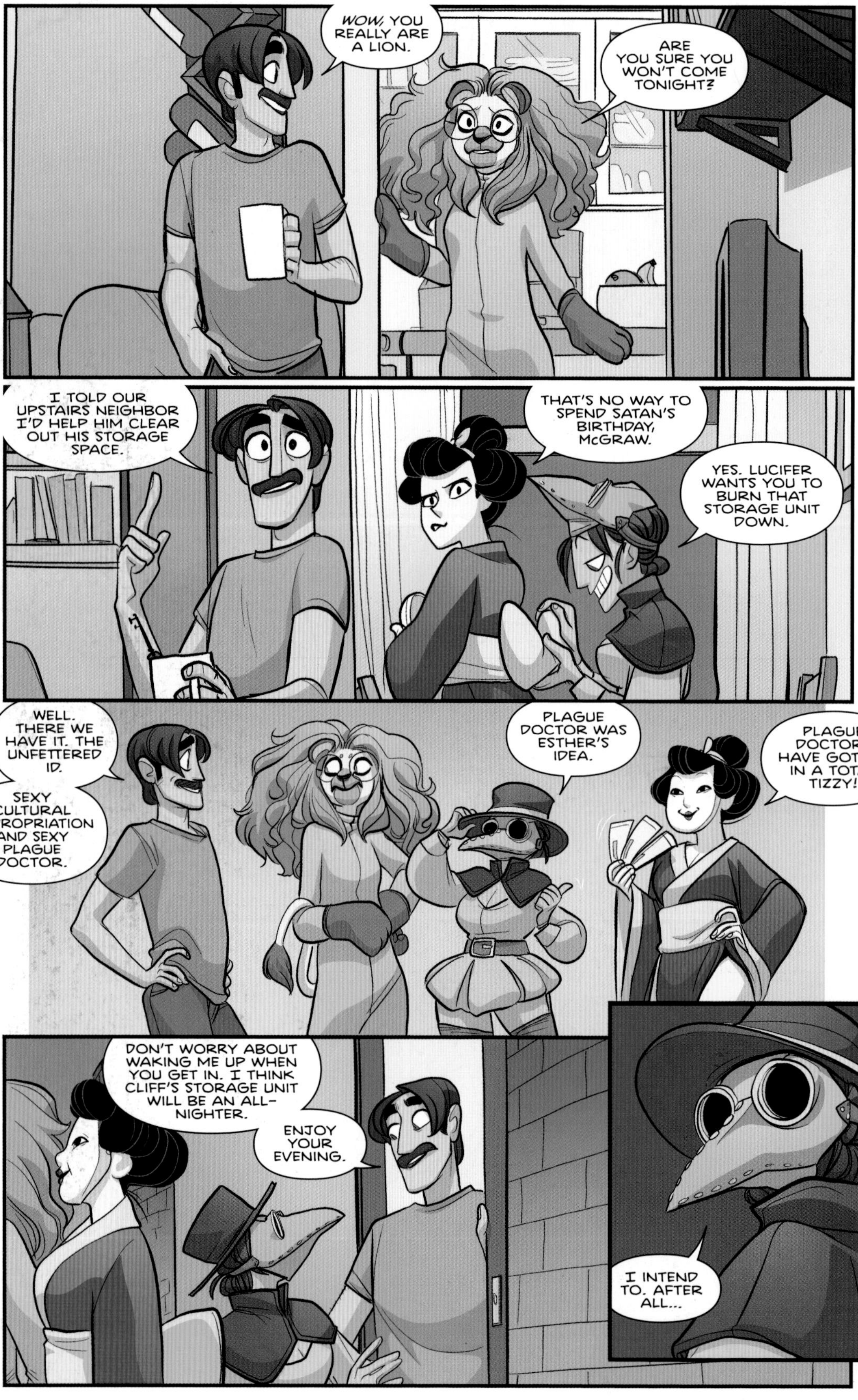
WOW, YOU REALLY ARE A LION.
ARE YOU SURE YOU WON'T COME TONIGHT?
I TOLD OUR UPSTAIRS NEIGHBOR I'D HELP HIM CLEAR OUT HIS STORAGE SPACE.
THAT'S NO WAY TO SPEND SATAN'S BIRTHDAY, McGRAW.
YES. LUCIFER WANTS YOU TO BURN THAT STORAGE UNIT DOWN.
WELL. THERE WE HAVE IT. THE UNFETTERED ID.
SEXY CULTURAL APPROPRIATION AND SEXY PLAGUE DOCTOR.
PLAGUE DOCTOR WAS ESTHER'S IDEA.
DON'T WORRY ABOUT WAKING ME UP WHEN YOU GET IN. I THINK CLIFF'S STORAGE UNIT WILL BE AN ALL-NIGHTER.
ENJOY YOUR EVENING.
I INTEND TO. AFTER ALL...

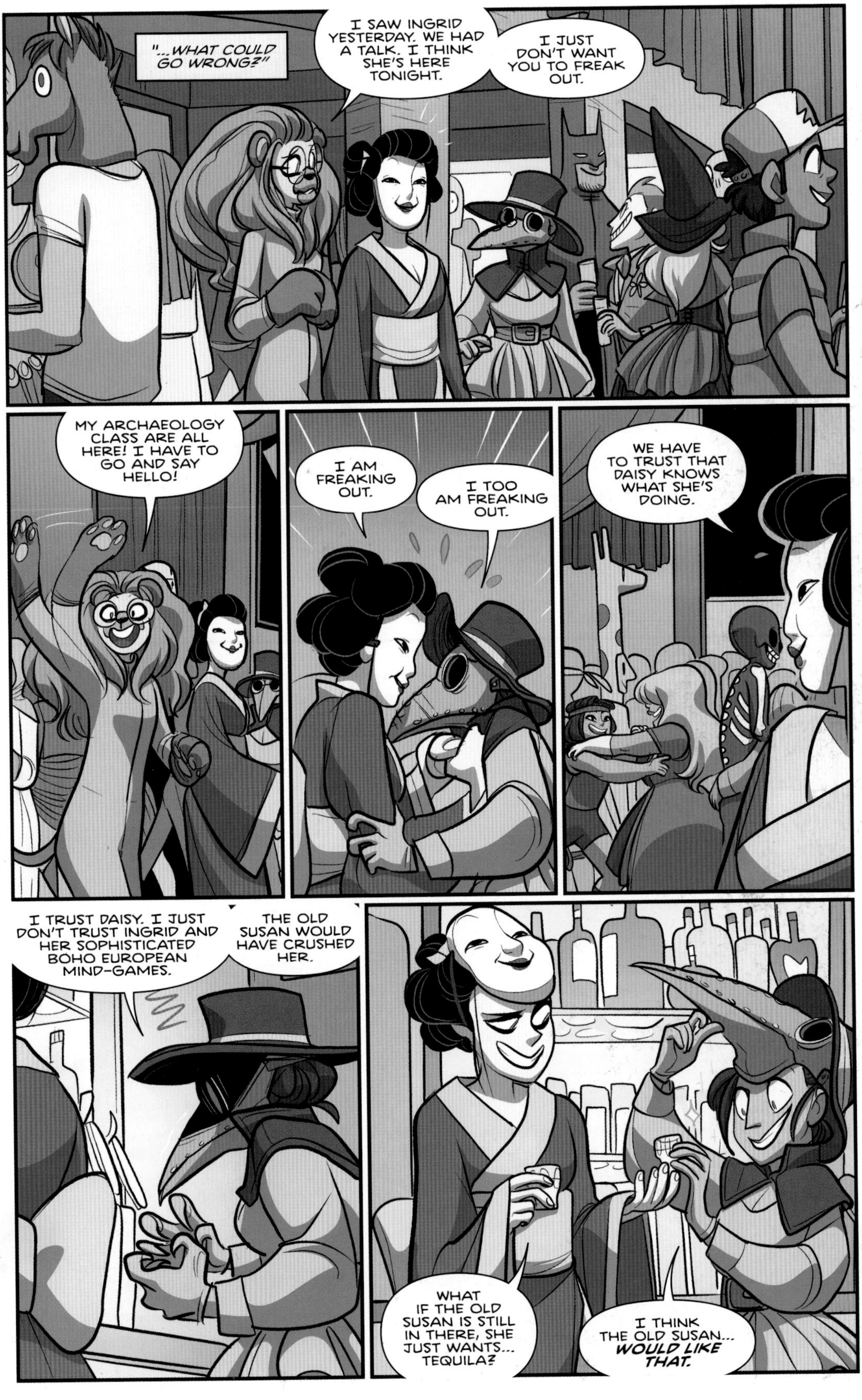
"...WHAT COULD GO WRONG?"
I SAW INGRID YESTERDAY. WE HAD A TALK. I THINK SHE'S HERE TONIGHT.
I JUST DON'T WANT YOU TO FREAK OUT.
MY ARCHAEOLOGY CLASS ARE ALL HERE! I HAVE TO GO AND SAY HELLO!
I AM FREAKING OUT.
I TOO AM FREAKING OUT.
WE HAVE TO TRUST THAT DAISY KNOWS WHAT SHE'S DOING.
I TRUST DAISY. I JUST DON'T TRUST INGRID AND HER SOPHISTICATED BOHO EUROPEAN MIND-GAMES.
THE OLD SUSAN WOULD HAVE CRUSHED HER.
WHAT IF THE OLD SUSAN IS STILL IN THERE, SHE JUST WANTS... TEQUILA?
I THINK THE OLD SUSAN... ***WOULD LIKE THAT.***

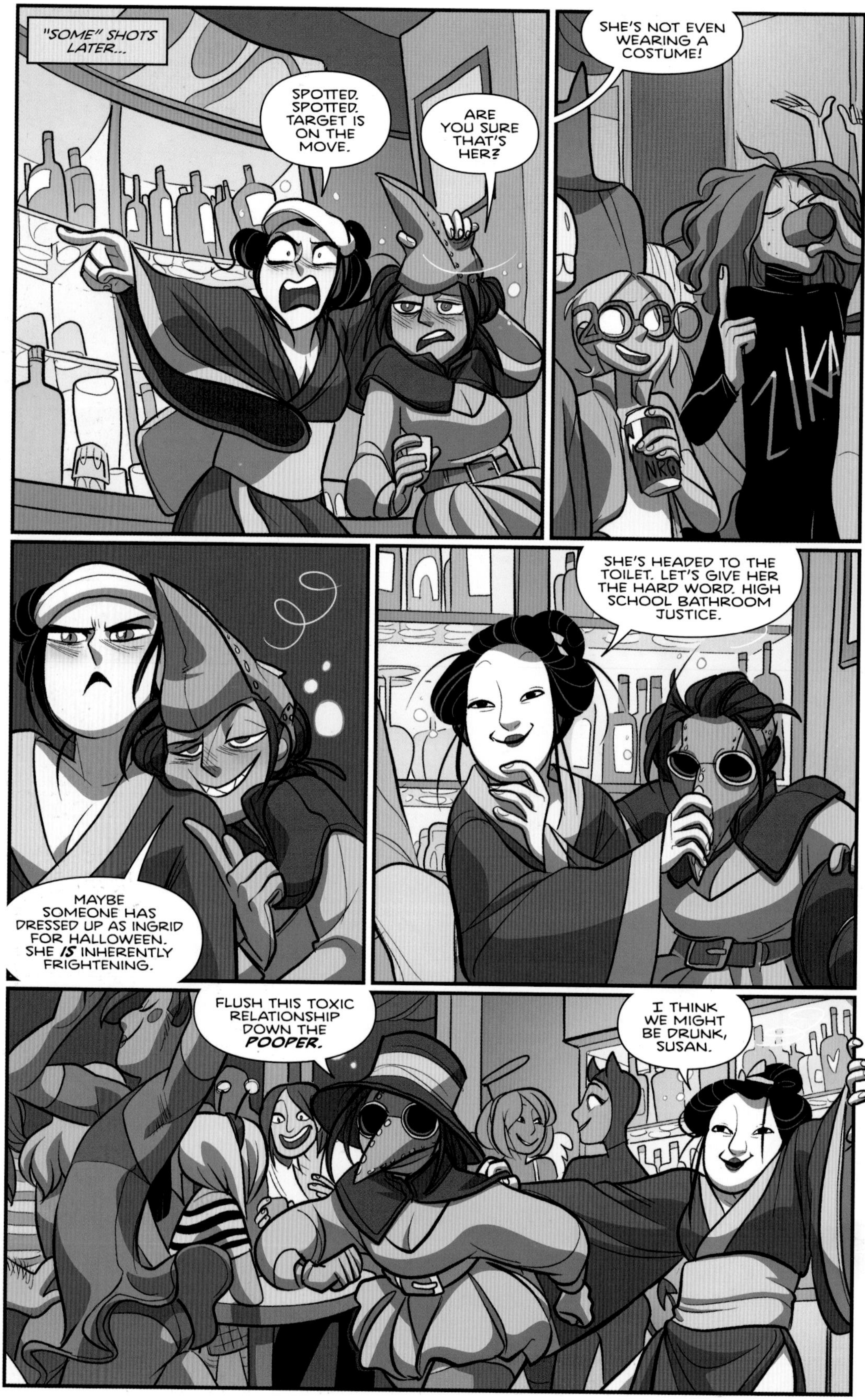
"SOME" SHOTS LATER...
SPOTTED. SPOTTED. TARGET IS ON THE MOVE.
ARE YOU SURE THAT'S HER?
SHE'S NOT EVEN WEARING A COSTUME!
2000
ZIKA
NRG
MAYBE SOMEONE HAS DRESSED UP AS INGRID FOR HALLOWEEN. SHE *IS* INHERENTLY FRIGHTENING.
SHE'S HEADED TO THE TOILET. LET'S GIVE HER THE HARD WORD. HIGH SCHOOL BATHROOM JUSTICE.
FLUSH THIS TOXIC RELATIONSHIP DOWN THE ***POOPER.***
I THINK WE MIGHT BE DRUNK, SUSAN.

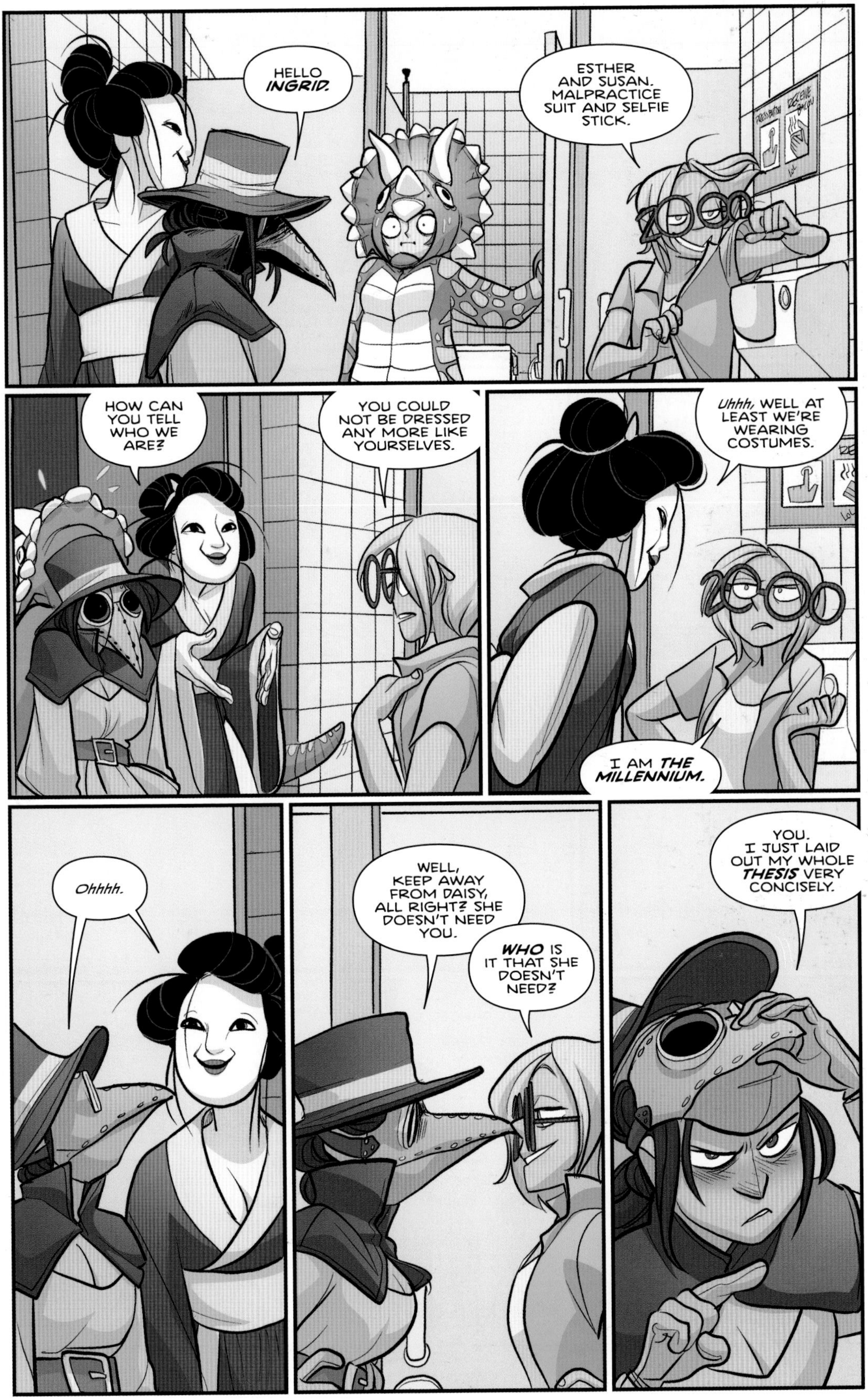
HELLO *INGRID.*
ESTHER AND SUSAN. MALPRACTICE SUIT AND SELFIE STICK.
HOW CAN YOU TELL WHO WE ARE?
YOU COULD NOT BE DRESSED ANY MORE LIKE YOURSELVES.
Uhhh, WELL AT LEAST WE'RE WEARING COSTUMES.
I AM *THE MILLENNIUM.*
Ohhhh.
WELL, KEEP AWAY FROM DAISY, ALL RIGHT? SHE DOESN'T NEED YOU.
WHO IS IT THAT SHE DOESN'T NEED?
YOU. I JUST LAID OUT MY WHOLE *THESIS* VERY CONCISELY.

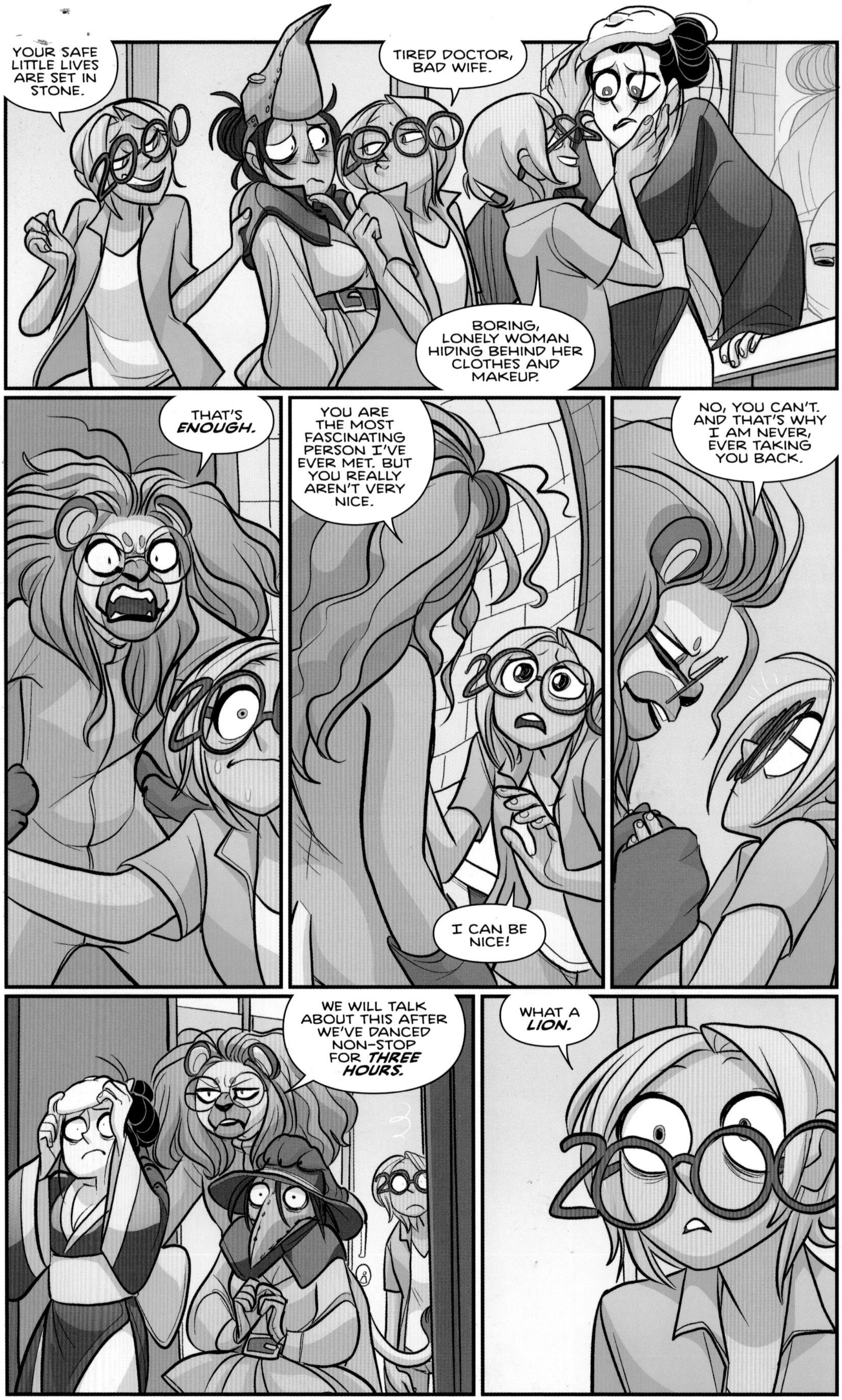
YOUR SAFE LITTLE LIVES ARE SET IN STONE.
TIRED DOCTOR, BAD WIFE.
BORING, LONELY WOMAN HIDING BEHIND HER CLOTHES AND MAKEUP.
THAT'S *ENOUGH.*
YOU ARE THE MOST FASCINATING PERSON I'VE EVER MET. BUT YOU REALLY AREN'T VERY NICE.
I CAN BE NICE!
NO, YOU CAN'T. AND THAT'S WHY I AM NEVER, EVER TAKING YOU BACK.
WE WILL TALK ABOUT THIS AFTER WE'VE DANCED NON-STOP FOR *THREE HOURS.*
WHAT A *LION.*

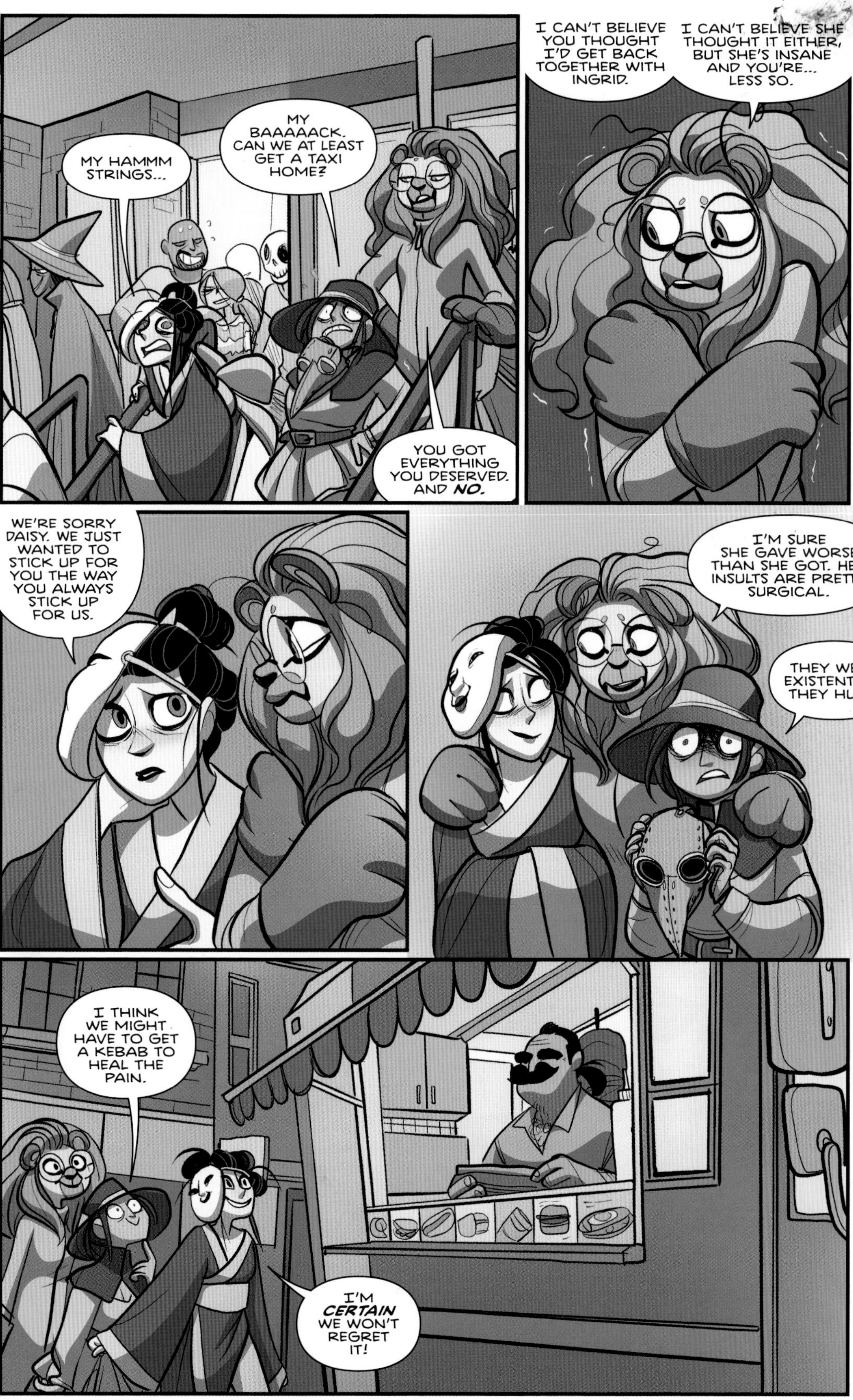
MY HAMMM STRINGS...
MY BAAAAAACK. CAN WE AT LEAST GET A TAXI HOME?
YOU GOT EVERYTHING YOU DESERVED. AND NO.
I CAN'T BELIEVE YOU THOUGHT I'D GET BACK TOGETHER WITH INGRID.
I CAN'T BELIEVE SHE THOUGHT IT EITHER, BUT SHE'S INSANE AND YOU'RE... LESS SO.
WE'RE SORRY DAISY. WE JUST WANTED TO STICK UP FOR YOU THE WAY YOU ALWAYS STICK UP FOR US.
I'M SURE SHE GAVE WORSE THAN SHE GOT. HER INSULTS ARE PRETTY SURGICAL.
THEY WERE EXISTENTIAL. THEY HURT.
I THINK WE MIGHT HAVE TO GET A KEBAB TO HEAL THE PAIN.
I'M CERTAIN WE WON'T REGRET IT!

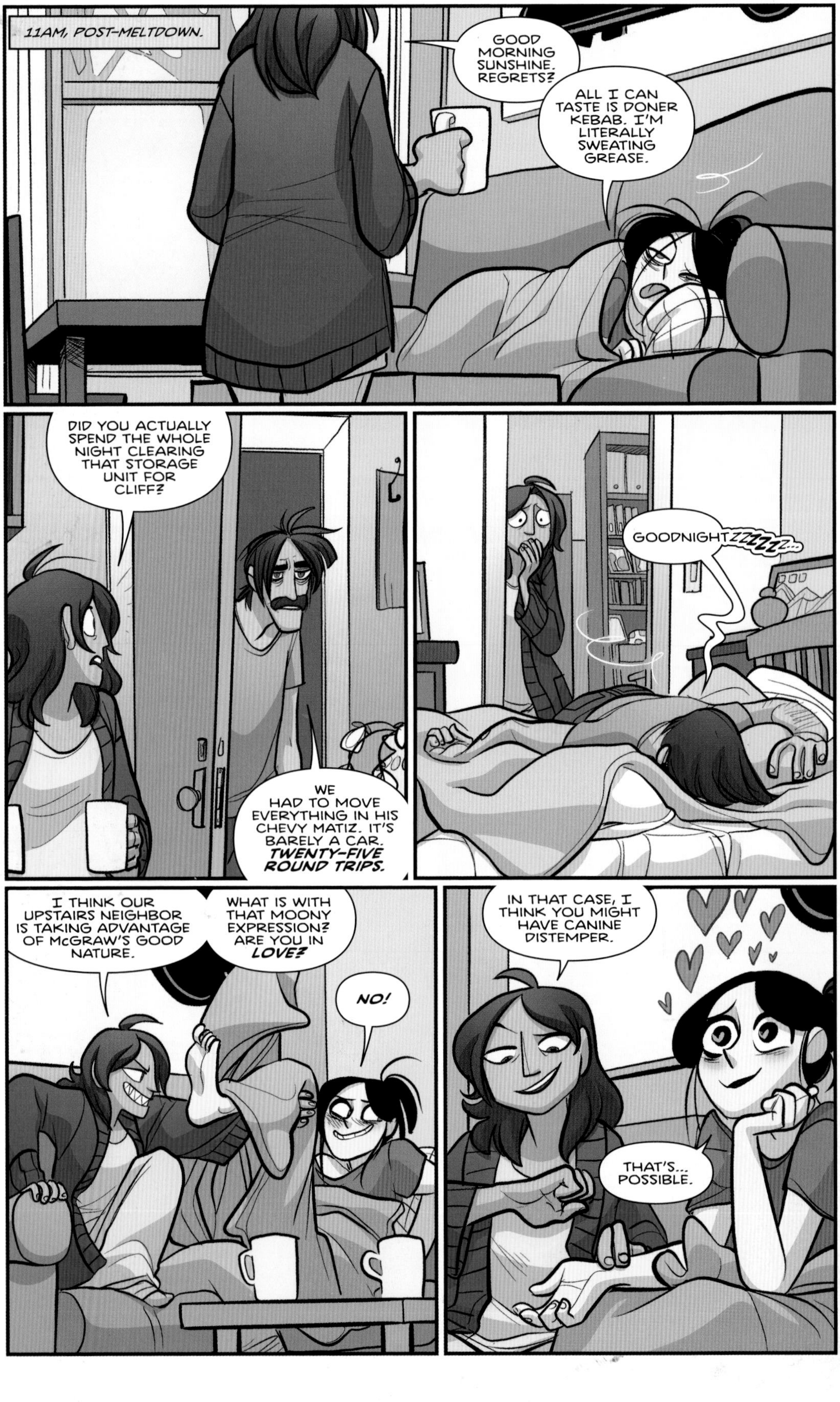
11AM, POST-MELTDOWN.
GOOD MORNING SUNSHINE. REGRETS?
ALL I CAN TASTE IS DONER KEBAB. I'M LITERALLY SWEATING GREASE.
DID YOU ACTUALLY SPEND THE WHOLE NIGHT CLEARING THAT STORAGE UNIT FOR CLIFF?
WE HAD TO MOVE EVERYTHING IN HIS CHEVY MATIZ. IT'S BARELY A CAR. TWENTY-FIVE ROUND TRIPS.
GOODNIGHTZZZZZZ...
I THINK OUR UPSTAIRS NEIGHBOR IS TAKING ADVANTAGE OF McGRAW'S GOOD NATURE.
WHAT IS WITH THAT MOONY EXPRESSION? ARE YOU IN LOVE?
NO!
IN THAT CASE, I THINK YOU MIGHT HAVE CANINE DISTEMPER.
THAT'S... POSSIBLE.

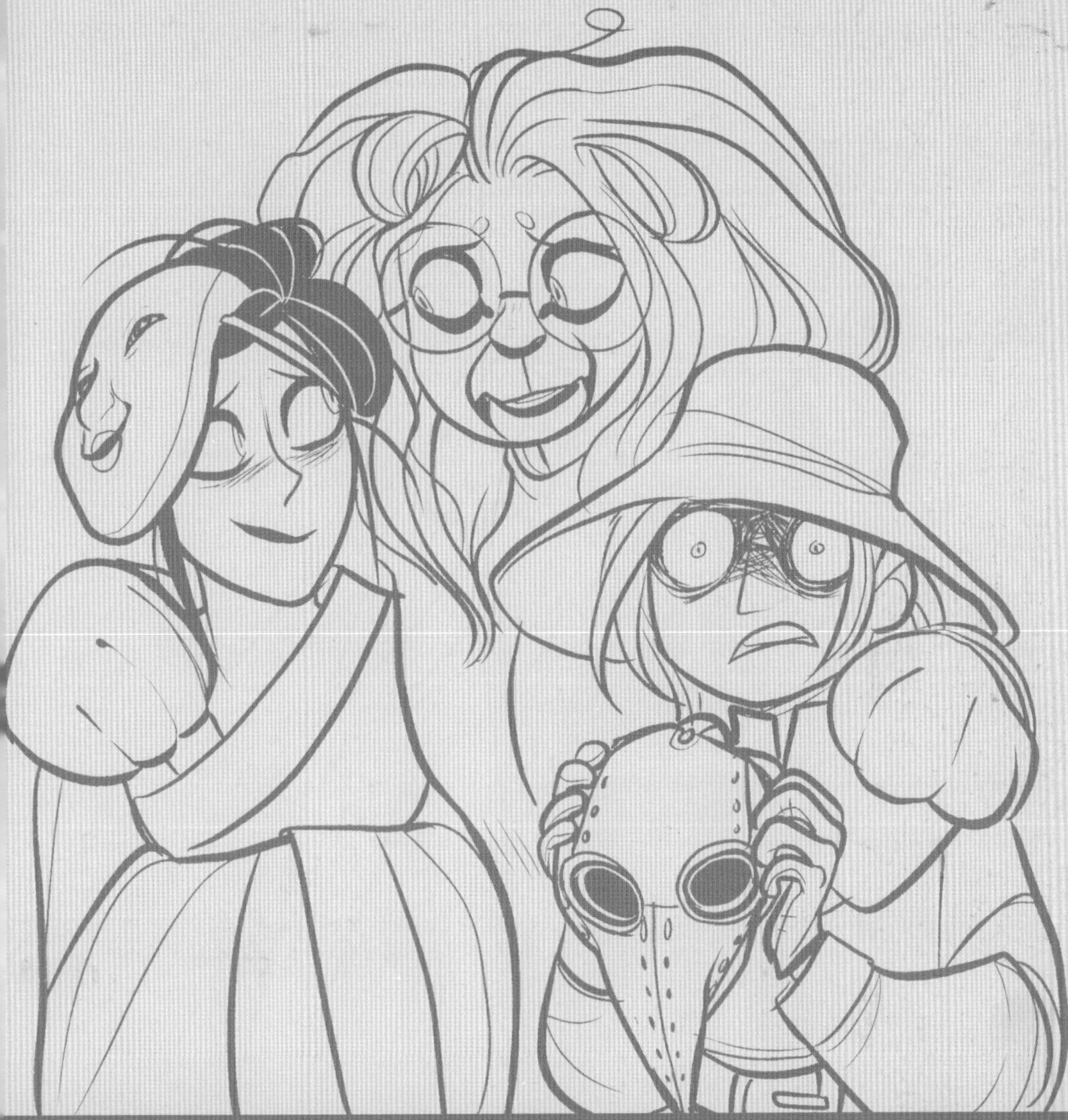

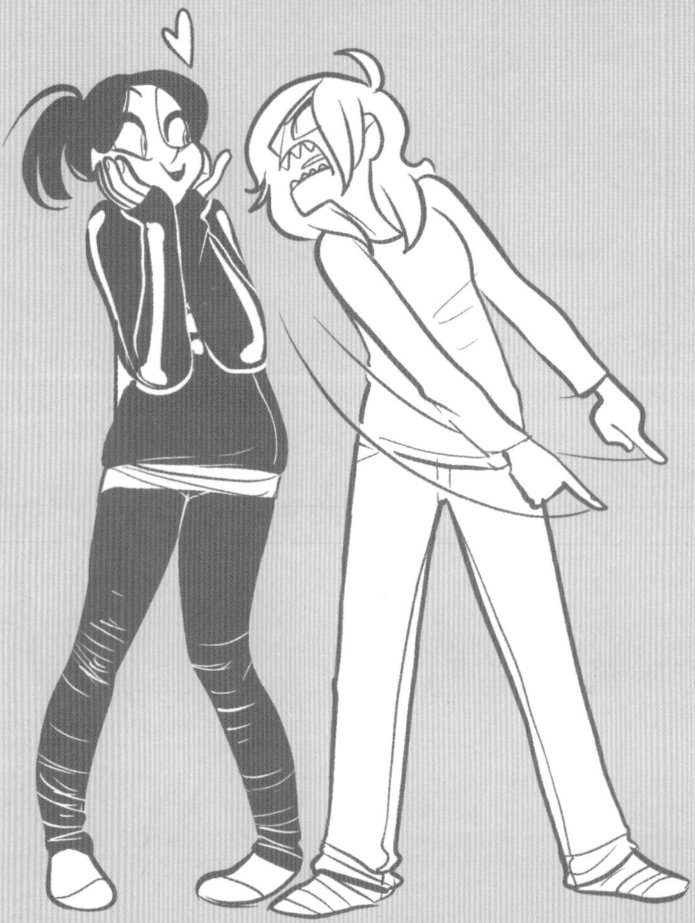

CHAPTER FORTY-TWO

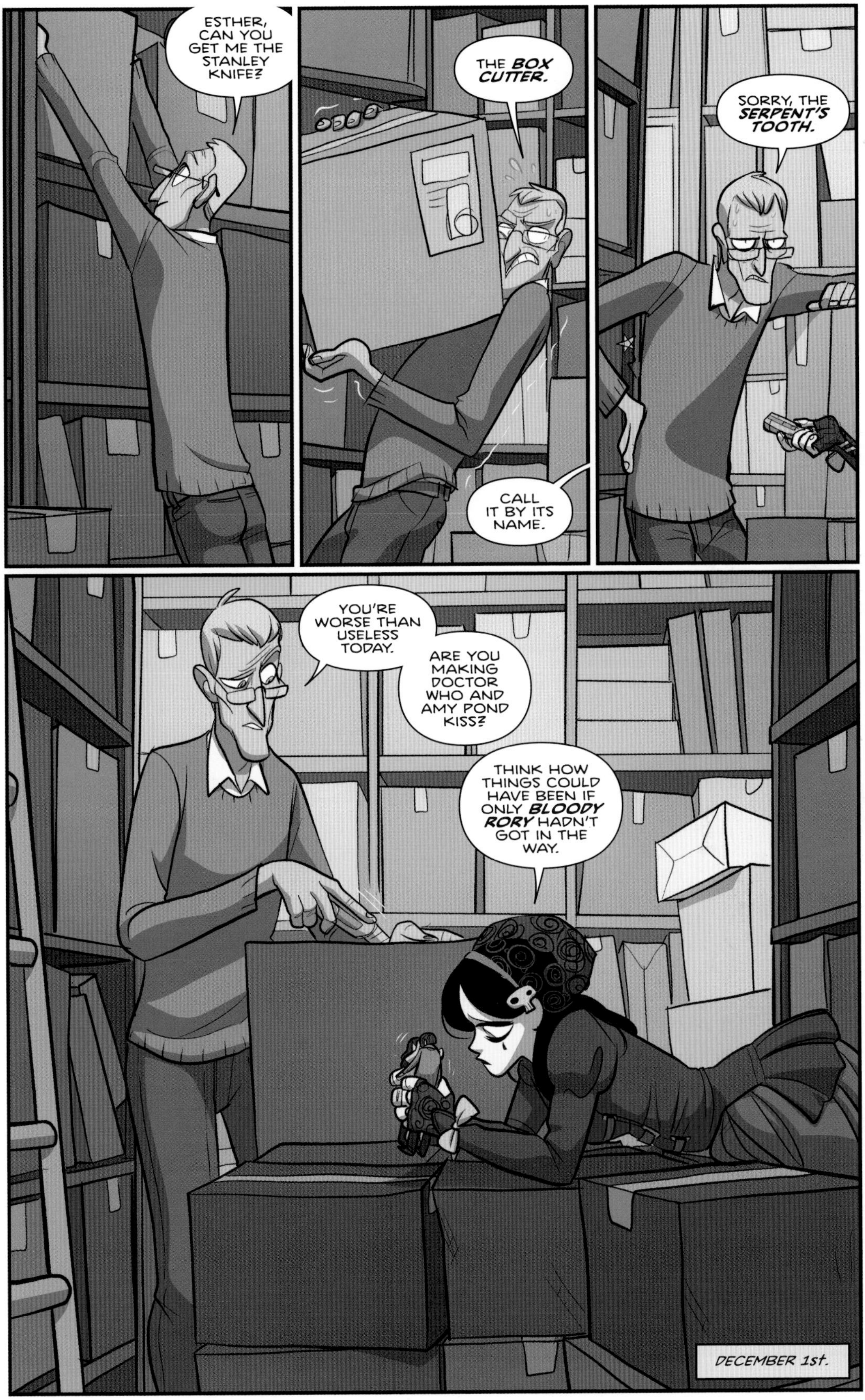

ESTHER, CAN YOU GET ME THE STANLEY KNIFE?
THE **BOX CUTTER.**
CALL IT BY ITS NAME.
SORRY, THE ***SERPENT'S TOOTH.***
YOU'RE WORSE THAN USELESS TODAY.
ARE YOU MAKING DOCTOR WHO AND AMY POND KISS?
THINK HOW THINGS COULD HAVE BEEN IF ONLY ***BLOODY RORY*** HADN'T GOT IN THE WAY.
DECEMBER 1st.

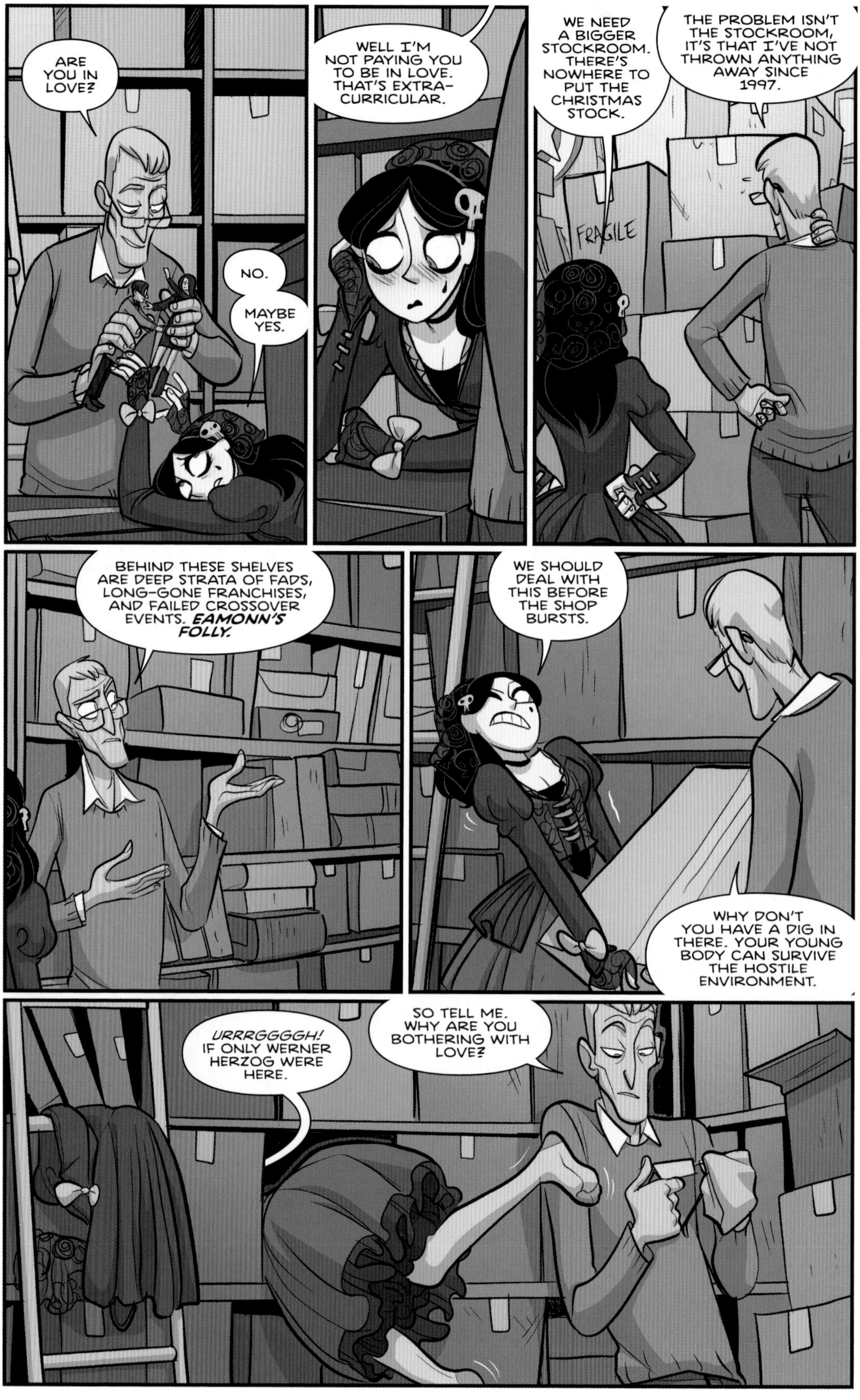
ARE YOU IN LOVE?
NO.
MAYBE YES.
WELL I'M NOT PAYING YOU TO BE IN LOVE. THAT'S EXTRA-CURRICULAR.
WE NEED A BIGGER STOCKROOM. THERE'S NOWHERE TO PUT THE CHRISTMAS STOCK.
THE PROBLEM ISN'T THE STOCKROOM, IT'S THAT I'VE NOT THROWN ANYTHING AWAY SINCE 1997.
FRAGILE
BEHIND THESE SHELVES ARE DEEP STRATA OF FADS, LONG-GONE FRANCHISES, AND FAILED CROSSOVER EVENTS. ***EAMONN'S FOLLY.***
WE SHOULD DEAL WITH THIS BEFORE THE SHOP BURSTS.
WHY DON'T YOU HAVE A DIG IN THERE. YOUR YOUNG BODY CAN SURVIVE THE HOSTILE ENVIRONMENT.
URRRGGGGH! IF ONLY WERNER HERZOG WERE HERE.
SO TELL ME. WHY ARE YOU BOTHERING WITH LOVE?

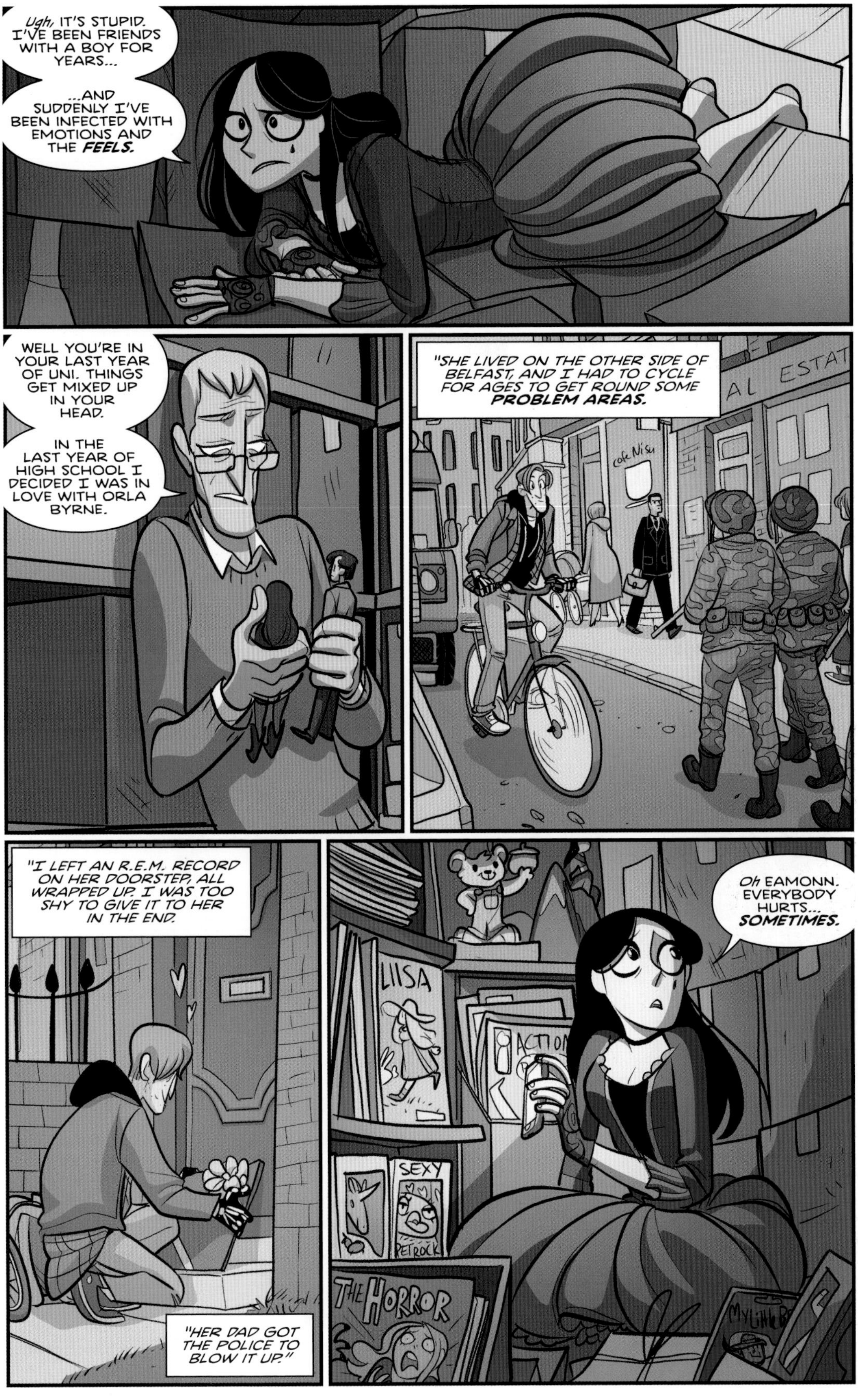
Ugh, IT'S STUPID. I'VE BEEN FRIENDS WITH A BOY FOR YEARS...
...AND SUDDENLY I'VE BEEN INFECTED WITH EMOTIONS AND THE FEELS.
WELL YOU'RE IN YOUR LAST YEAR OF UNI. THINGS GET MIXED UP IN YOUR HEAD.
IN THE LAST YEAR OF HIGH SCHOOL I DECIDED I WAS IN LOVE WITH ORLA BYRNE.
"SHE LIVED ON THE OTHER SIDE OF BELFAST, AND I HAD TO CYCLE FOR AGES TO GET ROUND SOME PROBLEM AREAS.
AL ESTAT
cafe Nisu
"I LEFT AN R.E.M. RECORD ON HER DOORSTEP, ALL WRAPPED UP. I WAS TOO SHY TO GIVE IT TO HER IN THE END.
"HER DAD GOT THE POLICE TO BLOW IT UP."
Oh EAMONN. EVERYBODY HURTS... SOMETIMES.
LIISA
ACTION
SEXY
PETROCK
THE HORROR

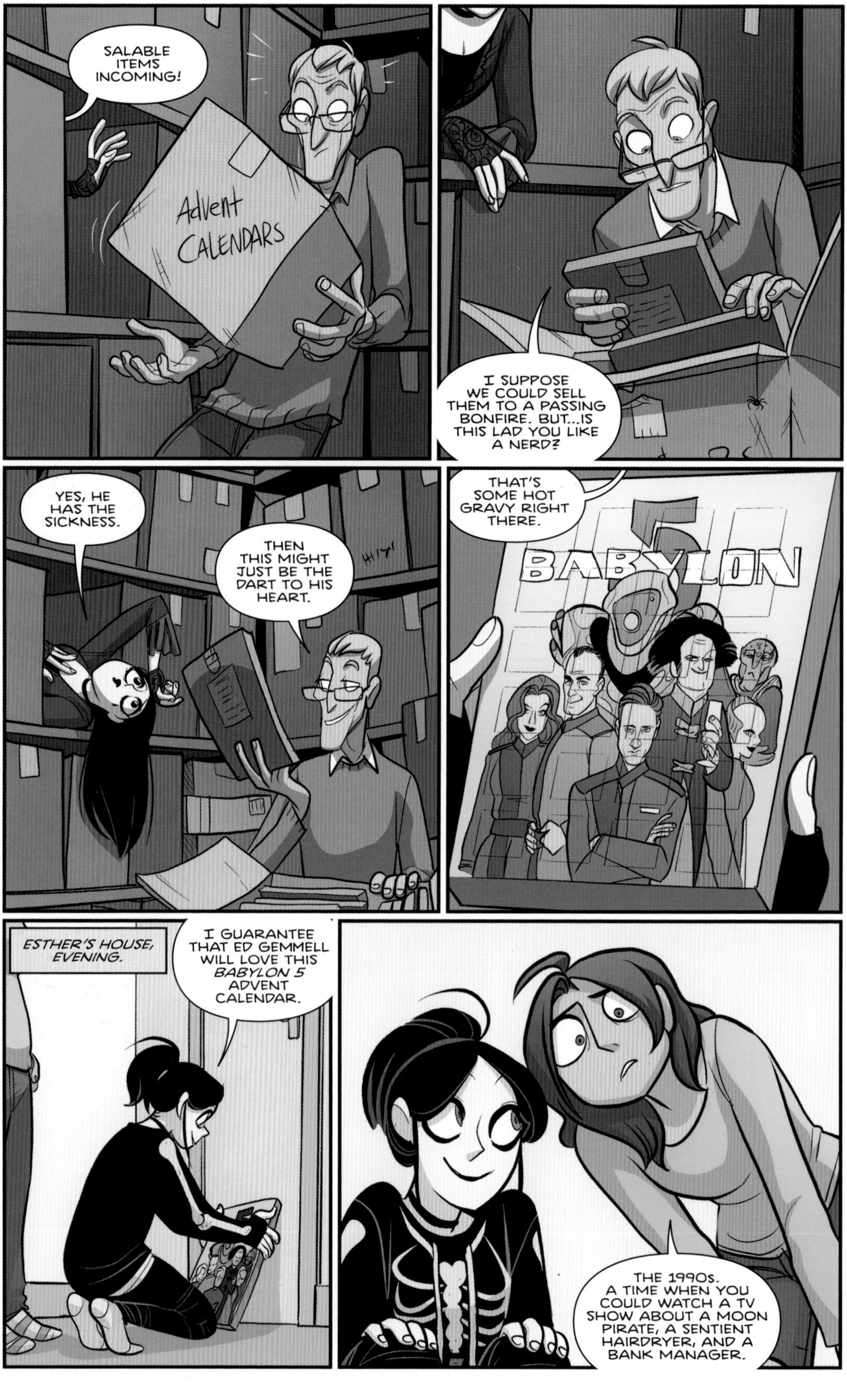
SALABLE ITEMS INCOMING!
Advent CALENDARS
I SUPPOSE WE COULD SELL THEM TO A PASSING BONFIRE. BUT...IS THIS LAD YOU LIKE A NERD?
YES, HE HAS THE SICKNESS.
THEN THIS MIGHT JUST BE THE DART TO HIS HEART.
THAT'S SOME HOT GRAVY RIGHT THERE.
BABYLON 5
ESTHER'S HOUSE, EVENING.
I GUARANTEE THAT ED GEMMELL WILL LOVE THIS *BABYLON 5* ADVENT CALENDAR.
THE 1990s. A TIME WHEN YOU COULD WATCH A TV SHOW ABOUT A MOON PIRATE, A SENTIENT HAIRDRYER, AND A BANK MANAGER.

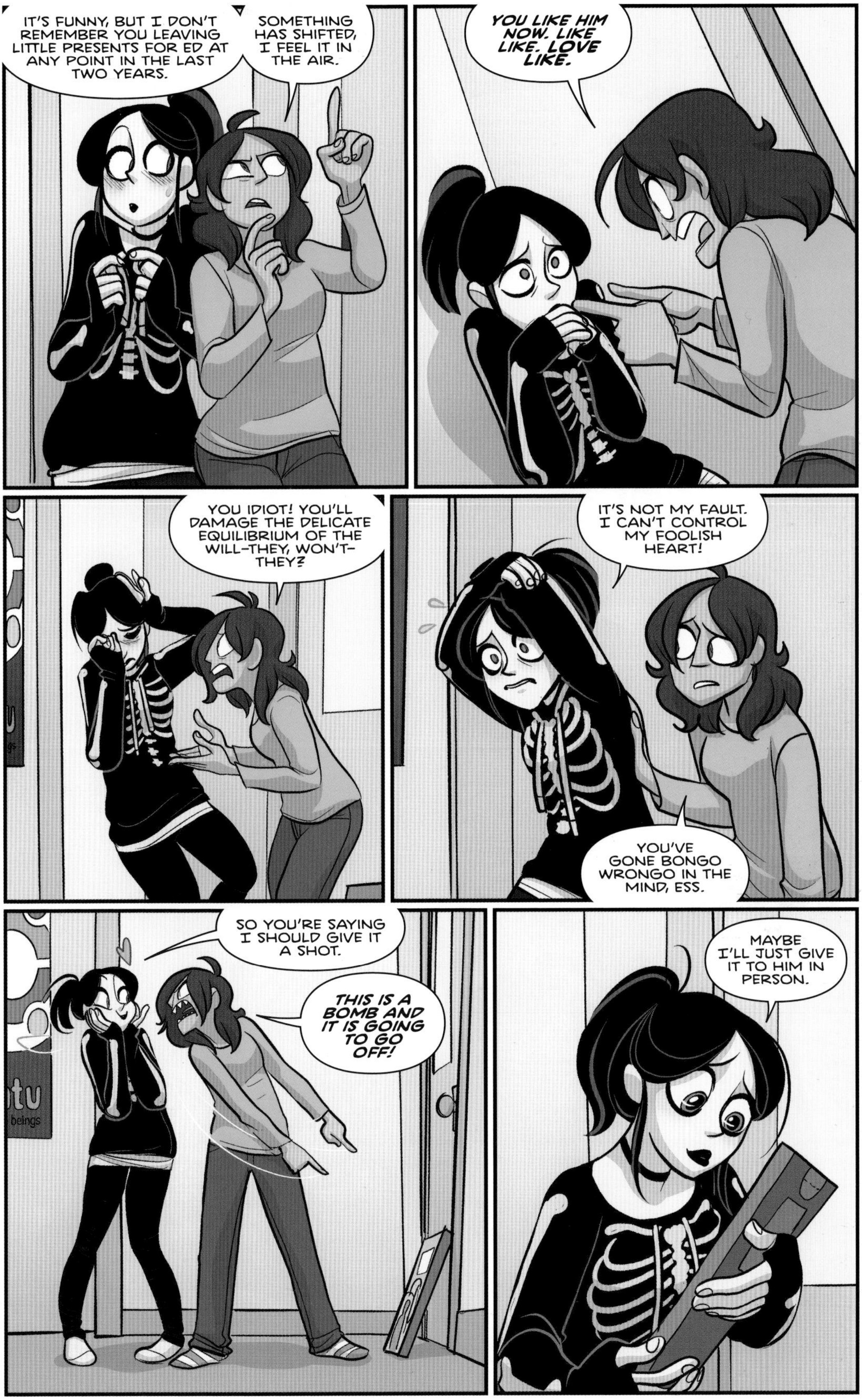
IT'S FUNNY, BUT I DON'T REMEMBER YOU LEAVING LITTLE PRESENTS FOR ED AT ANY POINT IN THE LAST TWO YEARS.
SOMETHING HAS SHIFTED, I FEEL IT IN THE AIR.
YOU LIKE HIM NOW. LIKE LIKE. LOVE LIKE.
YOU IDIOT! YOU'LL DAMAGE THE DELICATE EQUILIBRIUM OF THE WILL-THEY, WON'T-THEY?
IT'S NOT MY FAULT. I CAN'T CONTROL MY FOOLISH HEART!
YOU'VE GONE BONGO WRONGO IN THE MIND, ESS.
SO YOU'RE SAYING I SHOULD GIVE IT A SHOT.
THIS IS A BOMB AND IT IS GOING TO GO OFF!
MAYBE I'LL JUST GIVE IT TO HIM IN PERSON.

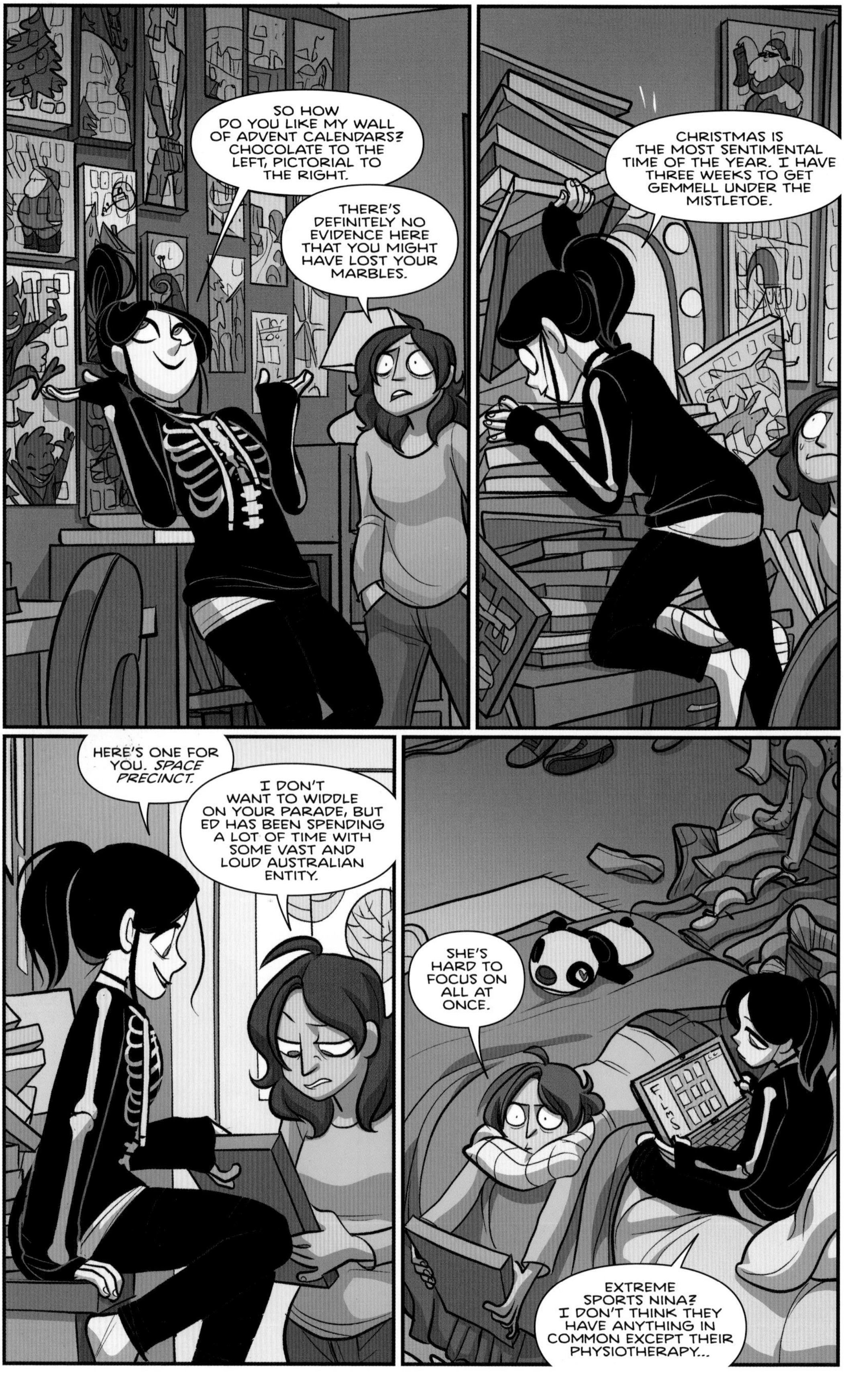
SO HOW DO YOU LIKE MY WALL OF ADVENT CALENDARS? CHOCOLATE TO THE LEFT, PICTORIAL TO THE RIGHT.
THERE'S DEFINITELY NO EVIDENCE HERE THAT YOU MIGHT HAVE LOST YOUR MARBLES.
CHRISTMAS IS THE MOST SENTIMENTAL TIME OF THE YEAR. I HAVE THREE WEEKS TO GET GEMMELL UNDER THE MISTLETOE.
HERE'S ONE FOR YOU. *SPACE PRECINCT.*
I DON'T WANT TO WIDDLE ON YOUR PARADE, BUT ED HAS BEEN SPENDING A LOT OF TIME WITH SOME VAST AND LOUD AUSTRALIAN ENTITY.
SHE'S HARD TO FOCUS ON ALL AT ONCE.
EXTREME SPORTS NINA? I DON'T THINK THEY HAVE ANYTHING IN COMMON EXCEPT THEIR PHYSIOTHERAPY...

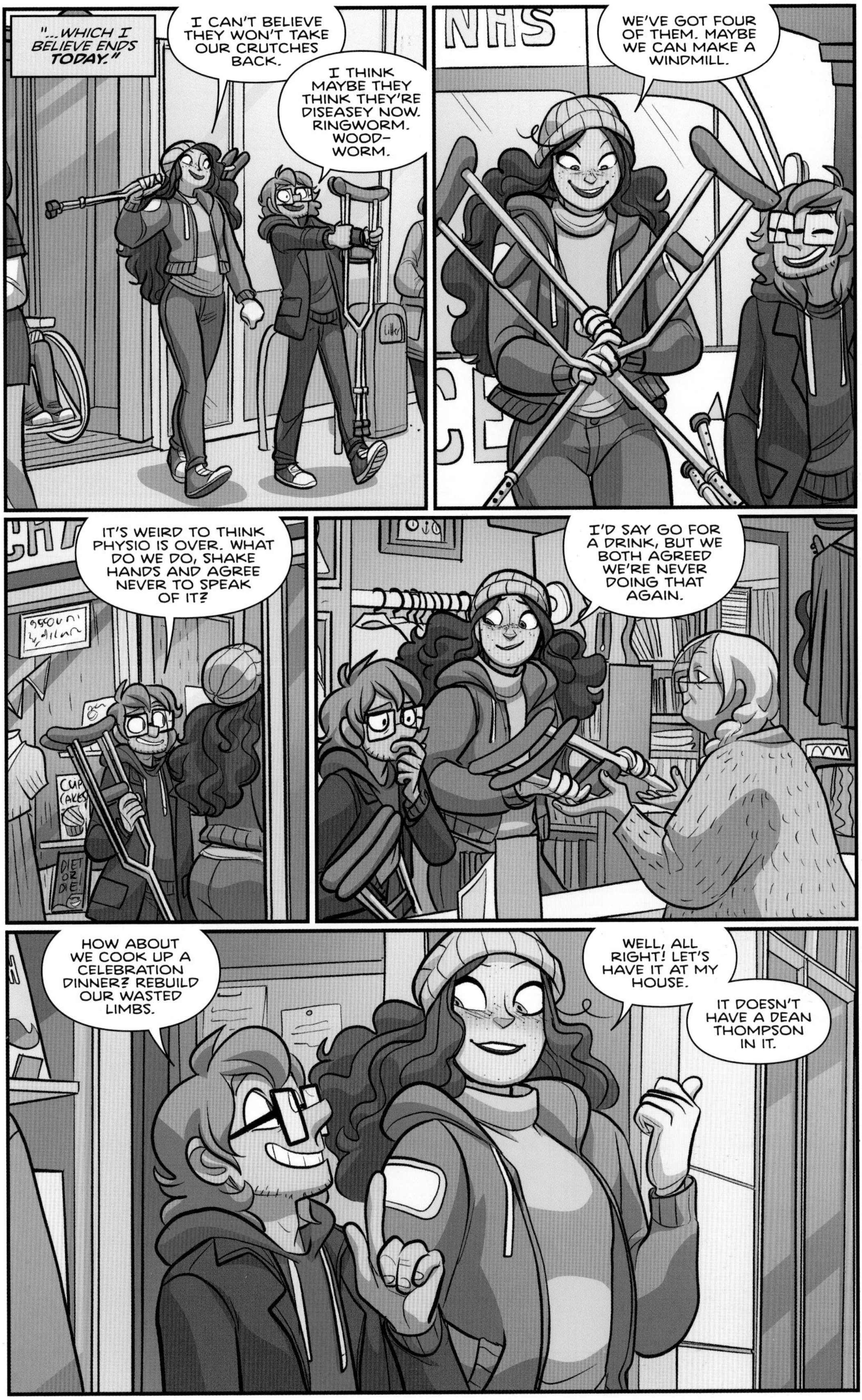
"...WHICH I BELIEVE ENDS TODAY."
I CAN'T BELIEVE THEY WON'T TAKE OUR CRUTCHES BACK.
I THINK MAYBE THEY THINK THEY'RE DISEASEY NOW. RINGWORM. WOOD-WORM.
NHS
WE'VE GOT FOUR OF THEM. MAYBE WE CAN MAKE A WINDMILL.
IT'S WEIRD TO THINK PHYSIO IS OVER. WHAT DO WE DO, SHAKE HANDS AND AGREE NEVER TO SPEAK OF IT?
CUP CAKES
DIET OR DIE!
I'D SAY GO FOR A DRINK, BUT WE BOTH AGREED WE'RE NEVER DOING THAT AGAIN.
HOW ABOUT WE COOK UP A CELEBRATION DINNER? REBUILD OUR WASTED LIMBS.
WELL, ALL RIGHT! LET'S HAVE IT AT MY HOUSE.
IT DOESN'T HAVE A DEAN THOMPSON IN IT.

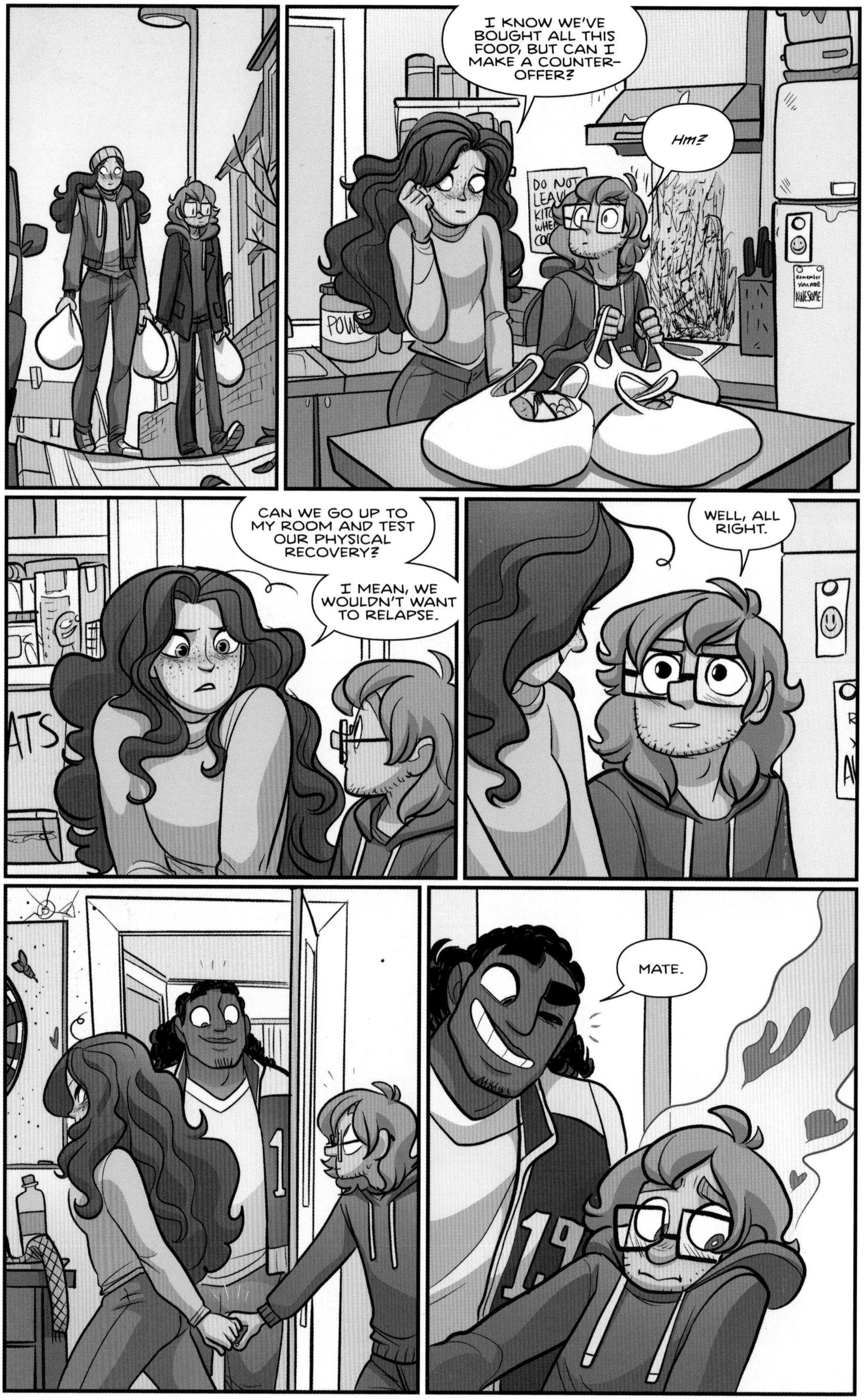
I KNOW WE'VE BOUGHT ALL THIS FOOD, BUT CAN I MAKE A COUNTER-OFFER?
Hm?
Remember YOU ARE AWESOME
CAN WE GO UP TO MY ROOM AND TEST OUR PHYSICAL RECOVERY?
I MEAN, WE WOULDN'T WANT TO RELAPSE.
WELL, ALL RIGHT.
MATE.

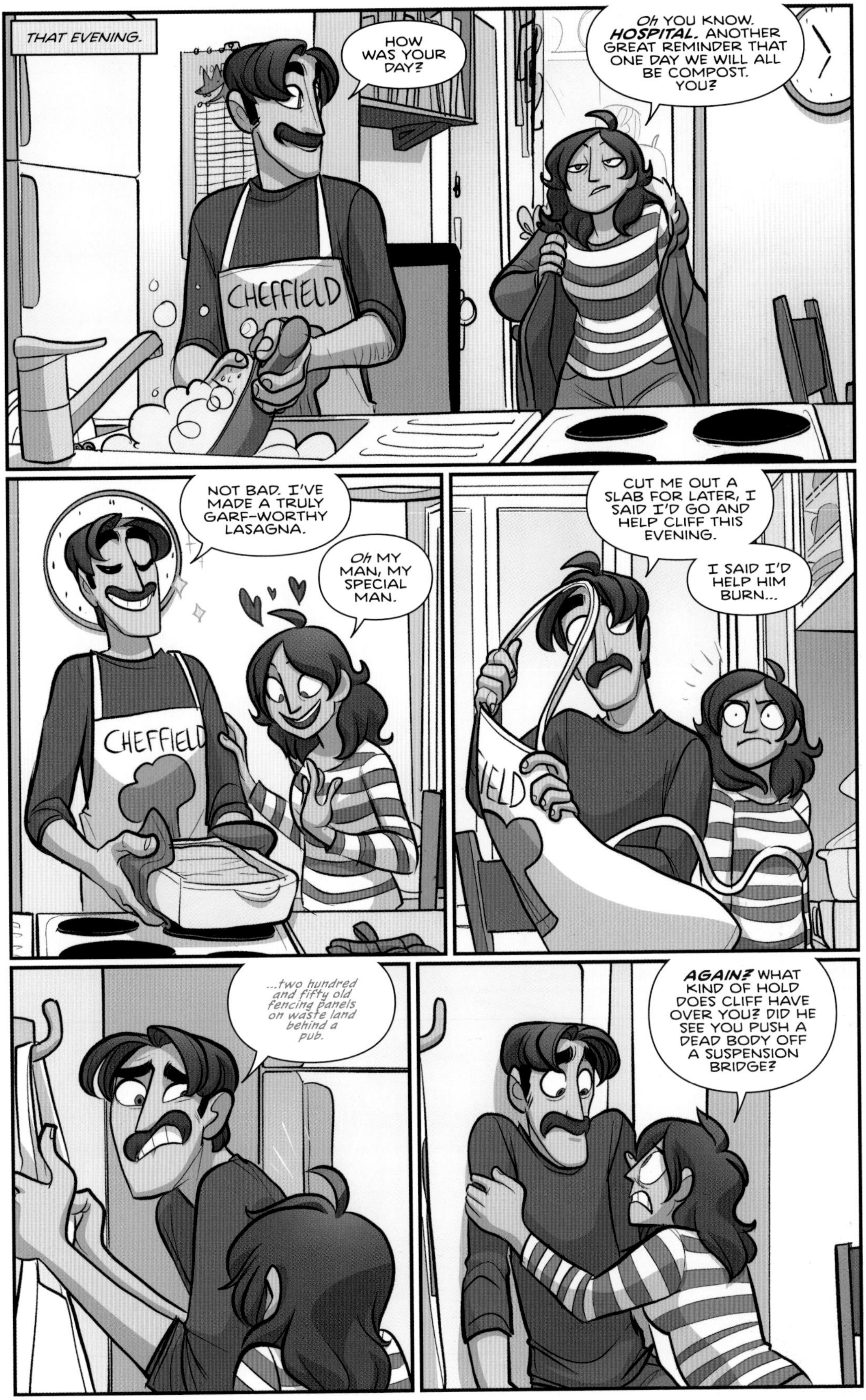
THAT EVENING.
HOW WAS YOUR DAY?
Oh YOU KNOW. HOSPITAL. ANOTHER GREAT REMINDER THAT ONE DAY WE WILL ALL BE COMPOST. YOU?
CHEFFIELD
NOT BAD. I'VE MADE A TRULY GARF-WORTHY LASAGNA.
Oh MY MAN, MY SPECIAL MAN.
CHEFFIELD
CUT ME OUT A SLAB FOR LATER, I SAID I'D GO AND HELP CLIFF THIS EVENING.
I SAID I'D HELP HIM BURN...
...two hundred and fifty old fencing panels on waste land behind a pub.
AGAIN? WHAT KIND OF HOLD DOES CLIFF HAVE OVER YOU? DID HE SEE YOU PUSH A DEAD BODY OFF A SUSPENSION BRIDGE?

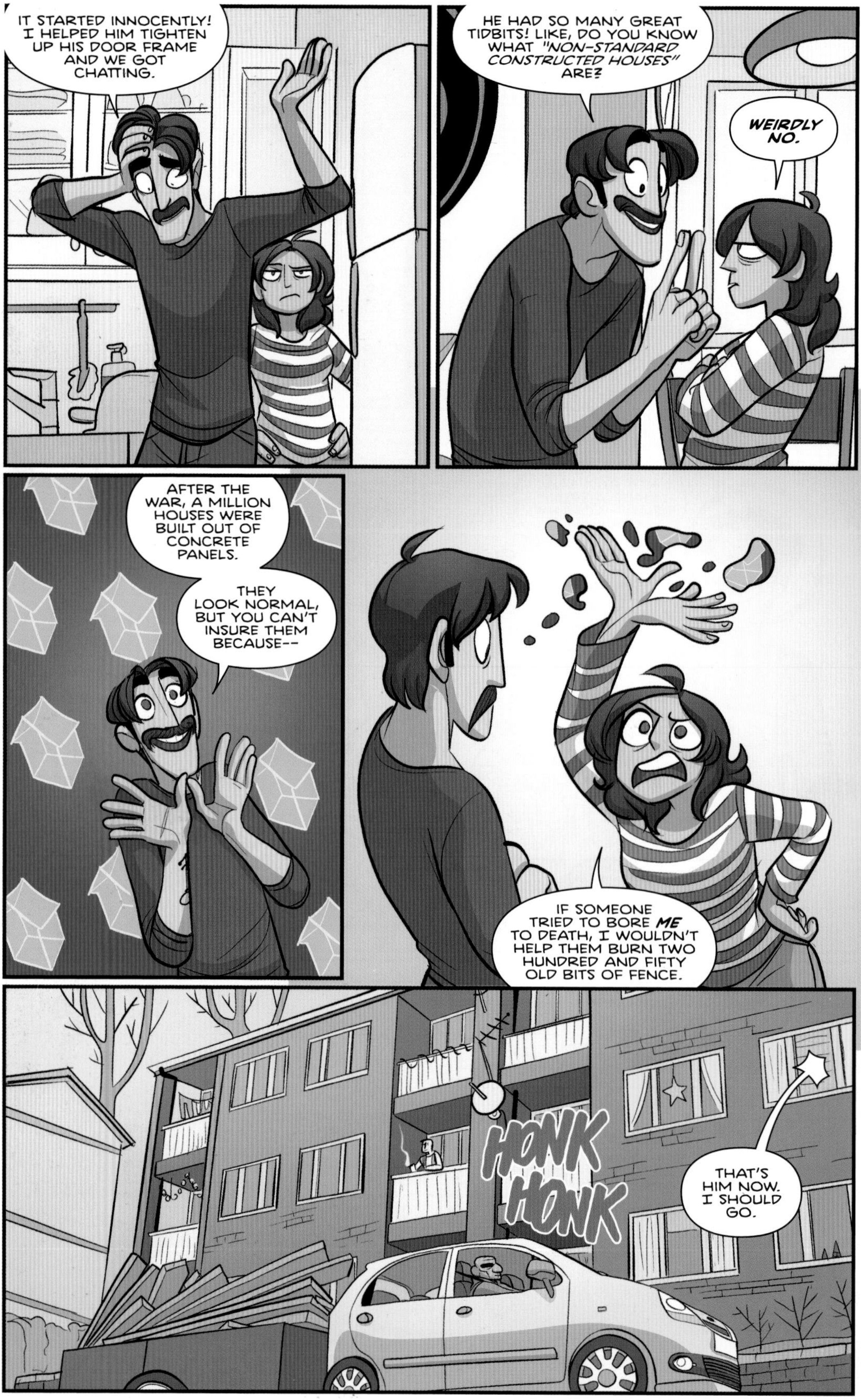
IT STARTED INNOCENTLY! I HELPED HIM TIGHTEN UP HIS DOOR FRAME AND WE GOT CHATTING.
HE HAD SO MANY GREAT TIDBITS! LIKE, DO YOU KNOW WHAT *"NON-STANDARD CONSTRUCTED HOUSES"* ARE?
WEIRDLY NO.
AFTER THE WAR, A MILLION HOUSES WERE BUILT OUT OF CONCRETE PANELS.
THEY LOOK NORMAL, BUT YOU CAN'T INSURE THEM BECAUSE--
IF SOMEONE TRIED TO BORE ***ME*** TO DEATH, I WOULDN'T HELP THEM BURN TWO HUNDRED AND FIFTY OLD BITS OF FENCE.
HONK HONK
THAT'S HIM NOW. I SHOULD GO.

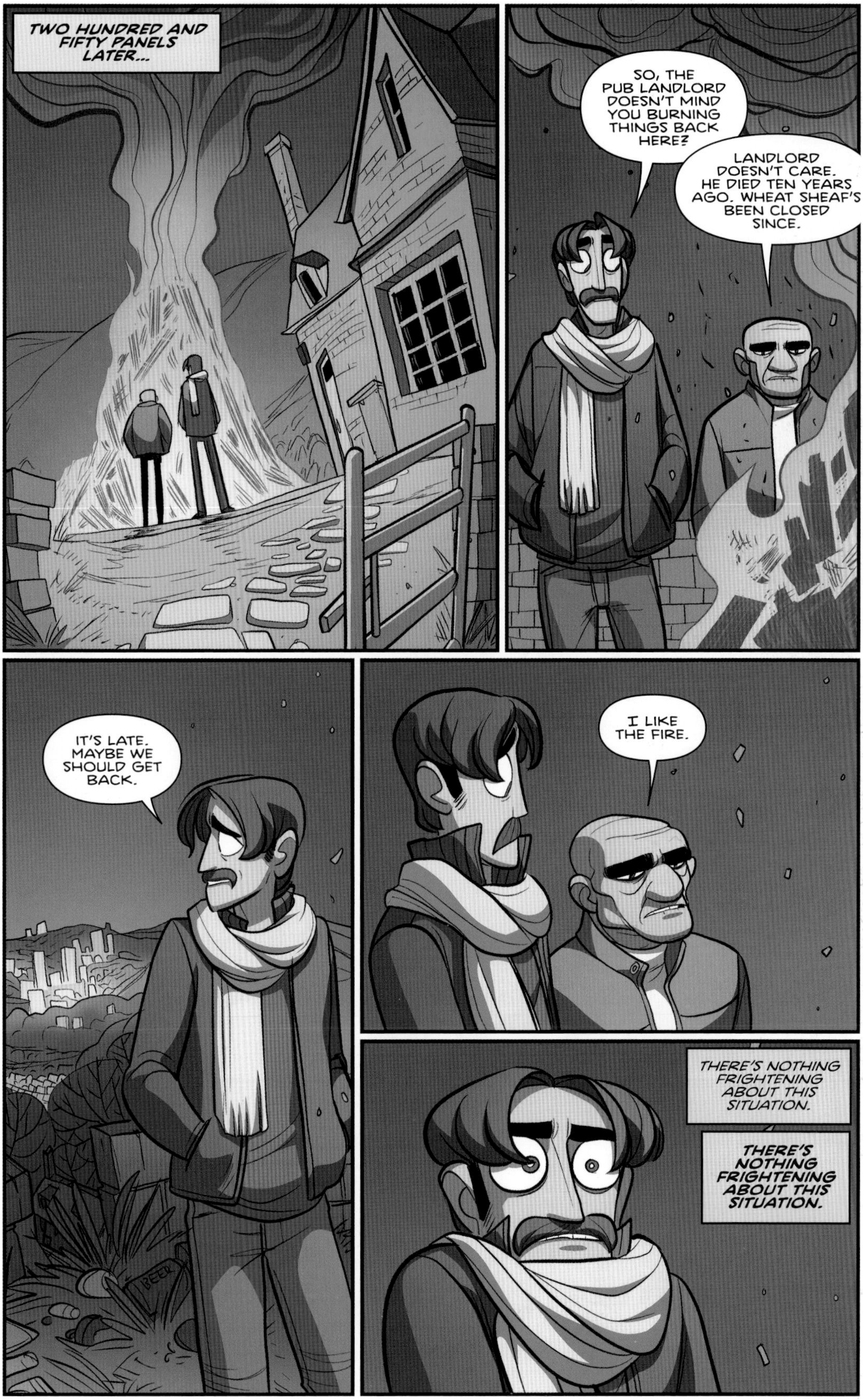
TWO HUNDRED AND FIFTY PANELS LATER...
SO, THE PUB LANDLORD DOESN'T MIND YOU BURNING THINGS BACK HERE?
LANDLORD DOESN'T CARE. HE DIED TEN YEARS AGO. WHEAT SHEAF'S BEEN CLOSED SINCE.
IT'S LATE. MAYBE WE SHOULD GET BACK.
I LIKE THE FIRE.
THERE'S NOTHING FRIGHTENING ABOUT THIS SITUATION.
THERE'S NOTHING FRIGHTENING ABOUT THIS SITUATION.

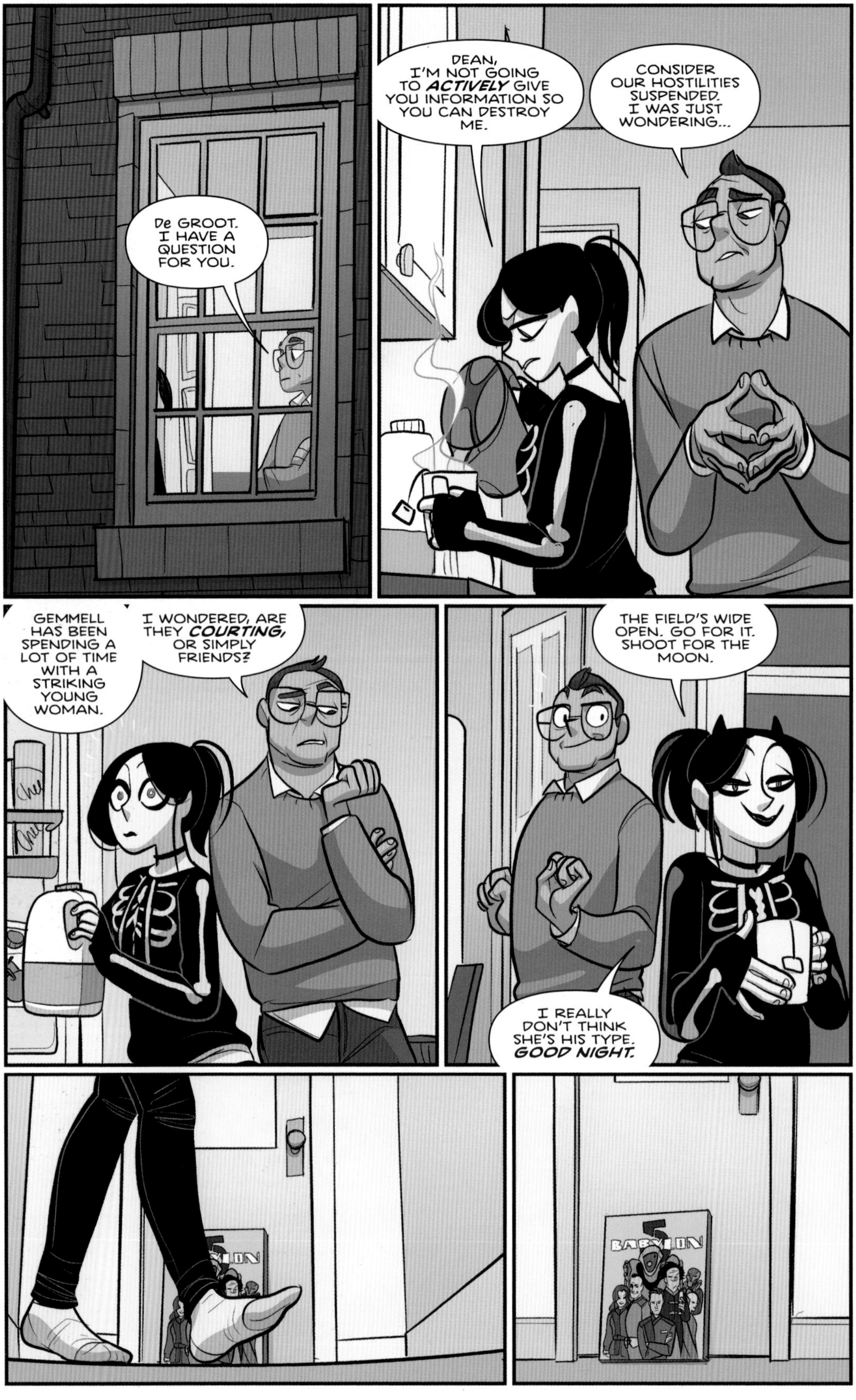
De GROOT. I HAVE A QUESTION FOR YOU.
DEAN, I'M NOT GOING TO ***ACTIVELY*** GIVE YOU INFORMATION SO YOU CAN DESTROY ME.
CONSIDER OUR HOSTILITIES SUSPENDED. I WAS JUST WONDERING...
GEMMELL HAS BEEN SPENDING A LOT OF TIME WITH A STRIKING YOUNG WOMAN.
I WONDERED, ARE THEY ***COURTING,*** OR SIMPLY FRIENDS?
THE FIELD'S WIDE OPEN. GO FOR IT. SHOOT FOR THE MOON.
I REALLY DON'T THINK SHE'S HIS TYPE. ***GOOD NIGHT.***
BABYLON 5

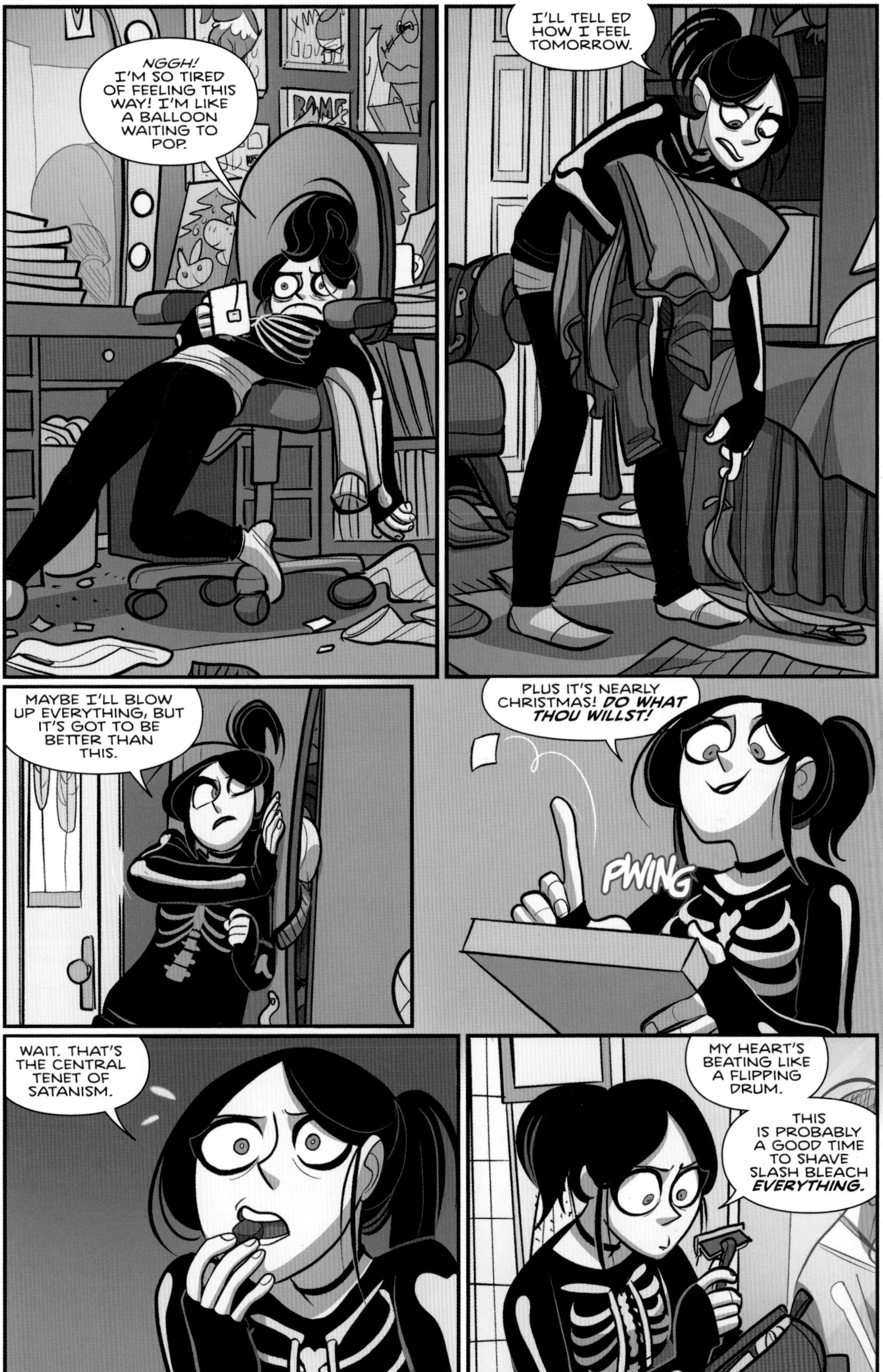

NGGH! I'M SO TIRED OF FEELING THIS WAY! I'M LIKE A BALLOON WAITING TO POP.
I'LL TELL ED HOW I FEEL TOMORROW.
MAYBE I'LL BLOW UP EVERYTHING, BUT IT'S GOT TO BE BETTER THAN THIS.
PLUS IT'S NEARLY CHRISTMAS! DO WHAT THOU WILLST!
PWING
WAIT. THAT'S THE CENTRAL TENET OF SATANISM.
MY HEART'S BEATING LIKE A FLIPPING DRUM.
THIS IS PROBABLY A GOOD TIME TO SHAVE SLASH BLEACH EVERYTHING.

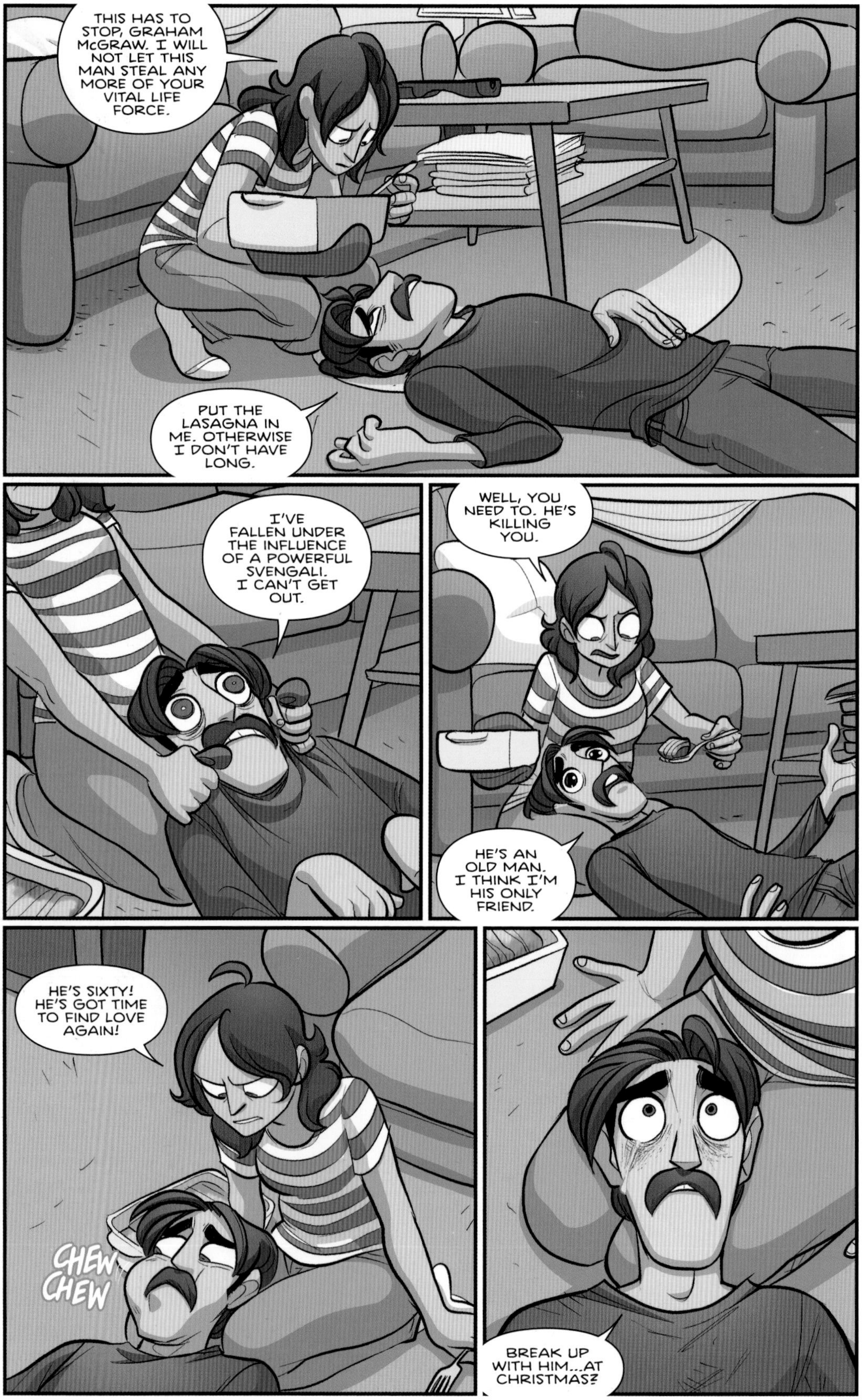
THIS HAS TO STOP, GRAHAM McGRAW. I WILL NOT LET THIS MAN STEAL ANY MORE OF YOUR VITAL LIFE FORCE.
PUT THE LASAGNA IN ME. OTHERWISE I DON'T HAVE LONG.
I'VE FALLEN UNDER THE INFLUENCE OF A POWERFUL SVENGALI. I CAN'T GET OUT.
WELL, YOU NEED TO. HE'S KILLING YOU.
HE'S AN OLD MAN. I THINK I'M HIS ONLY FRIEND.
HE'S SIXTY! HE'S GOT TIME TO FIND LOVE AGAIN!
CHEW CHEW
BREAK UP WITH HIM...AT CHRISTMAS?

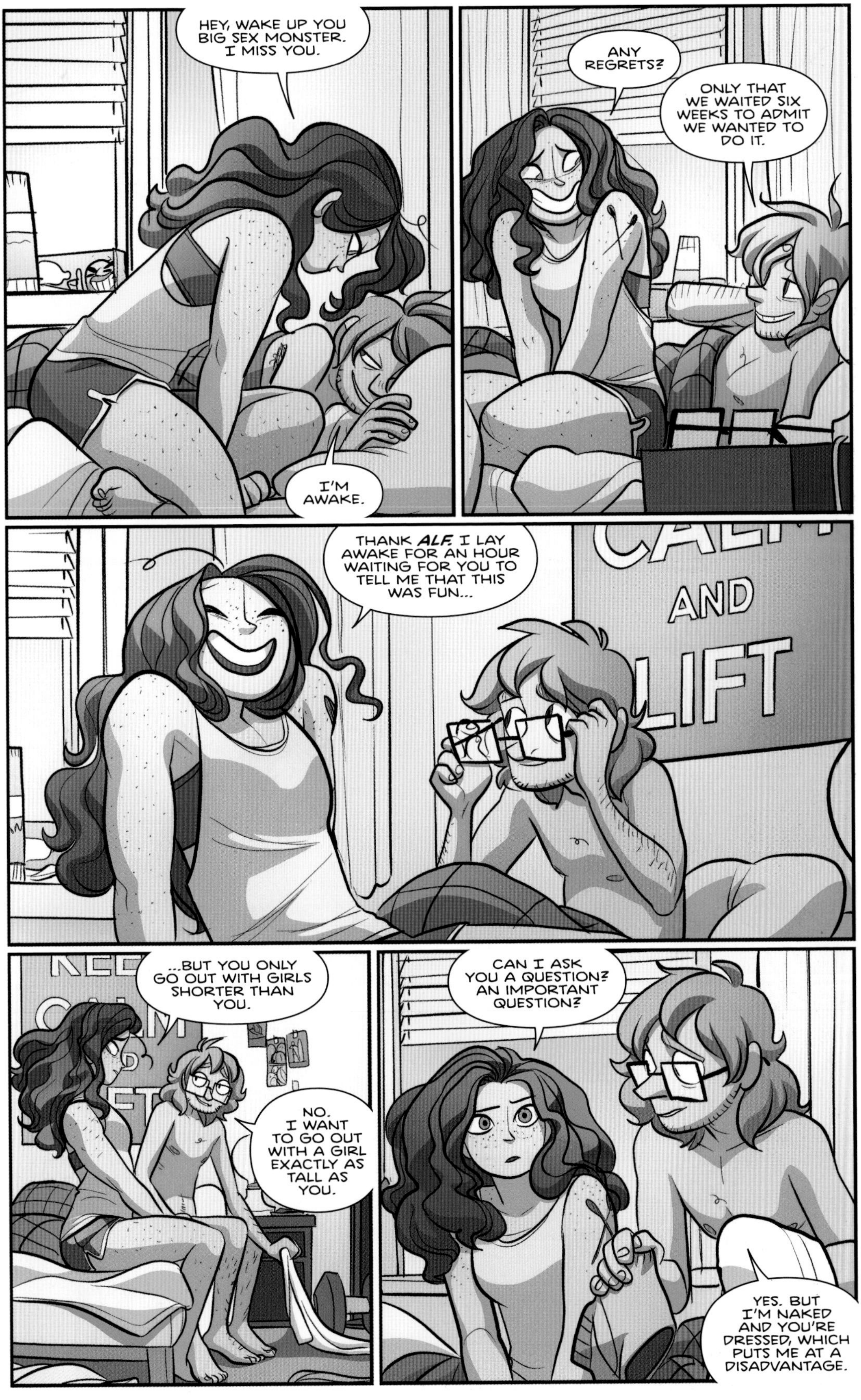
HEY, WAKE UP YOU BIG SEX MONSTER. I MISS YOU.
I'M AWAKE.
ANY REGRETS?
ONLY THAT WE WAITED SIX WEEKS TO ADMIT WE WANTED TO DO IT.
THANK *ALF*. I LAY AWAKE FOR AN HOUR WAITING FOR YOU TO TELL ME THAT THIS WAS FUN...
AND
...BUT YOU ONLY GO OUT WITH GIRLS SHORTER THAN YOU.
NO. I WANT TO GO OUT WITH A GIRL EXACTLY AS TALL AS YOU.
CAN I ASK YOU A QUESTION? AN IMPORTANT QUESTION?
YES. BUT I'M NAKED AND YOU'RE DRESSED, WHICH PUTS ME AT A DISADVANTAGE.

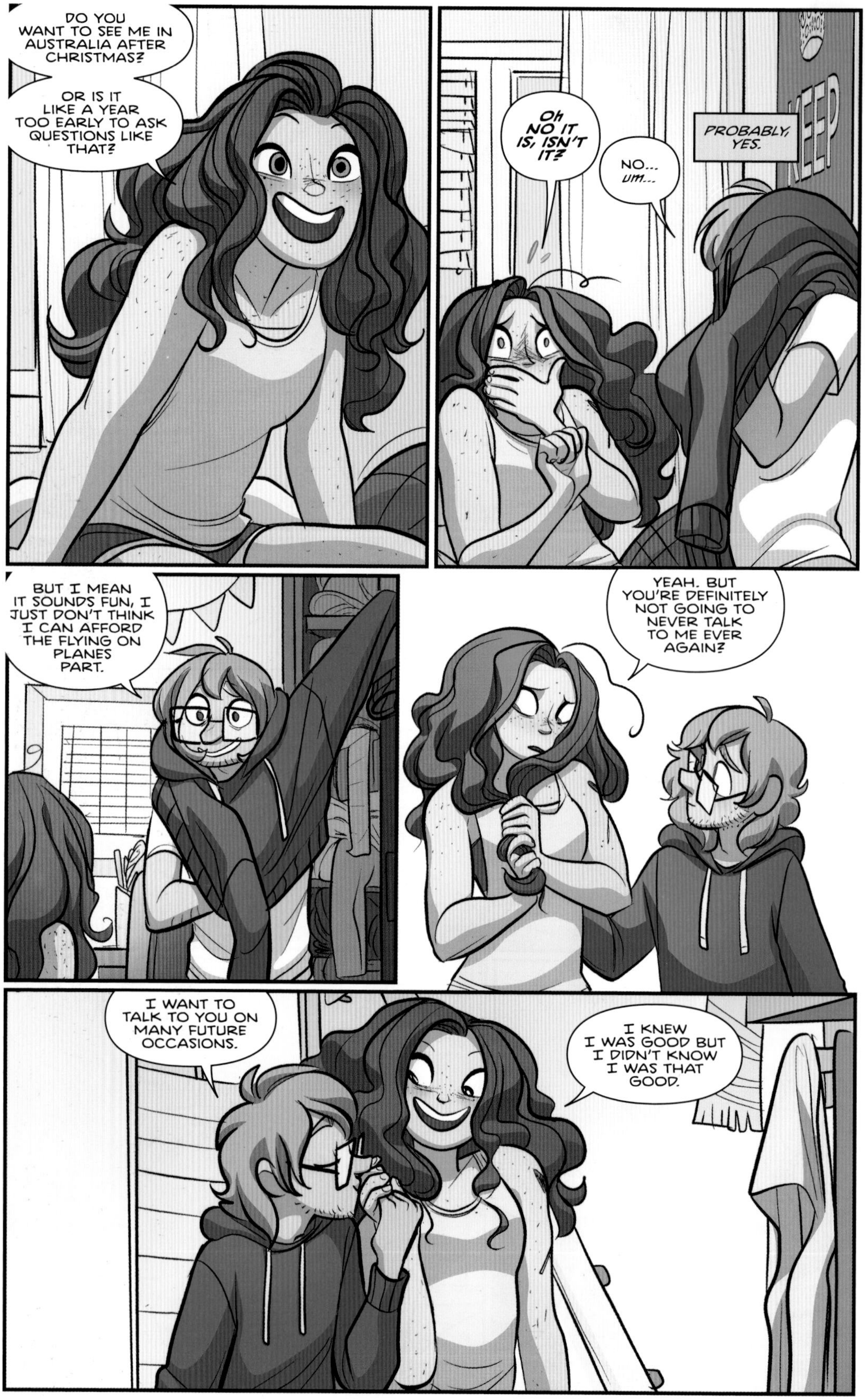

DO YOU WANT TO SEE ME IN AUSTRALIA AFTER CHRISTMAS?
OR IS IT LIKE A YEAR TOO EARLY TO ASK QUESTIONS LIKE THAT?
KEEP
Oh NO IT IS, ISN'T IT?
NO... um...
PROBABLY, YES.
BUT I MEAN IT SOUNDS FUN, I JUST DON'T THINK I CAN AFFORD THE FLYING ON PLANES PART.
YEAH. BUT YOU'RE DEFINITELY NOT GOING TO NEVER TALK TO ME EVER AGAIN?
I WANT TO TALK TO YOU ON MANY FUTURE OCCASIONS.
I KNEW I WAS GOOD BUT I DIDN'T KNOW I WAS THAT GOOD.

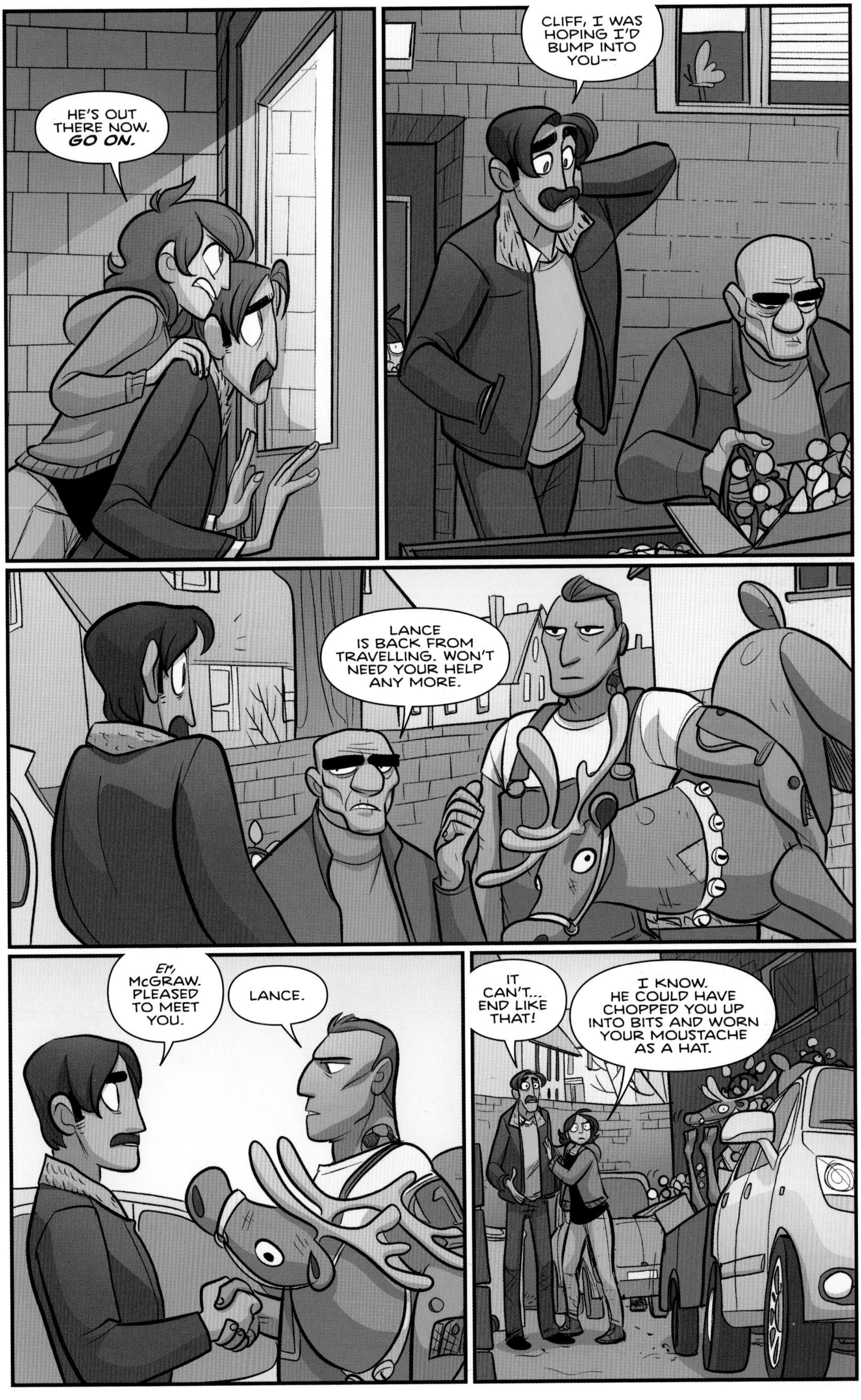
HE'S OUT THERE NOW. *GO ON.*
CLIFF, I WAS HOPING I'D BUMP INTO YOU--
LANCE IS BACK FROM TRAVELLING. WON'T NEED YOUR HELP ANY MORE.
Er, McGRAW. PLEASED TO MEET YOU.
LANCE.
IT CAN'T... END LIKE THAT!
I KNOW. HE COULD HAVE CHOPPED YOU UP INTO BITS AND WORN YOUR MOUSTACHE AS A HAT.

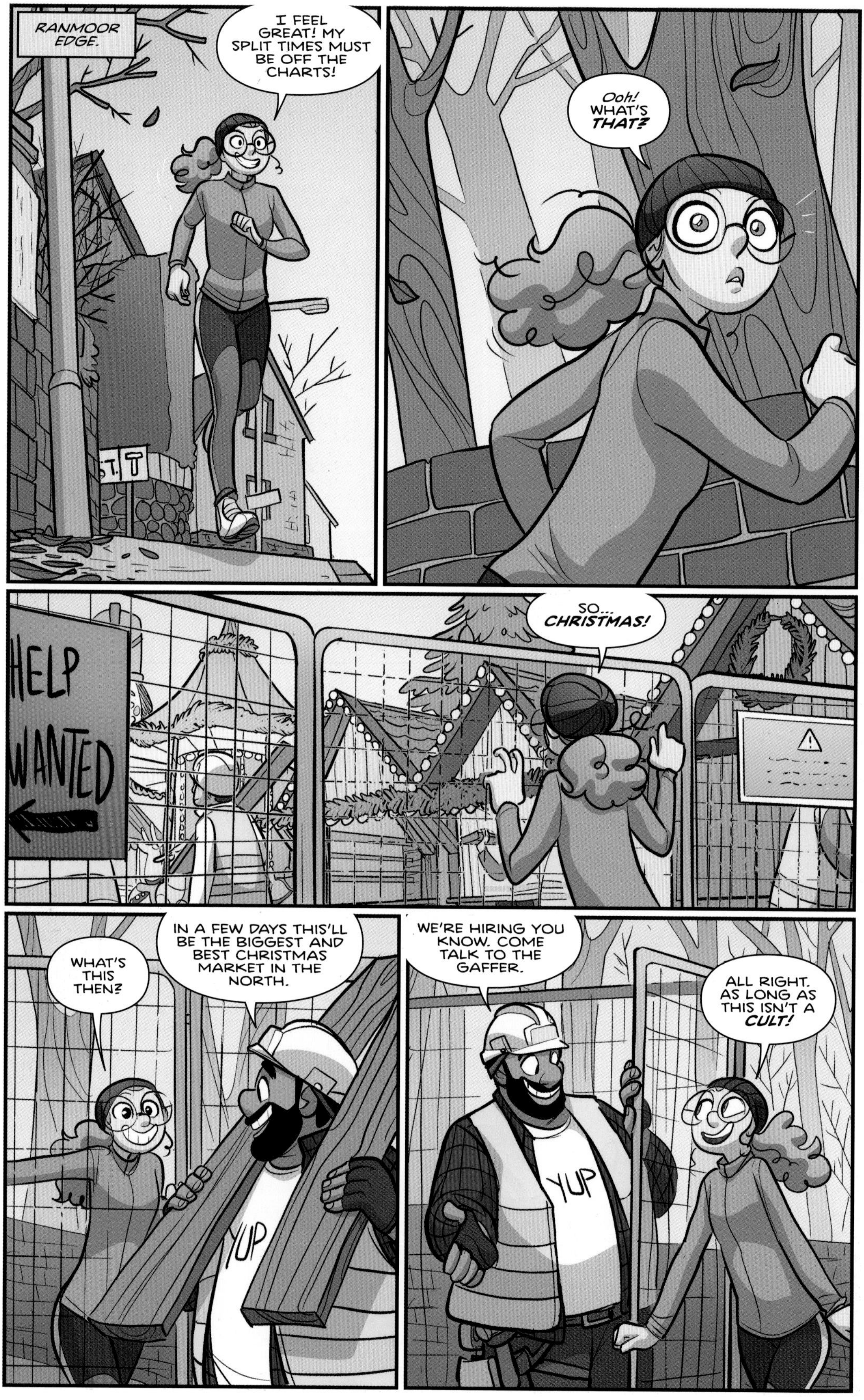
RANMOOR EDGE.
I FEEL GREAT! MY SPLIT TIMES MUST BE OFF THE CHARTS!
Ooh! WHAT'S THAT?
HELP WANTED
SO... CHRISTMAS!
WHAT'S THIS THEN?
IN A FEW DAYS THIS'LL BE THE BIGGEST AND BEST CHRISTMAS MARKET IN THE NORTH.
YUP
WE'RE HIRING YOU KNOW. COME TALK TO THE GAFFER.
ALL RIGHT. AS LONG AS THIS ISN'T A CULT!
YUP

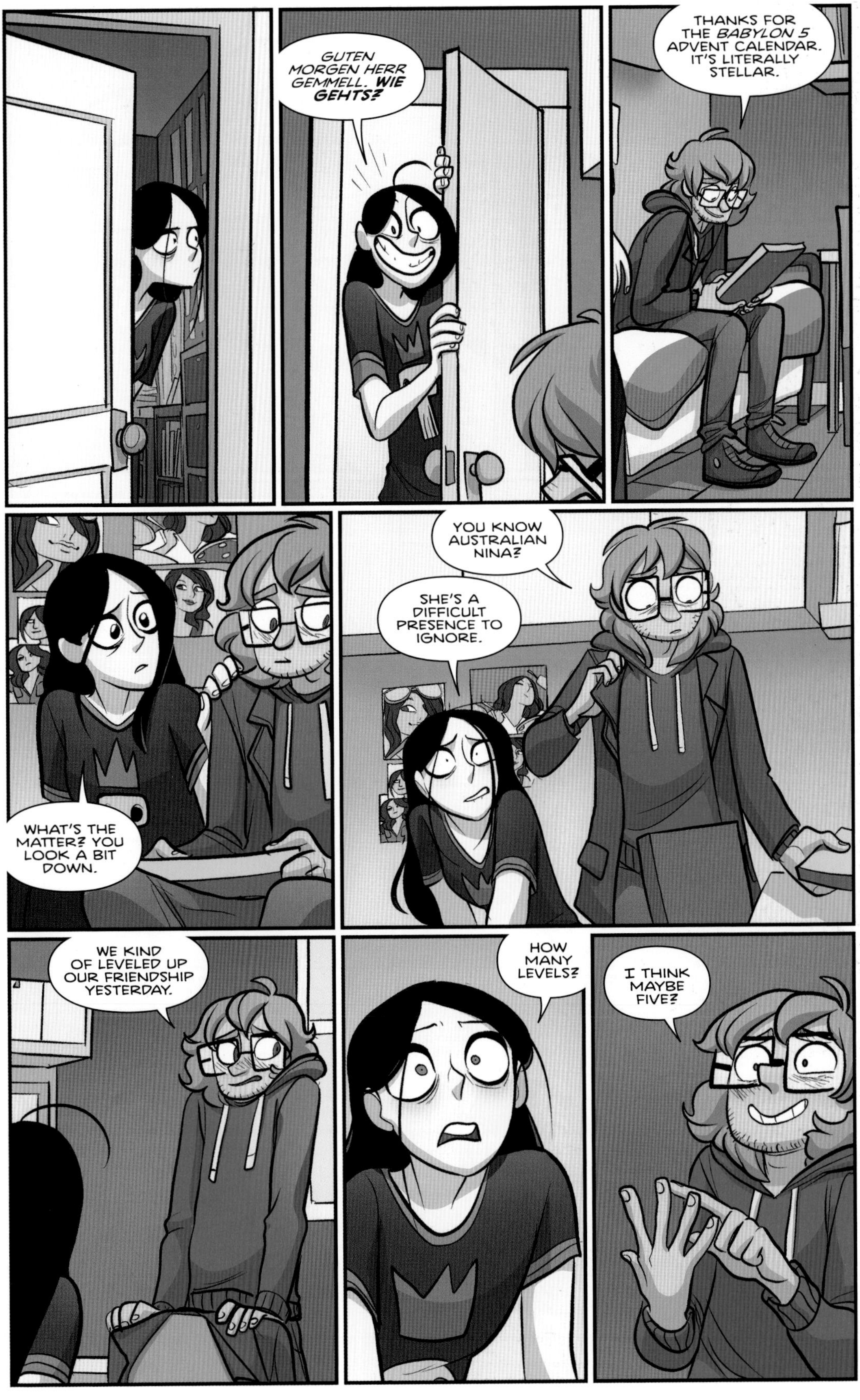
GUTEN MORGEN HERR GEMMELL. **WIE GEHTS?**
THANKS FOR THE *BABYLON 5* ADVENT CALENDAR. IT'S LITERALLY STELLAR.
WHAT'S THE MATTER? YOU LOOK A BIT DOWN.
YOU KNOW AUSTRALIAN NINA?
SHE'S A DIFFICULT PRESENCE TO IGNORE.
WE KIND OF LEVELED UP OUR FRIENDSHIP YESTERDAY.
HOW MANY LEVELS?
I THINK MAYBE FIVE?

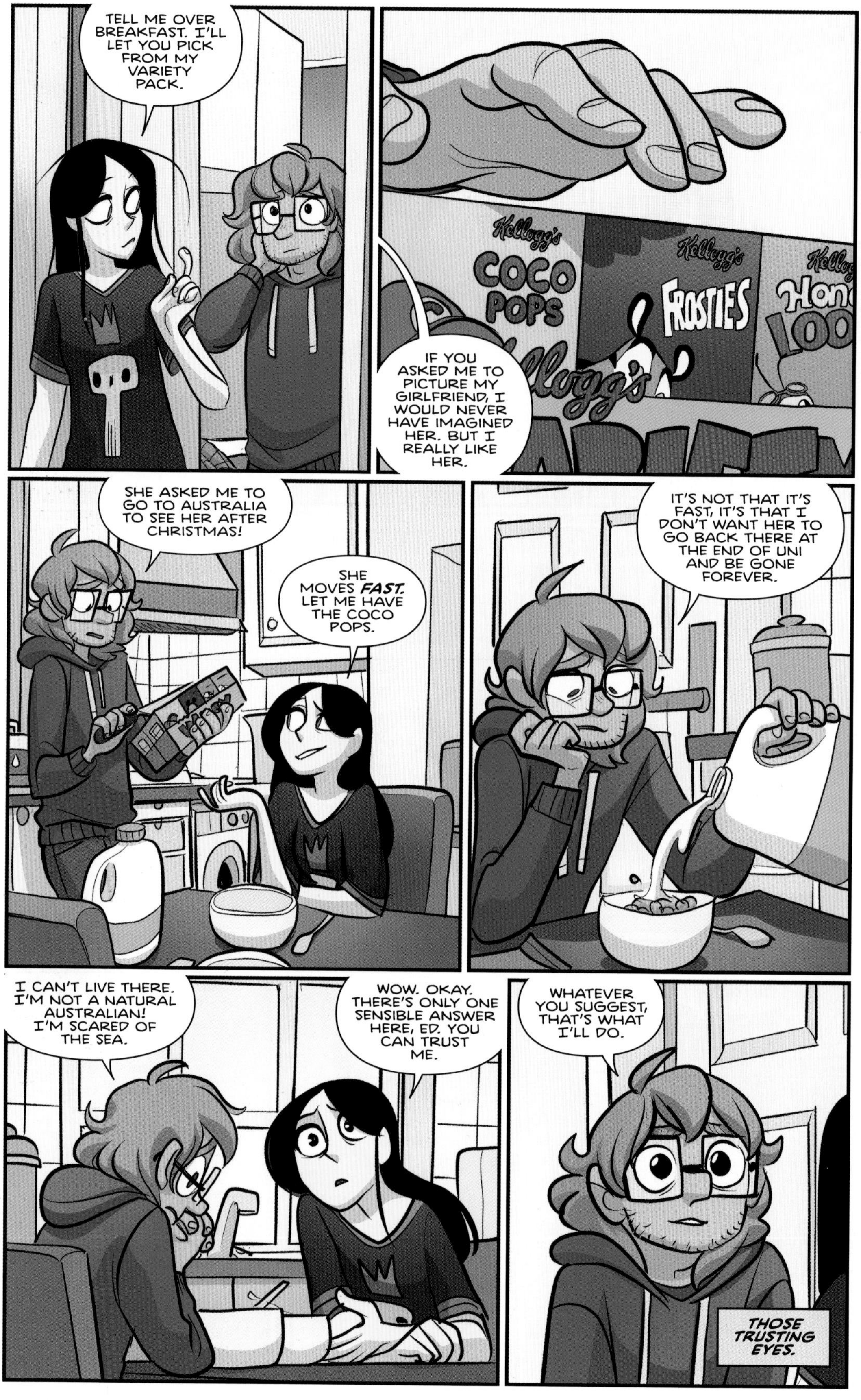
TELL ME OVER BREAKFAST. I'LL LET YOU PICK FROM MY VARIETY PACK.
Kellogg's COCO POPS
Kellogg's FROSTIES
IF YOU ASKED ME TO PICTURE MY GIRLFRIEND, I WOULD NEVER HAVE IMAGINED HER. BUT I REALLY LIKE HER.
SHE ASKED ME TO GO TO AUSTRALIA TO SEE HER AFTER CHRISTMAS!
SHE MOVES FAST. LET ME HAVE THE COCO POPS.
IT'S NOT THAT IT'S FAST, IT'S THAT I DON'T WANT HER TO GO BACK THERE AT THE END OF UNI AND BE GONE FOREVER.
I CAN'T LIVE THERE. I'M NOT A NATURAL AUSTRALIAN! I'M SCARED OF THE SEA.
WOW. OKAY. THERE'S ONLY ONE SENSIBLE ANSWER HERE, ED. YOU CAN TRUST ME.
WHATEVER YOU SUGGEST, THAT'S WHAT I'LL DO.
THOSE TRUSTING EYES.

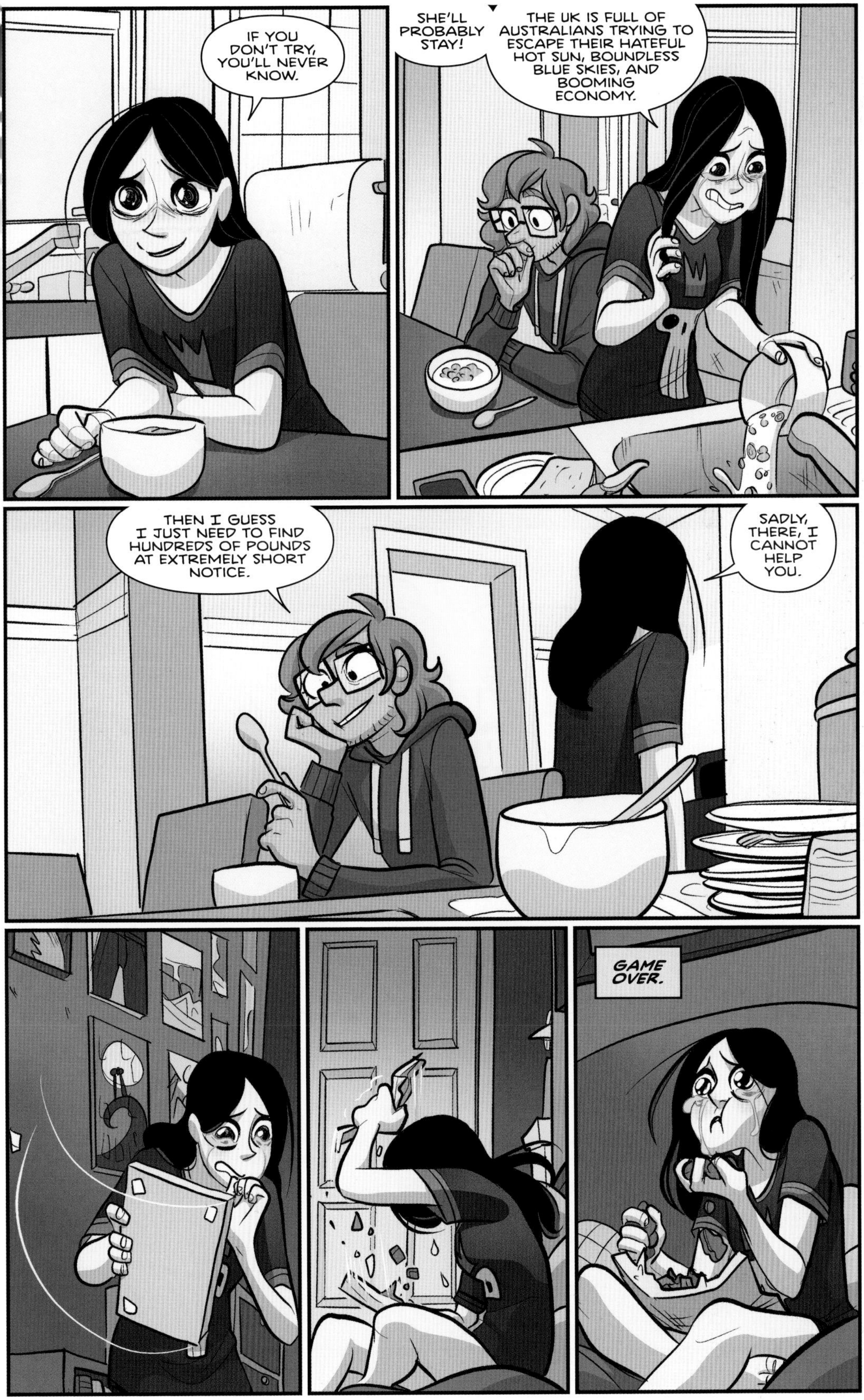
IF YOU DON'T TRY, YOU'LL NEVER KNOW.
SHE'LL PROBABLY STAY!
THE UK IS FULL OF AUSTRALIANS TRYING TO ESCAPE THEIR HATEFUL HOT SUN, BOUNDLESS BLUE SKIES, AND BOOMING ECONOMY.
THEN I GUESS I JUST NEED TO FIND HUNDREDS OF POUNDS AT EXTREMELY SHORT NOTICE.
SADLY, THERE, I CANNOT HELP YOU.
GAME OVER.

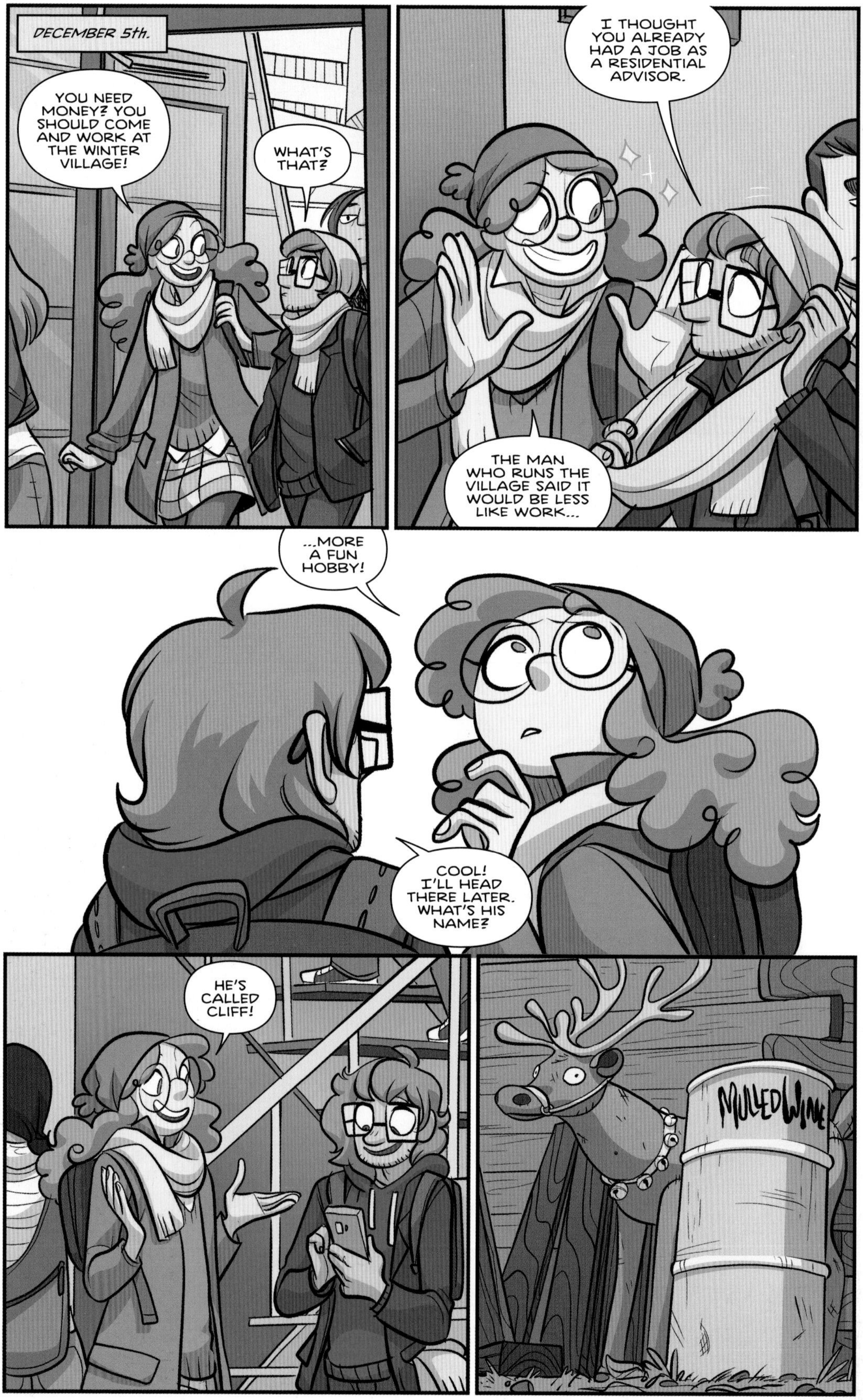
DECEMBER 5th.
YOU NEED MONEY? YOU SHOULD COME AND WORK AT THE WINTER VILLAGE!
WHAT'S THAT?
I THOUGHT YOU ALREADY HAD A JOB AS A RESIDENTIAL ADVISOR.
THE MAN WHO RUNS THE VILLAGE SAID IT WOULD BE LESS LIKE WORK...
...MORE A FUN HOBBY!
COOL! I'LL HEAD THERE LATER. WHAT'S HIS NAME?
HE'S CALLED CLIFF!
MULLED WINE

CHAPTER
FORTY-THREE

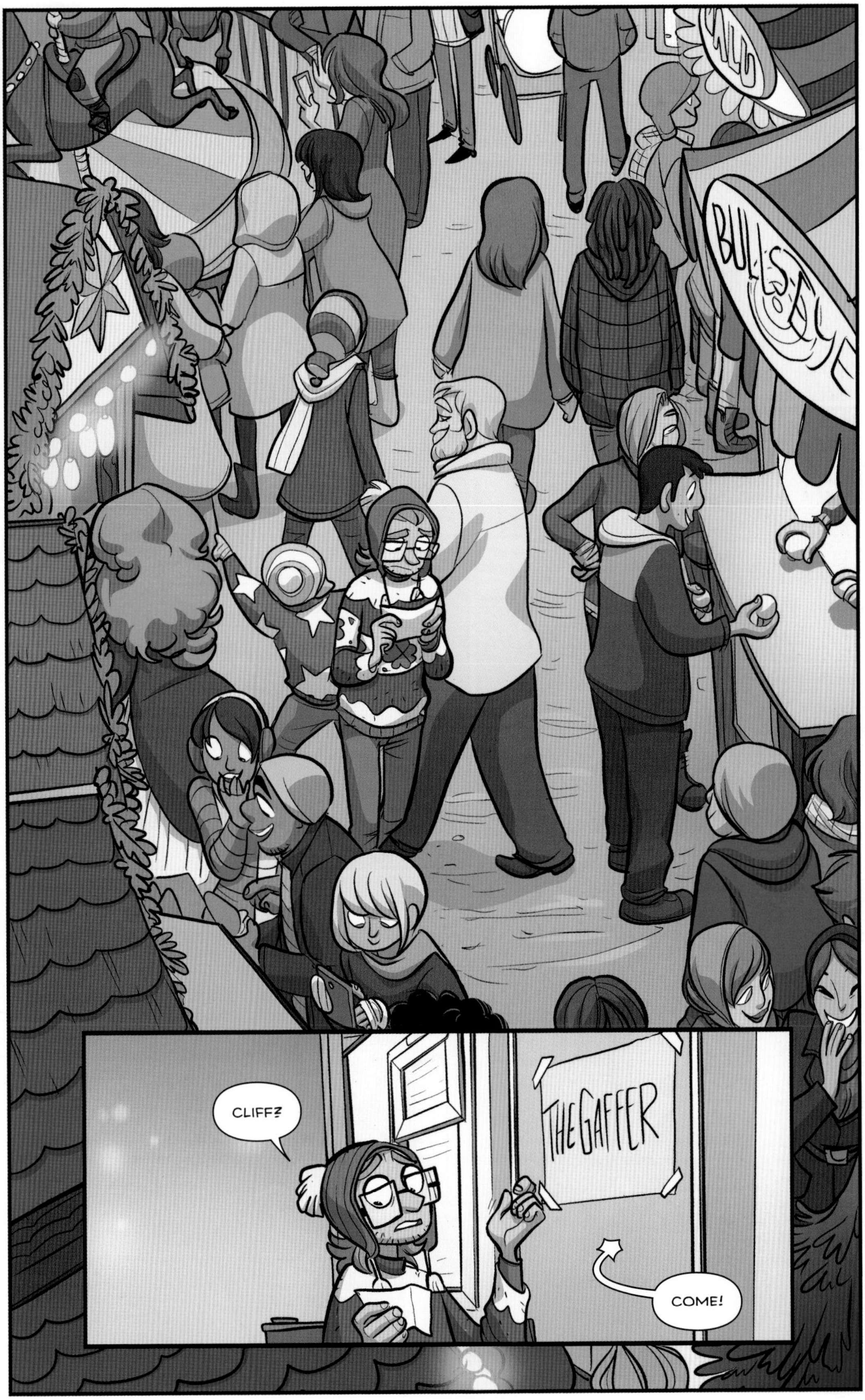
CALLO
BULL'S-EYE
CLIFF?
THE GAFFER
COME!

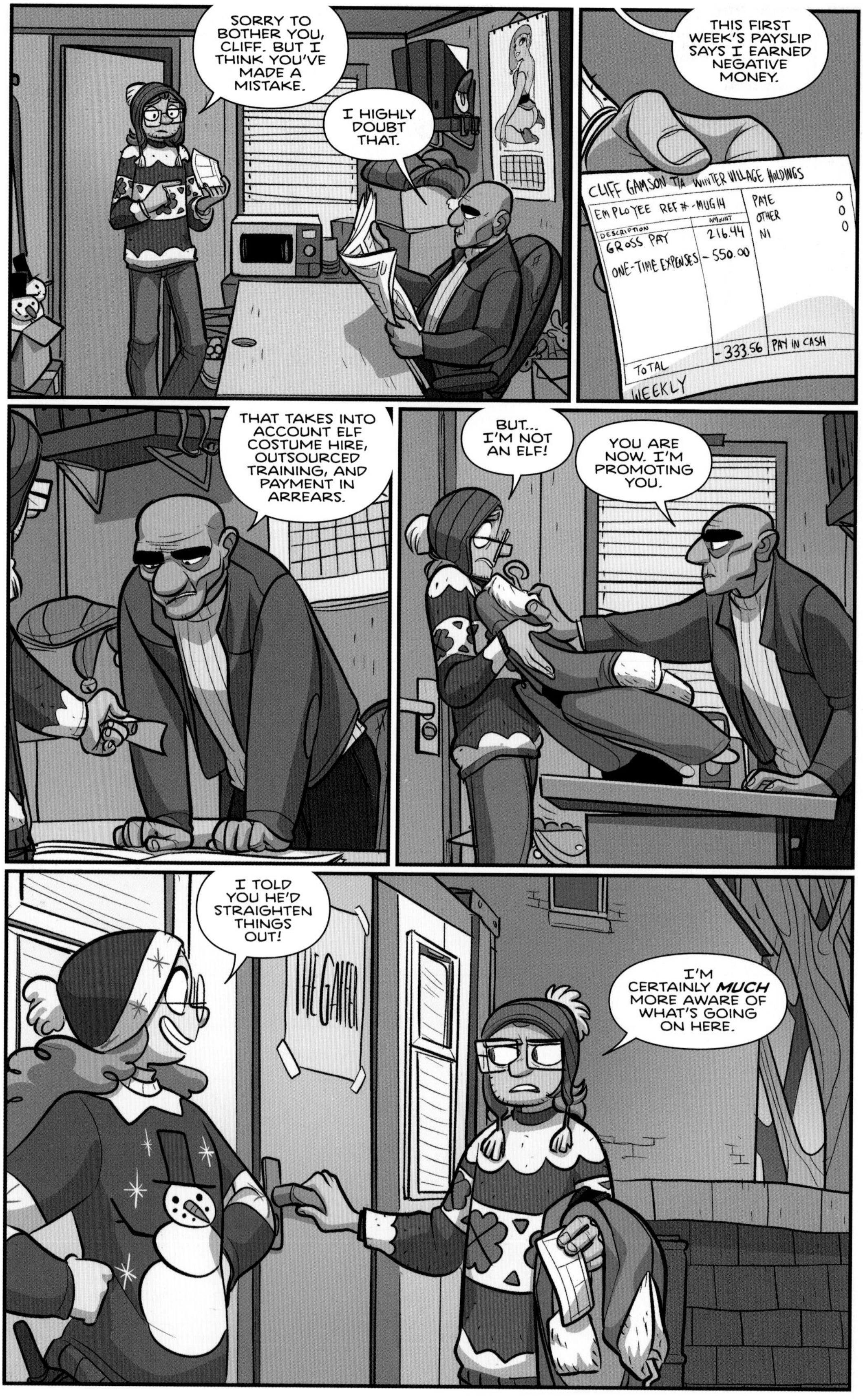
SORRY TO BOTHER YOU, CLIFF. BUT I THINK YOU'VE MADE A MISTAKE.
I HIGHLY DOUBT THAT.
THIS FIRST WEEK'S PAYSLIP SAYS I EARNED NEGATIVE MONEY.
CLIFF GAMSON T/A WINTER VILLAGE HOLDINGS
EMPLOYEE REF #-MUG14
PAYE 0
OTHER 0
NI 0
DESCRIPTION
AMOUNT
GROSS PAY 216.44
ONE-TIME EXPENSES -550.00
TOTAL -333.56 PAY IN CASH
WEEKLY
THAT TAKES INTO ACCOUNT ELF COSTUME HIRE, OUTSOURCED TRAINING, AND PAYMENT IN ARREARS.
BUT... I'M NOT AN ELF!
YOU ARE NOW. I'M PROMOTING YOU.
I TOLD YOU HE'D STRAIGHTEN THINGS OUT!
THE GAFFER
I'M CERTAINLY ***MUCH*** MORE AWARE OF WHAT'S GOING ON HERE.

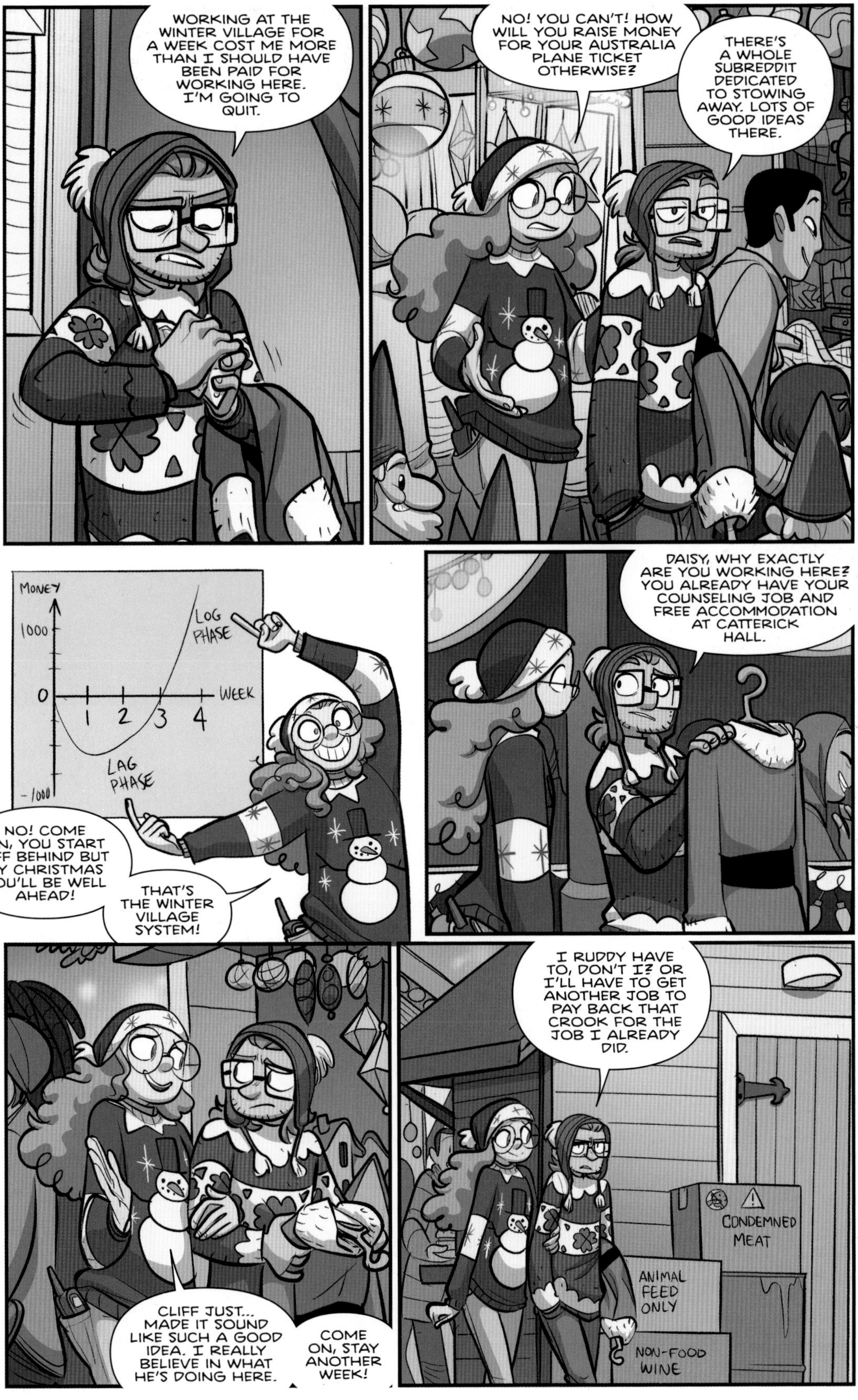
WORKING AT THE WINTER VILLAGE FOR A WEEK COST ME MORE THAN I SHOULD HAVE BEEN PAID FOR WORKING HERE. I'M GOING TO QUIT.
NO! YOU CAN'T! HOW WILL YOU RAISE MONEY FOR YOUR AUSTRALIA PLANE TICKET OTHERWISE?
THERE'S A WHOLE SUBREDDIT DEDICATED TO STOWING AWAY. LOTS OF GOOD IDEAS THERE.
MONEY
1000
0
-1000
WEEK
1 2 3 4
LOG PHASE
LAG PHASE
NO! COME
N, YOU START
FF BEHIND BUT
Y CHRISTMAS
OU'LL BE WELL
AHEAD!
THAT'S THE WINTER VILLAGE SYSTEM!
DAISY, WHY EXACTLY ARE YOU WORKING HERE? YOU ALREADY HAVE YOUR COUNSELING JOB AND FREE ACCOMMODATION AT CATTERICK HALL.
CLIFF JUST... MADE IT SOUND LIKE SUCH A GOOD IDEA. I REALLY BELIEVE IN WHAT HE'S DOING HERE.
COME ON, STAY ANOTHER WEEK!
I RUDDY HAVE TO, DON'T I? OR I'LL HAVE TO GET ANOTHER JOB TO PAY BACK THAT CROOK FOR THE JOB I ALREADY DID.
CONDEMNED MEAT
ANIMAL FEED ONLY
NON-FOOD WINE

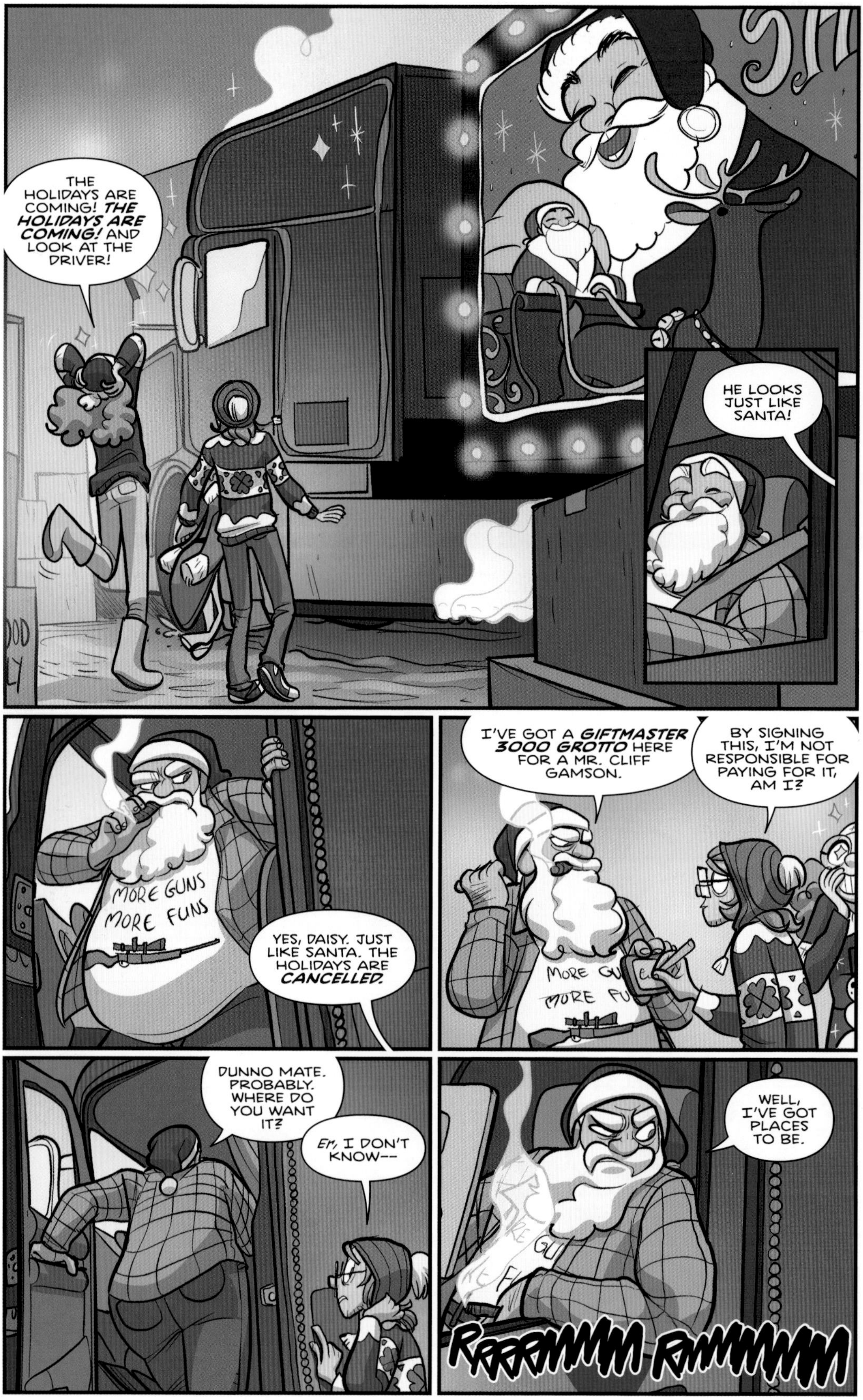
THE HOLIDAYS ARE COMING! THE HOLIDAYS ARE COMING! AND LOOK AT THE DRIVER!
HE LOOKS JUST LIKE SANTA!
YES, DAISY. JUST LIKE SANTA. THE HOLIDAYS ARE CANCELLED.
MORE GUNS MORE FUNS
I'VE GOT A GIFTMASTER 3000 GROTTO HERE FOR A MR. CLIFF GAMSON.
BY SIGNING THIS, I'M NOT RESPONSIBLE FOR PAYING FOR IT, AM I?
DUNNO MATE. PROBABLY. WHERE DO YOU WANT IT?
EM, I DON'T KNOW--
WELL, I'VE GOT PLACES TO BE.
RRRRMMM RMMMMM

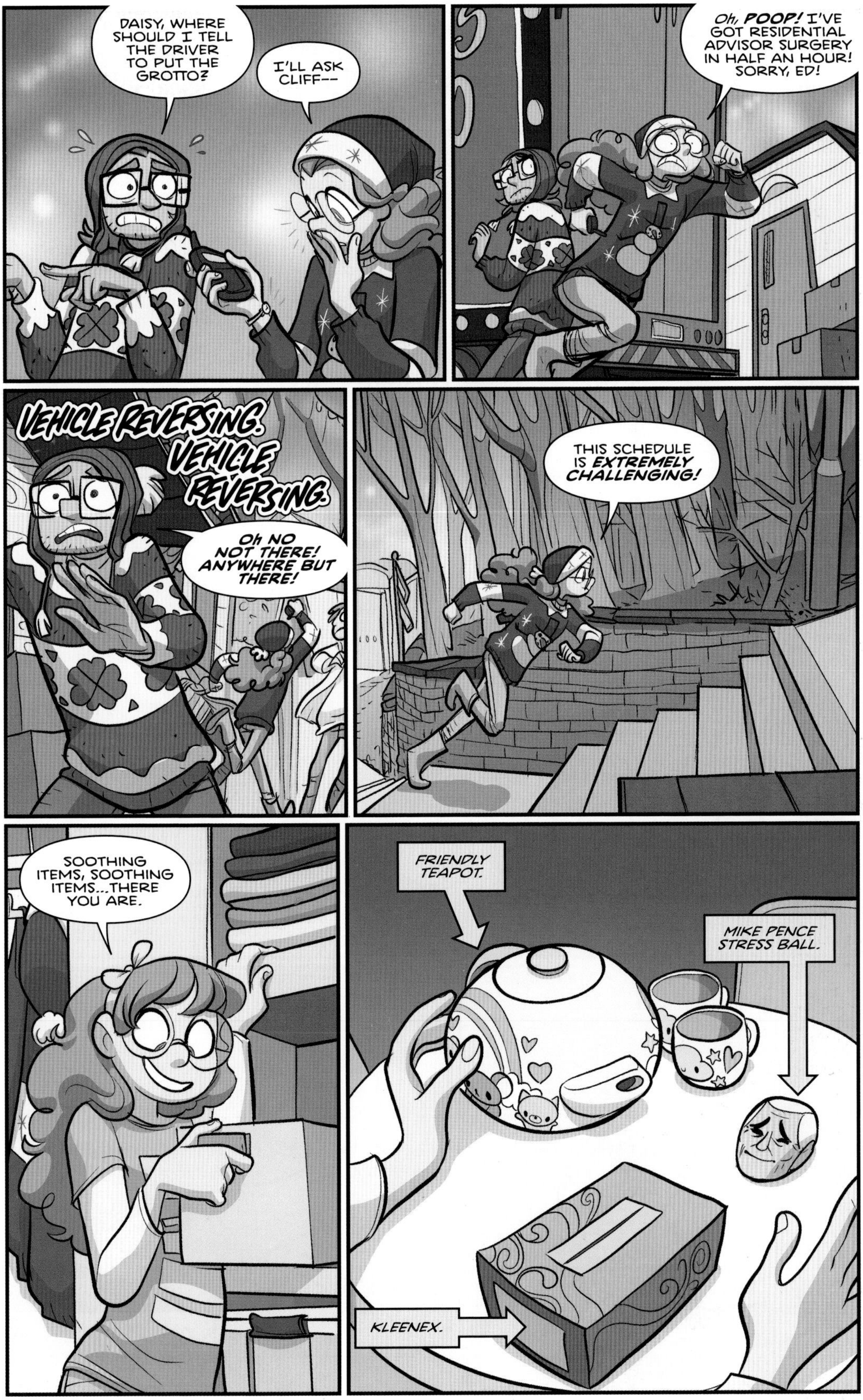

DAISY, WHERE SHOULD I TELL THE DRIVER TO PUT THE GROTTO?
I'LL ASK CLIFF--
Oh, POOP! I'VE GOT RESIDENTIAL ADVISOR SURGERY IN HALF AN HOUR! SORRY, ED!
VEHICLE REVERSING. VEHICLE REVERSING.
Oh NO NOT THERE! ANYWHERE BUT THERE!
THIS SCHEDULE IS EXTREMELY CHALLENGING!
SOOTHING ITEMS, SOOTHING ITEMS... THERE YOU ARE.
FRIENDLY TEAPOT.
MIKE PENCE STRESS BALL.
KLEENEX.

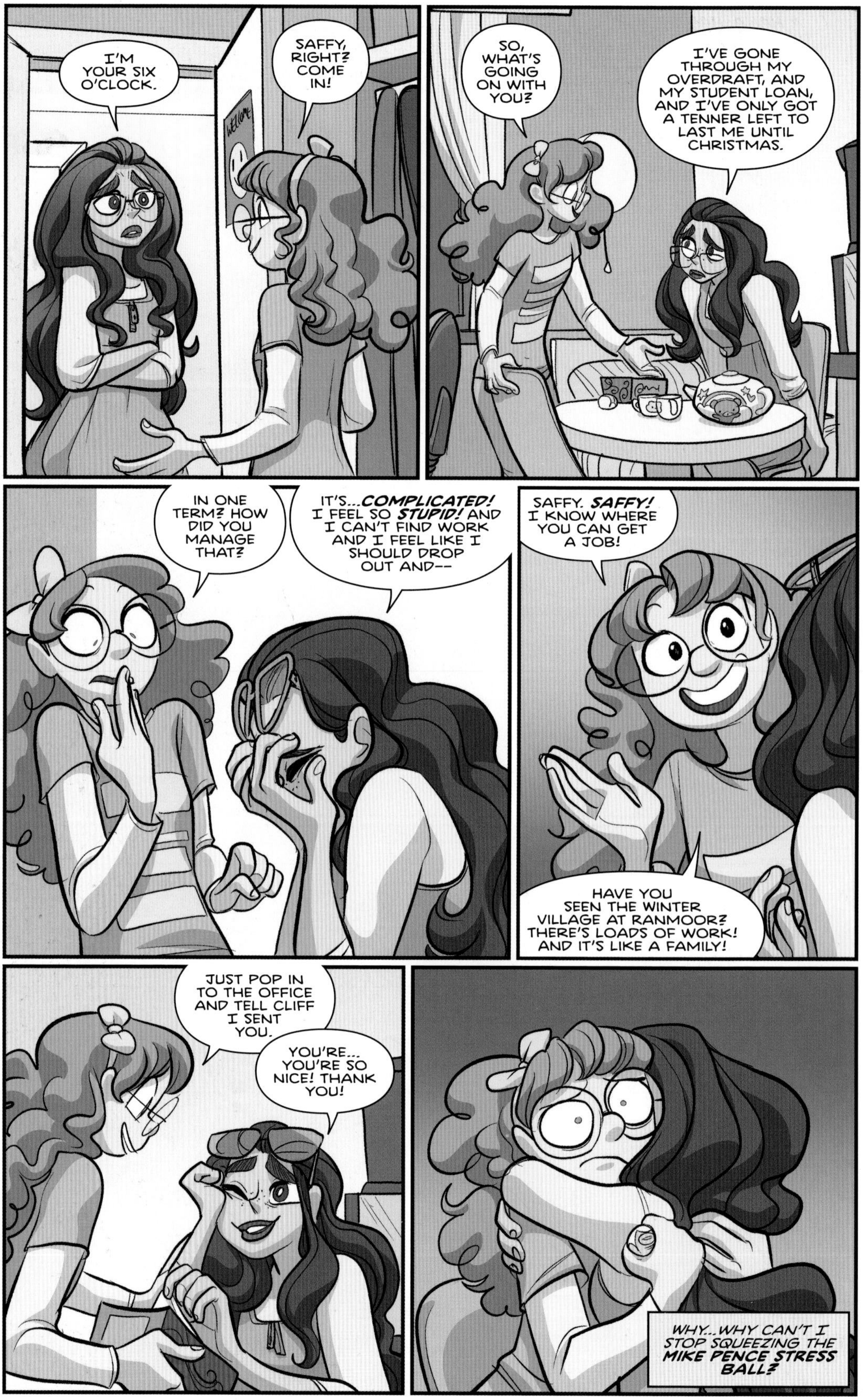
I'M YOUR SIX O'CLOCK.
SAFFY, RIGHT? COME IN!
SO, WHAT'S GOING ON WITH YOU?
I'VE GONE THROUGH MY OVERDRAFT, AND MY STUDENT LOAN, AND I'VE ONLY GOT A TENNER LEFT TO LAST ME UNTIL CHRISTMAS.
IN ONE TERM? HOW DID YOU MANAGE THAT?
IT'S...**COMPLICATED!** I FEEL SO **STUPID!** AND I CAN'T FIND WORK AND I FEEL LIKE I SHOULD DROP OUT AND--
SAFFY. **SAFFY!** I KNOW WHERE YOU CAN GET A JOB!
HAVE YOU SEEN THE WINTER VILLAGE AT RANMOOR? THERE'S LOADS OF WORK! AND IT'S LIKE A FAMILY!
JUST POP IN TO THE OFFICE AND TELL CLIFF I SENT YOU.
YOU'RE... YOU'RE SO NICE! THANK YOU!
*WHY...WHY CAN'T I STOP SQUEEZING THE **MIKE PENCE STRESS BALL?***

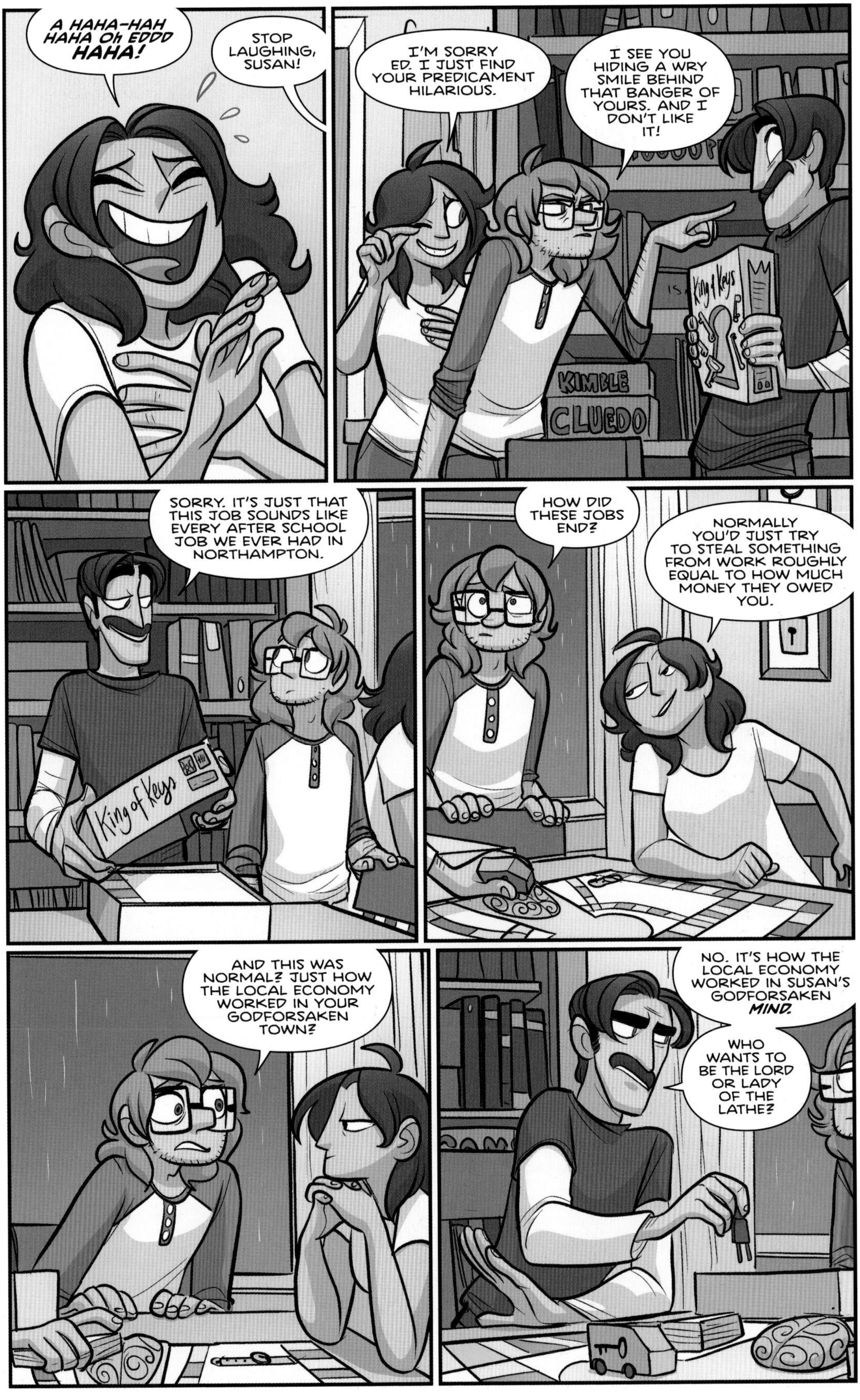

A HAHA-HAH HAHA Oh EDDD HAHA!
STOP LAUGHING, SUSAN!
I'M SORRY ED. I JUST FIND YOUR PREDICAMENT HILARIOUS.
I SEE YOU HIDING A WRY SMILE BEHIND THAT BANGER OF YOURS. AND I DON'T LIKE IT!
King of Keys
KIMBLE
CLUEDO
SORRY. IT'S JUST THAT THIS JOB SOUNDS LIKE EVERY AFTER SCHOOL JOB WE EVER HAD IN NORTHAMPTON.
King of Keys
HOW DID THESE JOBS END?
NORMALLY YOU'D JUST TRY TO STEAL SOMETHING FROM WORK ROUGHLY EQUAL TO HOW MUCH MONEY THEY OWED YOU.
AND THIS WAS NORMAL? JUST HOW THE LOCAL ECONOMY WORKED IN YOUR GODFORSAKEN TOWN?
NO. IT'S HOW THE LOCAL ECONOMY WORKED IN SUSAN'S GODFORSAKEN MIND.
WHO WANTS TO BE THE LORD OR LADY OF THE LATHE?

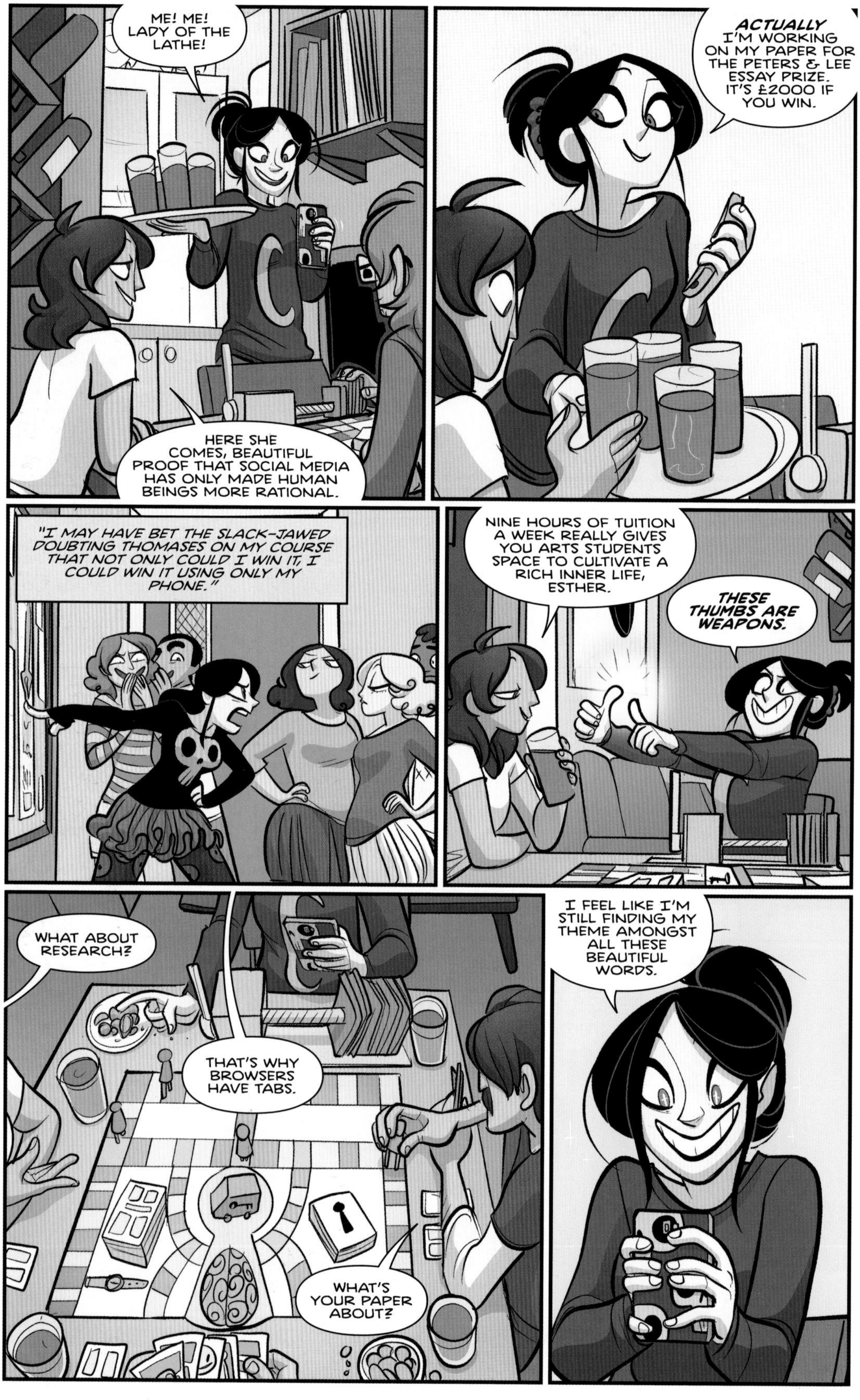

ME! ME! LADY OF THE LATHE!
HERE SHE COMES, BEAUTIFUL PROOF THAT SOCIAL MEDIA HAS ONLY MADE HUMAN BEINGS MORE RATIONAL.
ACTUALLY I'M WORKING ON MY PAPER FOR THE PETERS & LEE ESSAY PRIZE. IT'S £2000 IF YOU WIN.
"I MAY HAVE BET THE SLACK-JAWED DOUBTING THOMASES ON MY COURSE THAT NOT ONLY COULD I WIN IT, I COULD WIN IT USING ONLY MY PHONE."
NINE HOURS OF TUITION A WEEK REALLY GIVES YOU ARTS STUDENTS SPACE TO CULTIVATE A RICH INNER LIFE, ESTHER.
THESE THUMBS ARE WEAPONS.
WHAT ABOUT RESEARCH?
THAT'S WHY BROWSERS HAVE TABS.
WHAT'S YOUR PAPER ABOUT?
I FEEL LIKE I'M STILL FINDING MY THEME AMONGST ALL THESE BEAUTIFUL WORDS.

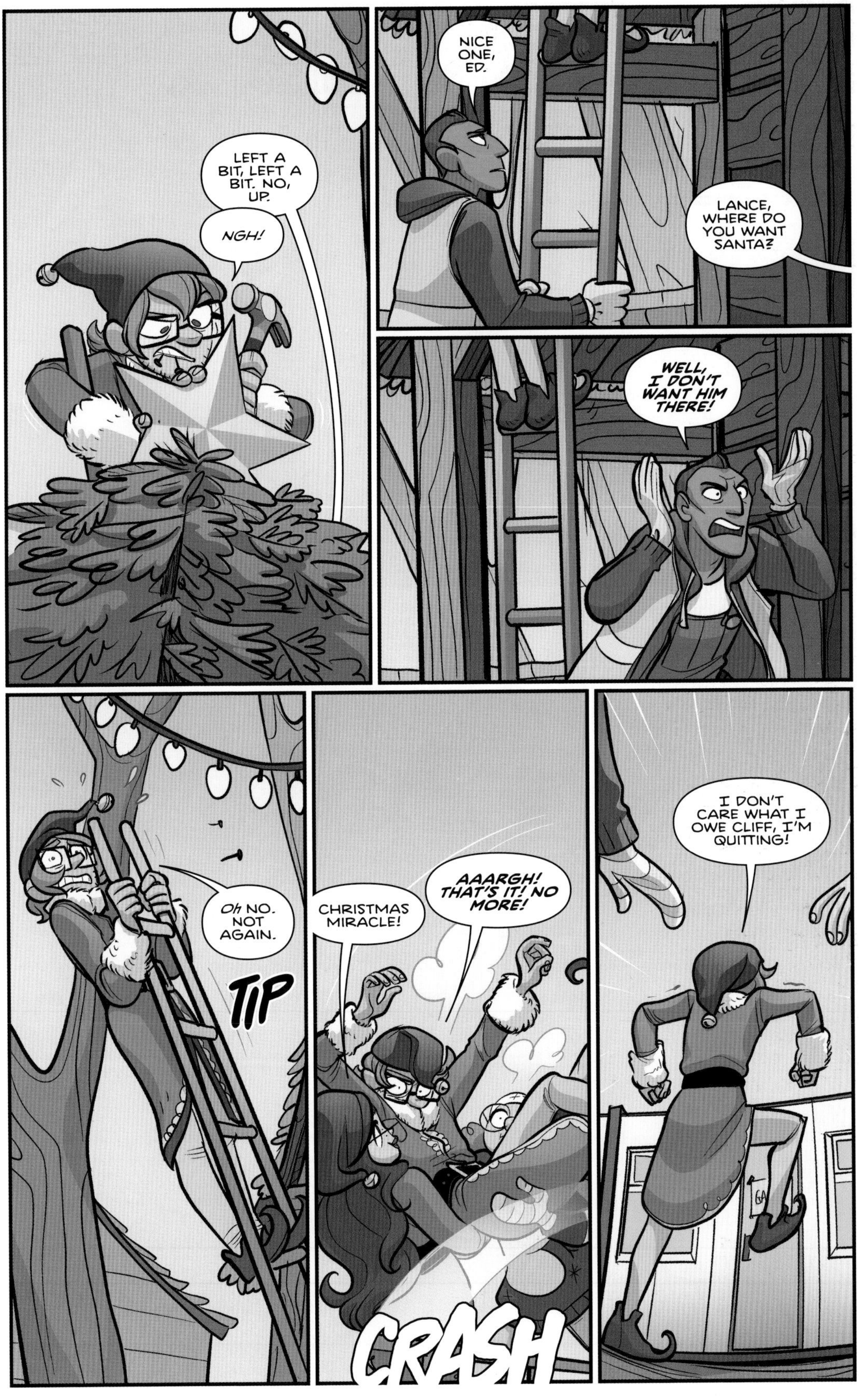
LEFT A BIT, LEFT A BIT. NO, UP.
NGH!
NICE ONE, ED.
LANCE, WHERE DO YOU WANT SANTA?
WELL, I DON'T WANT HIM THERE!
Oh NO. NOT AGAIN.
TIP
CHRISTMAS MIRACLE!
AAARGH! THAT'S IT! NO MORE!
CRASH
I DON'T CARE WHAT I OWE CLIFF, I'M QUITTING!

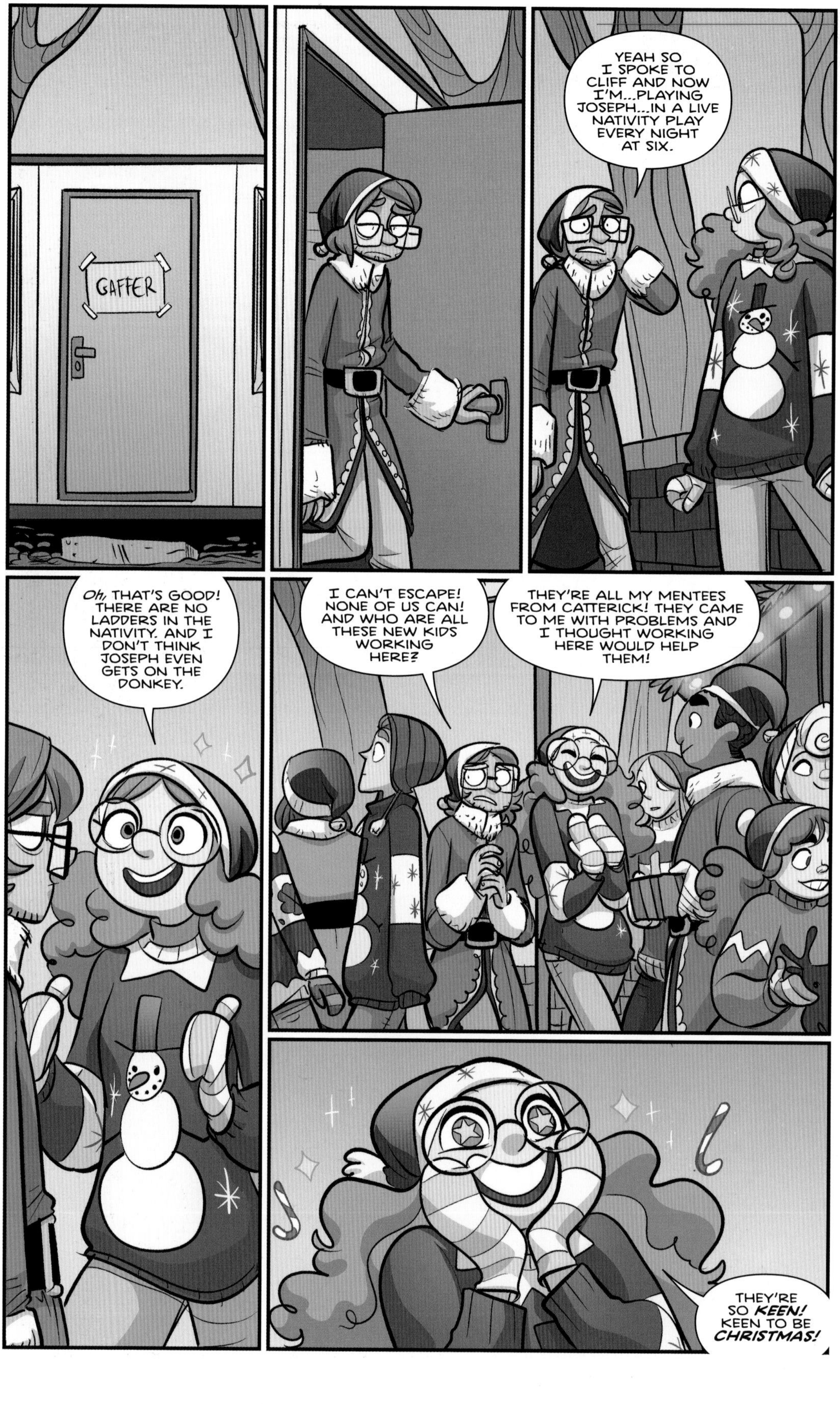
GAFFER
YEAH SO I SPOKE TO CLIFF AND NOW I'M...PLAYING JOSEPH...IN A LIVE NATIVITY PLAY EVERY NIGHT AT SIX.
Oh, THAT'S GOOD! THERE ARE NO LADDERS IN THE NATIVITY. AND I DON'T THINK JOSEPH EVEN GETS ON THE DONKEY.
I CAN'T ESCAPE! NONE OF US CAN! AND WHO ARE ALL THESE NEW KIDS WORKING HERE?
THEY'RE ALL MY MENTEES FROM CATTERICK! THEY CAME TO ME WITH PROBLEMS AND I THOUGHT WORKING HERE WOULD HELP THEM!
THEY'RE SO ***KEEN!*** KEEN TO BE ***CHRISTMAS!***

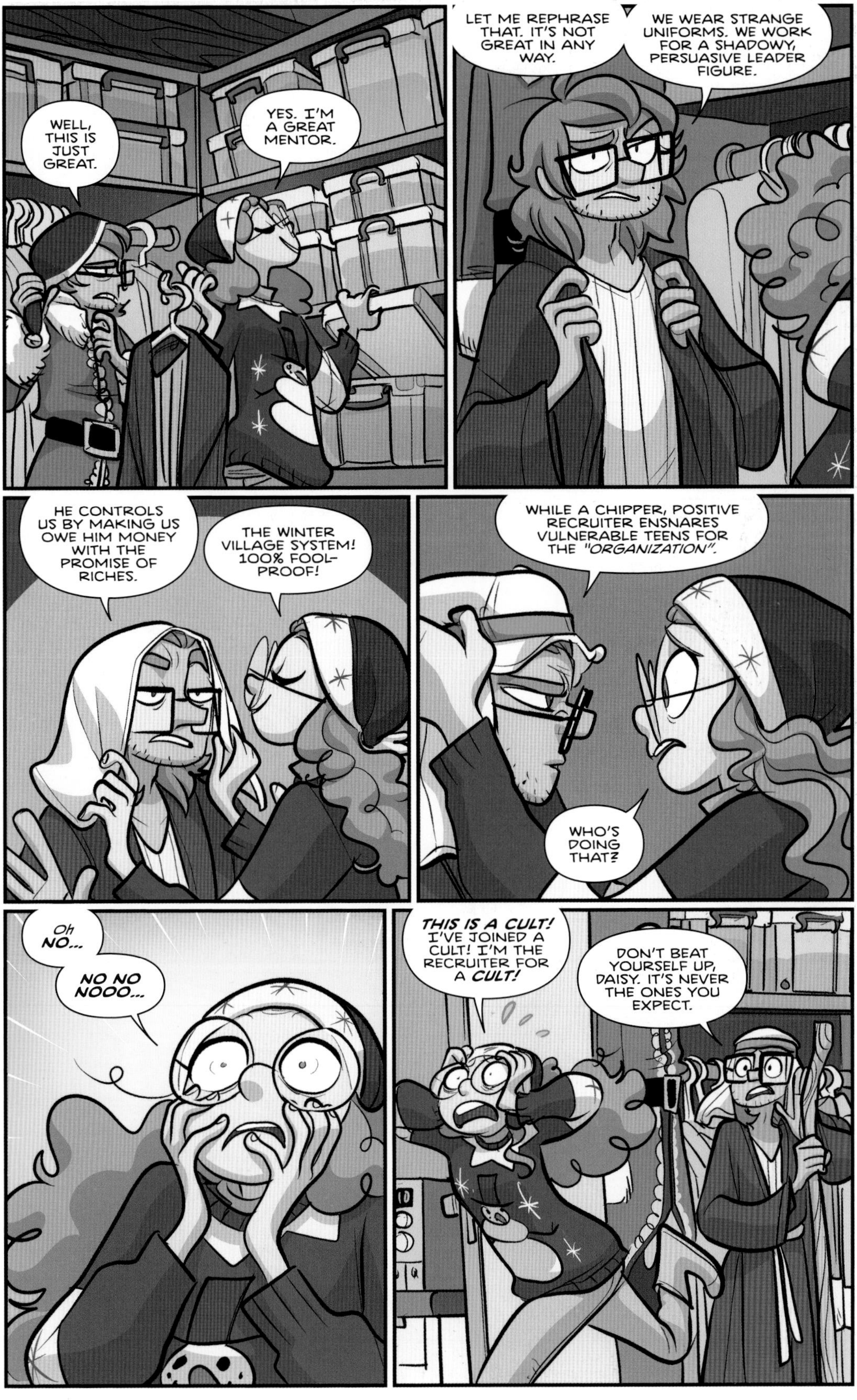
WELL, THIS IS JUST GREAT.
YES. I'M A GREAT MENTOR.
LET ME REPHRASE THAT. IT'S NOT GREAT IN ANY WAY.
WE WEAR STRANGE UNIFORMS. WE WORK FOR A SHADOWY, PERSUASIVE LEADER FIGURE.
HE CONTROLS US BY MAKING US OWE HIM MONEY WITH THE PROMISE OF RICHES.
THE WINTER VILLAGE SYSTEM! 100% FOOL-PROOF!
WHILE A CHIPPER, POSITIVE RECRUITER ENSNARES VULNERABLE TEENS FOR THE "ORGANIZATION".
WHO'S DOING THAT?
Oh NO...
NO NO NOOO...
THIS IS A CULT! I'VE JOINED A CULT! I'M THE RECRUITER FOR A CULT!
DON'T BEAT YOURSELF UP, DAISY. IT'S NEVER THE ONES YOU EXPECT.

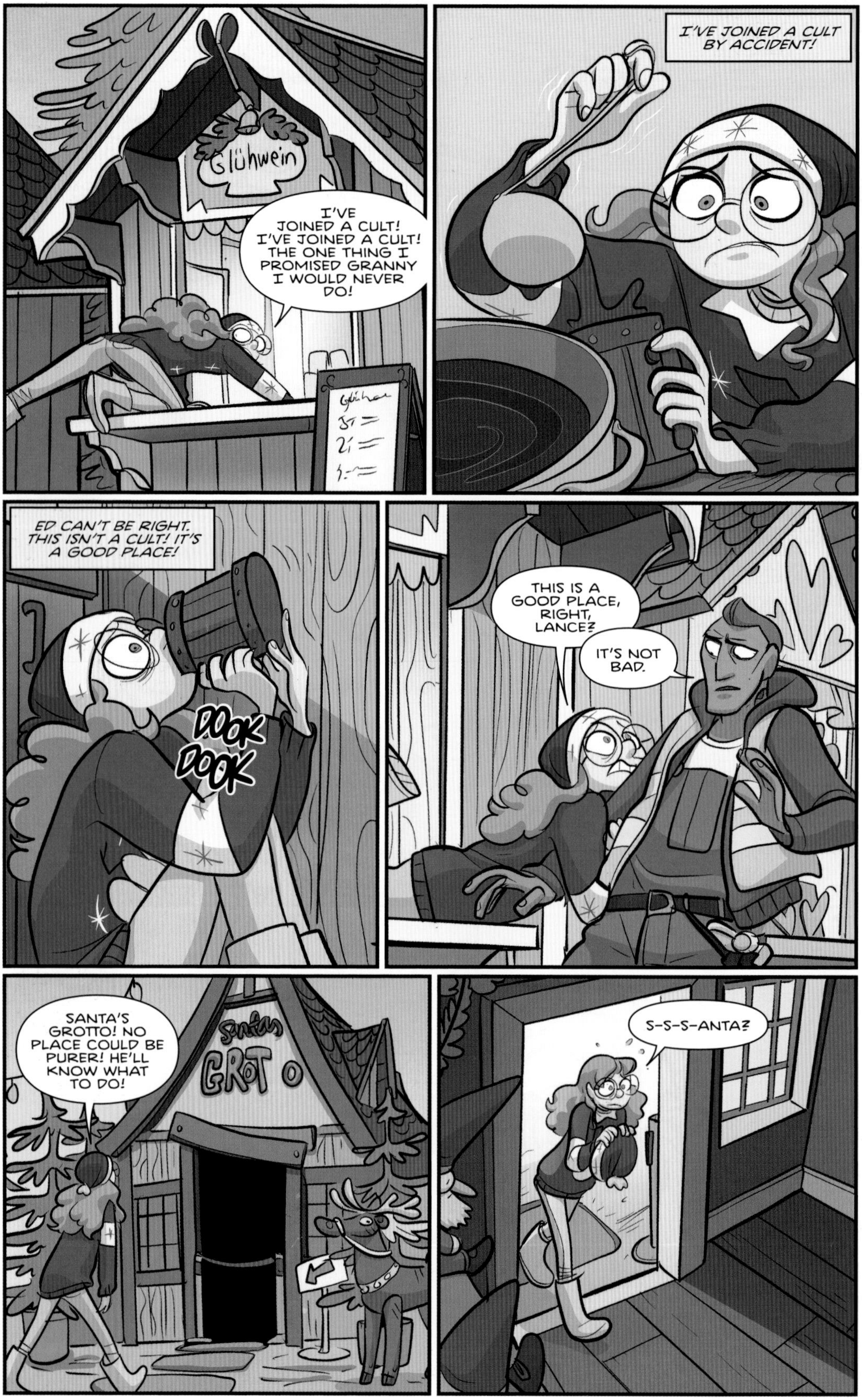
Glühwein
I'VE JOINED A CULT! I'VE JOINED A CULT! THE ONE THING I PROMISED GRANNY I WOULD NEVER DO!
I'VE JOINED A CULT BY ACCIDENT!
ED CAN'T BE RIGHT. THIS ISN'T A CULT! IT'S A GOOD PLACE!
DOOK DOOK
THIS IS A GOOD PLACE, RIGHT, LANCE?
IT'S NOT BAD.
SANTA'S GROTTO! NO PLACE COULD BE PURER! HE'LL KNOW WHAT TO DO!
Santas GROTTO
S-S-S-ANTA?

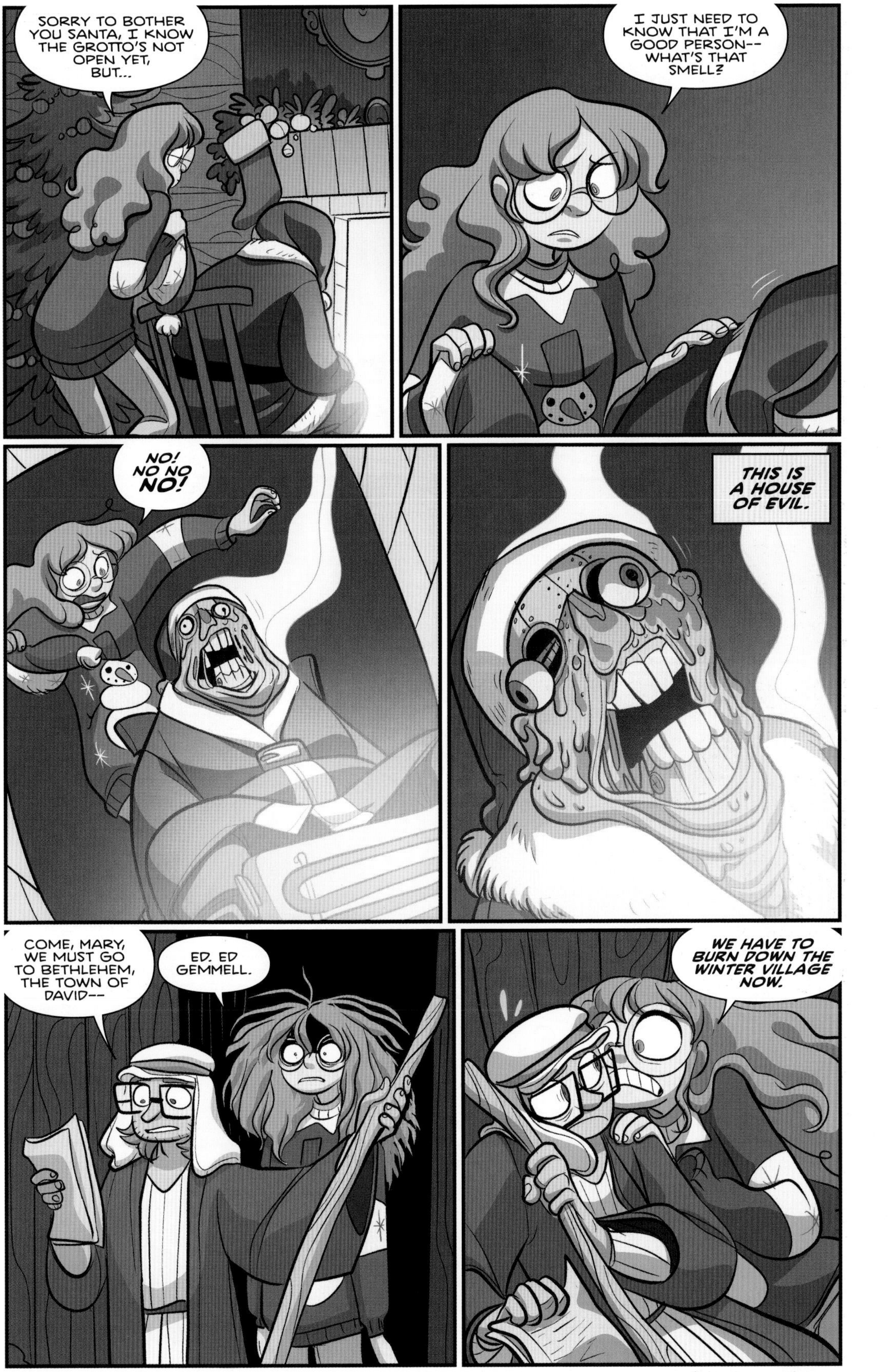
SORRY TO BOTHER YOU SANTA, I KNOW THE GROTTO'S NOT OPEN YET, BUT...
I JUST NEED TO KNOW THAT I'M A GOOD PERSON-- WHAT'S THAT SMELL?
NO! NO NO NO!
THIS IS A HOUSE OF EVIL.
COME, MARY, WE MUST GO TO BETHLEHEM, THE TOWN OF DAVID--
ED. ED GEMMELL.
WE HAVE TO BURN DOWN THE WINTER VILLAGE NOW.

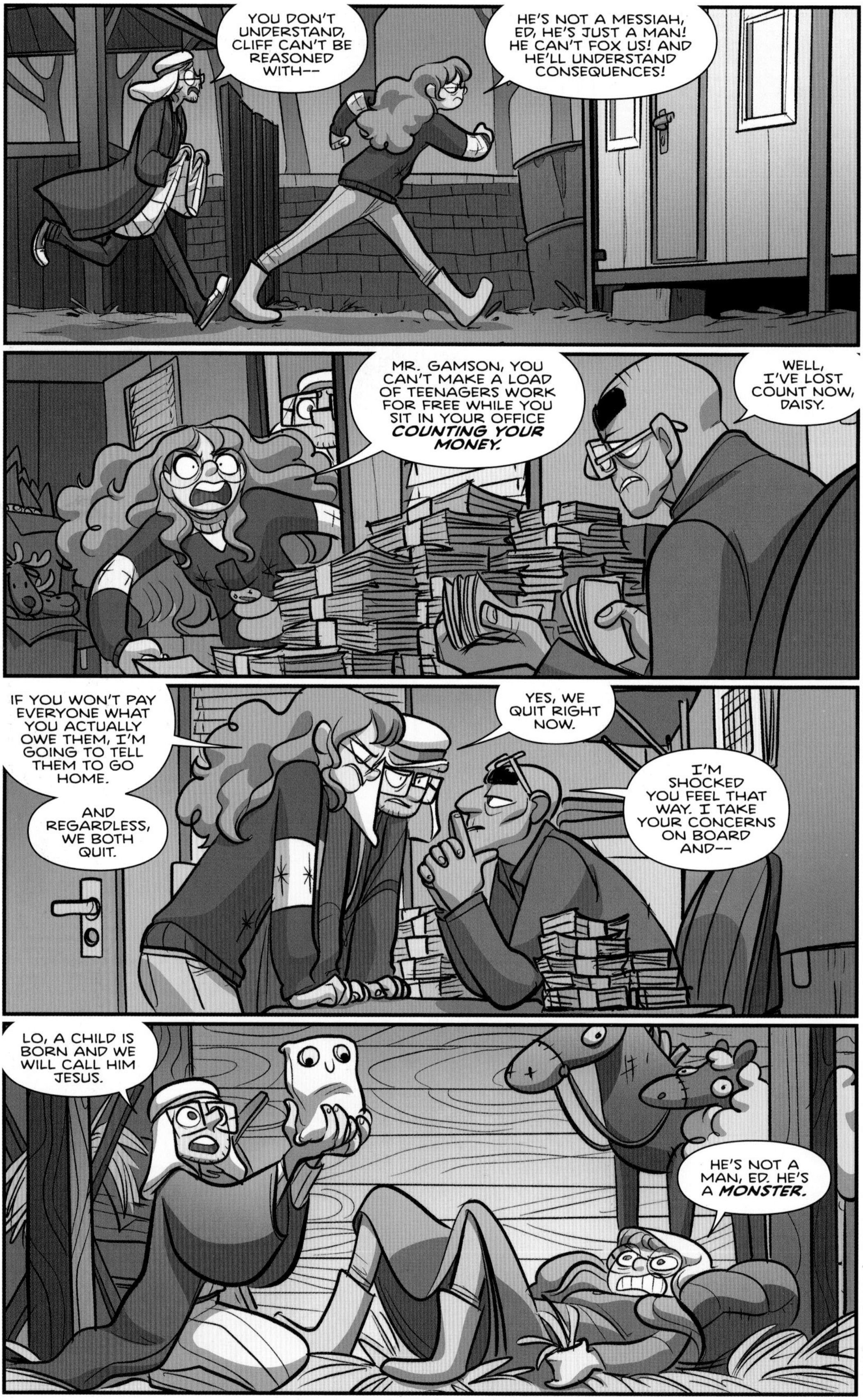
YOU DON'T UNDERSTAND, CLIFF CAN'T BE REASONED WITH--
HE'S NOT A MESSIAH, ED, HE'S JUST A MAN! HE CAN'T FOX US! AND HE'LL UNDERSTAND CONSEQUENCES!
MR. GAMSON, YOU CAN'T MAKE A LOAD OF TEENAGERS WORK FOR FREE WHILE YOU SIT IN YOUR OFFICE COUNTING YOUR MONEY.
WELL, I'VE LOST COUNT NOW, DAISY.
IF YOU WON'T PAY EVERYONE WHAT YOU ACTUALLY OWE THEM, I'M GOING TO TELL THEM TO GO HOME.
AND REGARDLESS, WE BOTH QUIT.
YES, WE QUIT RIGHT NOW.
I'M SHOCKED YOU FEEL THAT WAY. I TAKE YOUR CONCERNS ON BOARD AND--
LO, A CHILD IS BORN AND WE WILL CALL HIM JESUS.
HE'S NOT A MAN, ED. HE'S A MONSTER.

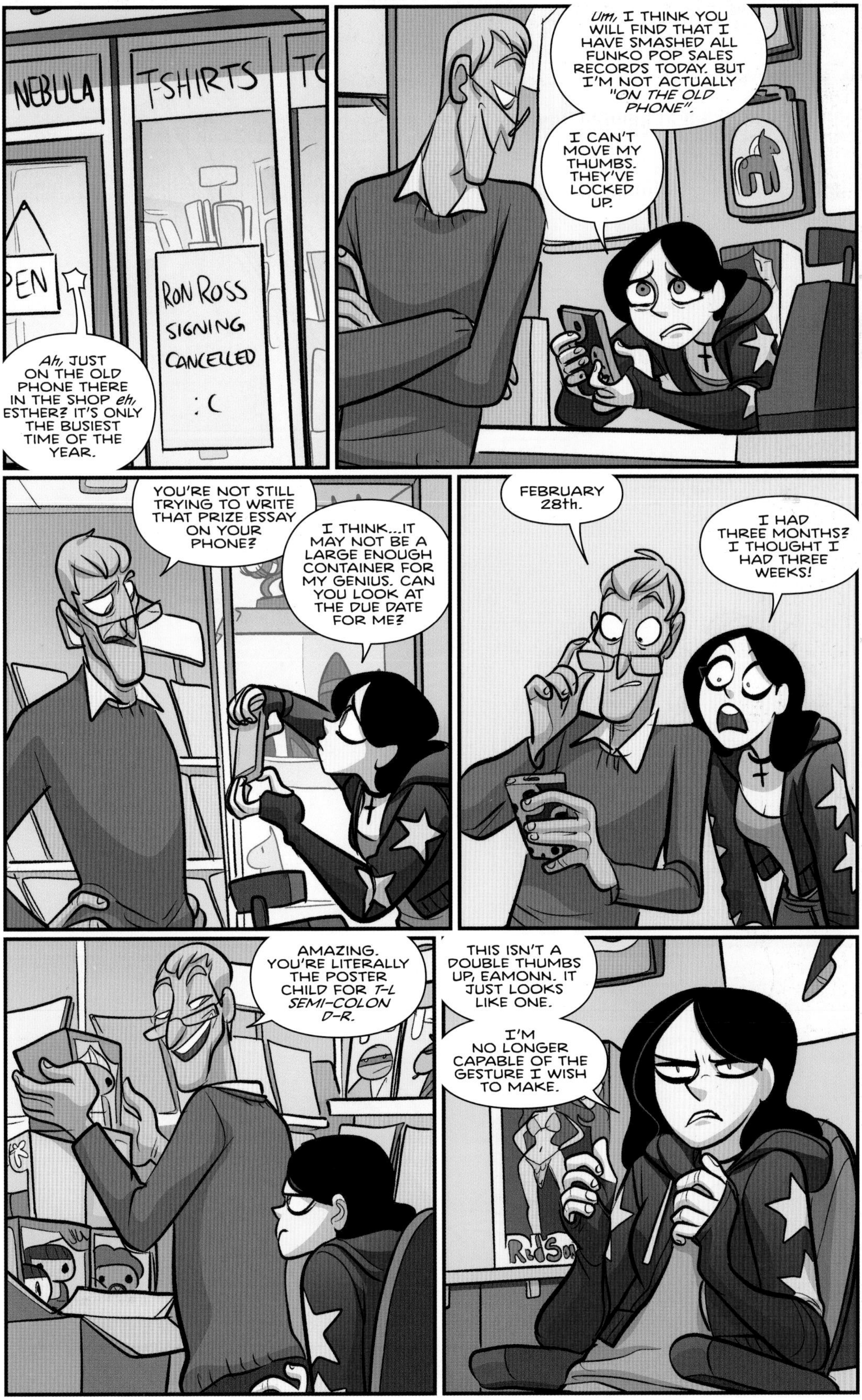
NEBULA
T-SHIRTS
OPEN
RON ROSS SIGNING CANCELLED :(
Ah, JUST ON THE OLD PHONE THERE IN THE SHOP eh, ESTHER? IT'S ONLY THE BUSIEST TIME OF THE YEAR.
Um, I THINK YOU WILL FIND THAT I HAVE SMASHED ALL FUNKO POP SALES RECORDS TODAY. BUT I'M NOT ACTUALLY "ON THE OLD PHONE".
I CAN'T MOVE MY THUMBS. THEY'VE LOCKED UP.
YOU'RE NOT STILL TRYING TO WRITE THAT PRIZE ESSAY ON YOUR PHONE?
I THINK...IT MAY NOT BE A LARGE ENOUGH CONTAINER FOR MY GENIUS. CAN YOU LOOK AT THE DUE DATE FOR ME?
FEBRUARY 28th.
I HAD THREE MONTHS? I THOUGHT I HAD THREE WEEKS!
AMAZING. YOU'RE LITERALLY THE POSTER CHILD FOR T-L SEMI-COLON D-R.
THIS ISN'T A DOUBLE THUMBS UP, EAMONN. IT JUST LOOKS LIKE ONE.
I'M NO LONGER CAPABLE OF THE GESTURE I WISH TO MAKE.

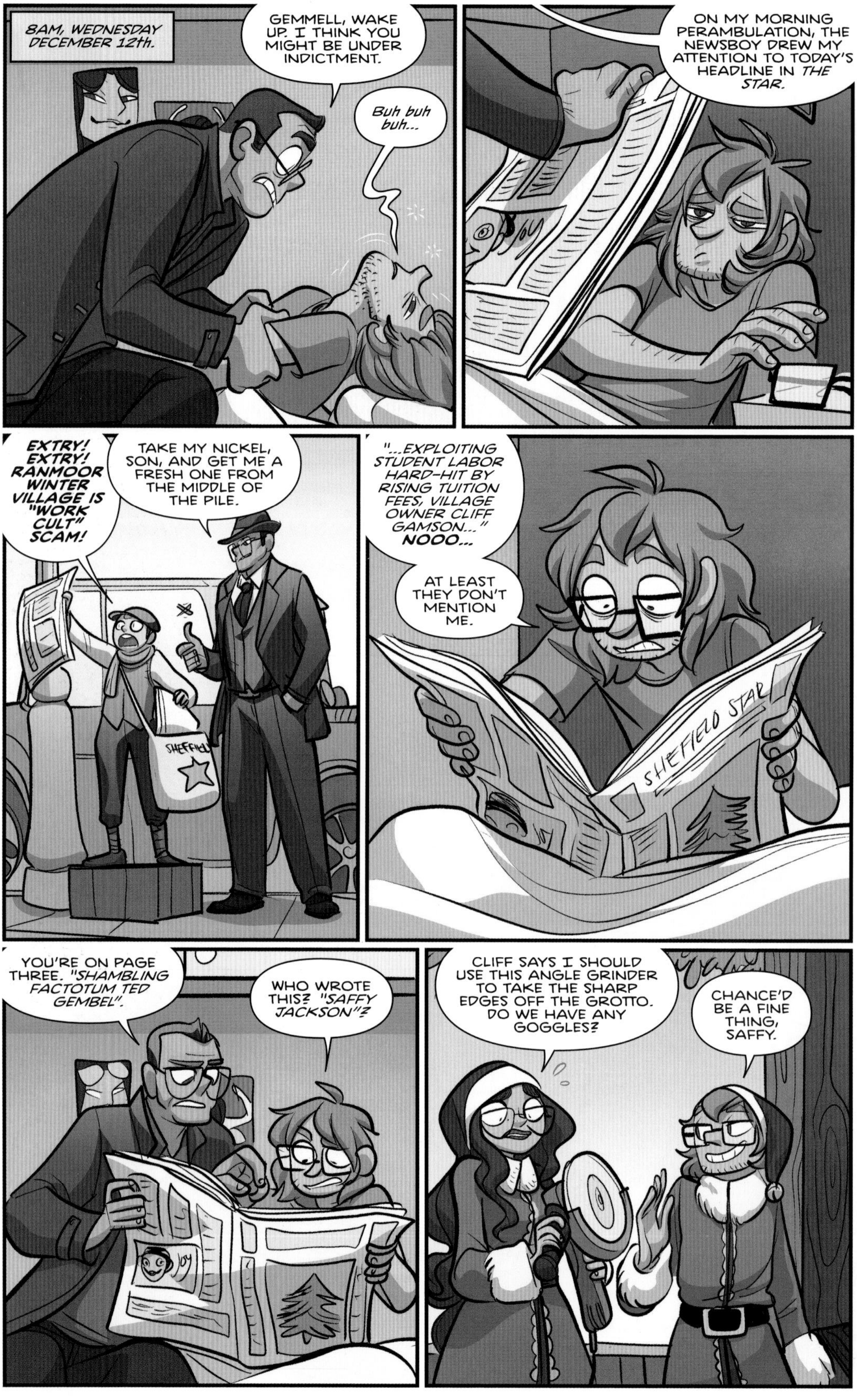
8AM, WEDNESDAY DECEMBER 12th.
GEMMELL, WAKE UP. I THINK YOU MIGHT BE UNDER INDICTMENT.
Buh buh buh...
ON MY MORNING PERAMBULATION, THE NEWSBOY DREW MY ATTENTION TO TODAY'S HEADLINE IN THE STAR.
EXTRY! EXTRY! RANMOOR WINTER VILLAGE IS "WORK CULT" SCAM!
TAKE MY NICKEL, SON, AND GET ME A FRESH ONE FROM THE MIDDLE OF THE PILE.
SHEFFIELD
"...EXPLOITING STUDENT LABOR HARD-HIT BY RISING TUITION FEES, VILLAGE OWNER CLIFF GAMSON..." NOOO...
AT LEAST THEY DON'T MENTION ME.
SHEFIELD STAR
YOU'RE ON PAGE THREE. "SHAMBLING FACTOTUM TED GEMBEL".
WHO WROTE THIS? "SAFFY JACKSON"?
CLIFF SAYS I SHOULD USE THIS ANGLE GRINDER TO TAKE THE SHARP EDGES OFF THE GROTTO. DO WE HAVE ANY GOGGLES?
CHANCE'D BE A FINE THING, SAFFY.

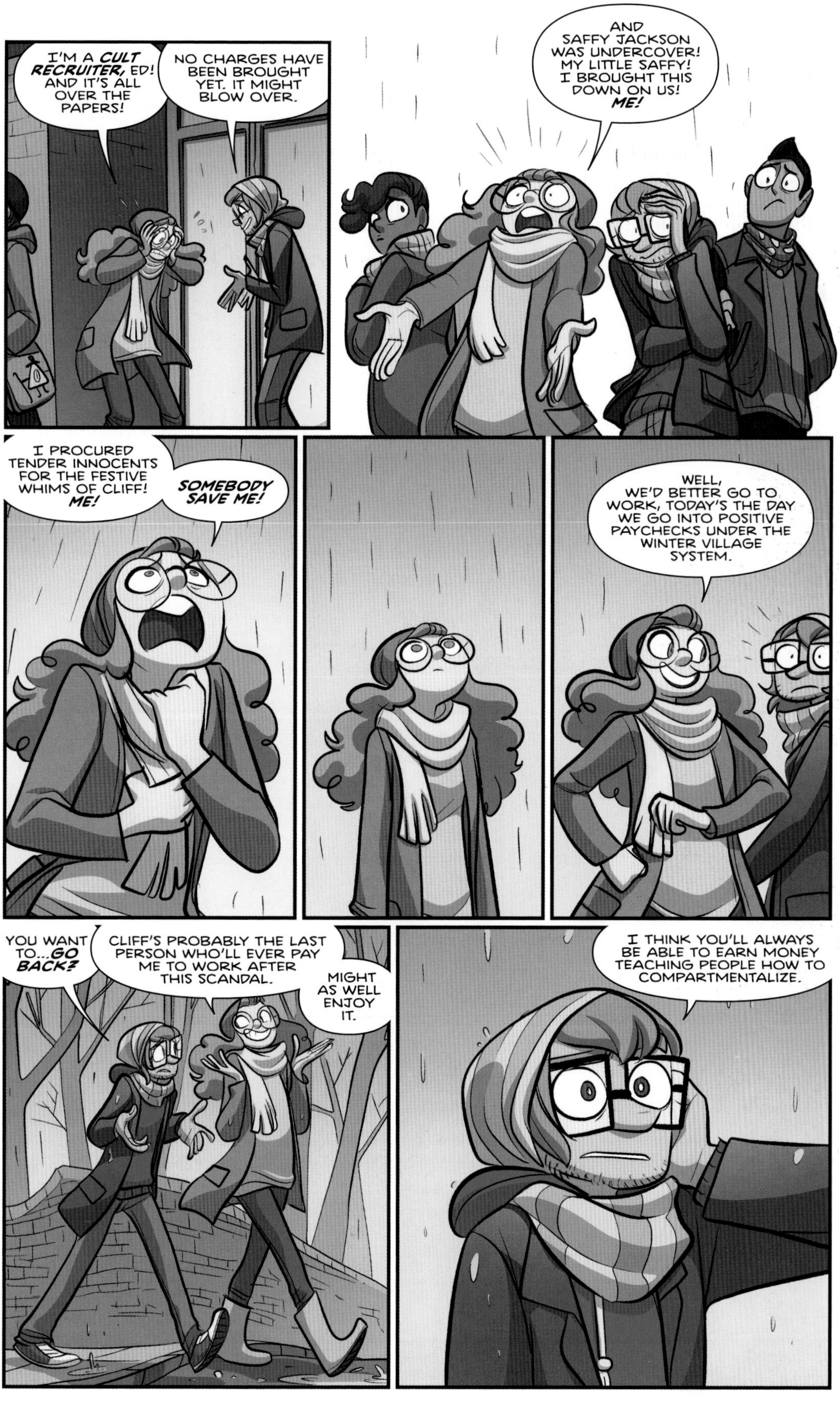

I'M A ***CULT RECRUITER,*** ED! AND IT'S ALL OVER THE PAPERS!
NO CHARGES HAVE BEEN BROUGHT YET. IT MIGHT BLOW OVER.
AND SAFFY JACKSON WAS UNDERCOVER! MY LITTLE SAFFY! I BROUGHT THIS DOWN ON US! ***ME!***
I PROCURED TENDER INNOCENTS FOR THE FESTIVE WHIMS OF CLIFF! ***ME!***
SOMEBODY SAVE ME!
WELL, WE'D BETTER GO TO WORK, TODAY'S THE DAY WE GO INTO POSITIVE PAYCHECKS UNDER THE WINTER VILLAGE SYSTEM.
YOU WANT TO...***GO BACK?***
CLIFF'S PROBABLY THE LAST PERSON WHO'LL EVER PAY ME TO WORK AFTER THIS SCANDAL.
MIGHT AS WELL ENJOY IT.
I THINK YOU'LL ALWAYS BE ABLE TO EARN MONEY TEACHING PEOPLE HOW TO COMPARTMENTALIZE.

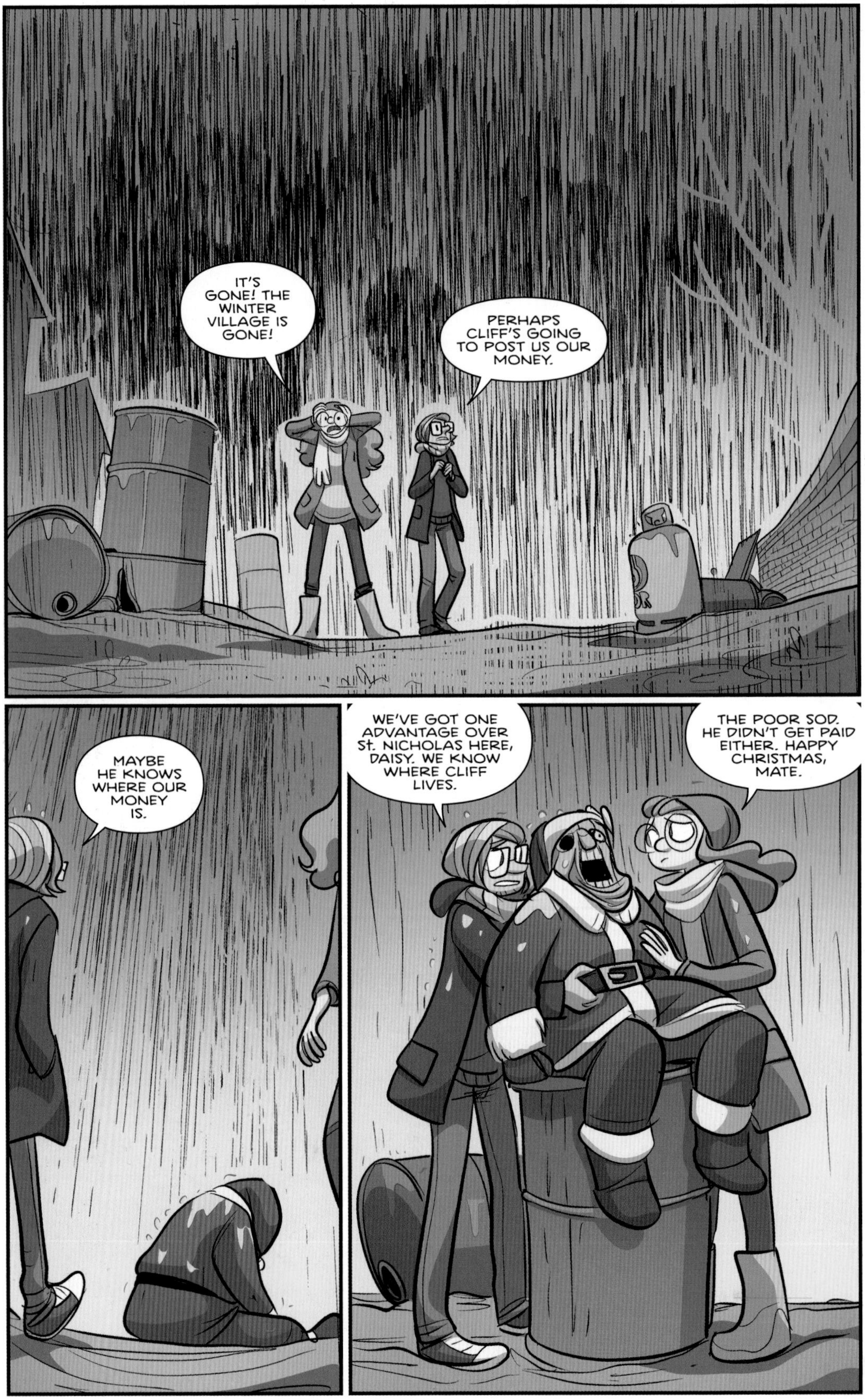
IT'S GONE! THE WINTER VILLAGE IS GONE!
PERHAPS CLIFF'S GOING TO POST US OUR MONEY.
MAYBE HE KNOWS WHERE OUR MONEY IS.
WE'VE GOT ONE ADVANTAGE OVER St. NICHOLAS HERE, DAISY. WE KNOW WHERE CLIFF LIVES.
THE POOR SOD. HE DIDN'T GET PAID EITHER. HAPPY CHRISTMAS, MATE.

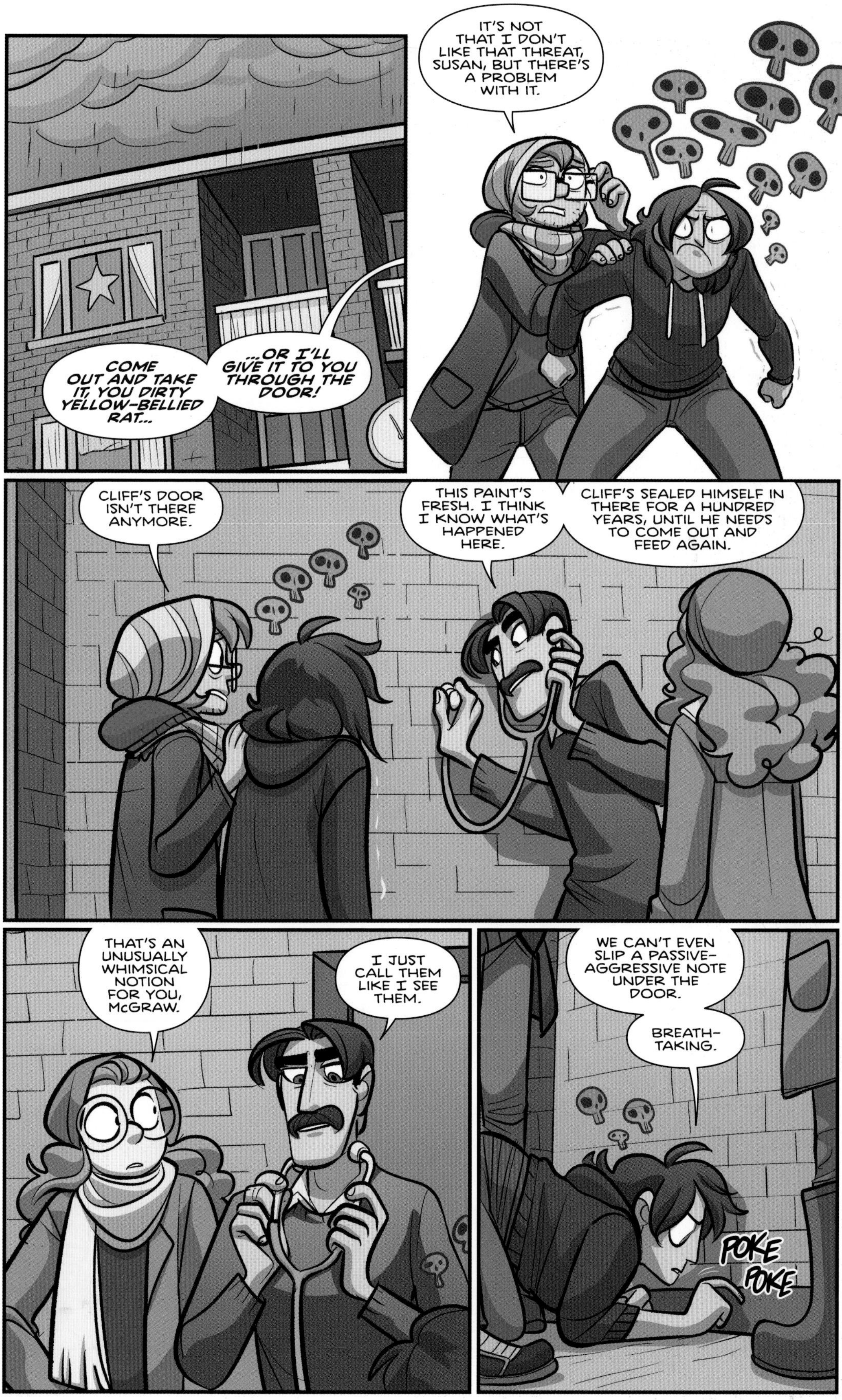
COME OUT AND TAKE IT, YOU DIRTY YELLOW-BELLIED RAT...
...OR I'LL GIVE IT TO YOU THROUGH THE DOOR!
IT'S NOT THAT I DON'T LIKE THAT THREAT, SUSAN, BUT THERE'S A PROBLEM WITH IT.
CLIFF'S DOOR ISN'T THERE ANYMORE.
THIS PAINT'S FRESH. I THINK I KNOW WHAT'S HAPPENED HERE.
CLIFF'S SEALED HIMSELF IN THERE FOR A HUNDRED YEARS, UNTIL HE NEEDS TO COME OUT AND FEED AGAIN.
THAT'S AN UNUSUALLY WHIMSICAL NOTION FOR YOU, McGRAW.
I JUST CALL THEM LIKE I SEE THEM.
WE CAN'T EVEN SLIP A PASSIVE-AGGRESSIVE NOTE UNDER THE DOOR.
BREATH-TAKING.
POKE
POKE

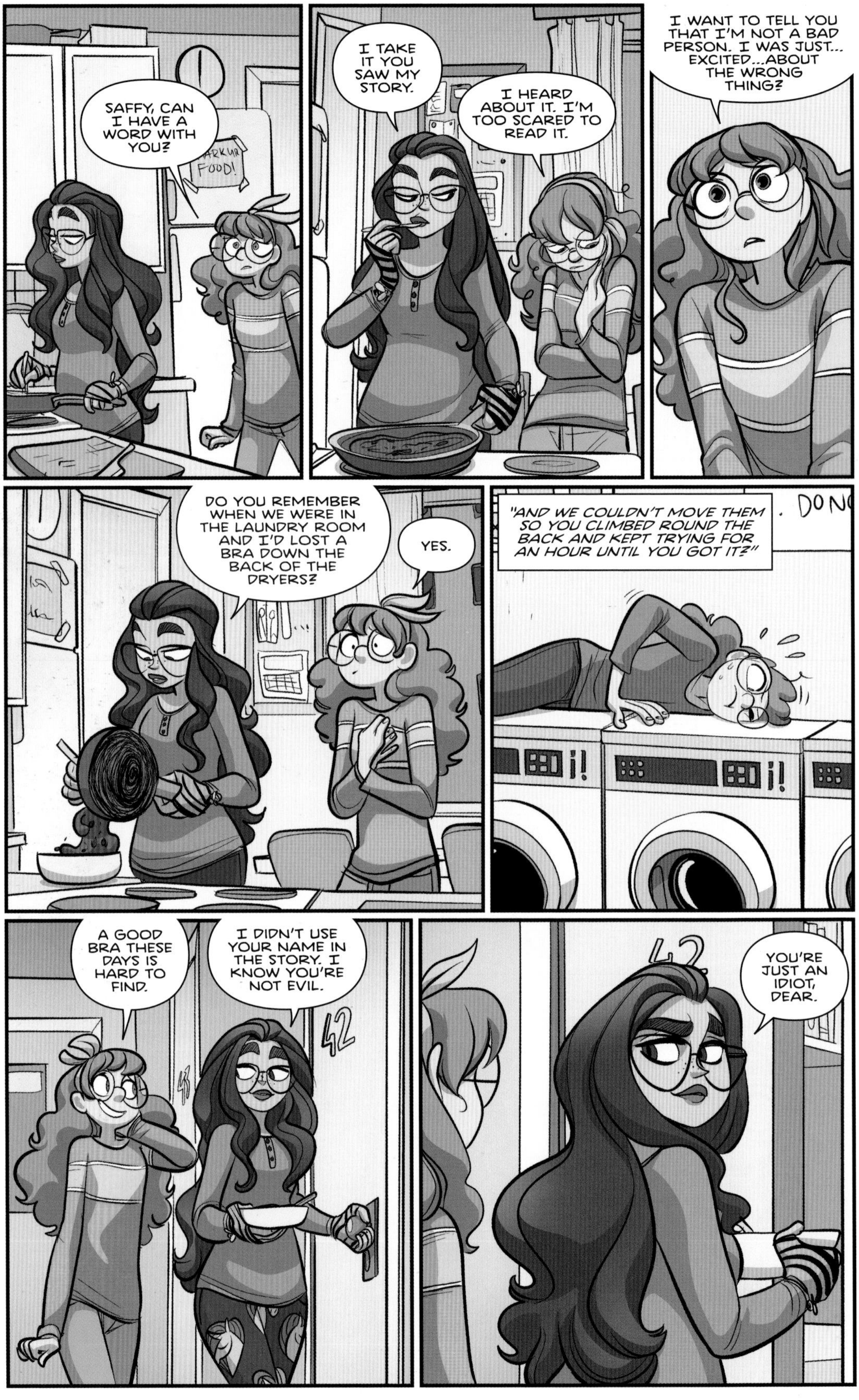
SAFFY, CAN I HAVE A WORD WITH YOU?
ARKUR FOOD!
I TAKE IT YOU SAW MY STORY.
I HEARD ABOUT IT. I'M TOO SCARED TO READ IT.
I WANT TO TELL YOU THAT I'M NOT A BAD PERSON. I WAS JUST... EXCITED...ABOUT THE WRONG THING?
DO YOU REMEMBER WHEN WE WERE IN THE LAUNDRY ROOM AND I'D LOST A BRA DOWN THE BACK OF THE DRYERS?
YES.
"AND WE COULDN'T MOVE THEM SO YOU CLIMBED ROUND THE BACK AND KEPT TRYING FOR AN HOUR UNTIL YOU GOT IT?"
A GOOD BRA THESE DAYS IS HARD TO FIND.
I DIDN'T USE YOUR NAME IN THE STORY. I KNOW YOU'RE NOT EVIL.
42
YOU'RE JUST AN IDIOT, DEAR.

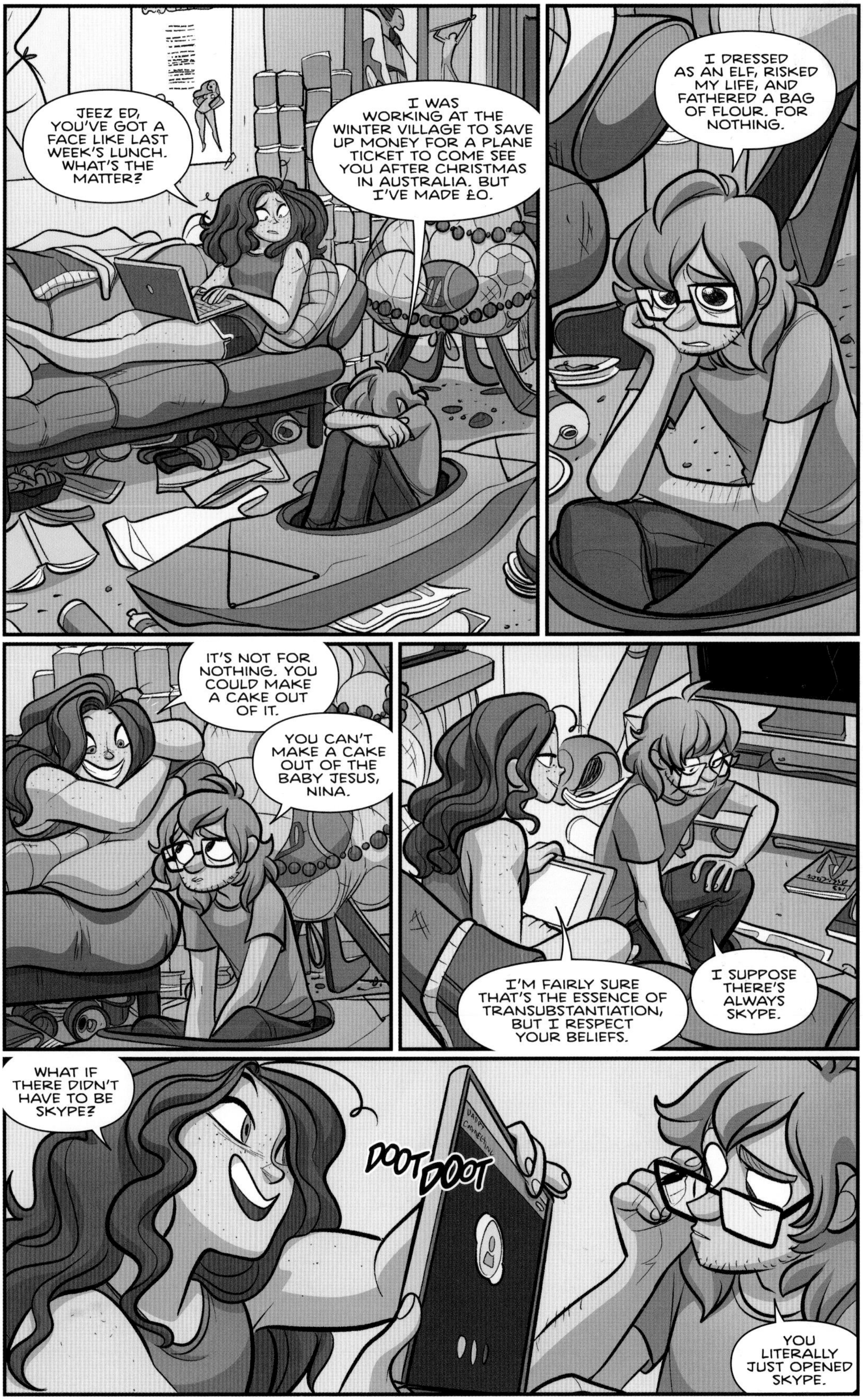
JEEZ ED, YOU'VE GOT A FACE LIKE LAST WEEK'S LUNCH. WHAT'S THE MATTER?
I WAS WORKING AT THE WINTER VILLAGE TO SAVE UP MONEY FOR A PLANE TICKET TO COME SEE YOU AFTER CHRISTMAS IN AUSTRALIA. BUT I'VE MADE £0.
I DRESSED AS AN ELF, RISKED MY LIFE, AND FATHERED A BAG OF FLOUR. FOR NOTHING.
IT'S NOT FOR NOTHING. YOU COULD MAKE A CAKE OUT OF IT.
YOU CAN'T MAKE A CAKE OUT OF THE BABY JESUS, NINA.
I'M FAIRLY SURE THAT'S THE ESSENCE OF TRANSUBSTANTIATION, BUT I RESPECT YOUR BELIEFS.
I SUPPOSE THERE'S ALWAYS SKYPE.
WHAT IF THERE DIDN'T HAVE TO BE SKYPE?
DOOT DOOT
YOU LITERALLY JUST OPENED SKYPE.

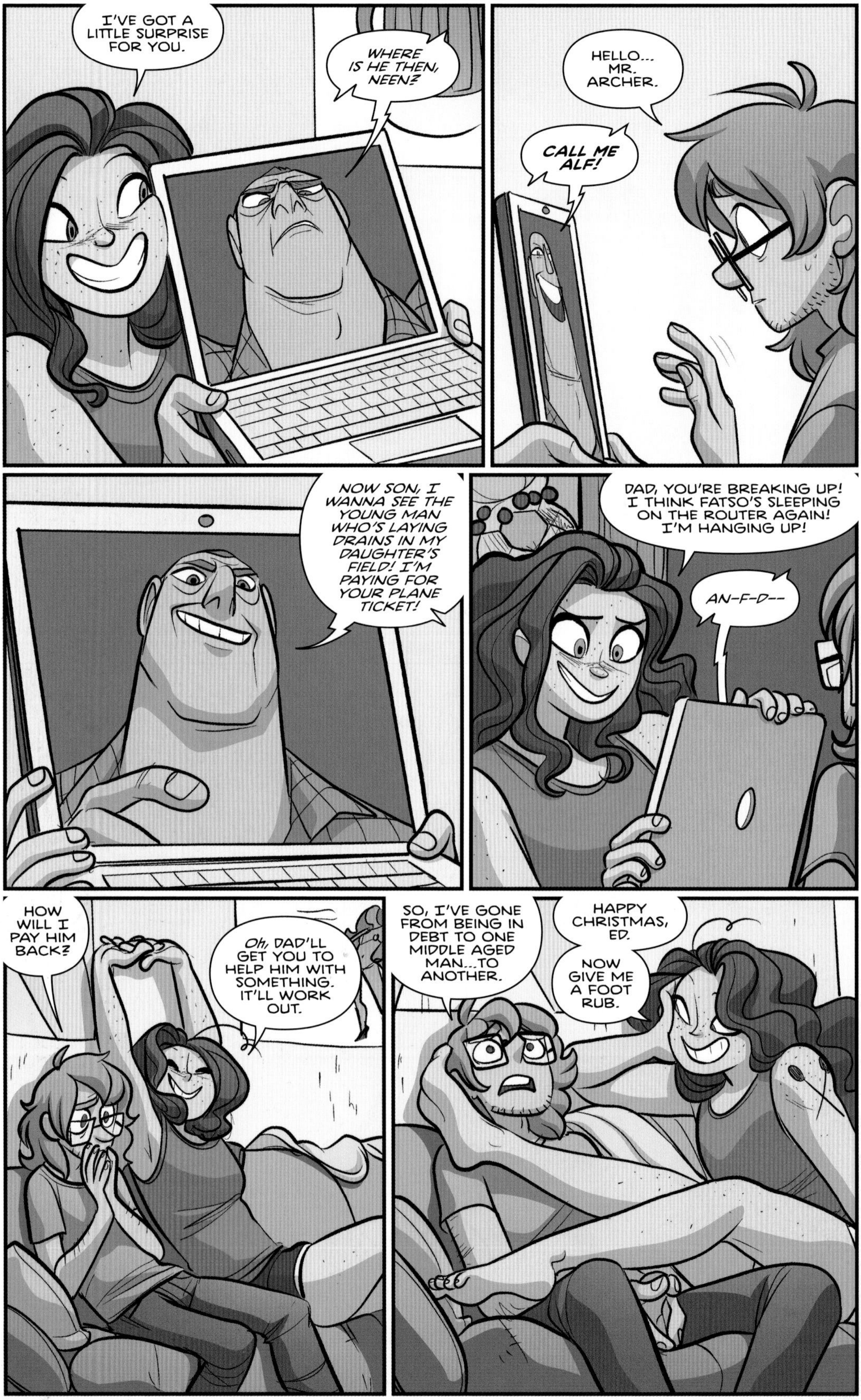
I'VE GOT A LITTLE SURPRISE FOR YOU.
WHERE IS HE THEN, NEEN?
HELLO... MR. ARCHER.
CALL ME ALF!
NOW SON, I WANNA SEE THE YOUNG MAN WHO'S LAYING DRAINS IN MY DAUGHTER'S FIELD! I'M PAYING FOR YOUR PLANE TICKET!
DAD, YOU'RE BREAKING UP! I THINK FATSO'S SLEEPING ON THE ROUTER AGAIN! I'M HANGING UP!
AN-F-D--
HOW WILL I PAY HIM BACK?
Oh, DAD'LL GET YOU TO HELP HIM WITH SOMETHING. IT'LL WORK OUT.
SO, I'VE GONE FROM BEING IN DEBT TO ONE MIDDLE AGED MAN...TO ANOTHER.
HAPPY CHRISTMAS, ED.
NOW GIVE ME A FOOT RUB.

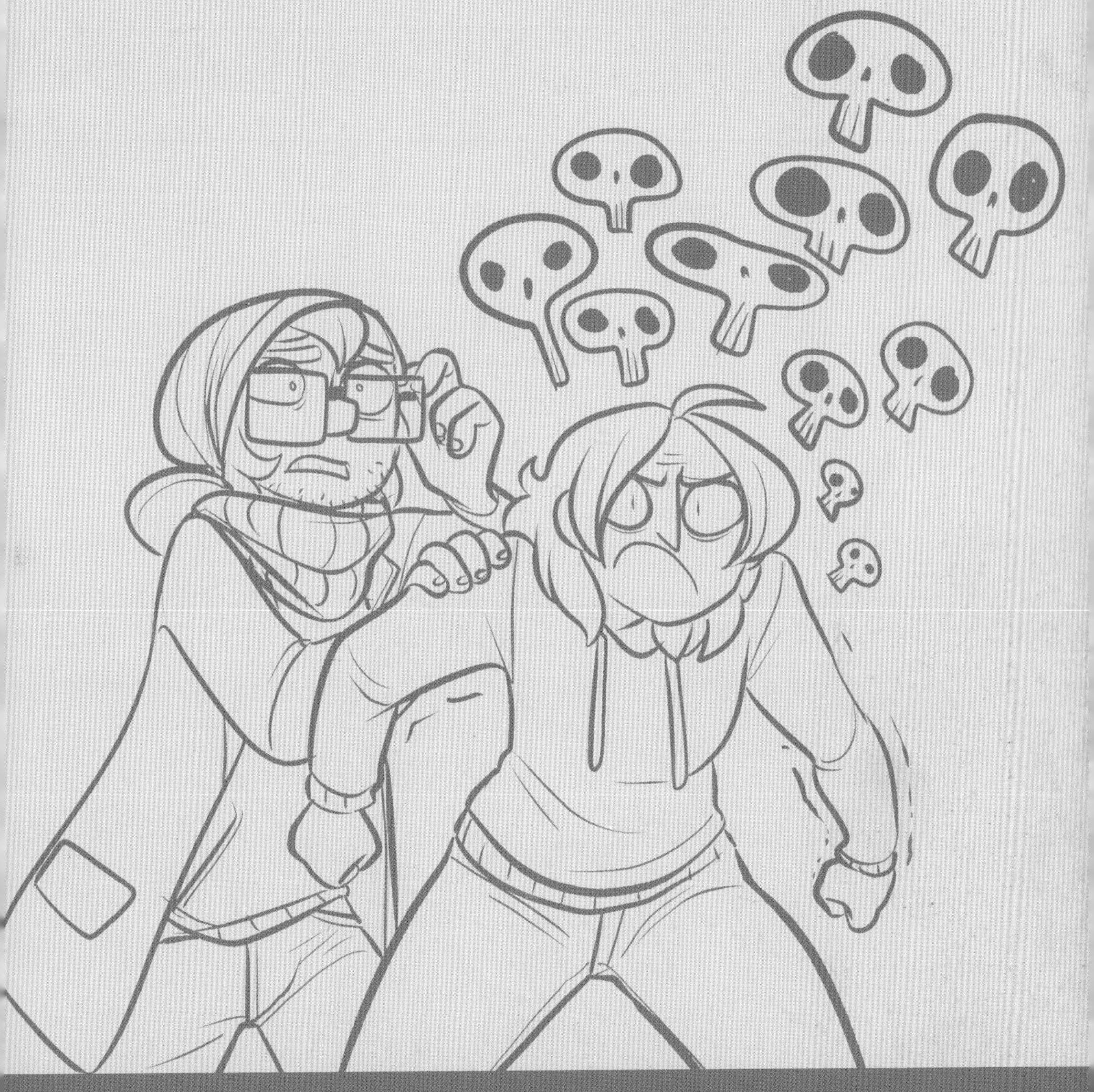

CHAPTER
FORTY-FOUR

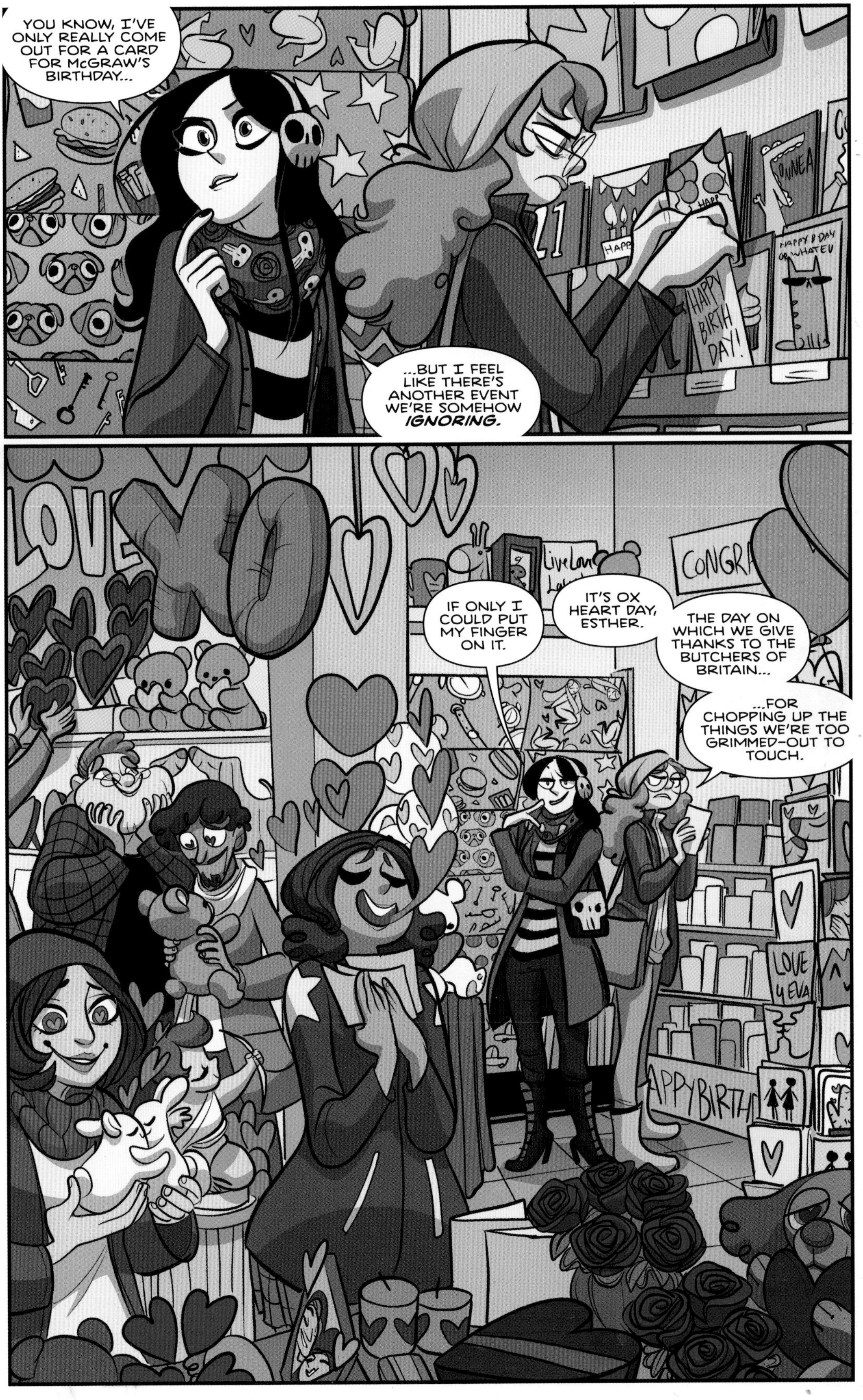
YOU KNOW, I'VE ONLY REALLY COME OUT FOR A CARD FOR McGRAW'S BIRTHDAY...
...BUT I FEEL LIKE THERE'S ANOTHER EVENT WE'RE SOMEHOW *IGNORING.*
HAPPY BIRTHDAY!
HAPPY B'DAY OR WHATEV
LOVE
XO
CONGRA
IF ONLY I COULD PUT MY FINGER ON IT.
IT'S OX HEART DAY, ESTHER.
THE DAY ON WHICH WE GIVE THANKS TO THE BUTCHERS OF BRITAIN...
...FOR CHOPPING UP THE THINGS WE'RE TOO GRIMMED-OUT TO TOUCH.
LOVE 4 EVA
APPY BIRTH

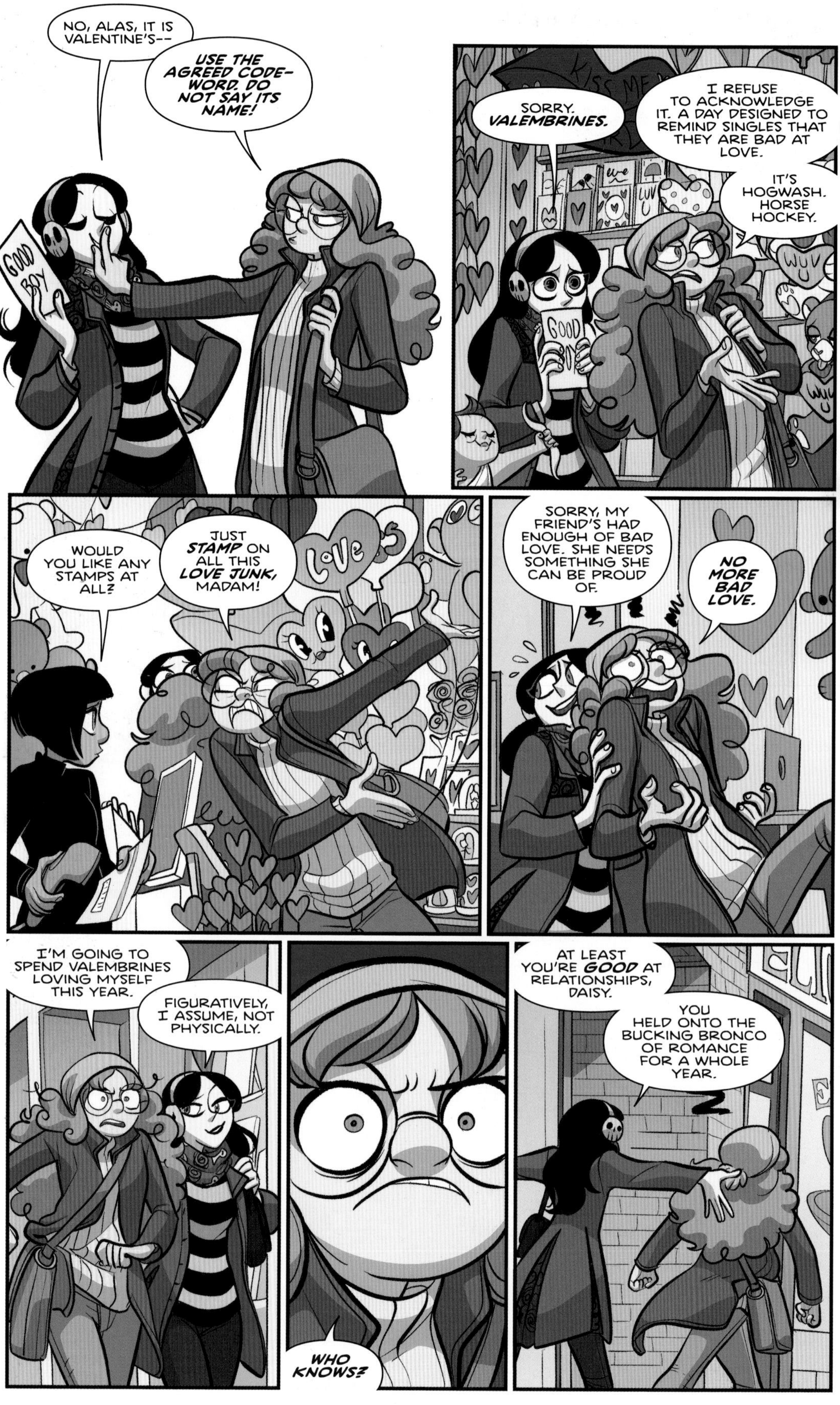
NO, ALAS, IT IS VALENTINE'S--
USE THE AGREED CODE-WORD. DO NOT SAY ITS NAME!
GOOD BOY
SORRY. VALEMBRINES.
I REFUSE TO ACKNOWLEDGE IT. A DAY DESIGNED TO REMIND SINGLES THAT THEY ARE BAD AT LOVE.
IT'S HOGWASH. HORSE HOCKEY.
WOULD YOU LIKE ANY STAMPS AT ALL?
JUST STAMP ON ALL THIS LOVE JUNK, MADAM!
SORRY, MY FRIEND'S HAD ENOUGH OF BAD LOVE. SHE NEEDS SOMETHING SHE CAN BE PROUD OF.
NO MORE BAD LOVE.
I'M GOING TO SPEND VALEMBRINES LOVING MYSELF THIS YEAR.
FIGURATIVELY, I ASSUME, NOT PHYSICALLY.
WHO KNOWS?
AT LEAST YOU'RE GOOD AT RELATIONSHIPS, DAISY.
YOU HELD ONTO THE BUCKING BRONCO OF ROMANCE FOR A WHOLE YEAR.

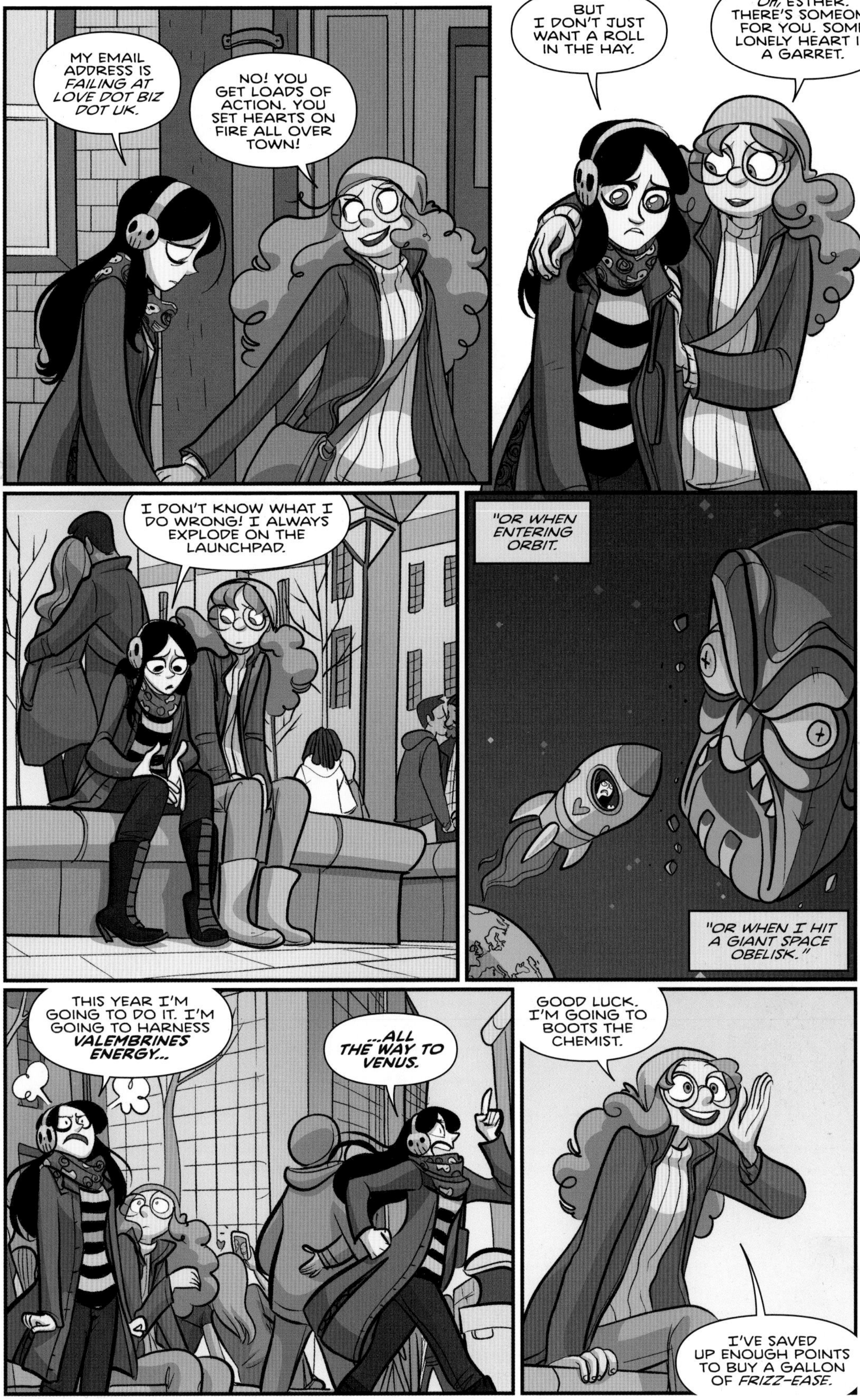
MY EMAIL ADDRESS IS *FAILING AT LOVE DOT BIZ DOT UK.*
NO! YOU GET LOADS OF ACTION. YOU SET HEARTS ON FIRE ALL OVER TOWN!
BUT I DON'T JUST WANT A ROLL IN THE HAY.
Oh, ESTHER. THERE'S SOMEONE FOR YOU. SOME LONELY HEART IN A GARRET.
I DON'T KNOW WHAT I DO WRONG! I ALWAYS EXPLODE ON THE LAUNCHPAD.
"OR WHEN ENTERING ORBIT.
"OR WHEN I HIT A GIANT SPACE OBELISK."
THIS YEAR I'M GOING TO DO IT. I'M GOING TO HARNESS ***VALEMBRINES ENERGY...***
...ALL THE WAY TO VENUS.
GOOD LUCK. I'M GOING TO BOOTS THE CHEMIST.
I'VE SAVED UP ENOUGH POINTS TO BUY A GALLON OF *FRIZZ-EASE.*

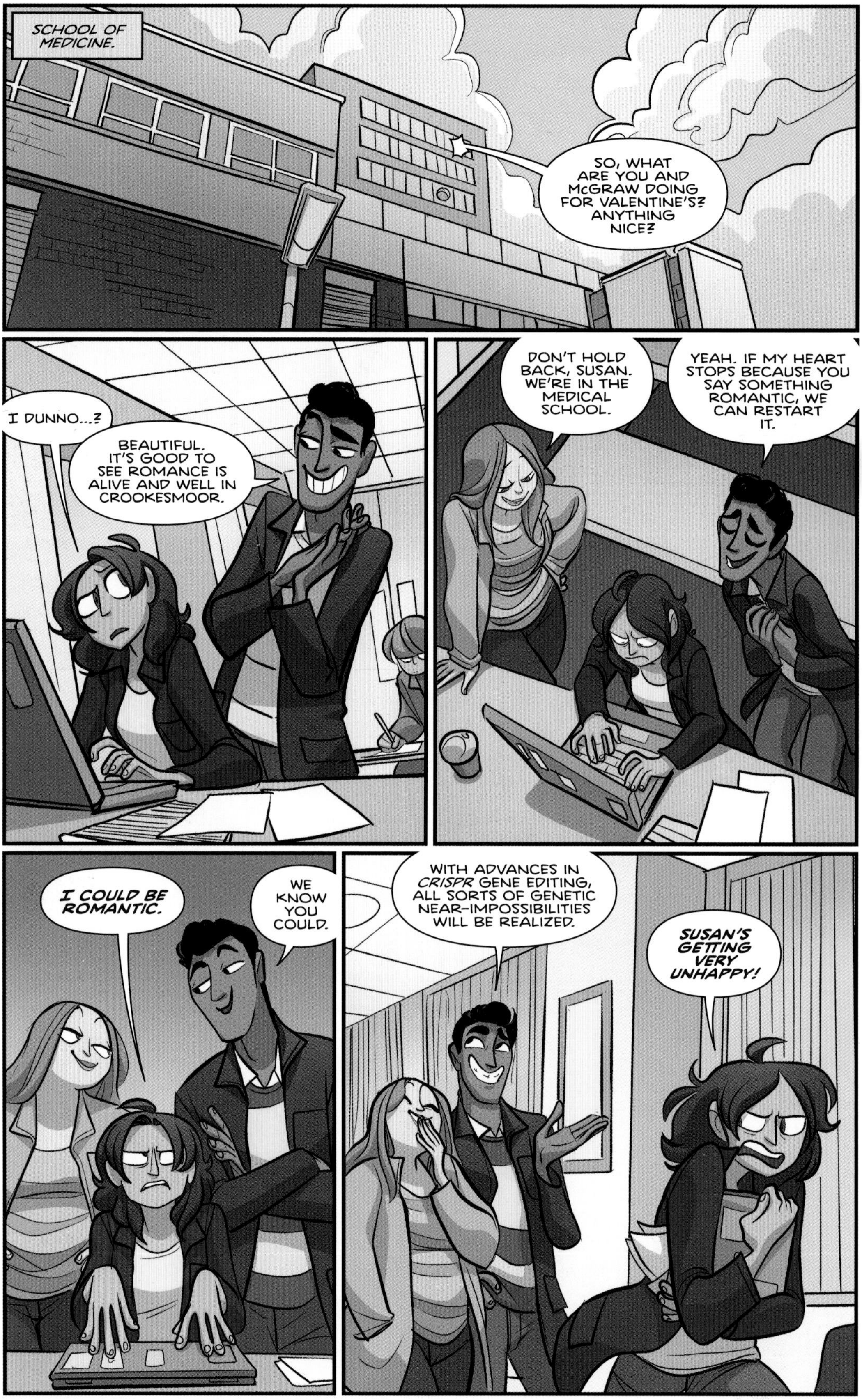
SCHOOL OF MEDICINE.
SO, WHAT ARE YOU AND McGRAW DOING FOR VALENTINE'S? ANYTHING NICE?
I DUNNO...?
BEAUTIFUL. IT'S GOOD TO SEE ROMANCE IS ALIVE AND WELL IN CROOKESMOOR.
DON'T HOLD BACK, SUSAN. WE'RE IN THE MEDICAL SCHOOL.
YEAH. IF MY HEART STOPS BECAUSE YOU SAY SOMETHING ROMANTIC, WE CAN RESTART IT.
I COULD BE ROMANTIC.
WE KNOW YOU COULD.
WITH ADVANCES IN CRISPR GENE EDITING, ALL SORTS OF GENETIC NEAR-IMPOSSIBILITIES WILL BE REALIZED.
SUSAN'S GETTING VERY UNHAPPY!

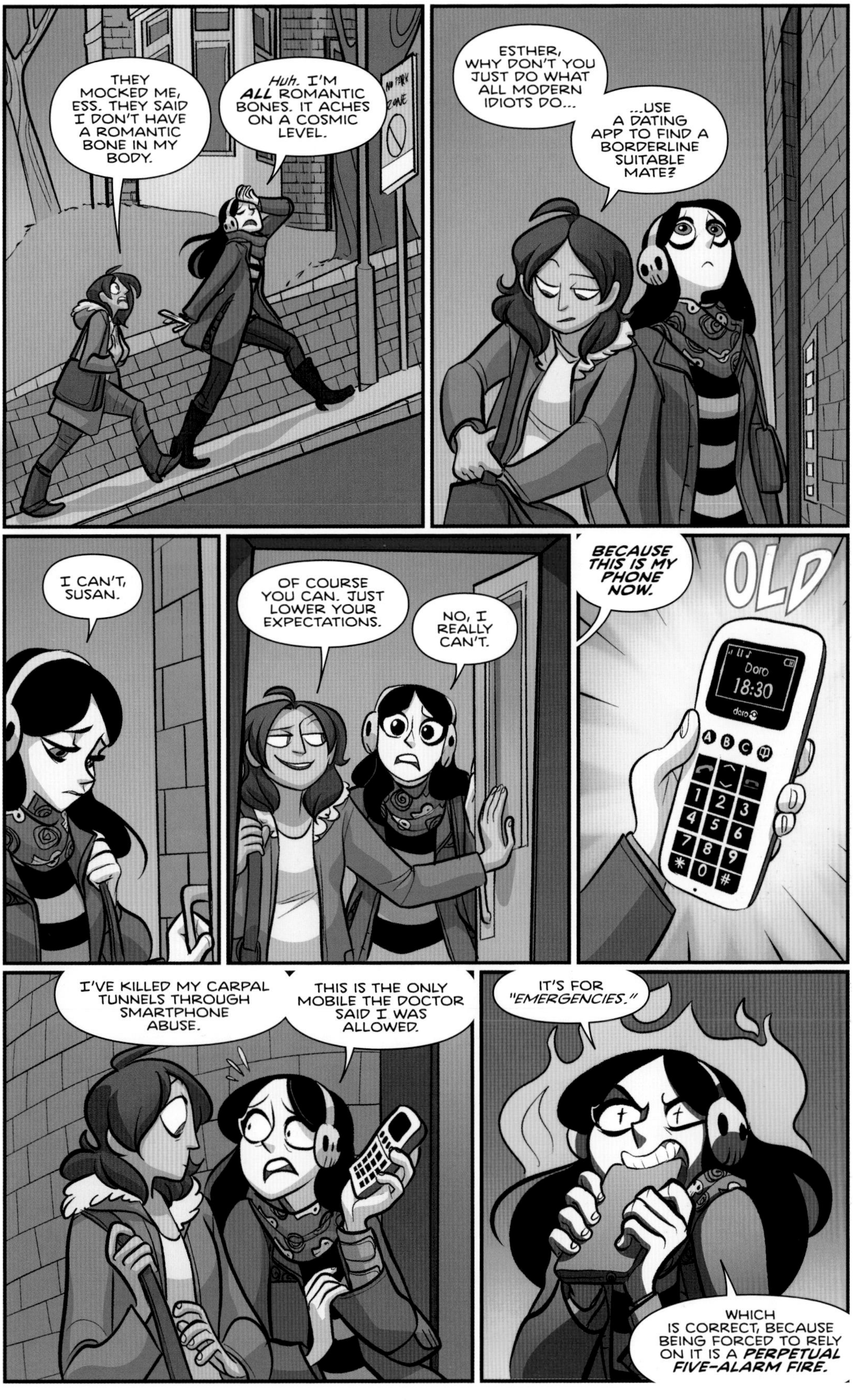

THEY MOCKED ME, ESS. THEY SAID I DON'T HAVE A ROMANTIC BONE IN MY BODY.
Huh. I'M **ALL** ROMANTIC BONES. IT ACHES ON A COSMIC LEVEL.
NO PARK ZONE
ESTHER, WHY DON'T YOU JUST DO WHAT ALL MODERN IDIOTS DO...
...USE A DATING APP TO FIND A BORDERLINE SUITABLE MATE?
I CAN'T, SUSAN.
OF COURSE YOU CAN. JUST LOWER YOUR EXPECTATIONS.
NO, I REALLY CAN'T.
BECAUSE THIS IS MY PHONE NOW.
OLD
Doro
18:30
doro
I'VE KILLED MY CARPAL TUNNELS THROUGH SMARTPHONE ABUSE.
THIS IS THE ONLY MOBILE THE DOCTOR SAID I WAS ALLOWED.
IT'S FOR *"EMERGENCIES."*
WHICH IS CORRECT, BECAUSE BEING FORCED TO RELY ON IT IS A ***PERPETUAL FIVE-ALARM FIRE.***

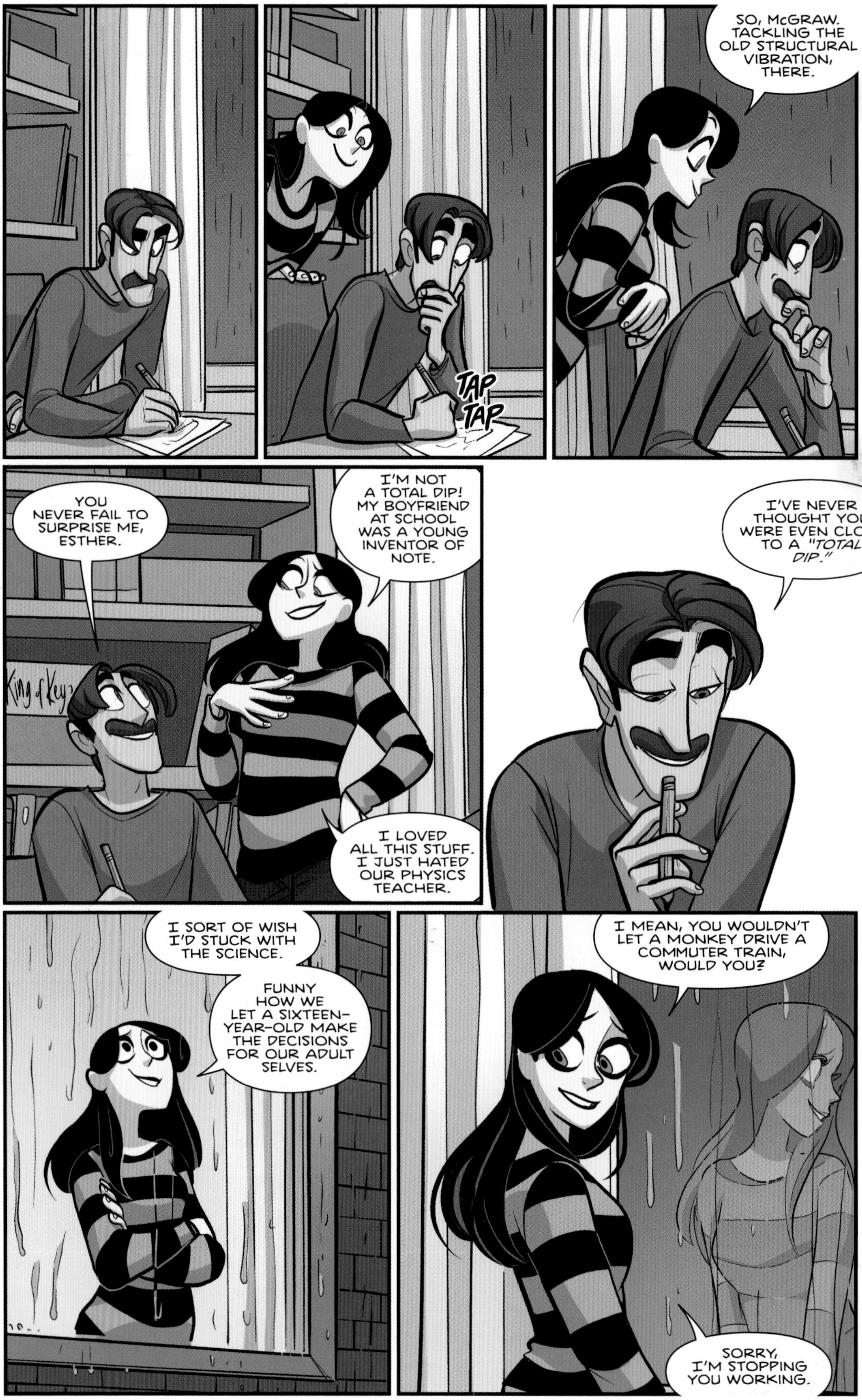
TAP
TAP
SO, McGRAW. TACKLING THE OLD STRUCTURAL VIBRATION, THERE.
YOU NEVER FAIL TO SURPRISE ME, ESTHER.
I'M NOT A TOTAL DIP! MY BOYFRIEND AT SCHOOL WAS A YOUNG INVENTOR OF NOTE.
I LOVED ALL THIS STUFF. I JUST HATED OUR PHYSICS TEACHER.
I'VE NEVER THOUGHT YOU WERE EVEN CLOSE TO A "TOTAL DIP."
I SORT OF WISH I'D STUCK WITH THE SCIENCE.
FUNNY HOW WE LET A SIXTEEN-YEAR-OLD MAKE THE DECISIONS FOR OUR ADULT SELVES.
I MEAN, YOU WOULDN'T LET A MONKEY DRIVE A COMMUTER TRAIN, WOULD YOU?
SORRY, I'M STOPPING YOU WORKING.

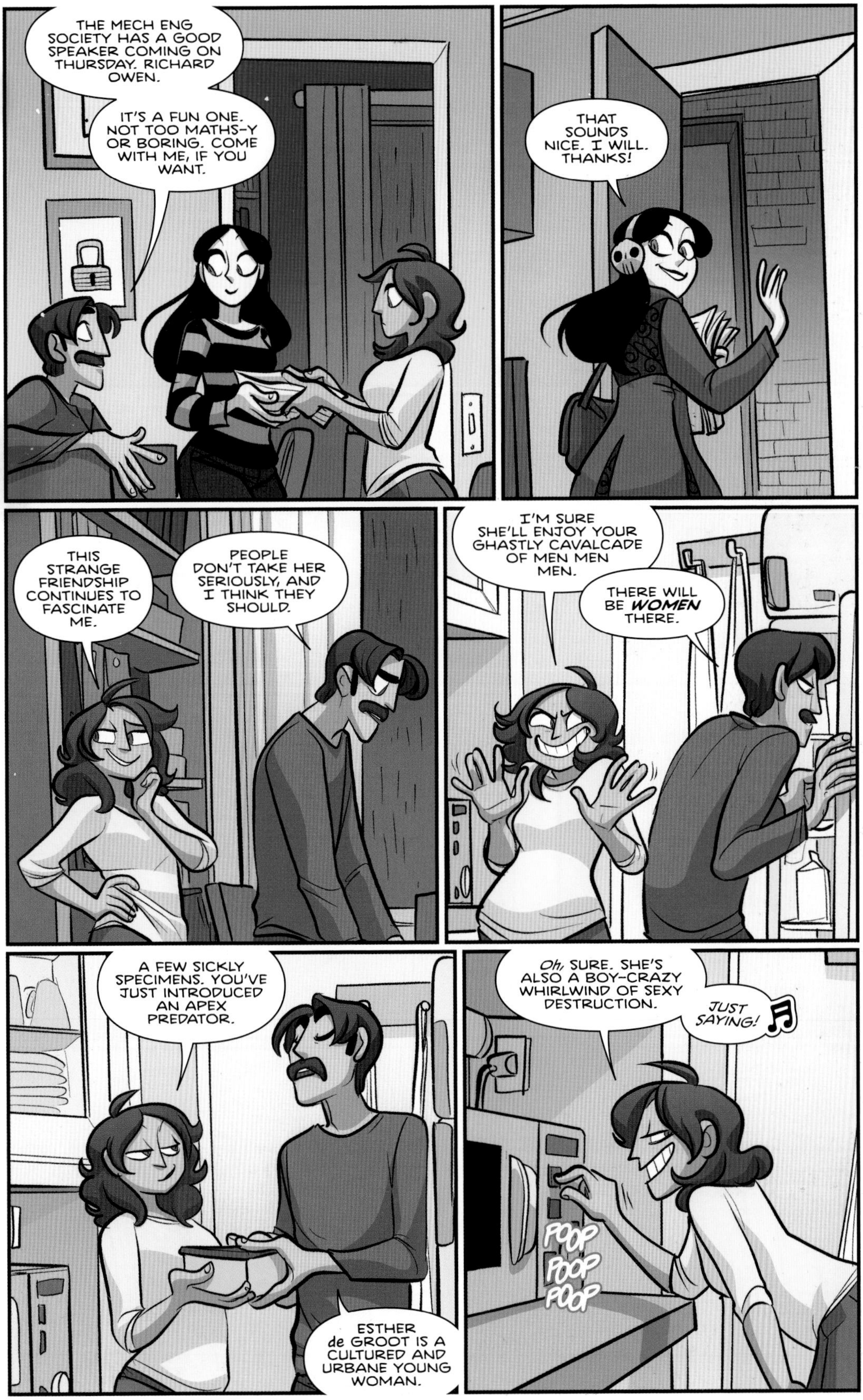
THE MECH ENG SOCIETY HAS A GOOD SPEAKER COMING ON THURSDAY. RICHARD OWEN.
IT'S A FUN ONE. NOT TOO MATHS-Y OR BORING. COME WITH ME, IF YOU WANT.
THAT SOUNDS NICE. I WILL. THANKS!
THIS STRANGE FRIENDSHIP CONTINUES TO FASCINATE ME.
PEOPLE DON'T TAKE HER SERIOUSLY, AND I THINK THEY SHOULD.
I'M SURE SHE'LL ENJOY YOUR GHASTLY CAVALCADE OF MEN MEN MEN.
THERE WILL BE ***WOMEN*** THERE.
A FEW SICKLY SPECIMENS. YOU'VE JUST INTRODUCED AN APEX PREDATOR.
ESTHER de GROOT IS A CULTURED AND URBANE YOUNG WOMAN.
Oh, SURE. SHE'S ALSO A BOY-CRAZY WHIRLWIND OF SEXY DESTRUCTION.
JUST SAYING!
POOP POOP POOP

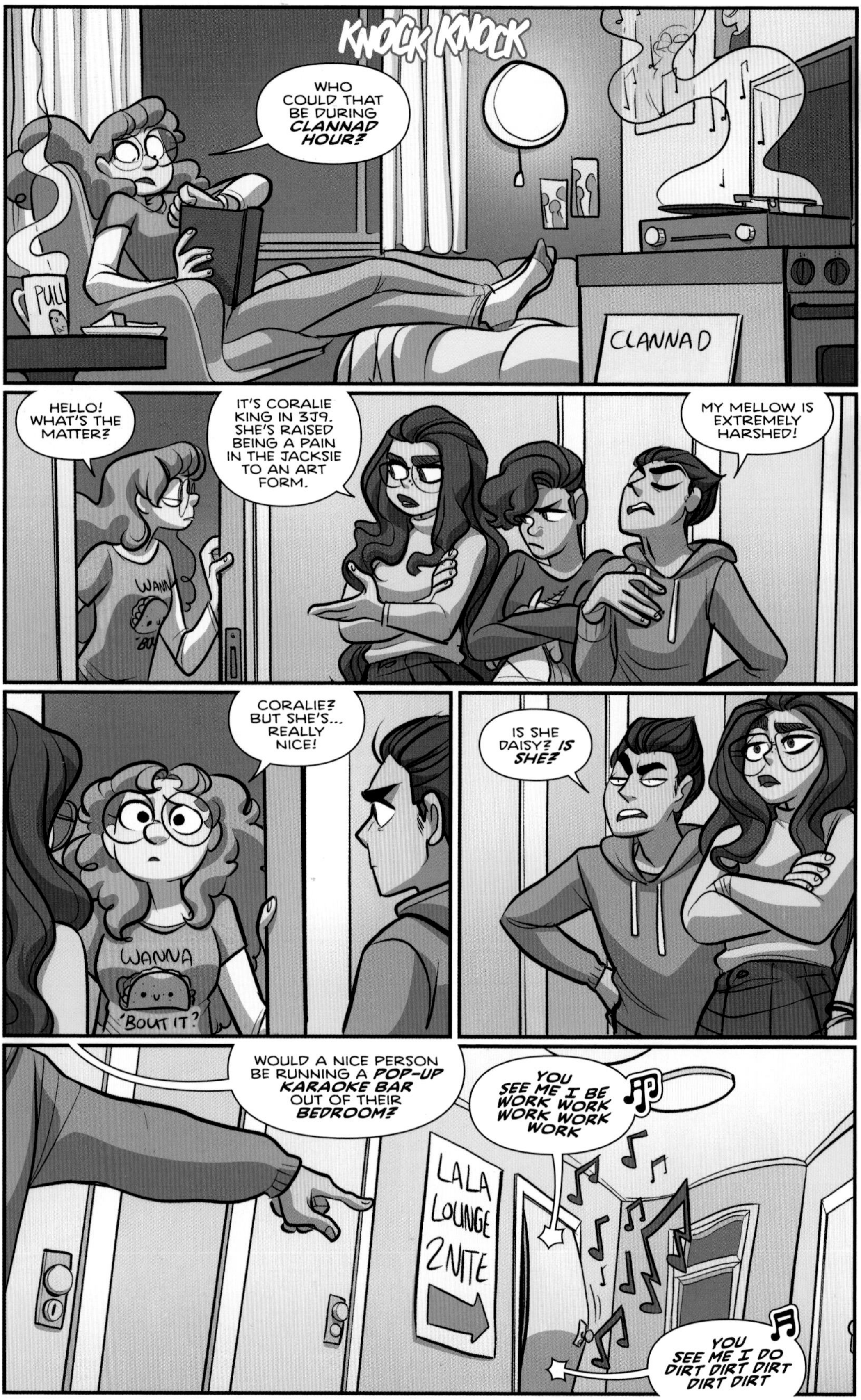
KNOCK KNOCK
WHO COULD THAT BE DURING ***CLANNAD HOUR?***
CLANNAD
HELLO! WHAT'S THE MATTER?
IT'S CORALIE KING IN 3J9. SHE'S RAISED BEING A PAIN IN THE JACKSIE TO AN ART FORM.
MY MELLOW IS EXTREMELY HARSHED!
CORALIE? BUT SHE'S... REALLY NICE!
WANNA 'BOUT IT?
IS SHE DAISY? ***IS SHE?***
WOULD A NICE PERSON BE RUNNING A ***POP-UP KARAOKE BAR*** OUT OF THEIR ***BEDROOM?***
YOU SEE ME I BE WORK WORK WORK WORK WORK
LALA LOUNGE 2NITE
YOU SEE ME I DO DIRT DIRT DIRT DIRT DIRT

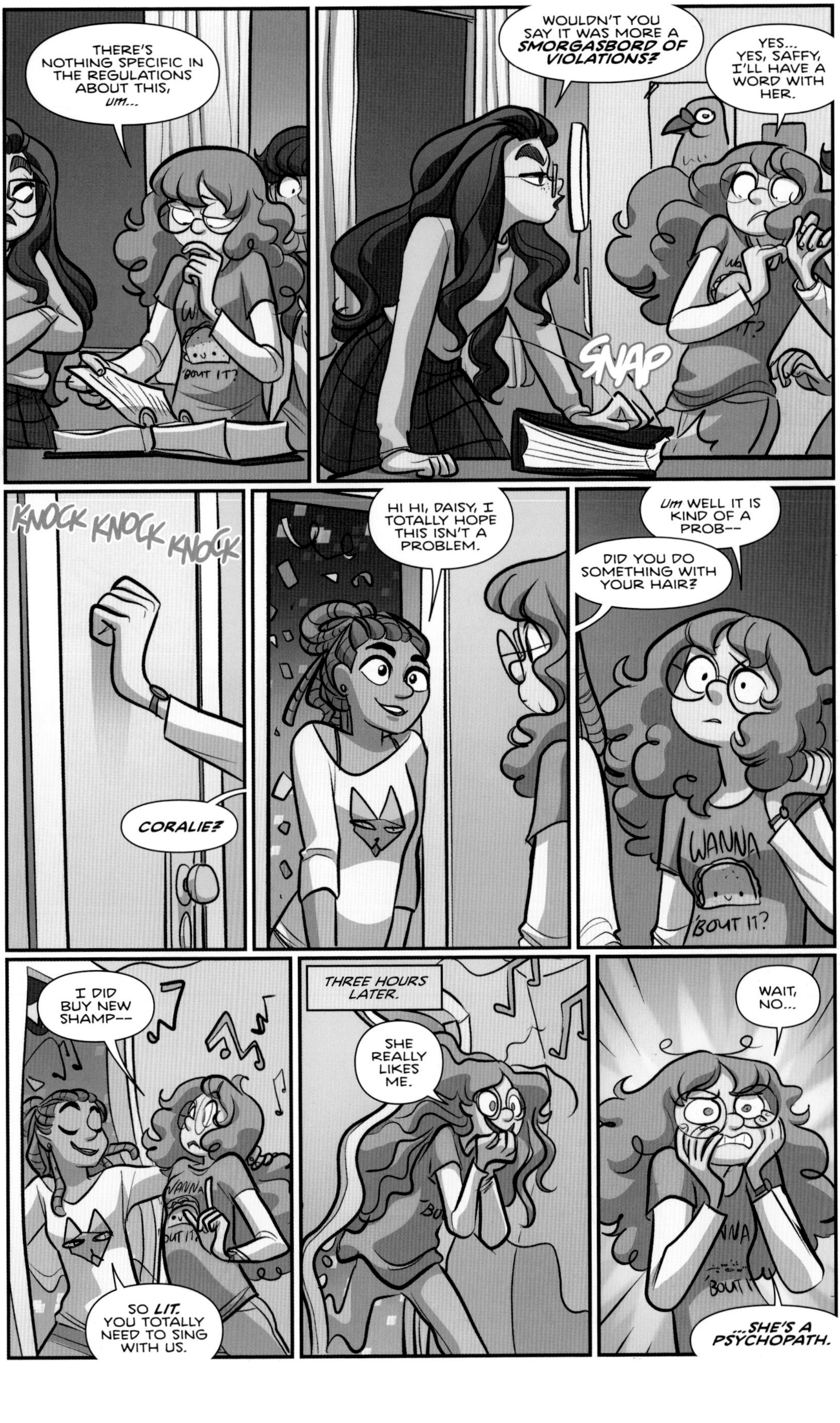

THERE'S NOTHING SPECIFIC IN THE REGULATIONS ABOUT THIS, *UM...*
WOULDN'T YOU SAY IT WAS MORE A ***SMORGASBORD OF VIOLATIONS?***
YES... YES, SAFFY, I'LL HAVE A WORD WITH HER.
SNAP
KNOCK KNOCK KNOCK
CORALIE?
HI HI, DAISY, I TOTALLY HOPE THIS ISN'T A PROBLEM.
UM WELL IT IS KIND OF A PROB--
DID YOU DO SOMETHING WITH YOUR HAIR?
WANNA 'BOUT IT?
I DID BUY NEW SHAMP--
SO ***LIT.*** YOU TOTALLY NEED TO SING WITH US.
THREE HOURS LATER.
SHE REALLY LIKES ME.
WAIT, NO...
...SHE'S A PSYCHOPATH.

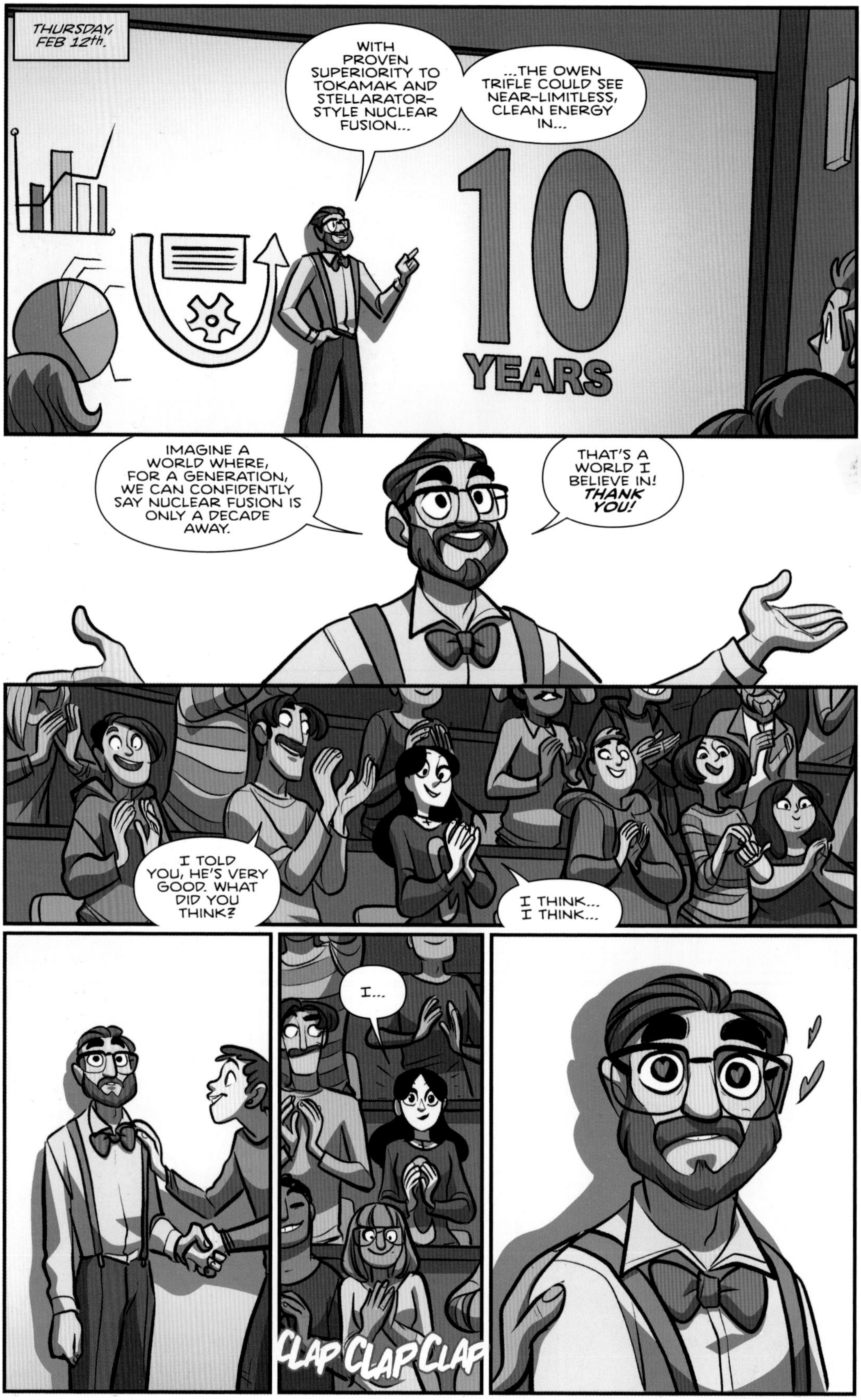
THURSDAY, FEB 12th.
WITH PROVEN SUPERIORITY TO TOKAMAK AND STELLARATOR-STYLE NUCLEAR FUSION...
...THE OWEN TRIFLE COULD SEE NEAR-LIMITLESS, CLEAN ENERGY IN...
10 YEARS
IMAGINE A WORLD WHERE, FOR A GENERATION, WE CAN CONFIDENTLY SAY NUCLEAR FUSION IS ONLY A DECADE AWAY.
THAT'S A WORLD I BELIEVE IN! THANK YOU!
I TOLD YOU, HE'S VERY GOOD. WHAT DID YOU THINK?
I THINK... I THINK...
I...
CLAP CLAP CLAP

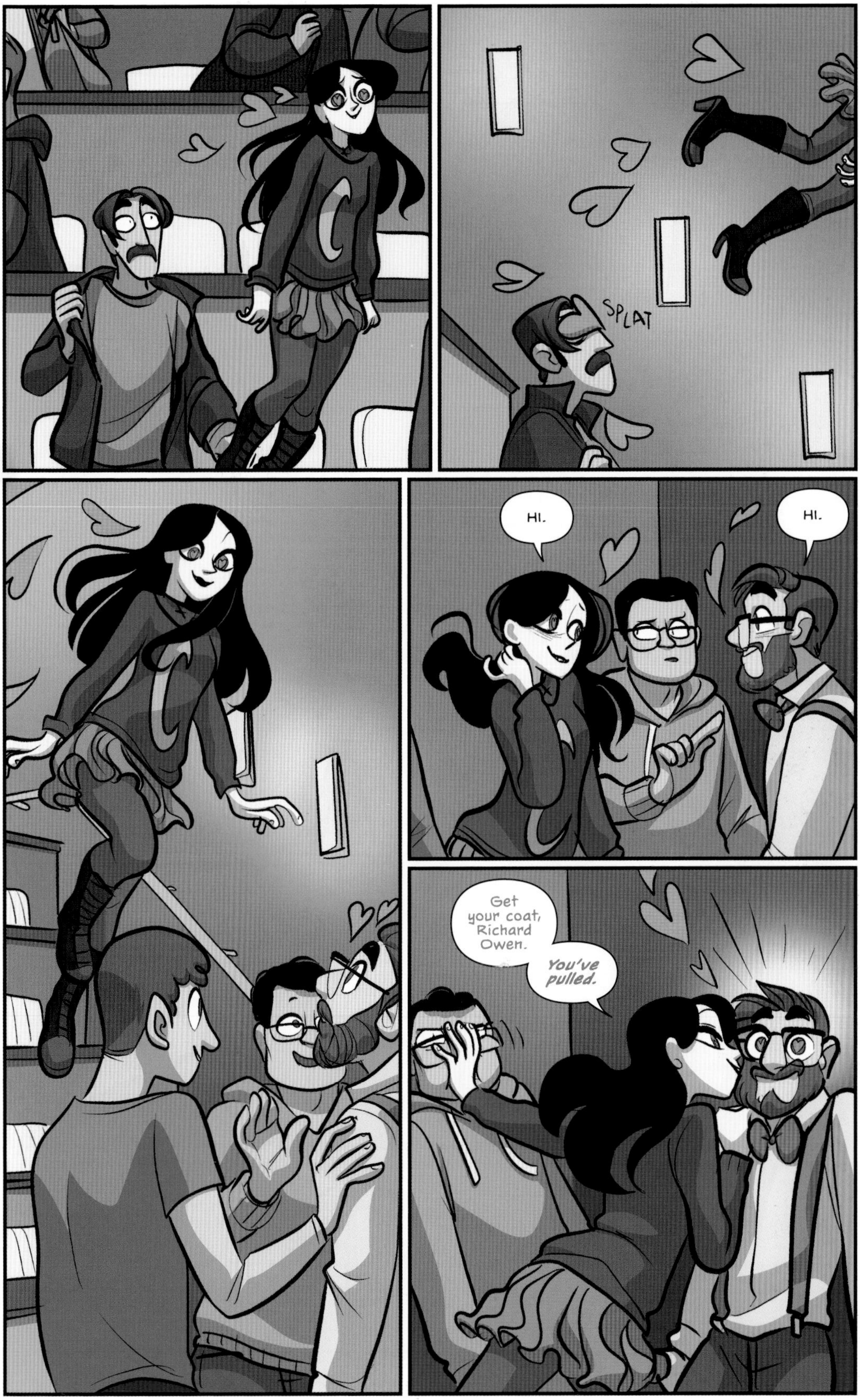
SPLAT
HI.
HI.
Get your coat, Richard Owen.
You've pulled.

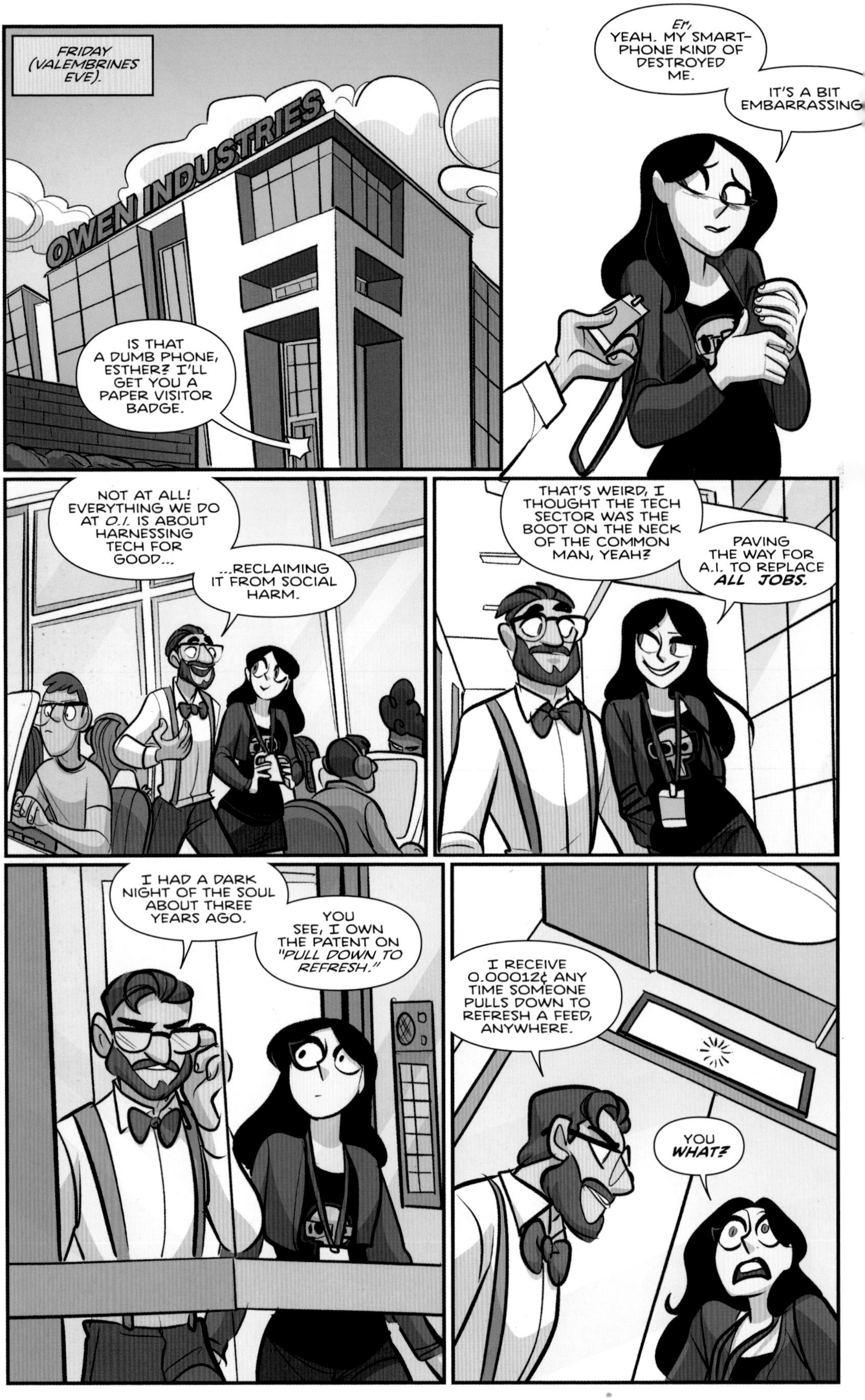
FRIDAY (VALEMBRINES EVE).
OWEN INDUSTRIES
IS THAT A DUMB PHONE, ESTHER? I'LL GET YOU A PAPER VISITOR BADGE.
Er, YEAH. MY SMART-PHONE KIND OF DESTROYED ME.
IT'S A BIT EMBARRASSING
NOT AT ALL! EVERYTHING WE DO AT O.I. IS ABOUT HARNESSING TECH FOR GOOD...
...RECLAIMING IT FROM SOCIAL HARM.
THAT'S WEIRD, I THOUGHT THE TECH SECTOR WAS THE BOOT ON THE NECK OF THE COMMON MAN, YEAH?
PAVING THE WAY FOR A.I. TO REPLACE ALL JOBS.
I HAD A DARK NIGHT OF THE SOUL ABOUT THREE YEARS AGO.
YOU SEE, I OWN THE PATENT ON "PULL DOWN TO REFRESH."
I RECEIVE 0.00012¢ ANY TIME SOMEONE PULLS DOWN TO REFRESH A FEED, ANYWHERE.
YOU WHAT?

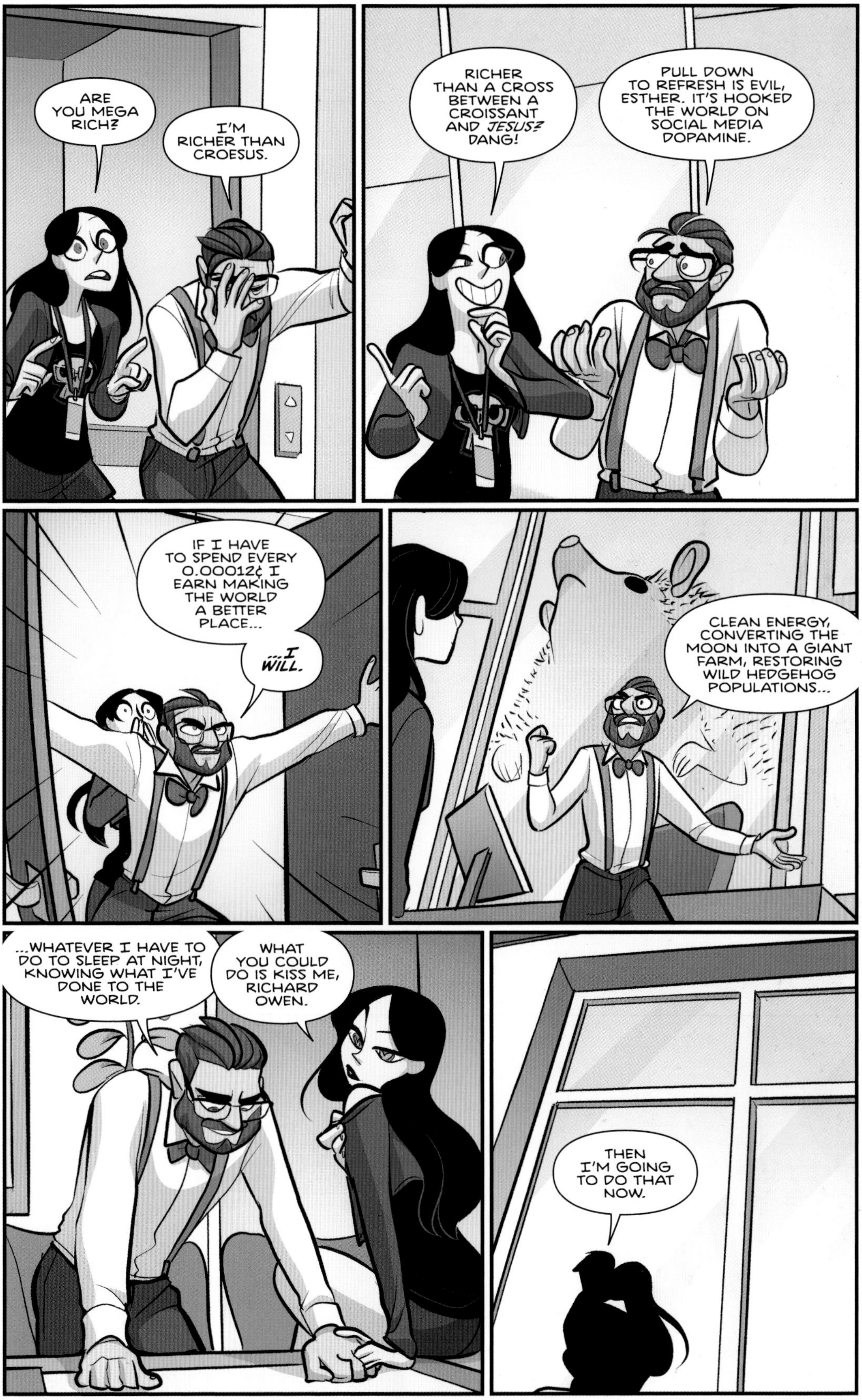
ARE YOU MEGA RICH?
I'M RICHER THAN CROESUS.
RICHER THAN A CROSS BETWEEN A CROISSANT AND *JESUS?* DANG!
PULL DOWN TO REFRESH IS EVIL, ESTHER. IT'S HOOKED THE WORLD ON SOCIAL MEDIA DOPAMINE.
IF I HAVE TO SPEND EVERY 0.00012¢ I EARN MAKING THE WORLD A BETTER PLACE...
...I *WILL.*
CLEAN ENERGY, CONVERTING THE MOON INTO A GIANT FARM, RESTORING WILD HEDGEHOG POPULATIONS...
...WHATEVER I HAVE TO DO TO SLEEP AT NIGHT, KNOWING WHAT I'VE DONE TO THE WORLD.
WHAT YOU COULD DO IS KISS ME, RICHARD OWEN.
THEN I'M GOING TO DO THAT NOW.

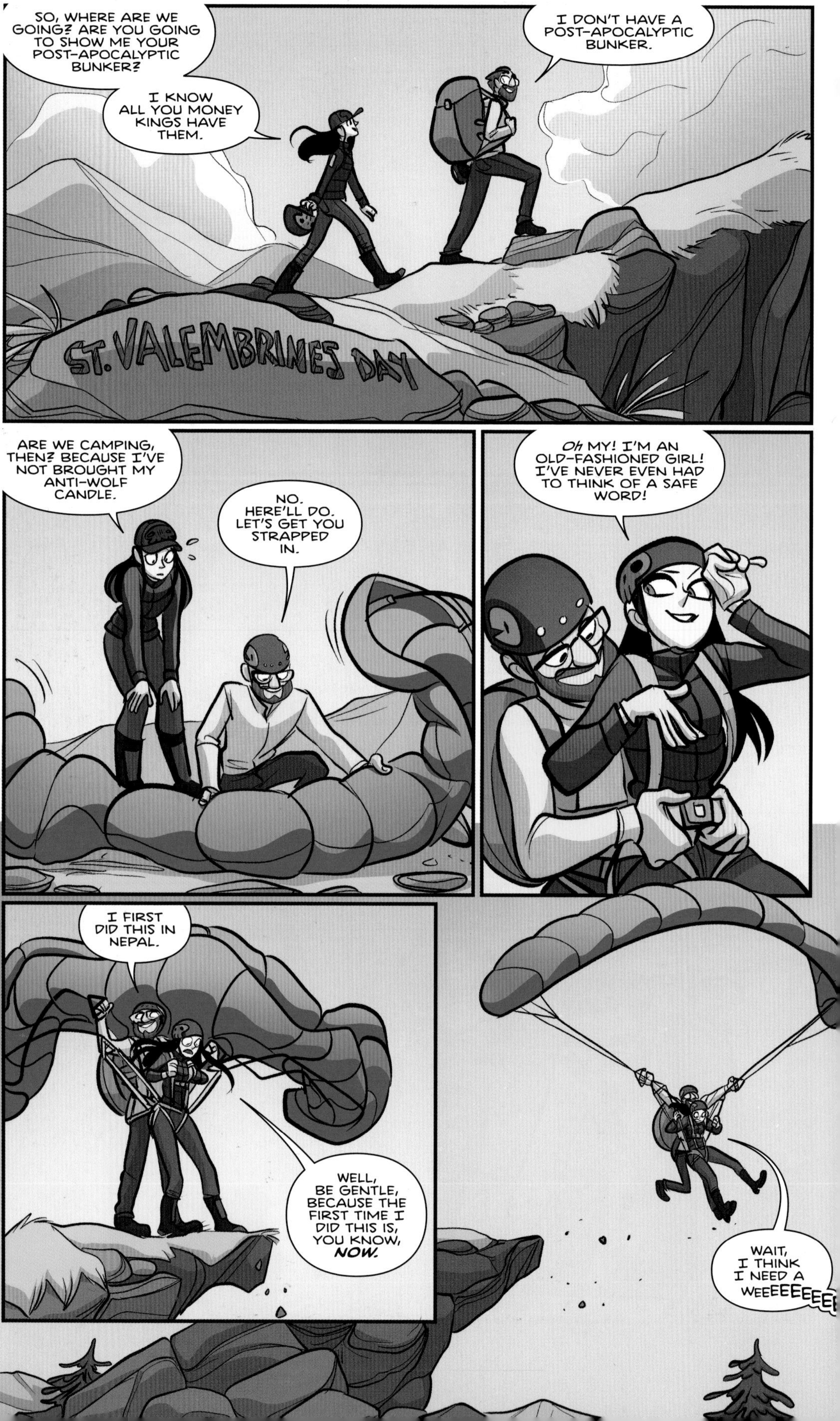
SO, WHERE ARE WE GOING? ARE YOU GOING TO SHOW ME YOUR POST-APOCALYPTIC BUNKER?
I KNOW ALL YOU MONEY KINGS HAVE THEM.
I DON'T HAVE A POST-APOCALYPTIC BUNKER.
ST. VALEMBRINES DAY
ARE WE CAMPING, THEN? BECAUSE I'VE NOT BROUGHT MY ANTI-WOLF CANDLE.
NO. HERE'LL DO. LET'S GET YOU STRAPPED IN.
Oh MY! I'M AN OLD-FASHIONED GIRL! I'VE NEVER EVEN HAD TO THINK OF A SAFE WORD!
I FIRST DID THIS IN NEPAL.
WELL, BE GENTLE, BECAUSE THE FIRST TIME I DID THIS IS, YOU KNOW, ***NOW.***
WAIT, I THINK I NEED A WEEEEEEEEE

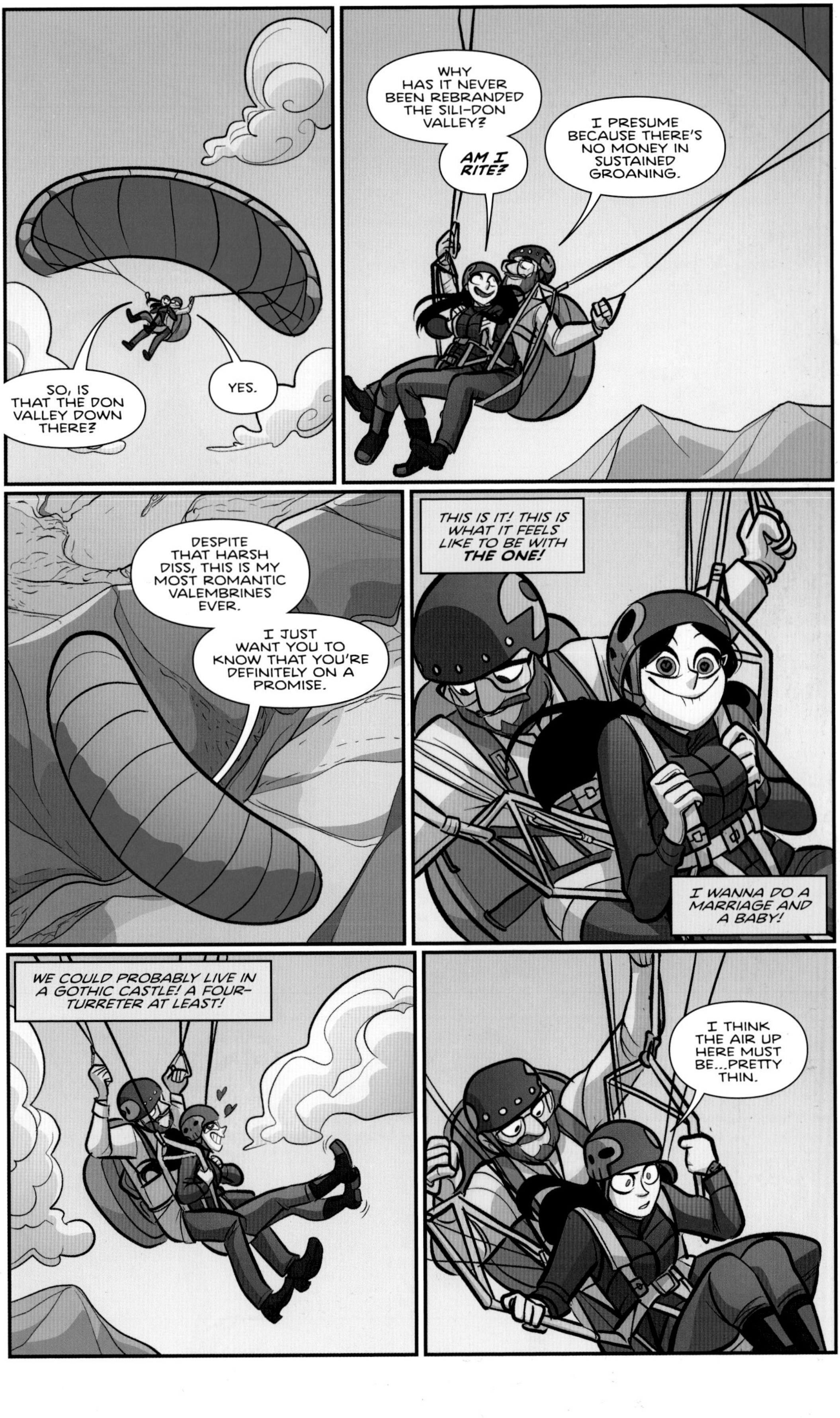
SO, IS
THAT THE DON
VALLEY DOWN
THERE?
YES.
WHY
HAS IT NEVER
BEEN REBRANDED
THE SILI-DON
VALLEY?
AM I
RITE?
I PRESUME
BECAUSE THERE'S
NO MONEY IN
SUSTAINED
GROANING.
DESPITE
THAT HARSH
DISS, THIS IS MY
MOST ROMANTIC
VALEMBRINES
EVER.
I JUST
WANT YOU TO
KNOW THAT YOU'RE
DEFINITELY ON A
PROMISE.
THIS IS IT! THIS IS
WHAT IT FEELS
LIKE TO BE WITH
THE ONE!
I WANNA DO A
MARRIAGE AND
A BABY!
WE COULD PROBABLY LIVE IN
A GOTHIC CASTLE! A FOUR-
TURRETER AT LEAST!
I THINK
THE AIR UP
HERE MUST
BE...PRETTY
THIN.

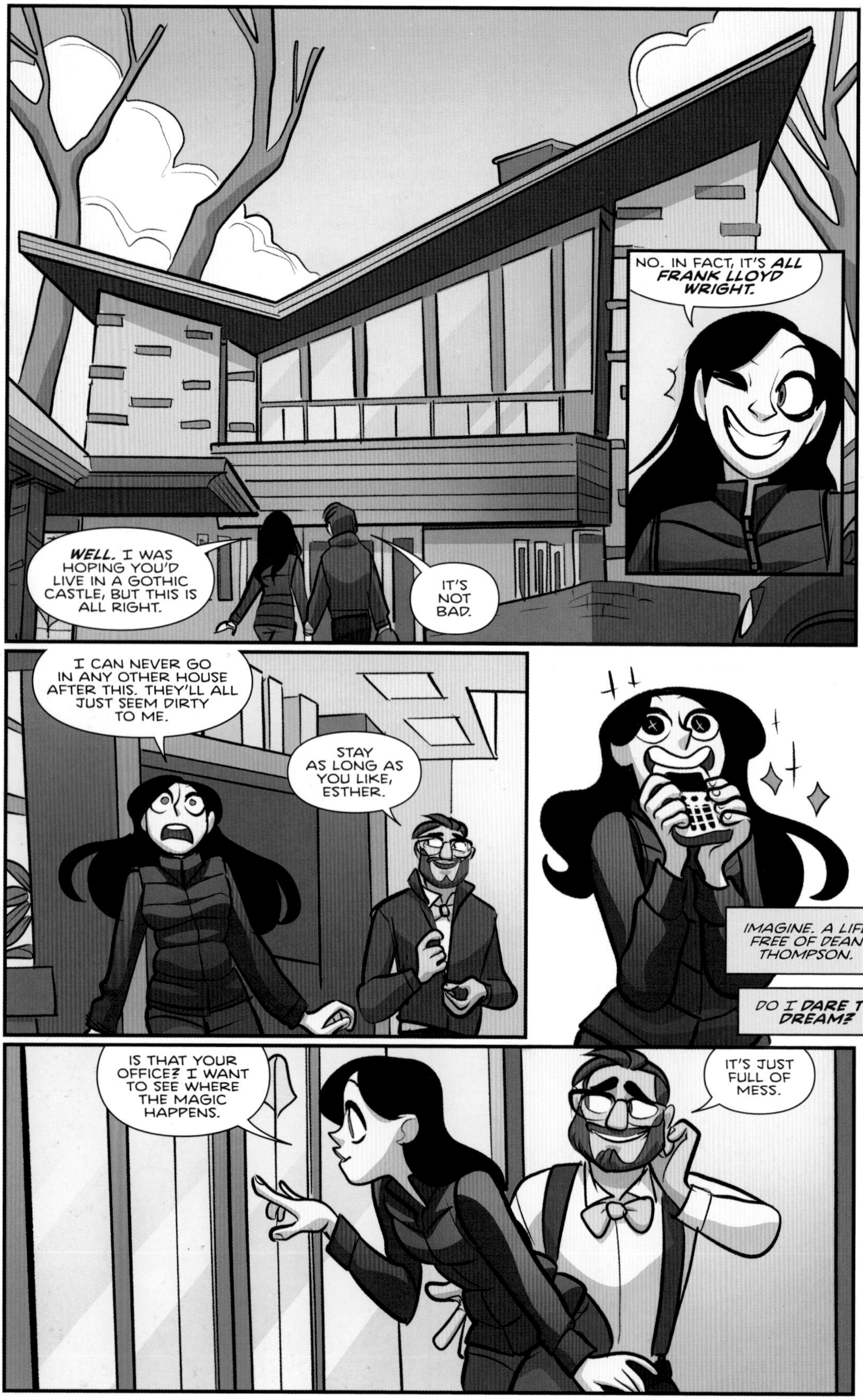
WELL. I WAS HOPING YOU'D LIVE IN A GOTHIC CASTLE, BUT THIS IS ALL RIGHT.
IT'S NOT BAD.
NO. IN FACT, IT'S ALL FRANK LLOYD WRIGHT.
I CAN NEVER GO IN ANY OTHER HOUSE AFTER THIS. THEY'LL ALL JUST SEEM DIRTY TO ME.
STAY AS LONG AS YOU LIKE, ESTHER.
IMAGINE. A LIFE FREE OF DEAN THOMPSON.
DO I DARE TO DREAM?
IS THAT YOUR OFFICE? I WANT TO SEE WHERE THE MAGIC HAPPENS.
IT'S JUST FULL OF MESS.

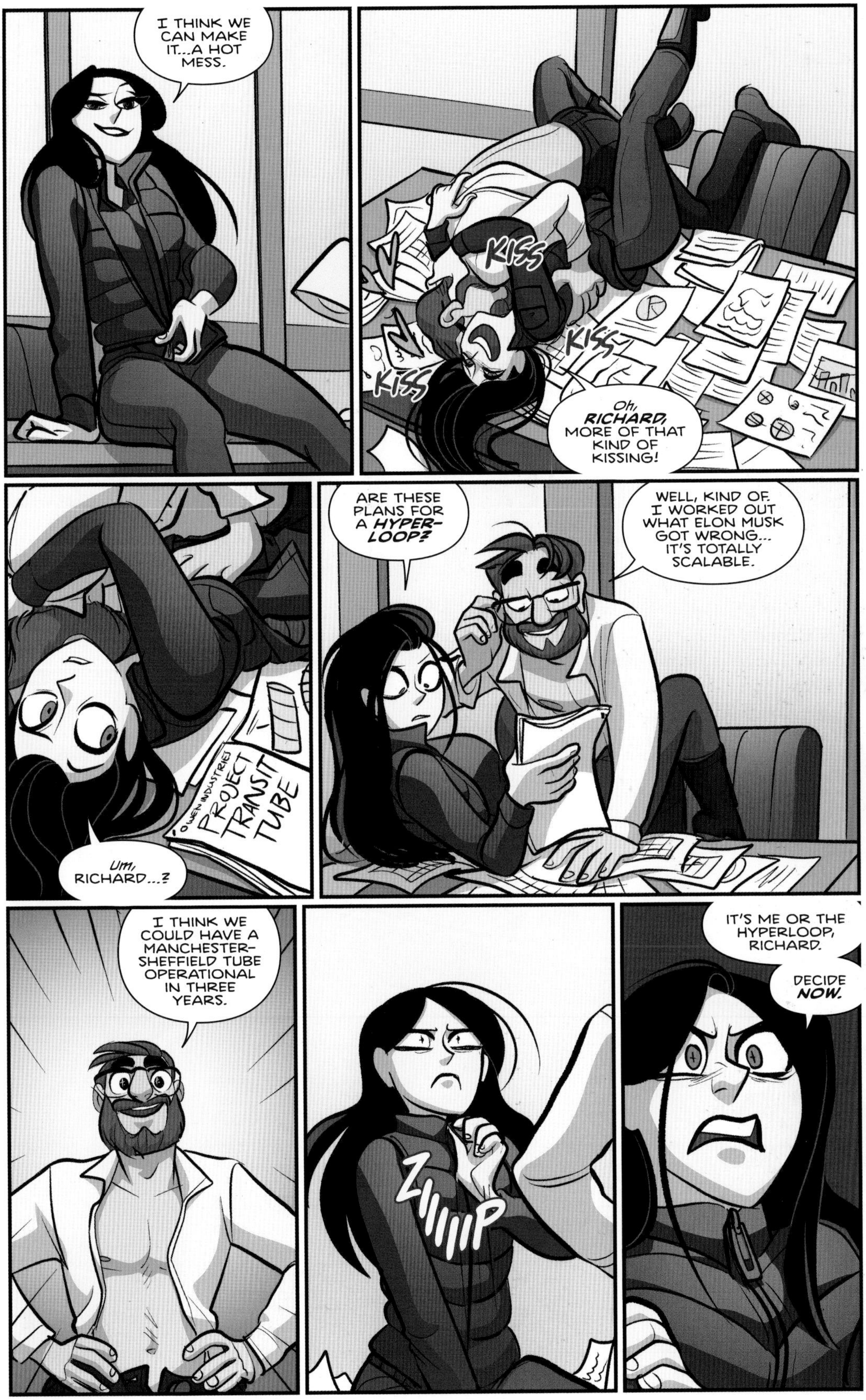
I THINK WE CAN MAKE IT...A HOT MESS.
KISS
KISS
KISS
Oh, **RICHARD,** MORE OF THAT KIND OF KISSING!
OWEN INDUSTRIES PROJECT TRANSIT TUBE
Um, RICHARD...?
ARE THESE PLANS FOR A ***HYPER-LOOP?***
WELL, KIND OF. I WORKED OUT WHAT ELON MUSK GOT WRONG... IT'S TOTALLY SCALABLE.
I THINK WE COULD HAVE A MANCHESTER-SHEFFIELD TUBE OPERATIONAL IN THREE YEARS.
ZIIIIIP
IT'S ME OR THE HYPERLOOP, RICHARD.
DECIDE ***NOW.***

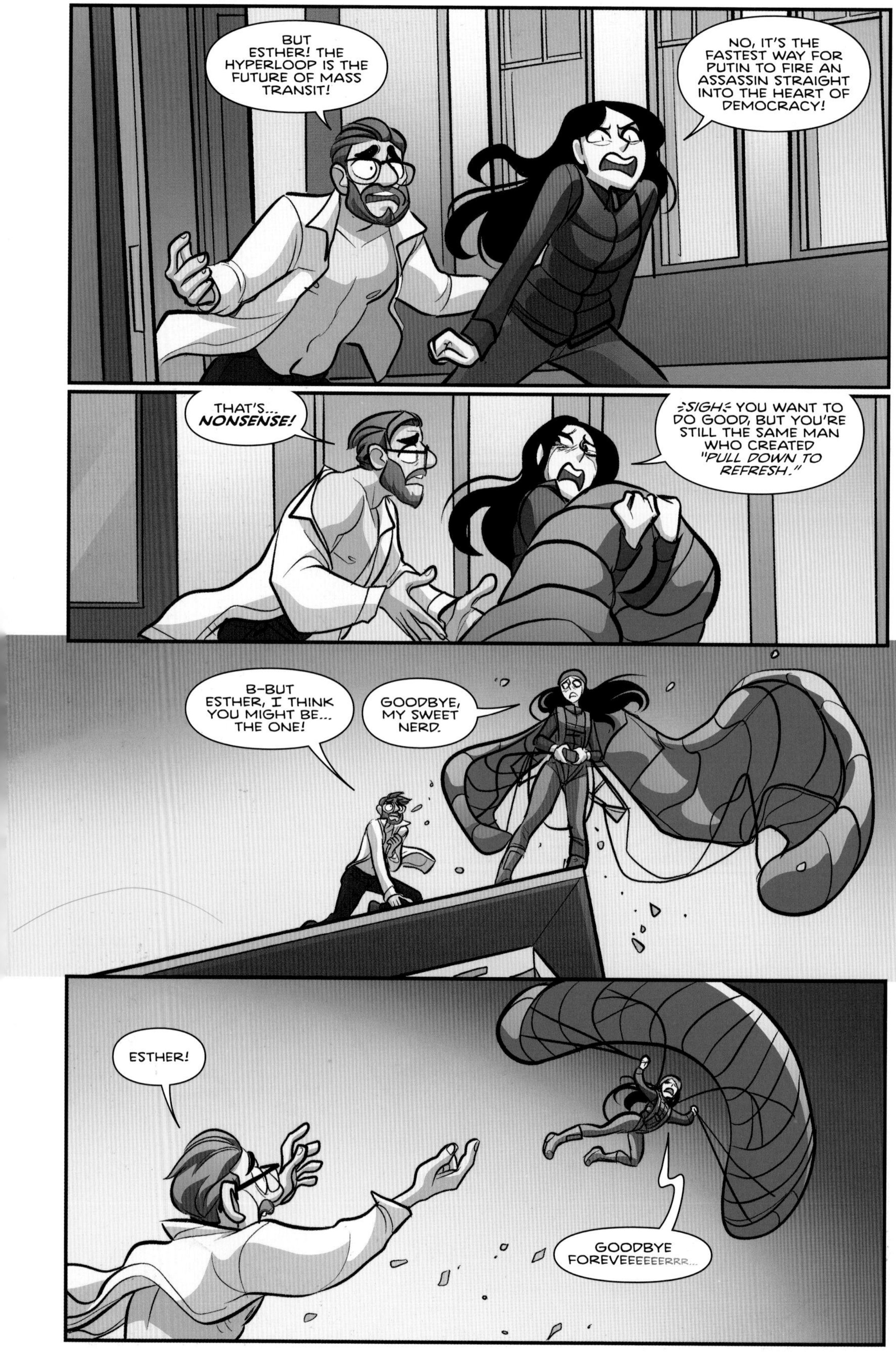
BUT ESTHER! THE HYPERLOOP IS THE FUTURE OF MASS TRANSIT!
NO, IT'S THE FASTEST WAY FOR PUTIN TO FIRE AN ASSASSIN STRAIGHT INTO THE HEART OF DEMOCRACY!
THAT'S... NONSENSE!
SIGH YOU WANT TO DO GOOD, BUT YOU'RE STILL THE SAME MAN WHO CREATED "PULL DOWN TO REFRESH."
B-BUT ESTHER, I THINK YOU MIGHT BE... THE ONE!
GOODBYE, MY SWEET NERD.
ESTHER!
GOODBYE FOREVEEEEEERRR...

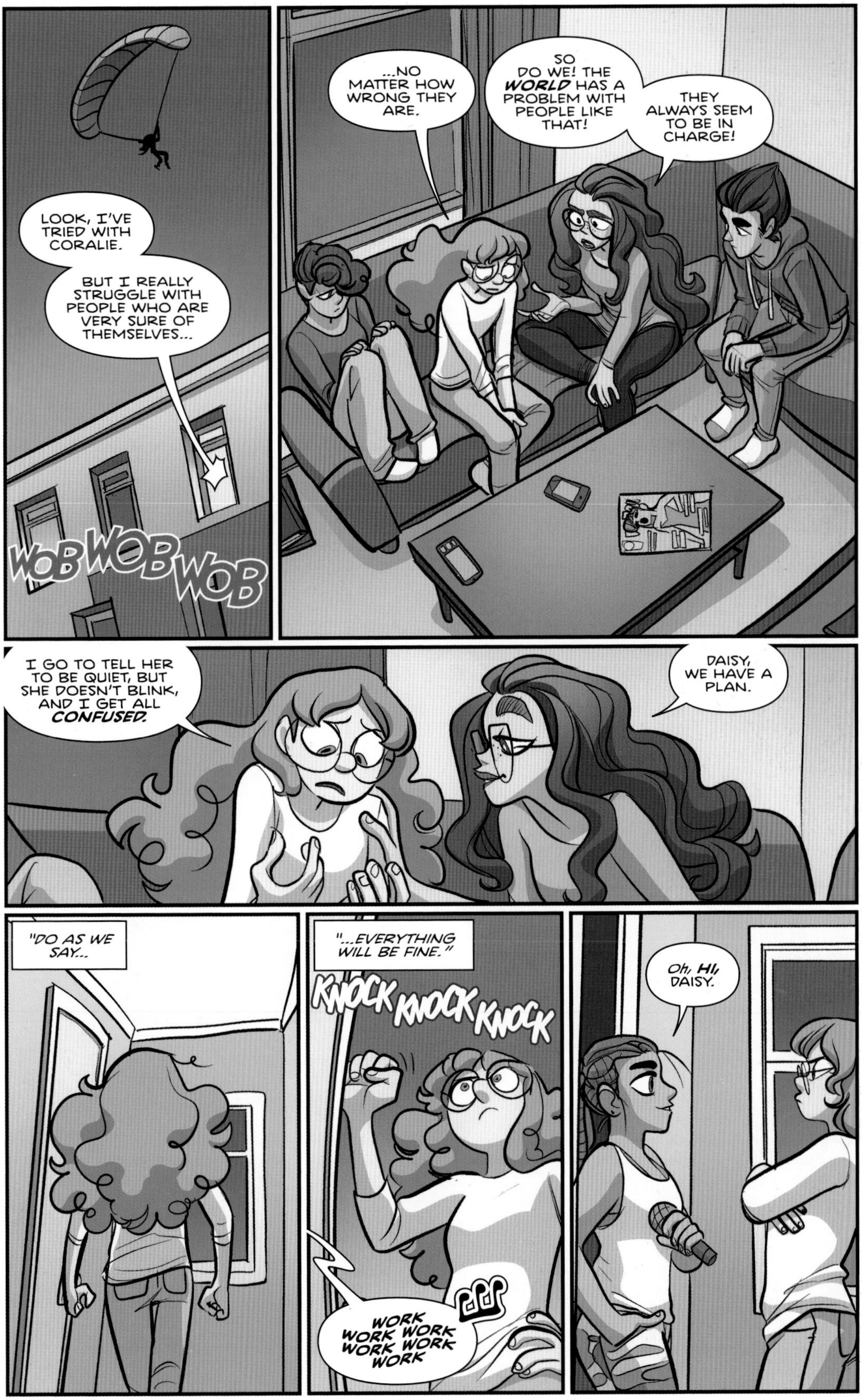
LOOK, I'VE TRIED WITH CORALIE.
BUT I REALLY STRUGGLE WITH PEOPLE WHO ARE VERY SURE OF THEMSELVES...
WOB WOB WOB WOB
...NO MATTER HOW WRONG THEY ARE.
SO DO WE! THE WORLD HAS A PROBLEM WITH PEOPLE LIKE THAT!
THEY ALWAYS SEEM TO BE IN CHARGE!
I GO TO TELL HER TO BE QUIET, BUT SHE DOESN'T BLINK, AND I GET ALL CONFUSED.
DAISY, WE HAVE A PLAN.
"DO AS WE SAY...
"...EVERYTHING WILL BE FINE."
KNOCK KNOCK KNOCK
WORK WORK WORK WORK WORK WORK
Oh, HI, DAISY.

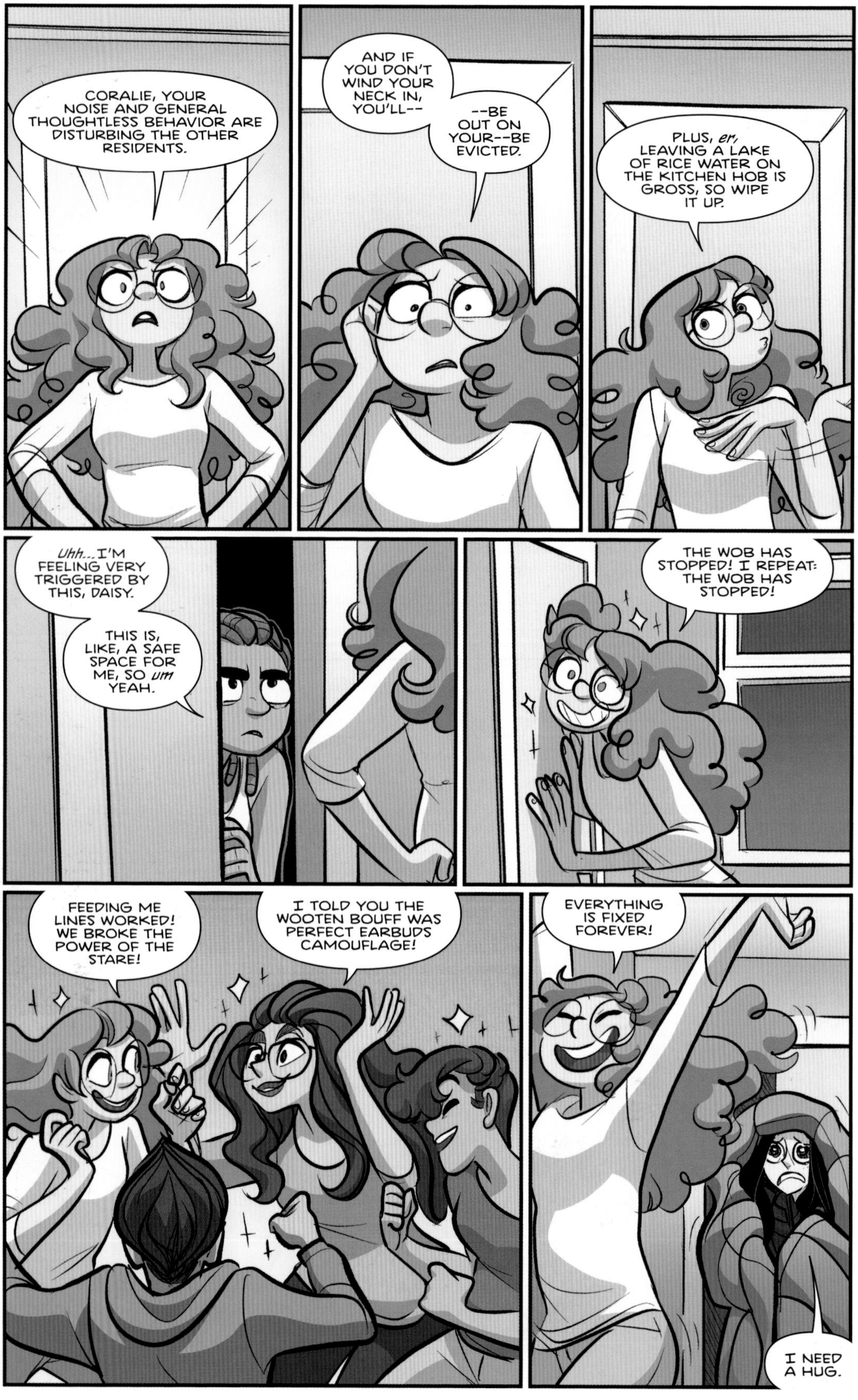
CORALIE, YOUR NOISE AND GENERAL THOUGHTLESS BEHAVIOR ARE DISTURBING THE OTHER RESIDENTS.
AND IF YOU DON'T WIND YOUR NECK IN, YOU'LL--
--BE OUT ON YOUR--BE EVICTED.
PLUS, *er*, LEAVING A LAKE OF RICE WATER ON THE KITCHEN HOB IS GROSS, SO WIPE IT UP.
Uhh... I'M FEELING VERY TRIGGERED BY THIS, DAISY.
THIS IS, LIKE, A SAFE SPACE FOR ME, SO *um* YEAH.
THE WOB HAS STOPPED! I REPEAT: THE WOB HAS STOPPED!
FEEDING ME LINES WORKED! WE BROKE THE POWER OF THE STARE!
I TOLD YOU THE WOOTEN BOUFF WAS PERFECT EARBUDS CAMOUFLAGE!
EVERYTHING IS FIXED FOREVER!
I NEED A HUG.

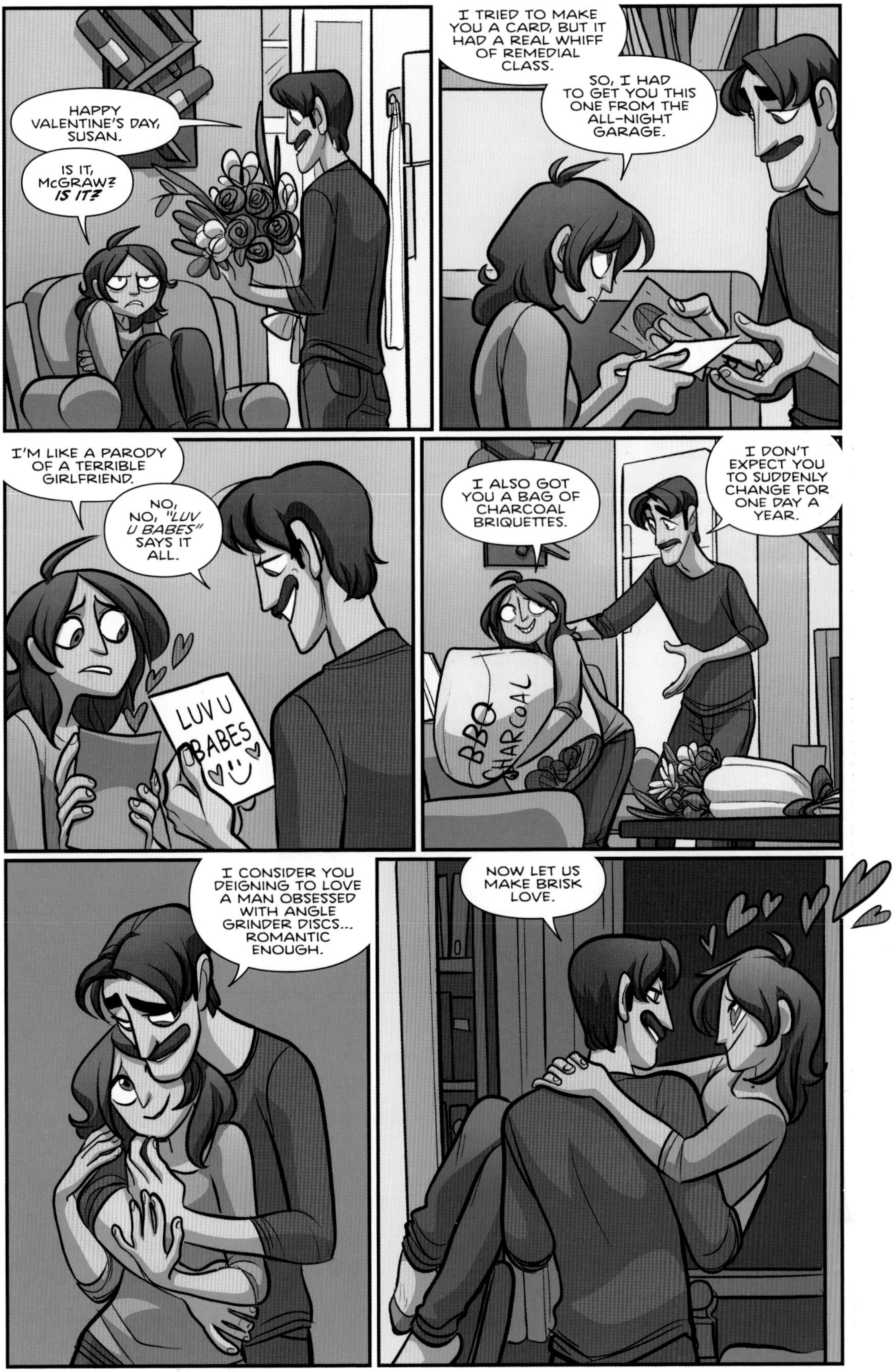
HAPPY VALENTINE'S DAY, SUSAN.
IS IT, McGRAW? *IS IT?*
I TRIED TO MAKE YOU A CARD, BUT IT HAD A REAL WHIFF OF REMEDIAL CLASS.
SO, I HAD TO GET YOU THIS ONE FROM THE ALL-NIGHT GARAGE.
I'M LIKE A PARODY OF A TERRIBLE GIRLFRIEND.
NO, NO, *"LUV U BABES"* SAYS IT ALL.
LUV U BABES
I ALSO GOT YOU A BAG OF CHARCOAL BRIQUETTES.
I DON'T EXPECT YOU TO SUDDENLY CHANGE FOR ONE DAY A YEAR.
BBQ CHARCOAL
I CONSIDER YOU DEIGNING TO LOVE A MAN OBSESSED WITH ANGLE GRINDER DISCS... ROMANTIC ENOUGH.
NOW LET US MAKE BRISK LOVE.

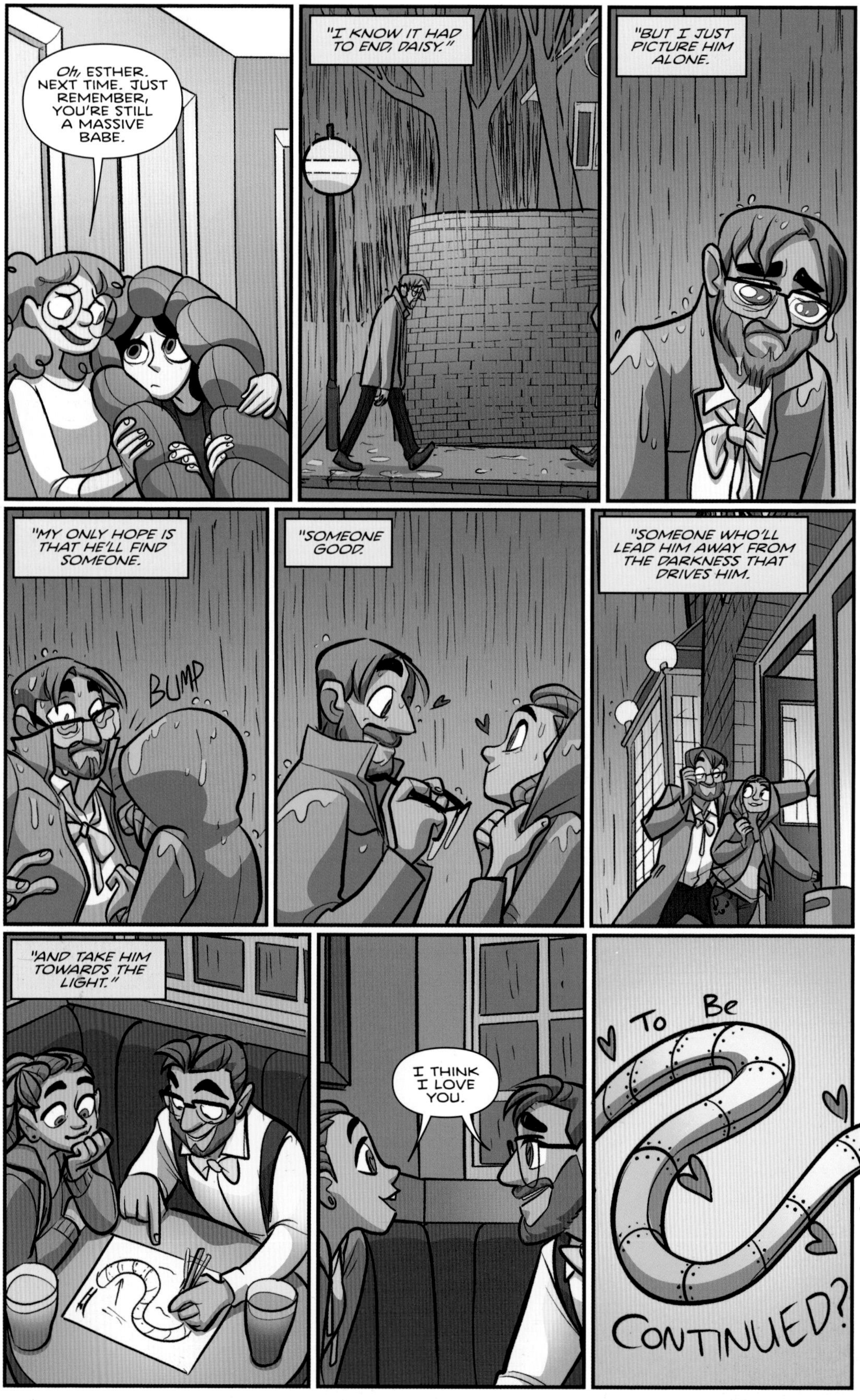
Oh, ESTHER. NEXT TIME. JUST REMEMBER, YOU'RE STILL A MASSIVE BABE.
"I KNOW IT HAD TO END, DAISY."
"BUT I JUST PICTURE HIM ALONE.
"MY ONLY HOPE IS THAT HE'LL FIND SOMEONE.
BUMP
"SOMEONE GOOD.
"SOMEONE WHO'LL LEAD HIM AWAY FROM THE DARKNESS THAT DRIVES HIM.
"AND TAKE HIM TOWARDS THE LIGHT."
I THINK I LOVE YOU.
To Be
CONTINUED?

WHERE WOMEN GLOW
AND MEN PLUNDER

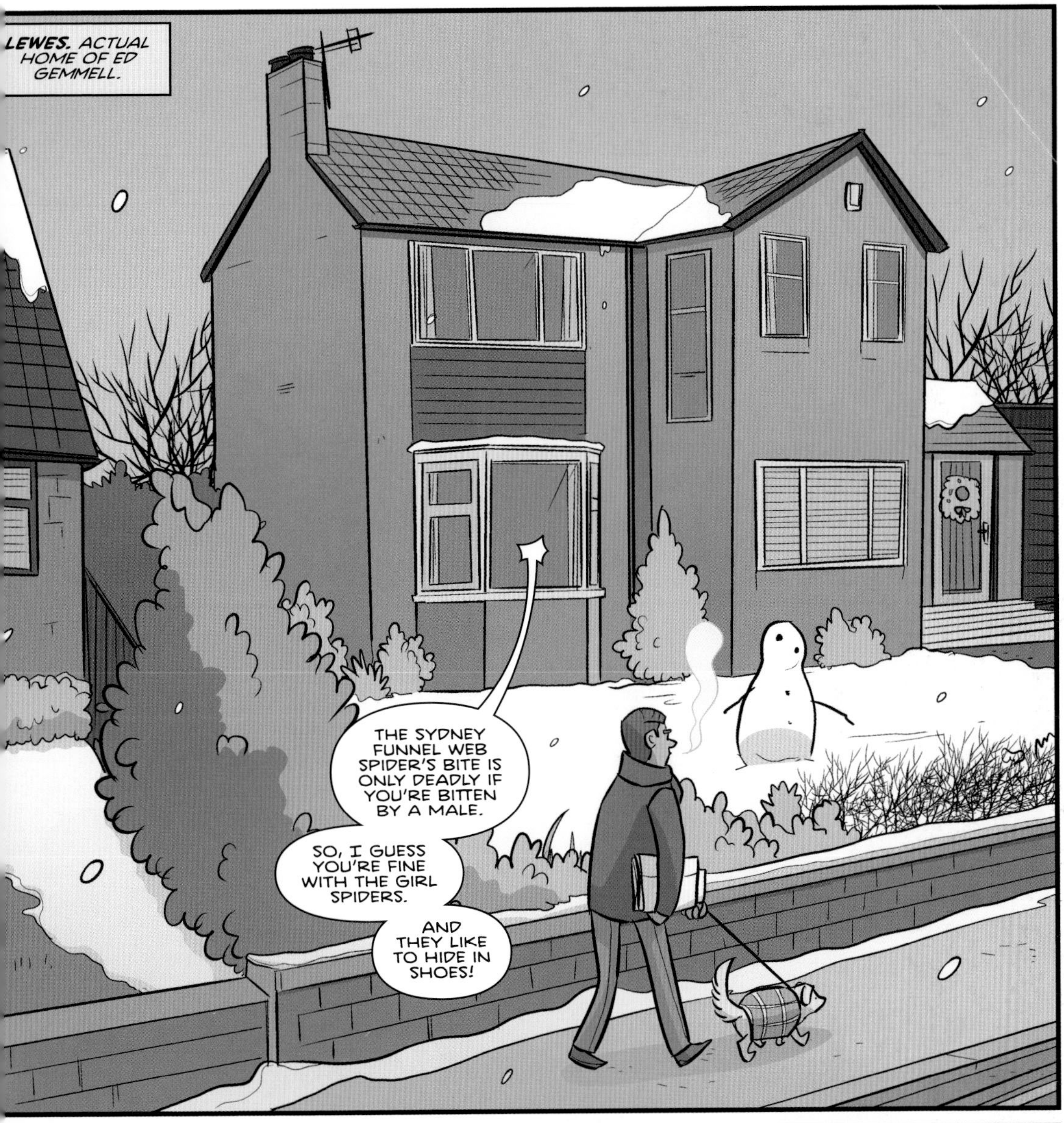
LEWES. ACTUAL HOME OF ED GEMMELL.
THE SYDNEY FUNNEL WEB SPIDER'S BITE IS ONLY DEADLY IF YOU'RE BITTEN BY A MALE.
SO, I GUESS YOU'RE FINE WITH THE GIRL SPIDERS.
AND THEY LIKE TO HIDE IN SHOES!

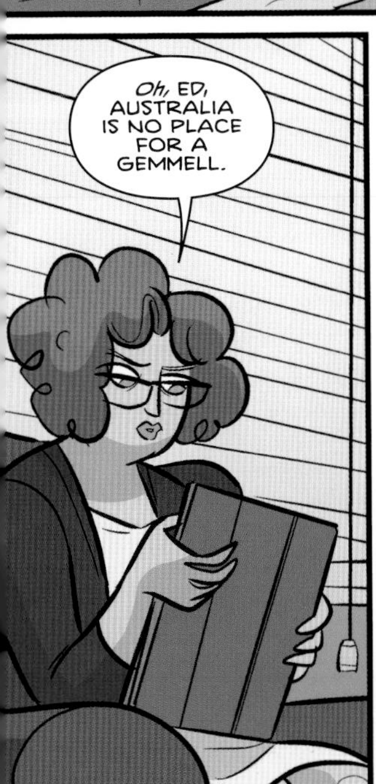
Oh, ED, AUSTRALIA IS NO PLACE FOR A GEMMELL.

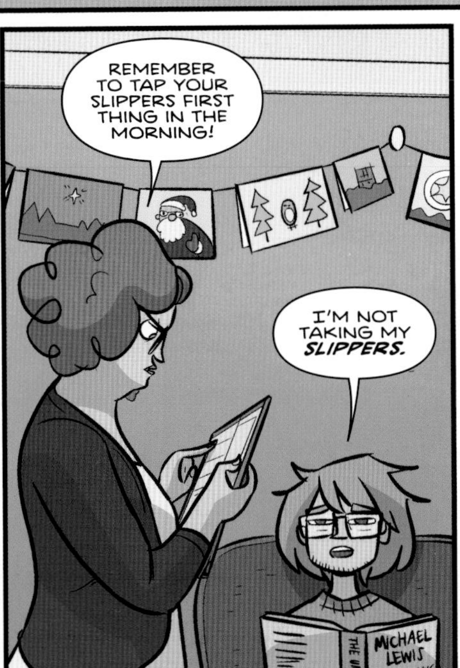
REMEMBER TO TAP YOUR SLIPPERS FIRST THING IN THE MORNING!
I'M NOT TAKING MY SLIPPERS.
MICHAEL LEWIS THE UNDOING PROJECT

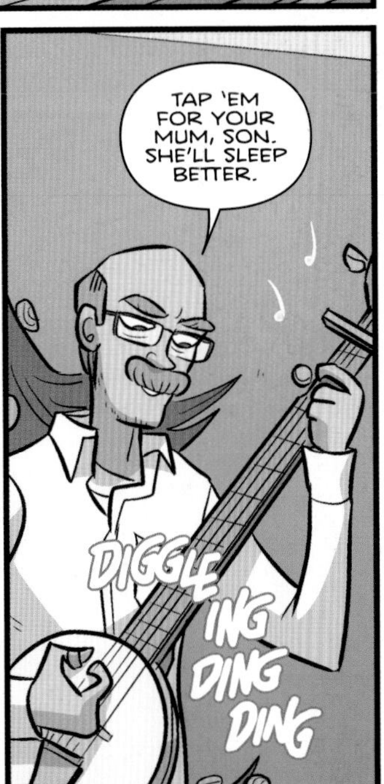
TAP 'EM FOR YOUR MUM, SON. SHE'LL SLEEP BETTER.
DIGGLE ING DING DING

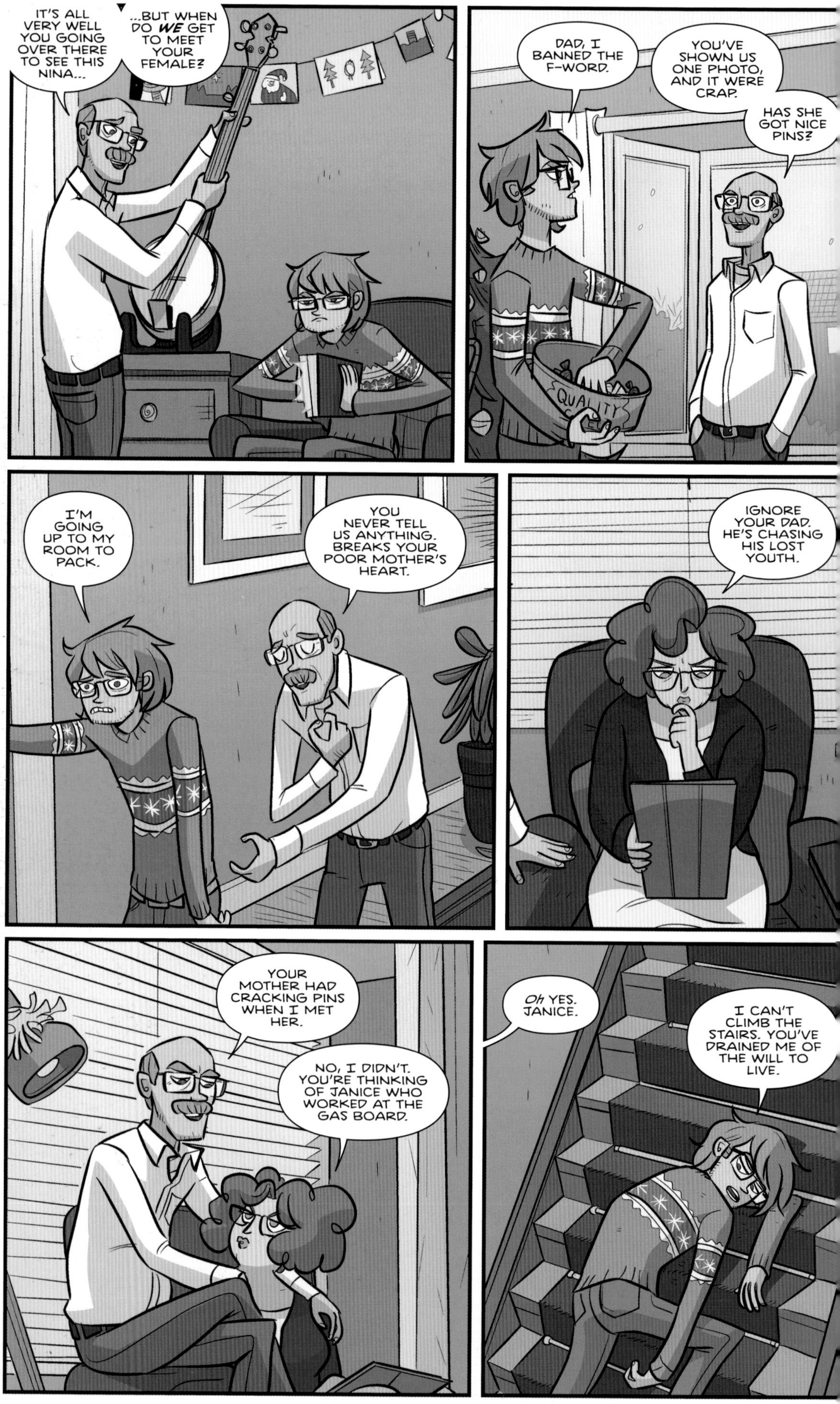
IT'S ALL VERY WELL YOU GOING OVER THERE TO SEE THIS NINA...
...BUT WHEN DO *WE* GET TO MEET YOUR FEMALE?
DAD, I BANNED THE F-WORD.
YOU'VE SHOWN US ONE PHOTO, AND IT WERE CRAP.
HAS SHE GOT NICE PINS?
QUALITY
I'M GOING UP TO MY ROOM TO PACK.
YOU NEVER TELL US ANYTHING. BREAKS YOUR POOR MOTHER'S HEART.
IGNORE YOUR DAD. HE'S CHASING HIS LOST YOUTH.
YOUR MOTHER HAD CRACKING PINS WHEN I MET HER.
NO, I DIDN'T. YOU'RE THINKING OF JANICE WHO WORKED AT THE GAS BOARD.
Oh YES. JANICE.
I CAN'T CLIMB THE STAIRS. YOU'VE DRAINED ME OF THE WILL TO LIVE.

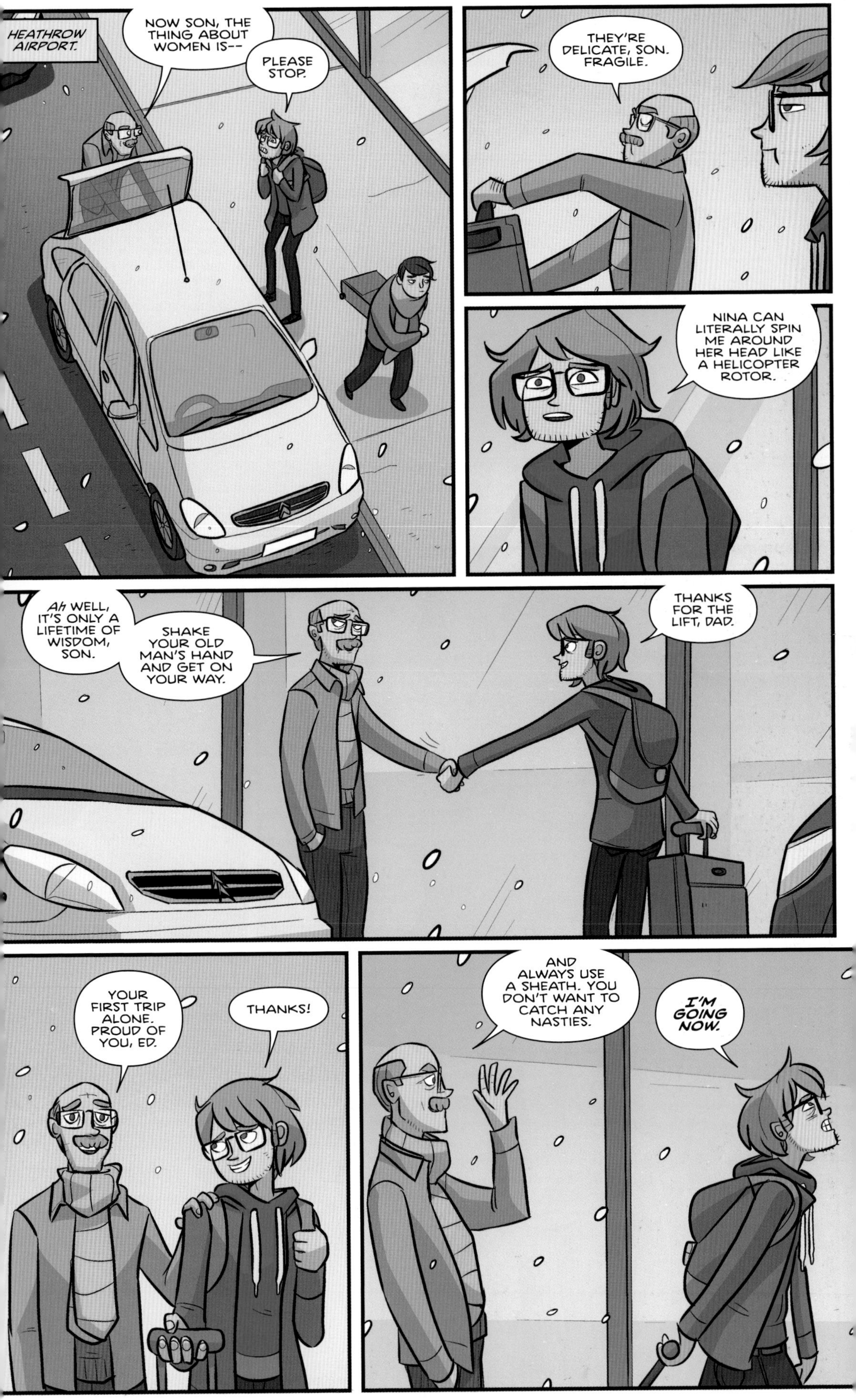
HEATHROW AIRPORT.
NOW SON, THE THING ABOUT WOMEN IS--
PLEASE STOP.
THEY'RE DELICATE, SON. FRAGILE.
NINA CAN LITERALLY SPIN ME AROUND HER HEAD LIKE A HELICOPTER ROTOR.
Ah WELL, IT'S ONLY A LIFETIME OF WISDOM, SON.
SHAKE YOUR OLD MAN'S HAND AND GET ON YOUR WAY.
THANKS FOR THE LIFT, DAD.
YOUR FIRST TRIP ALONE. PROUD OF YOU, ED.
THANKS!
AND ALWAYS USE A SHEATH. YOU DON'T WANT TO CATCH ANY NASTIES.
I'M GOING NOW.

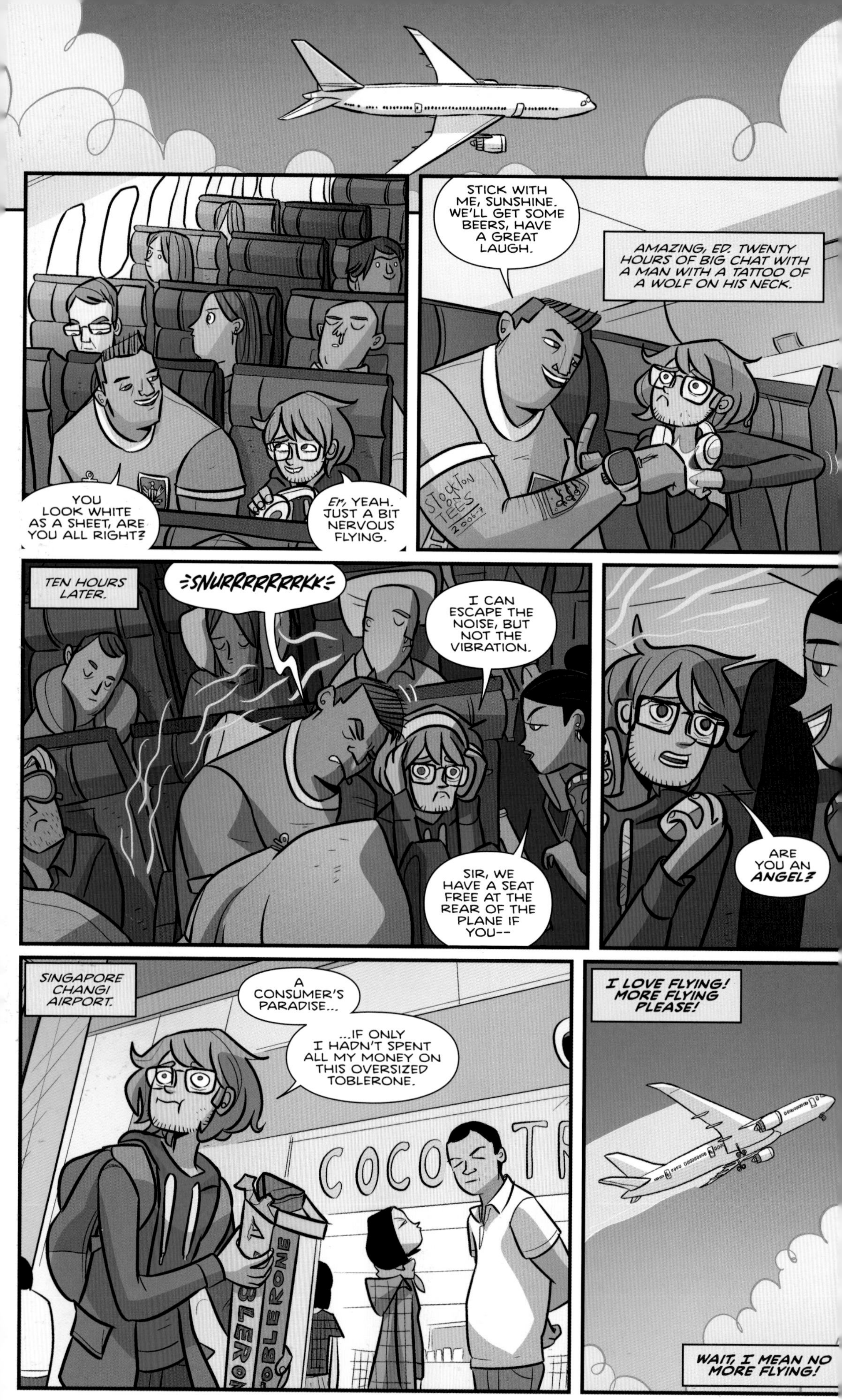
YOU LOOK WHITE AS A SHEET, ARE YOU ALL RIGHT?
ER, YEAH. JUST A BIT NERVOUS FLYING.
STICK WITH ME, SUNSHINE. WE'LL GET SOME BEERS, HAVE A GREAT LAUGH.
AMAZING, ED. TWENTY HOURS OF BIG CHAT WITH A MAN WITH A TATTOO OF A WOLF ON HIS NECK.
STOCKTON ON TEES 2006-7
TEN HOURS LATER.
SNURRRRRRRKK
I CAN ESCAPE THE NOISE, BUT NOT THE VIBRATION.
SIR, WE HAVE A SEAT FREE AT THE REAR OF THE PLANE IF YOU--
ARE YOU AN ANGEL?
SINGAPORE CHANGI AIRPORT.
A CONSUMER'S PARADISE...
...IF ONLY I HADN'T SPENT ALL MY MONEY ON THIS OVERSIZED TOBLERONE.
COCO TR
TOBLERONE
I LOVE FLYING! MORE FLYING PLEASE!
WAIT, I MEAN NO MORE FLYING!

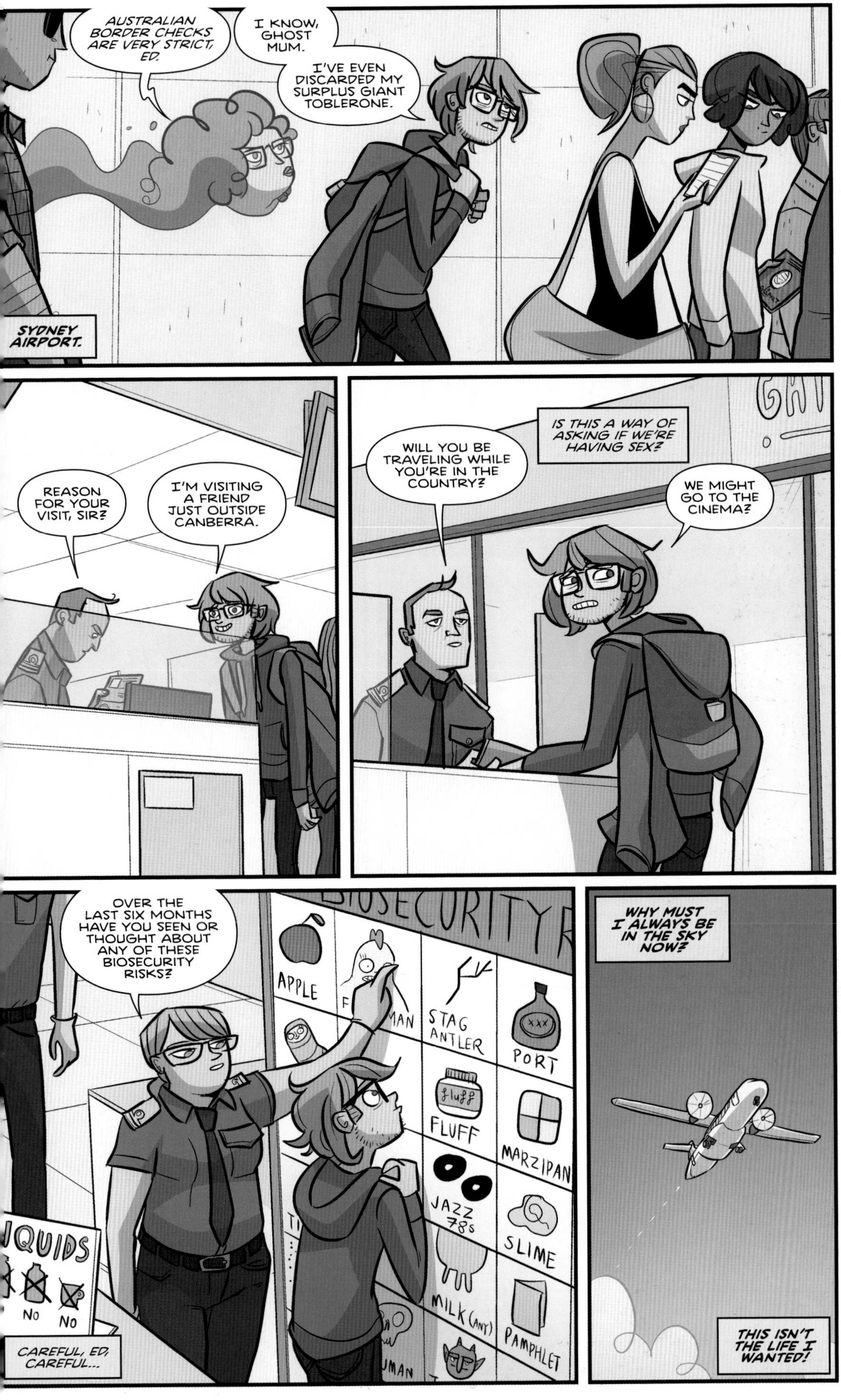

AUSTRALIAN BORDER CHECKS ARE VERY STRICT, ED.
I KNOW, GHOST MUM.
I'VE EVEN DISCARDED MY SURPLUS GIANT TOBLERONE.
SYDNEY AIRPORT.
REASON FOR YOUR VISIT, SIR?
I'M VISITING A FRIEND JUST OUTSIDE CANBERRA.
WILL YOU BE TRAVELING WHILE YOU'RE IN THE COUNTRY?
IS THIS A WAY OF ASKING IF WE'RE HAVING SEX?
WE MIGHT GO TO THE CINEMA?
OVER THE LAST SIX MONTHS HAVE YOU SEEN OR THOUGHT ABOUT ANY OF THESE BIOSECURITY RISKS?
BIOSECURITY
APPLE
STAG ANTLER
PORT
FLUFF
MARZIPAN
JAZZ 78s
SLIME
MILK (ANY)
PAMPHLET
IQUIDS
NO
NO
CAREFUL, ED, CAREFUL...
WHY MUST I ALWAYS BE IN THE SKY NOW?
THIS ISN'T THE LIFE I WANTED!

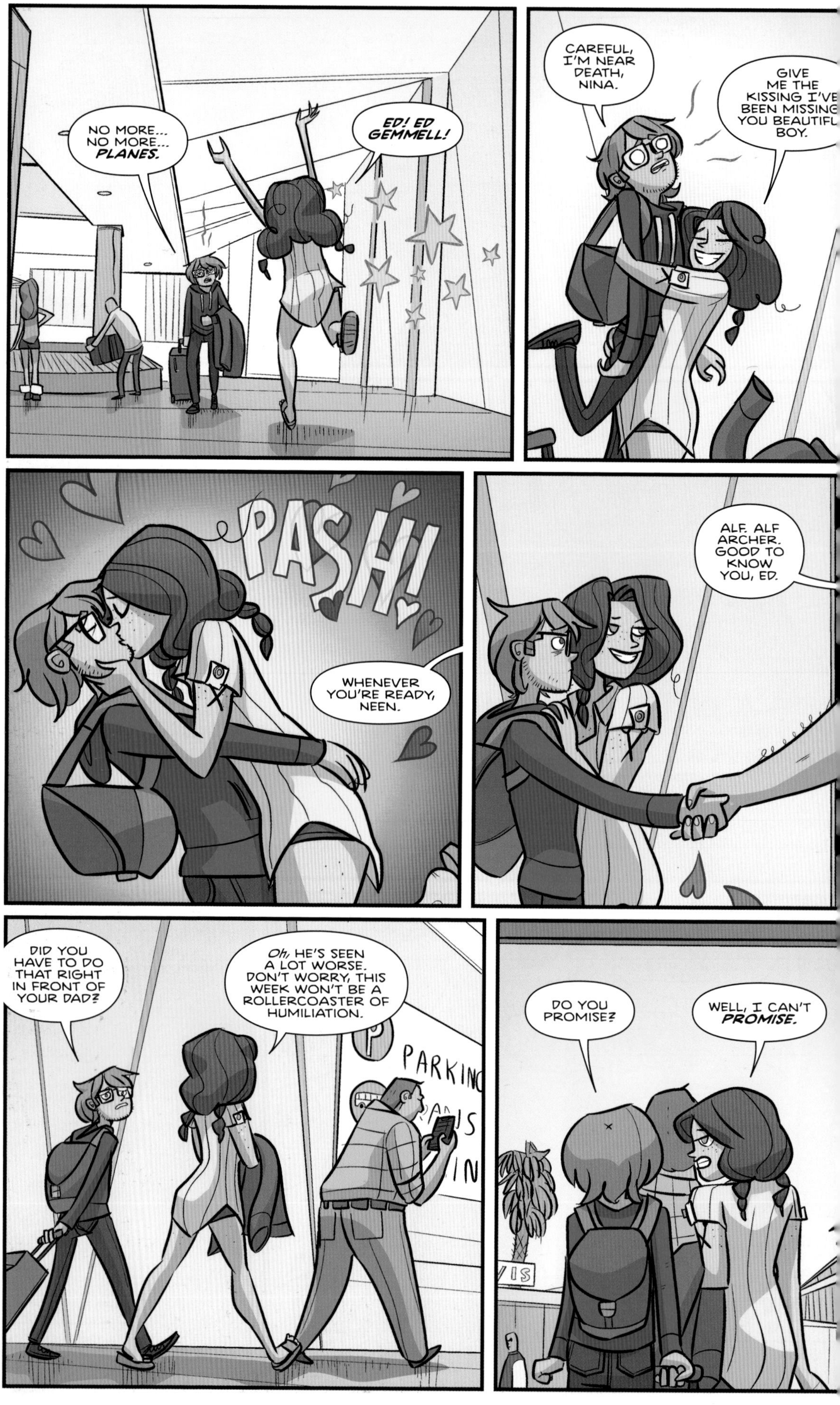
NO MORE... NO MORE... *PLANES.*
ED! ED GEMMELL!
CAREFUL, I'M NEAR DEATH, NINA.
GIVE ME THE KISSING I'VE BEEN MISSING YOU BEAUTIFUL BOY.
PASH!
WHENEVER YOU'RE READY, NEEN.
ALF. ALF ARCHER. GOOD TO KNOW YOU, ED.
DID YOU HAVE TO DO THAT RIGHT IN FRONT OF YOUR DAD?
Oh, HE'S SEEN A LOT WORSE. DON'T WORRY, THIS WEEK WON'T BE A ROLLERCOASTER OF HUMILIATION.
PARKING
DO YOU PROMISE?
WELL, I CAN'T *PROMISE.*

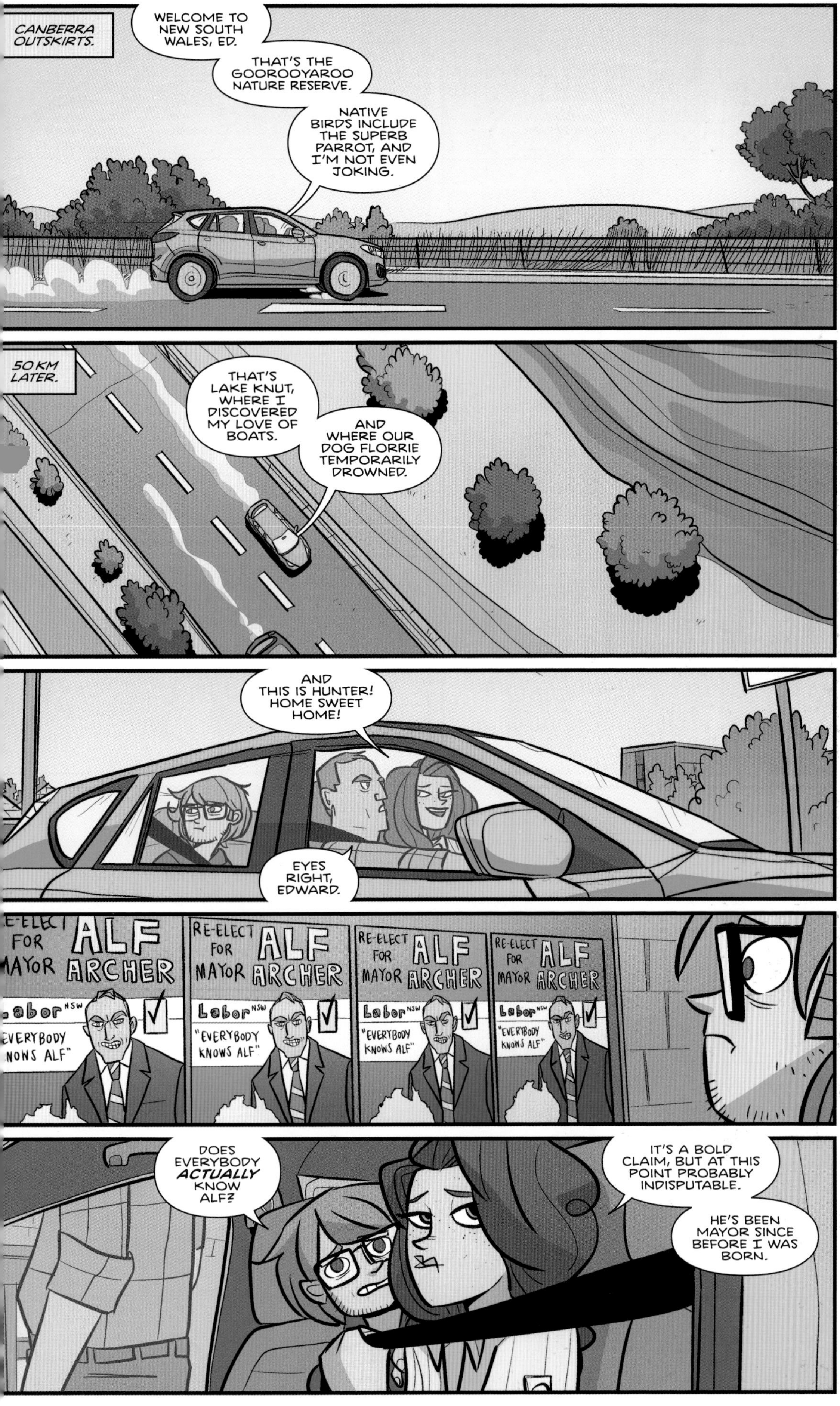
CANBERRA OUTSKIRTS.
WELCOME TO NEW SOUTH WALES, ED.
THAT'S THE GOOROOYAROO NATURE RESERVE.
NATIVE BIRDS INCLUDE THE SUPERB PARROT, AND I'M NOT EVEN JOKING.
50 KM LATER.
THAT'S LAKE KNUT, WHERE I DISCOVERED MY LOVE OF BOATS.
AND WHERE OUR DOG FLORRIE TEMPORARILY DROWNED.
AND THIS IS HUNTER! HOME SWEET HOME!
EYES RIGHT, EDWARD.
RE-ELECT FOR MAYOR ALF ARCHER
Labor NSW
"EVERYBODY KNOWS ALF"
DOES EVERYBODY ***ACTUALLY*** KNOW ALF?
IT'S A BOLD CLAIM, BUT AT THIS POINT PROBABLY INDISPUTABLE.
HE'S BEEN MAYOR SINCE BEFORE I WAS BORN.

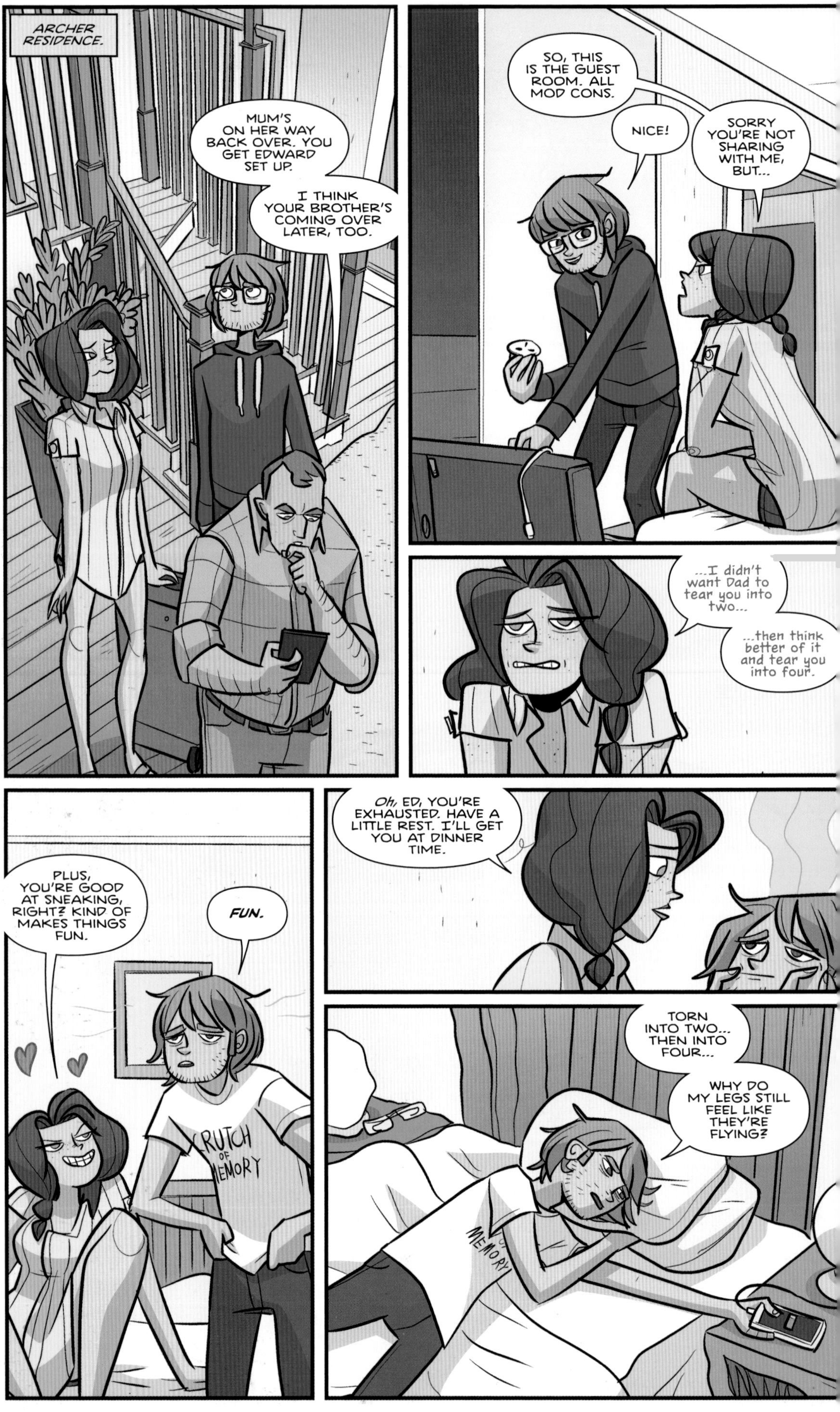
ARCHER RESIDENCE.
MUM'S ON HER WAY BACK OVER. YOU GET EDWARD SET UP.
I THINK YOUR BROTHER'S COMING OVER LATER, TOO.
SO, THIS IS THE GUEST ROOM. ALL MOD CONS.
NICE!
SORRY YOU'RE NOT SHARING WITH ME, BUT...
...I didn't want Dad to tear you into two...
...then think better of it and tear you into four.
PLUS, YOU'RE GOOD AT SNEAKING, RIGHT? KIND OF MAKES THINGS FUN.
FUN.
CRUTCH OF MEMORY
Oh, ED, YOU'RE EXHAUSTED. HAVE A LITTLE REST. I'LL GET YOU AT DINNER TIME.
TORN INTO TWO... THEN INTO FOUR...
WHY DO MY LEGS STILL FEEL LIKE THEY'RE FLYING?
MEMORY

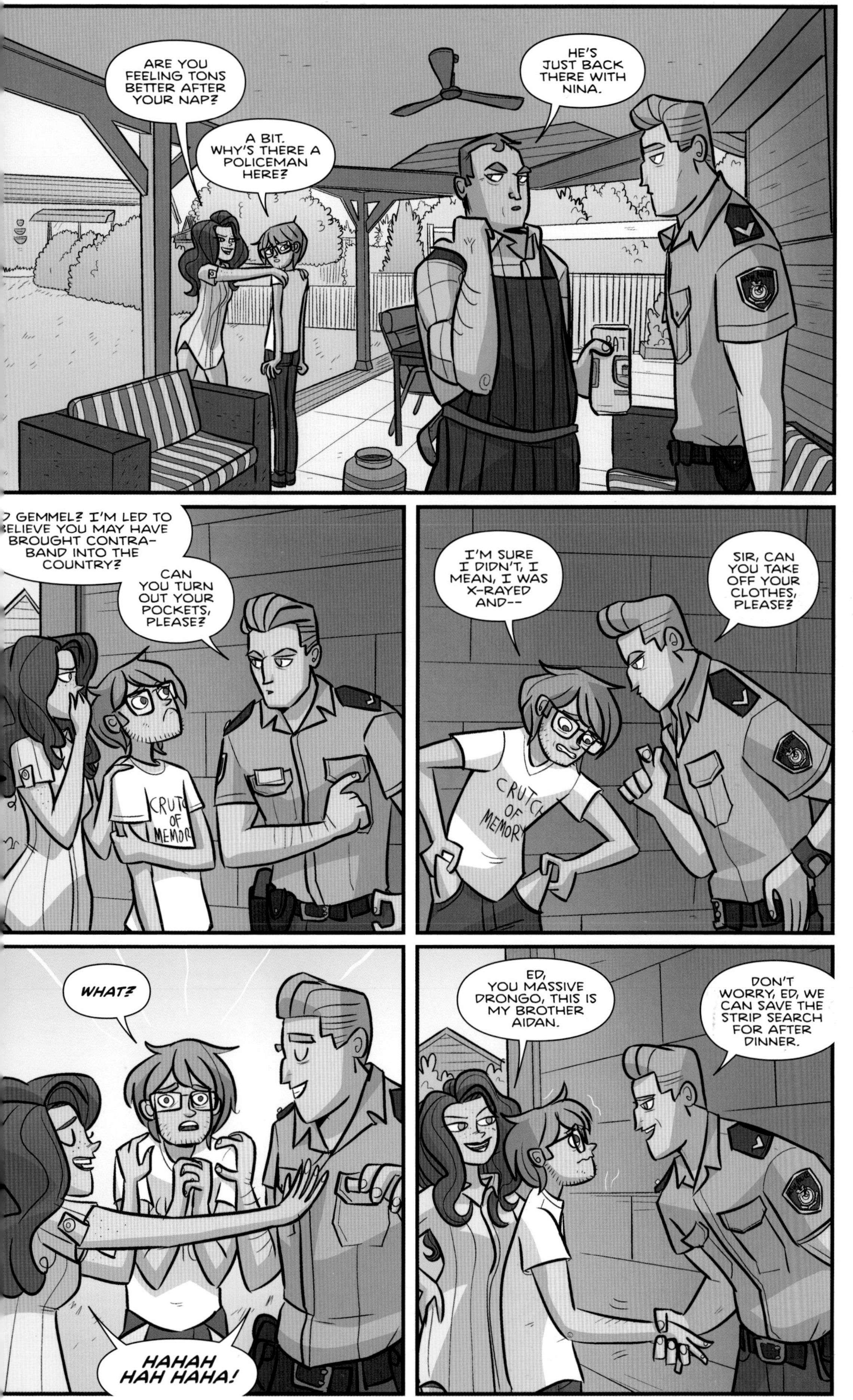
ARE YOU FEELING TONS BETTER AFTER YOUR NAP?
A BIT. WHY'S THERE A POLICEMAN HERE?
HE'S JUST BACK THERE WITH NINA.
GEMMEL? I'M LED TO BELIEVE YOU MAY HAVE BROUGHT CONTRA-BAND INTO THE COUNTRY?
CAN YOU TURN OUT YOUR POCKETS, PLEASE?
I'M SURE I DIDN'T, I MEAN, I WAS X-RAYED AND--
SIR, CAN YOU TAKE OFF YOUR CLOTHES, PLEASE?
WHAT?
HAHAH HAH HAHA!
ED, YOU MASSIVE DRONGO, THIS IS MY BROTHER AIDAN.
DON'T WORRY, ED, WE CAN SAVE THE STRIP SEARCH FOR AFTER DINNER.

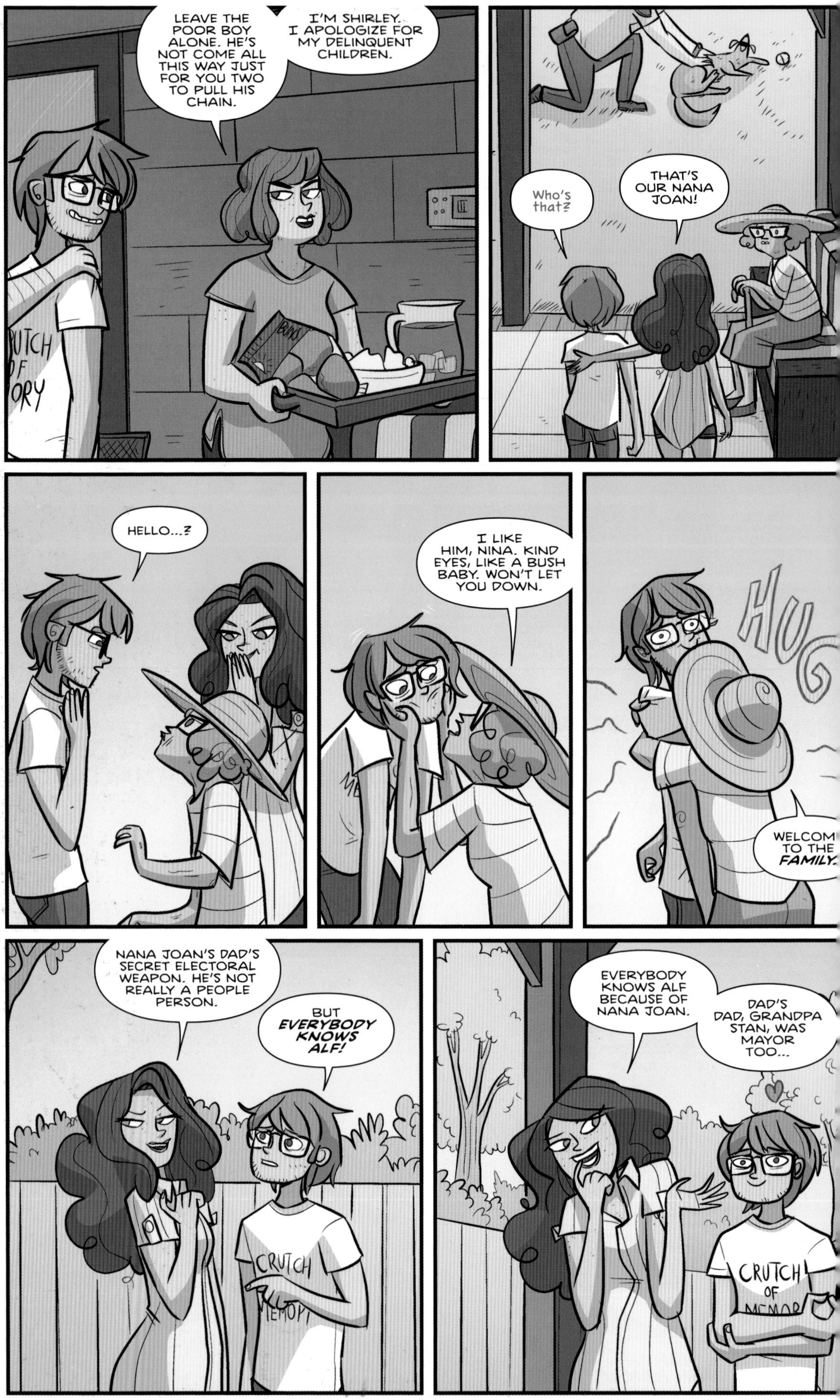
LEAVE THE POOR BOY ALONE. HE'S NOT COME ALL THIS WAY JUST FOR YOU TWO TO PULL HIS CHAIN.
I'M SHIRLEY. I APOLOGIZE FOR MY DELINQUENT CHILDREN.
BUNS
Who's that?
THAT'S OUR NANA JOAN!
HELLO...?
I LIKE HIM, NINA. KIND EYES, LIKE A BUSH BABY. WON'T LET YOU DOWN.
HUG
WELCOM TO THE FAMILY.
NANA JOAN'S DAD'S SECRET ELECTORAL WEAPON. HE'S NOT REALLY A PEOPLE PERSON.
BUT EVERYBODY KNOWS ALF!
CRUTCH
EVERYBODY KNOWS ALF BECAUSE OF NANA JOAN.
DAD'S DAD, GRANDPA STAN, WAS MAYOR TOO...
CRUTCH OF

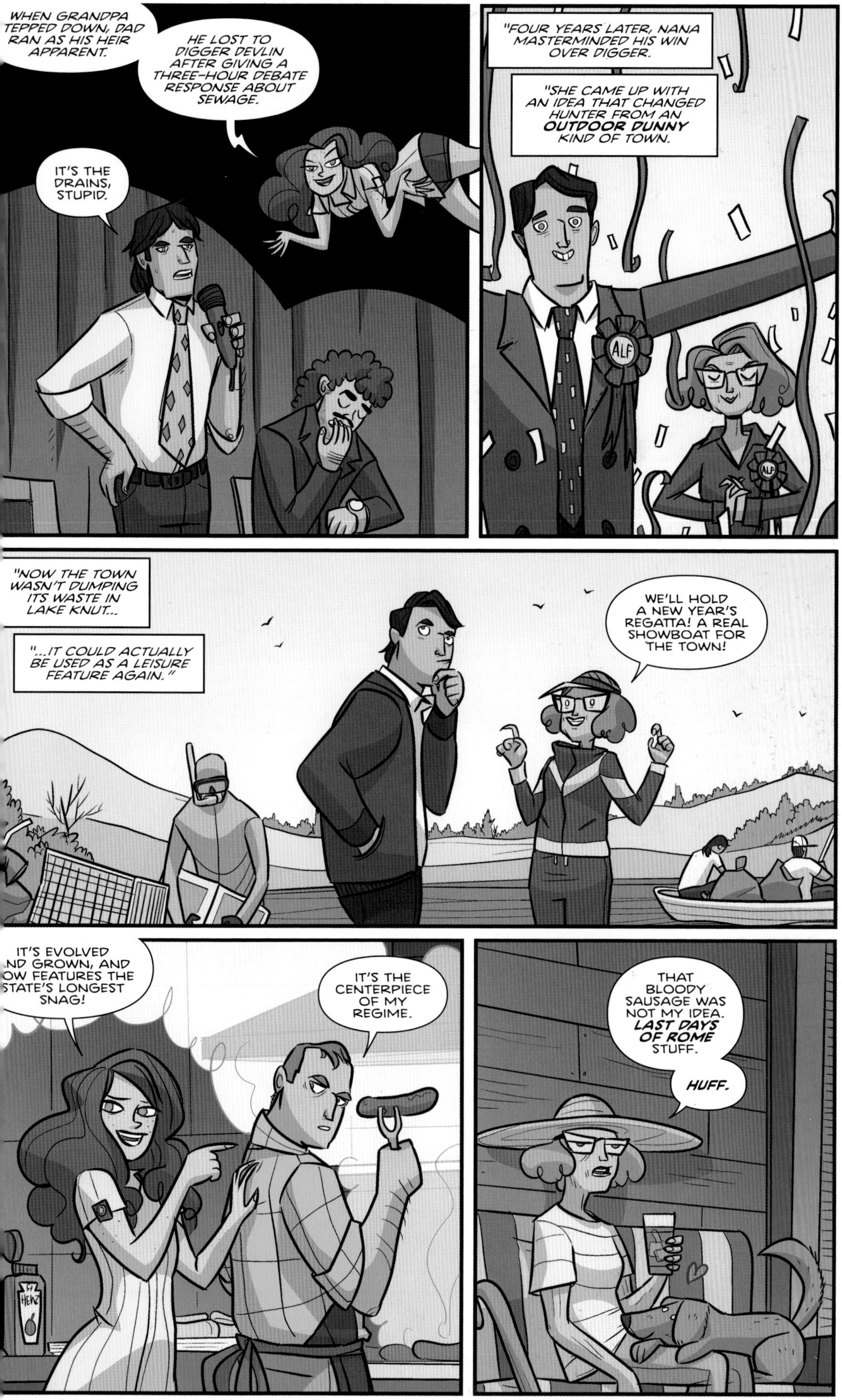
WHEN GRANDPA TEPPED DOWN, DAD RAN AS HIS HEIR APPARENT.
HE LOST TO DIGGER DEVLIN AFTER GIVING A THREE-HOUR DEBATE RESPONSE ABOUT SEWAGE.
IT'S THE DRAINS, STUPID.
"FOUR YEARS LATER, NANA MASTERMINDED HIS WIN OVER DIGGER.
"SHE CAME UP WITH AN IDEA THAT CHANGED HUNTER FROM AN OUTDOOR DUNNY KIND OF TOWN.
ALF
ALF
"NOW THE TOWN WASN'T DUMPING ITS WASTE IN LAKE KNUT...
"...IT COULD ACTUALLY BE USED AS A LEISURE FEATURE AGAIN."
WE'LL HOLD A NEW YEAR'S REGATTA! A REAL SHOWBOAT FOR THE TOWN!
IT'S EVOLVED ND GROWN, AND OW FEATURES THE STATE'S LONGEST SNAG!
IT'S THE CENTERPIECE OF MY REGIME.
HEINZ
THAT BLOODY SAUSAGE WAS NOT MY IDEA. LAST DAYS OF ROME STUFF.
HUFF.

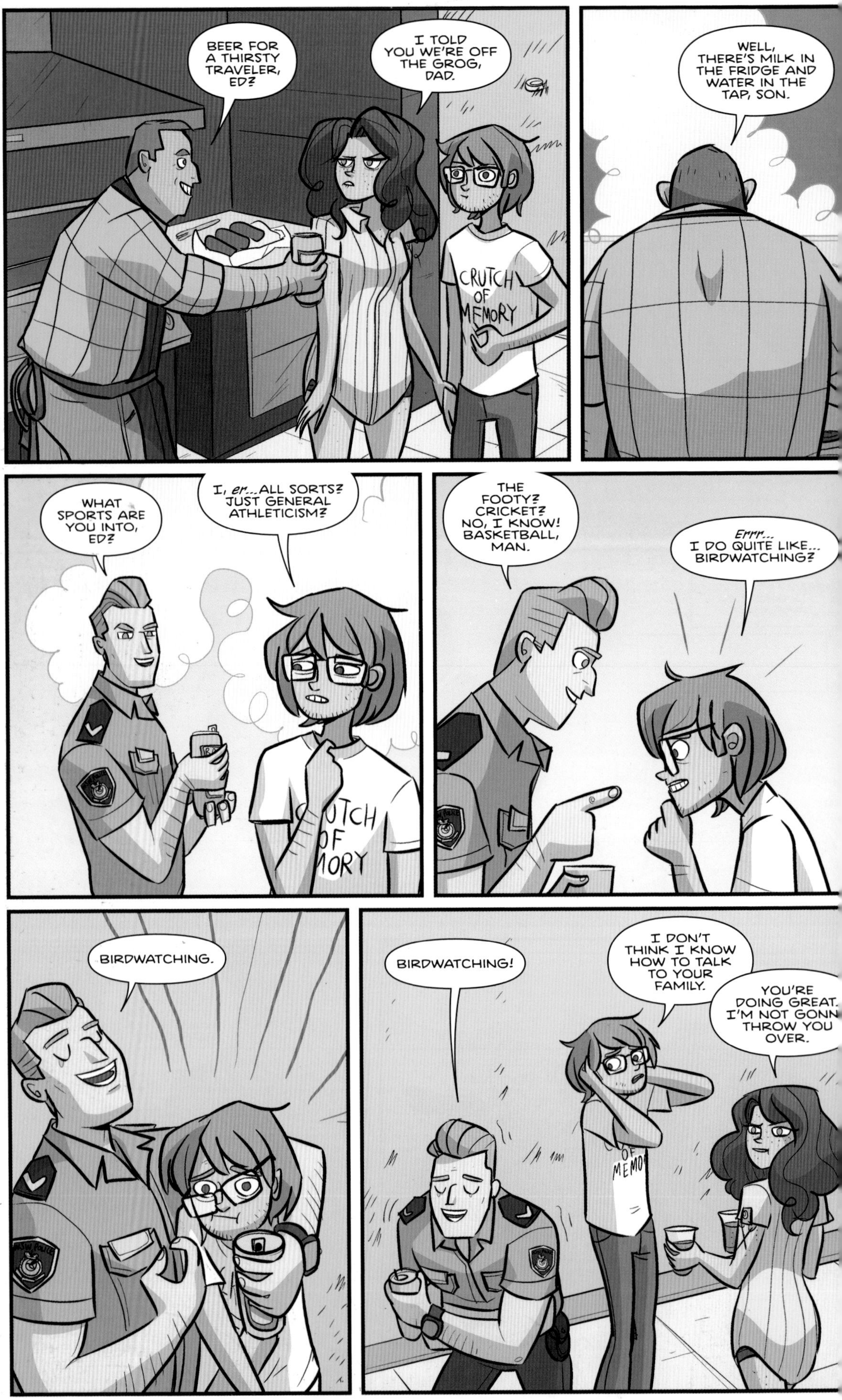
BEER FOR A THIRSTY TRAVELER, ED?
I TOLD YOU WE'RE OFF THE GROG, DAD.
CRUTCH OF MEMORY
WELL, THERE'S MILK IN THE FRIDGE AND WATER IN THE TAP, SON.
WHAT SPORTS ARE YOU INTO, ED?
I, *er*... ALL SORTS? JUST GENERAL ATHLETICISM?
THE FOOTY? CRICKET? NO, I KNOW! BASKETBALL, MAN.
Errr... I DO QUITE LIKE... BIRDWATCHING?
BIRDWATCHING.
BIRDWATCHING!
I DON'T THINK I KNOW HOW TO TALK TO YOUR FAMILY.
YOU'RE DOING GREAT. I'M NOT GONN THROW YOU OVER.

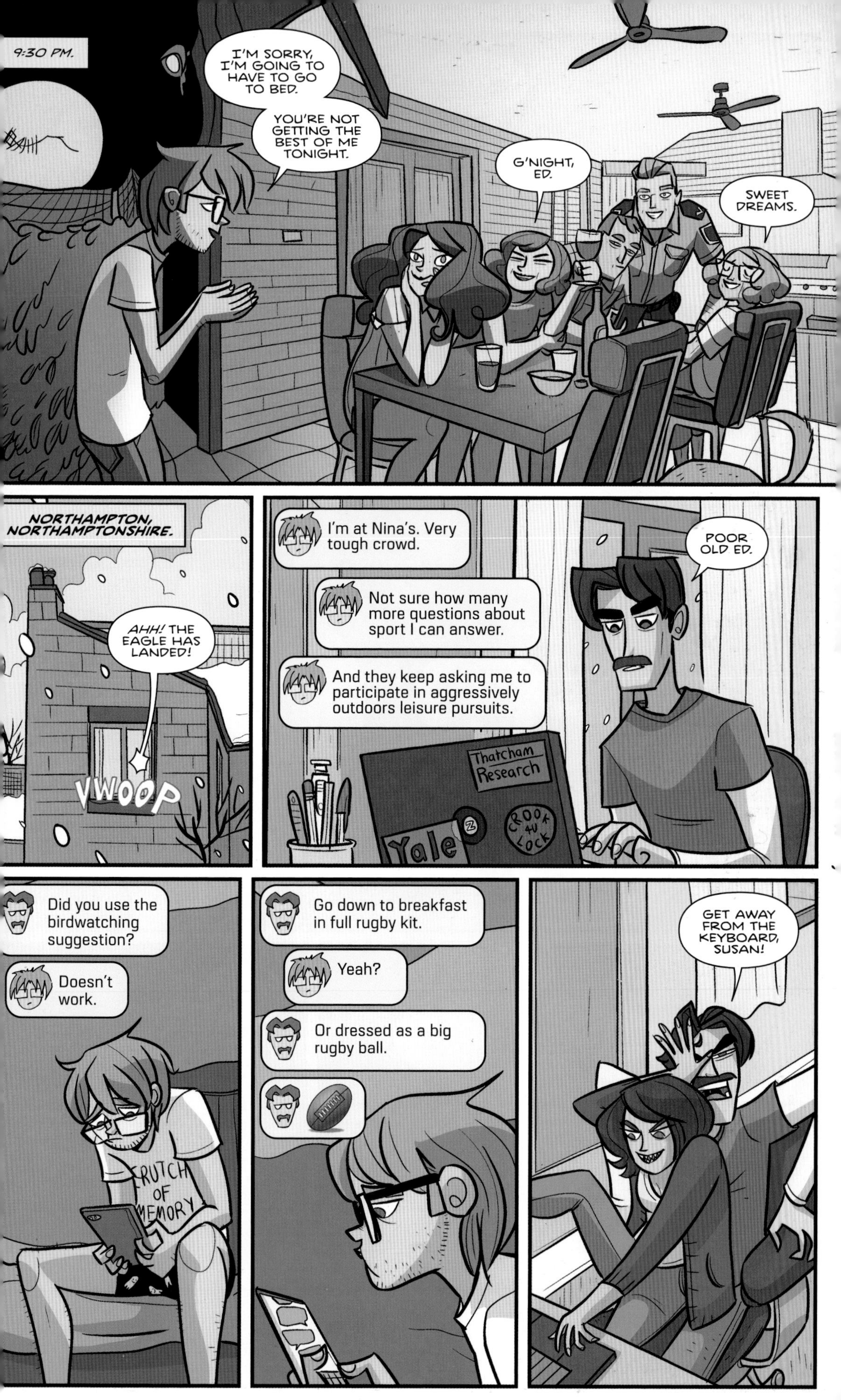
9:30 PM.
I'M SORRY, I'M GOING TO HAVE TO GO TO BED.
YOU'RE NOT GETTING THE BEST OF ME TONIGHT.
G'NIGHT, ED.
SWEET DREAMS.
NORTHAMPTON, NORTHAMPTONSHIRE.
AHH! THE EAGLE HAS LANDED!
VWOOP
I'm at Nina's. Very tough crowd.
Not sure how many more questions about sport I can answer.
And they keep asking me to participate in aggressively outdoors leisure pursuits.
POOR OLD ED.
Thatcham Research
CROOK 4U LOCK
Yale
Did you use the birdwatching suggestion?
Doesn't work.
CRUTCH OF MEMORY
Go down to breakfast in full rugby kit.
Yeah?
Or dressed as a big rugby ball.
GET AWAY FROM THE KEYBOARD, SUSAN!

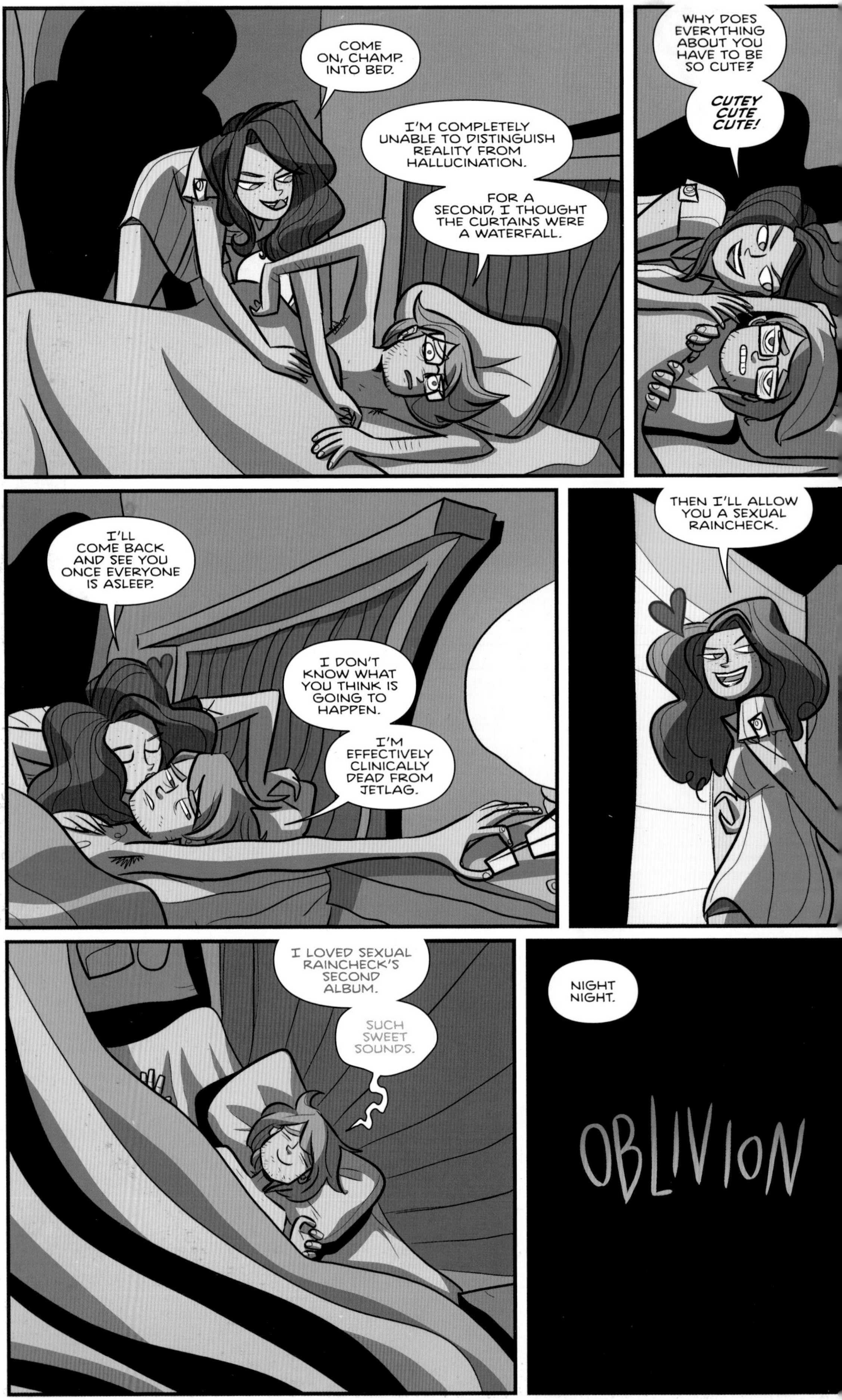
COME ON, CHAMP. INTO BED.
I'M COMPLETELY UNABLE TO DISTINGUISH REALITY FROM HALLUCINATION.
FOR A SECOND, I THOUGHT THE CURTAINS WERE A WATERFALL.
WHY DOES EVERYTHING ABOUT YOU HAVE TO BE SO CUTE?
CUTEY CUTE CUTE!
I'LL COME BACK AND SEE YOU ONCE EVERYONE IS ASLEEP.
I DON'T KNOW WHAT YOU THINK IS GOING TO HAPPEN.
I'M EFFECTIVELY CLINICALLY DEAD FROM JETLAG.
THEN I'LL ALLOW YOU A SEXUAL RAINCHECK.
I LOVED SEXUAL RAINCHECK'S SECOND ALBUM.
SUCH SWEET SOUNDS.
NIGHT NIGHT.
OBLIVION

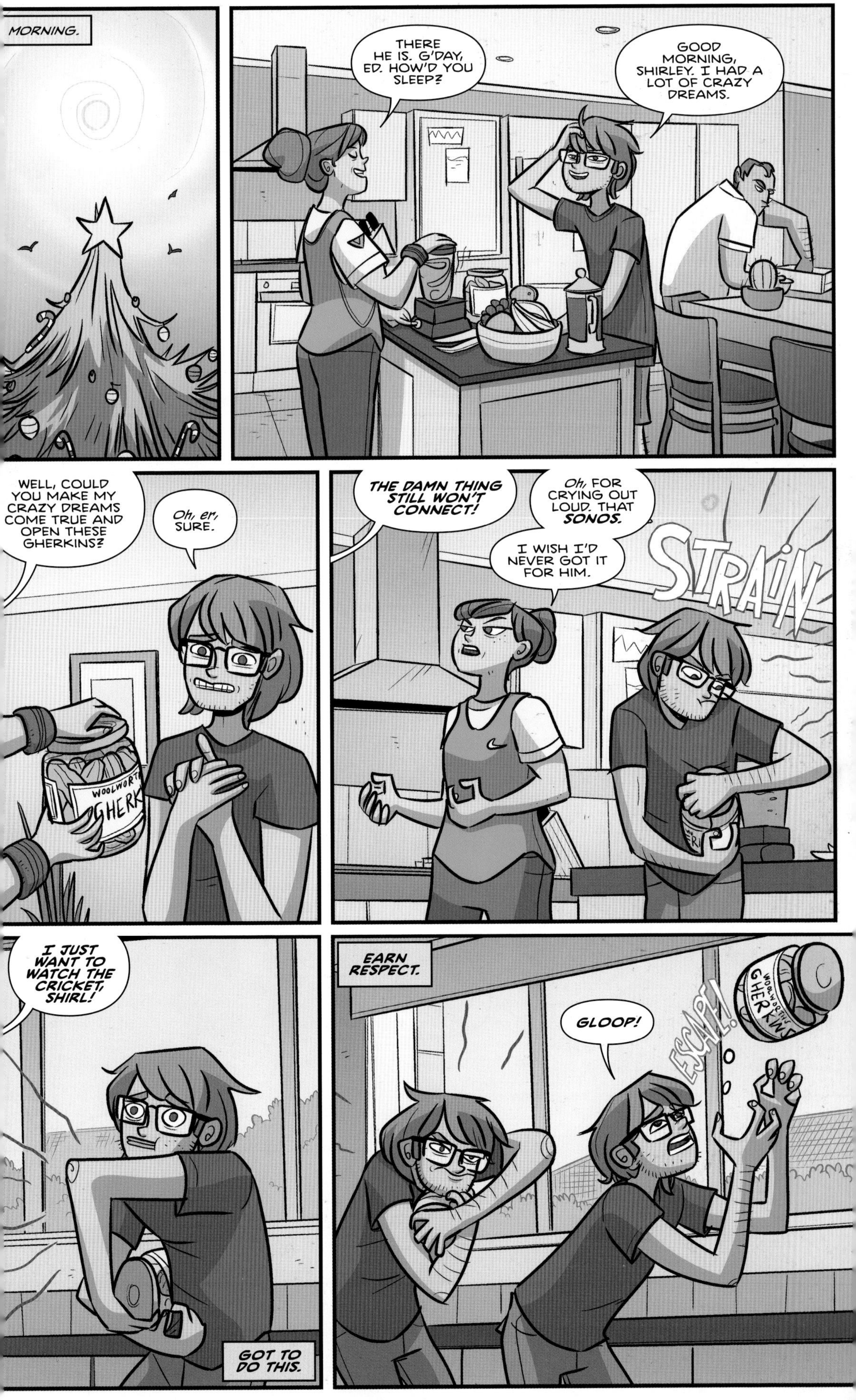
MORNING.
THERE HE IS. G'DAY, ED. HOW'D YOU SLEEP?
GOOD MORNING, SHIRLEY. I HAD A LOT OF CRAZY DREAMS.
WELL, COULD YOU MAKE MY CRAZY DREAMS COME TRUE AND OPEN THESE GHERKINS?
Oh, er, SURE.
WOOLWORTHS GHERK
THE DAMN THING STILL WON'T CONNECT!
Oh, FOR CRYING OUT LOUD. THAT SONOS.
I WISH I'D NEVER GOT IT FOR HIM.
STRAIN
I JUST WANT TO WATCH THE CRICKET, SHIRL!
GOT TO DO THIS.
EARN RESPECT.
GLOOP!
ESCAPE!
WOOLWORTHS GHERKINS

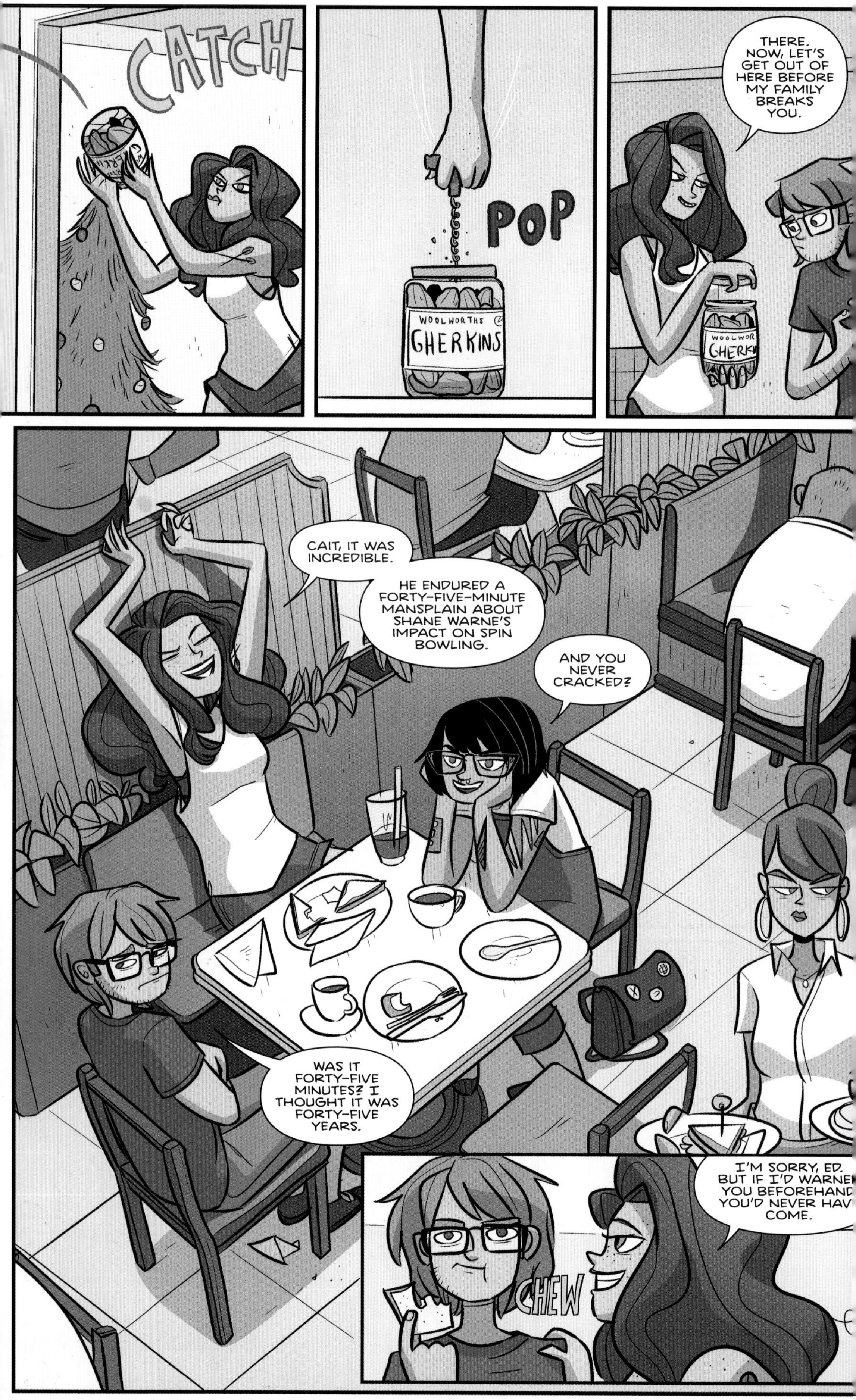
CATCH
POP
WOOLWORTHS
GHERKINS
THERE. NOW, LET'S GET OUT OF HERE BEFORE MY FAMILY BREAKS YOU.
CAIT, IT WAS INCREDIBLE.
HE ENDURED A FORTY-FIVE-MINUTE MANSPLAIN ABOUT SHANE WARNE'S IMPACT ON SPIN BOWLING.
AND YOU NEVER CRACKED?
WAS IT FORTY-FIVE MINUTES? I THOUGHT IT WAS FORTY-FIVE YEARS.
I'M SORRY, ED. BUT IF I'D WARNE
YOU BEFOREHAND
YOU'D NEVER HAV
COME.
CHEW

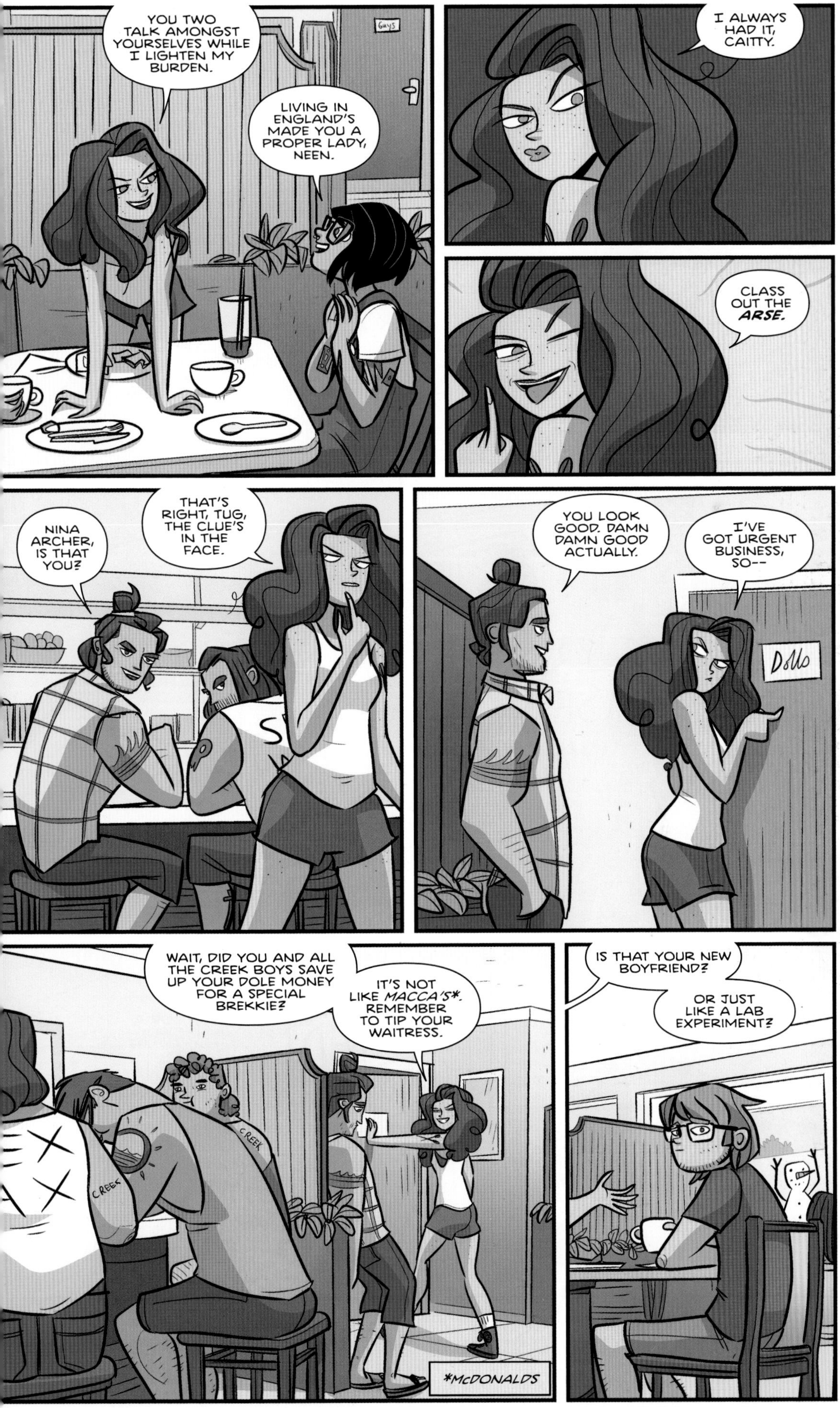

GUYS
YOU TWO TALK AMONGST YOURSELVES WHILE I LIGHTEN MY BURDEN.
LIVING IN ENGLAND'S MADE YOU A PROPER LADY, NEEN.
I ALWAYS HAD IT, CAITTY.
CLASS OUT THE *ARSE.*
NINA ARCHER, IS THAT YOU?
THAT'S RIGHT, TUG, THE CLUE'S IN THE FACE.
YOU LOOK GOOD. DAMN DAMN GOOD ACTUALLY.
I'VE GOT URGENT BUSINESS, SO--
Dolls
WAIT, DID YOU AND ALL THE CREEK BOYS SAVE UP YOUR DOLE MONEY FOR A SPECIAL BREKKIE?
IT'S NOT LIKE *MACCA'S**. REMEMBER TO TIP YOUR WAITRESS.
CREEK
CREEK
*McDONALDS
IS THAT YOUR NEW BOYFRIEND?
OR JUST LIKE A LAB EXPERIMENT?

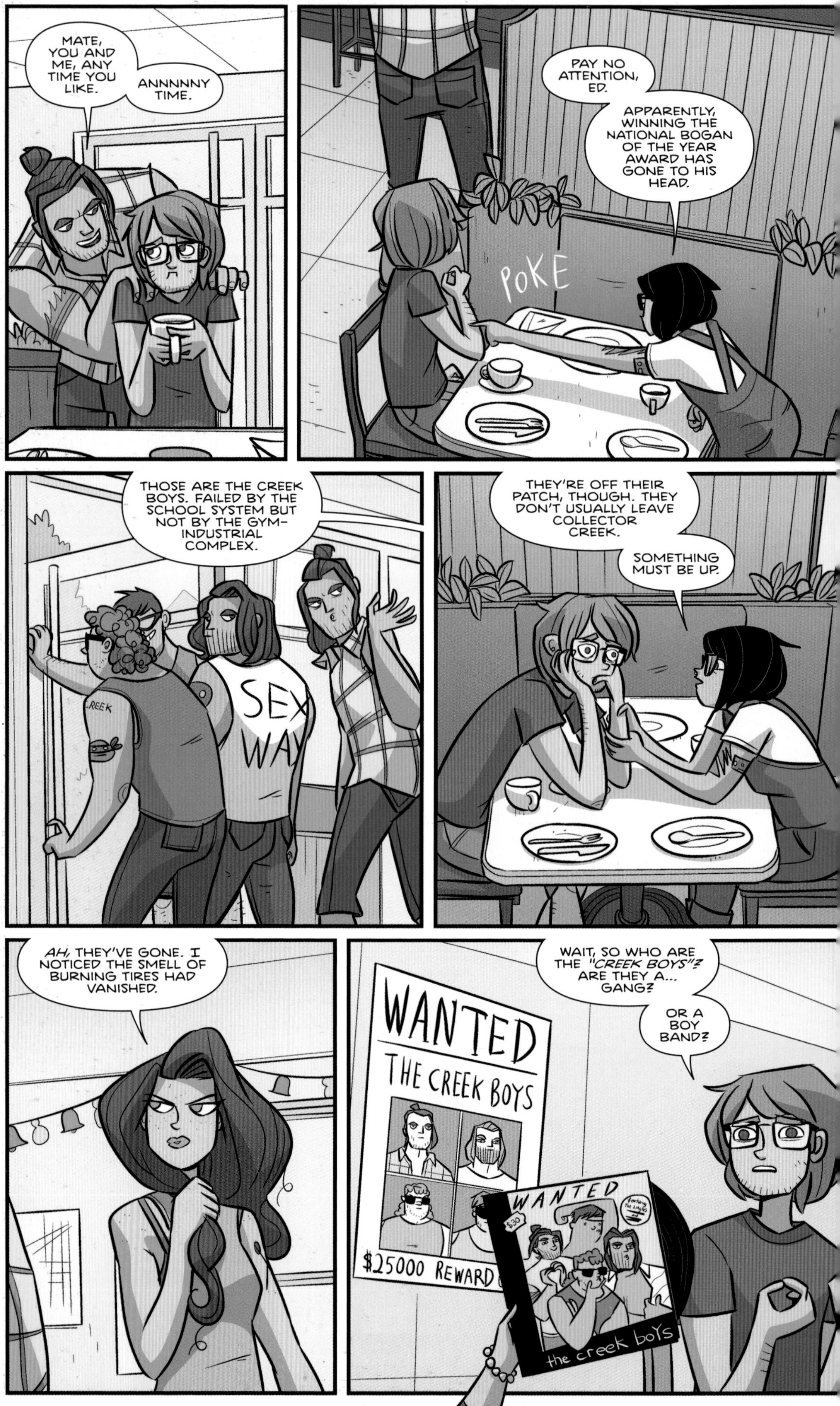

MATE, YOU AND ME, ANY TIME YOU LIKE.
ANNNNNY TIME.
PAY NO ATTENTION, ED.
APPARENTLY, WINNING THE NATIONAL BOGAN OF THE YEAR AWARD HAS GONE TO HIS HEAD.
POKE
THOSE ARE THE CREEK BOYS. FAILED BY THE SCHOOL SYSTEM BUT NOT BY THE GYM-INDUSTRIAL COMPLEX.
CREEK
SEX WA
THEY'RE OFF THEIR PATCH, THOUGH. THEY DON'T USUALLY LEAVE COLLECTOR CREEK.
SOMETHING MUST BE UP.
AH, THEY'VE GONE. I NOTICED THE SMELL OF BURNING TIRES HAD VANISHED.
WAIT, SO WHO ARE THE *"CREEK BOYS"*? ARE THEY A... GANG?
OR A BOY BAND?
WANTED
THE CREEK BOYS
$25000 REWARD
WANTED
$20
the creek boys

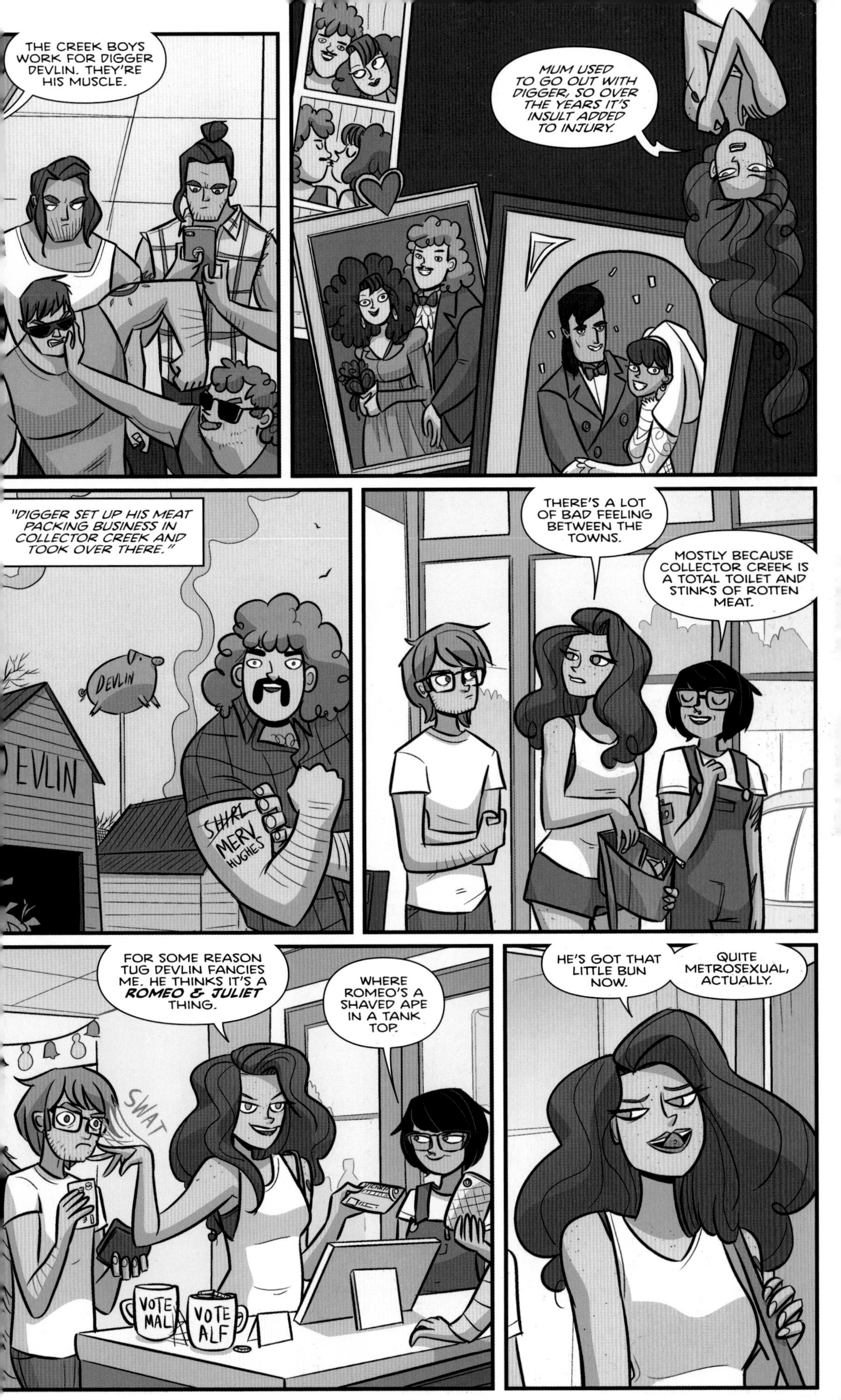
THE CREEK BOYS WORK FOR DIGGER DEVLIN. THEY'RE HIS MUSCLE.
MUM USED TO GO OUT WITH DIGGER, SO OVER THE YEARS IT'S INSULT ADDED TO INJURY.
"DIGGER SET UP HIS MEAT PACKING BUSINESS IN COLLECTOR CREEK AND TOOK OVER THERE."
DEVLIN
DEVLIN
SHIRL
MERV HUGHES
THERE'S A LOT OF BAD FEELING BETWEEN THE TOWNS.
MOSTLY BECAUSE COLLECTOR CREEK IS A TOTAL TOILET AND STINKS OF ROTTEN MEAT.
FOR SOME REASON TUG DEVLIN FANCIES ME. HE THINKS IT'S A **ROMEO & JULIET** THING.
WHERE ROMEO'S A SHAVED APE IN A TANK TOP.
SWAT
VOTE MAL
VOTE ALF
HE'S GOT THAT LITTLE BUN NOW.
QUITE METROSEXUAL, ACTUALLY.

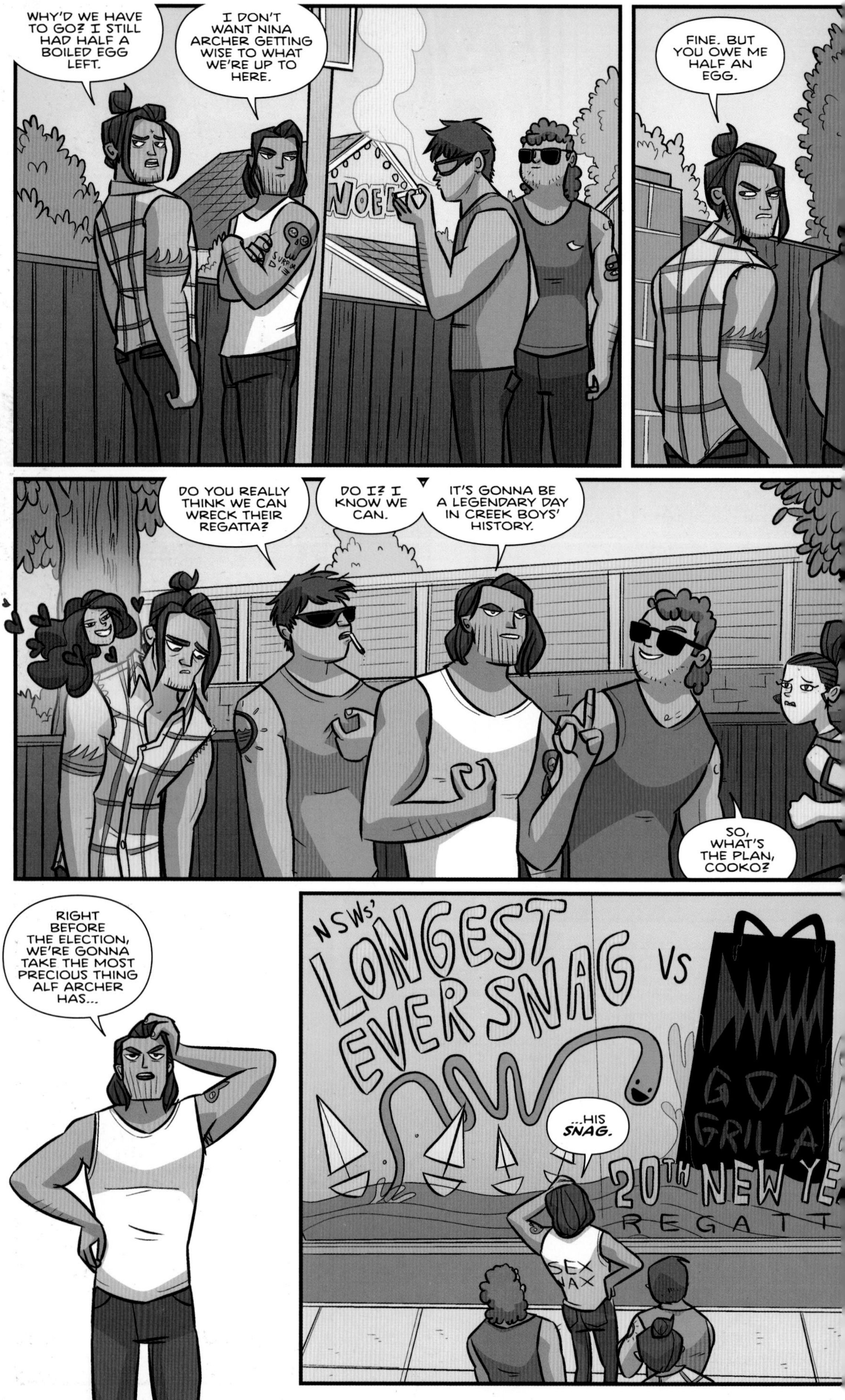
WHY'D WE HAVE TO GO? I STILL HAD HALF A BOILED EGG LEFT.
I DON'T WANT NINA ARCHER GETTING WISE TO WHAT WE'RE UP TO HERE.
NOEL
FINE. BUT YOU OWE ME HALF AN EGG.
DO YOU REALLY THINK WE CAN WRECK THEIR REGATTA?
DO I? I KNOW WE CAN.
IT'S GONNA BE A LEGENDARY DAY IN CREEK BOYS' HISTORY.
SO, WHAT'S THE PLAN, COOKO?
RIGHT BEFORE THE ELECTION, WE'RE GONNA TAKE THE MOST PRECIOUS THING ALF ARCHER HAS...
NSWS' LONGEST EVER SNAG VS
GOD GRILLA
20TH NEW YE
REGATT
...HIS ***SNAG.***
SEX WAX

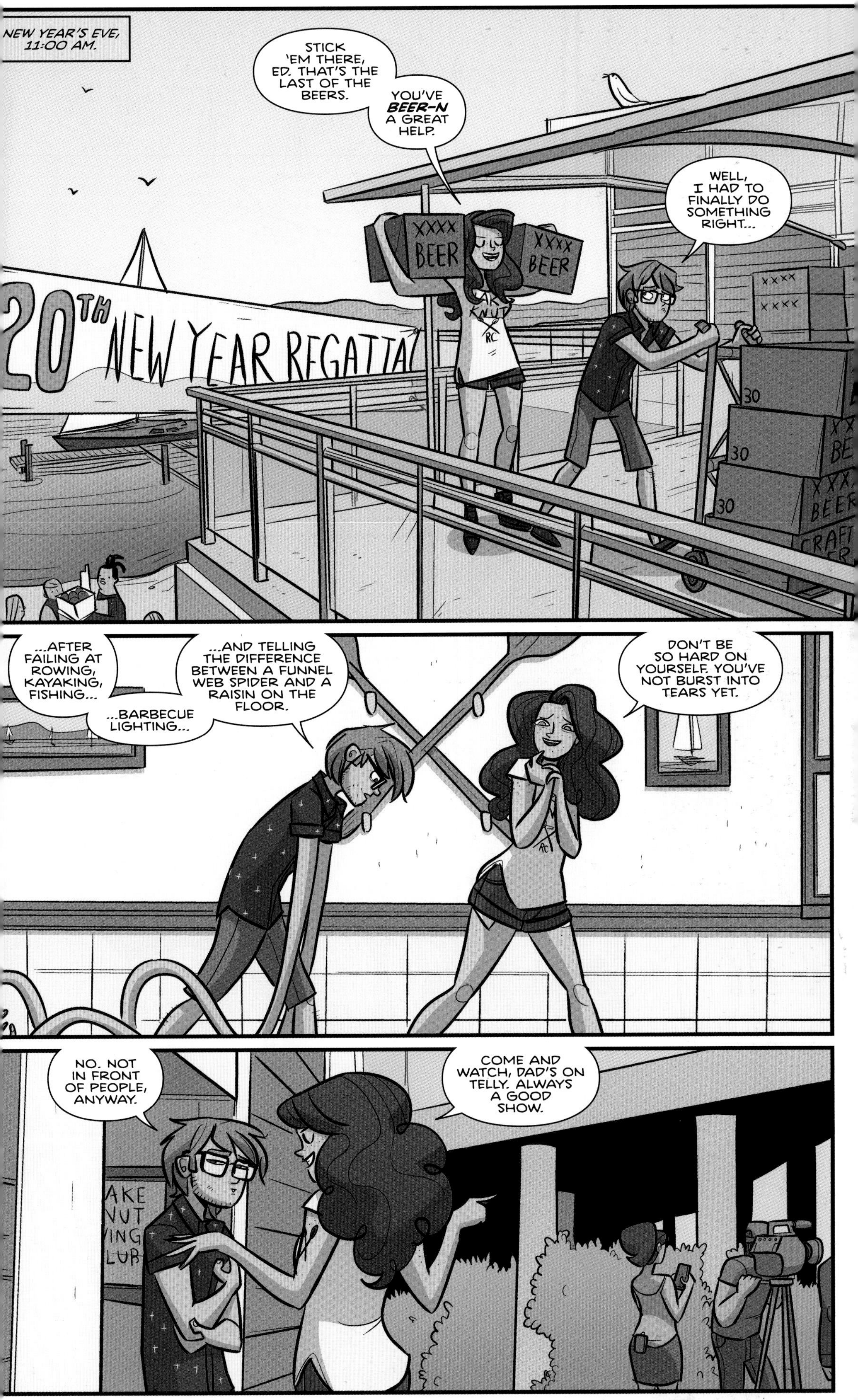
NEW YEAR'S EVE, 11:00 AM.
STICK 'EM THERE, ED. THAT'S THE LAST OF THE BEERS.
YOU'VE BEER-N A GREAT HELP.
WELL, I HAD TO FINALLY DO SOMETHING RIGHT...
XXXX BEER
XXXX BEER
20TH NEW YEAR REGATTA
...AFTER FAILING AT ROWING, KAYAKING, FISHING...
...BARBECUE LIGHTING...
...AND TELLING THE DIFFERENCE BETWEEN A FUNNEL WEB SPIDER AND A RAISIN ON THE FLOOR.
DON'T BE SO HARD ON YOURSELF. YOU'VE NOT BURST INTO TEARS YET.
NO. NOT IN FRONT OF PEOPLE, ANYWAY.
COME AND WATCH, DAD'S ON TELLY. ALWAYS A GOOD SHOW.

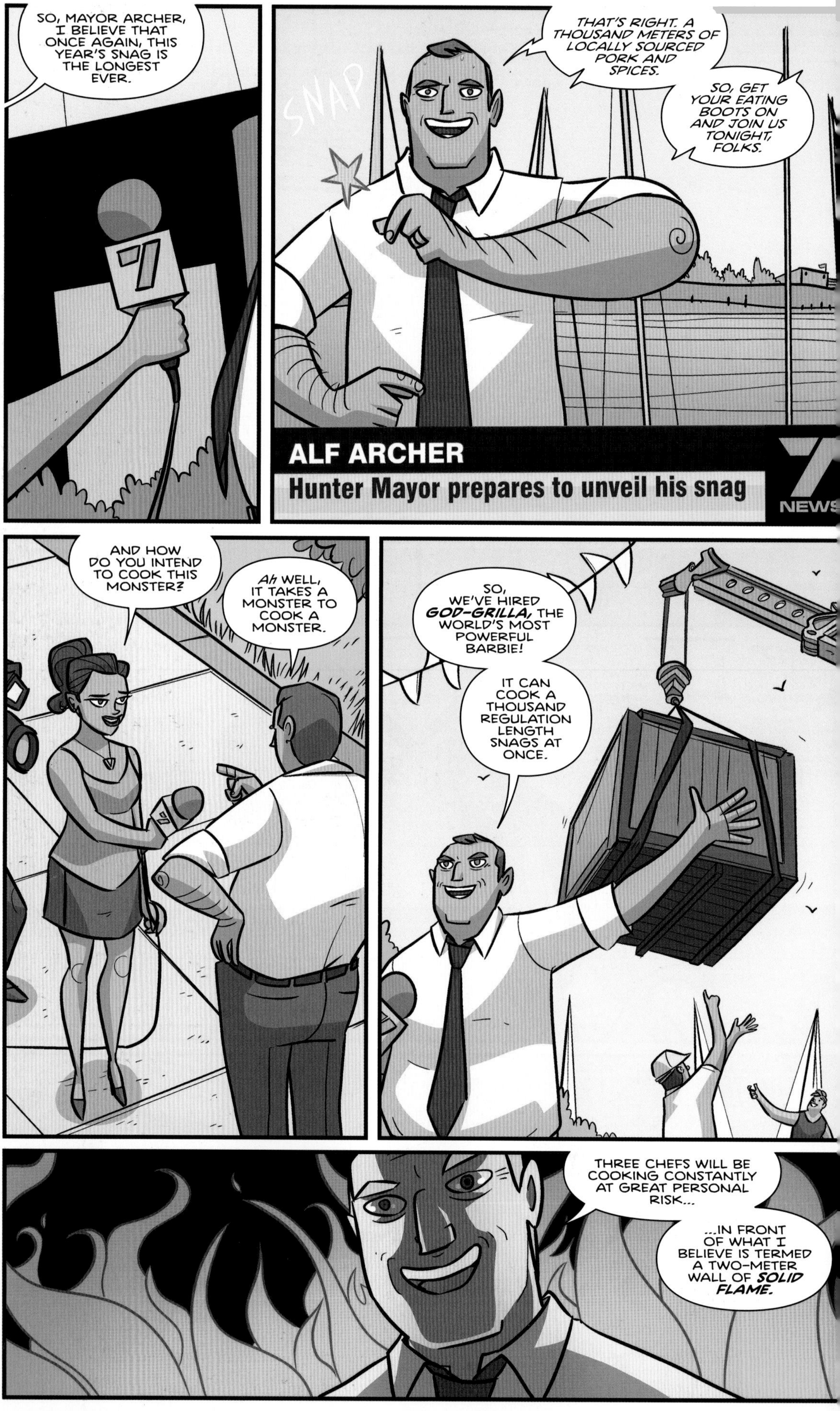
SO, MAYOR ARCHER, I BELIEVE THAT ONCE AGAIN, THIS YEAR'S SNAG IS THE LONGEST EVER.
THAT'S RIGHT. A THOUSAND METERS OF LOCALLY SOURCED PORK AND SPICES.
SO, GET YOUR EATING BOOTS ON AND JOIN US TONIGHT, FOLKS.
SNAP
ALF ARCHER
Hunter Mayor prepares to unveil his snag
7
NEWS
AND HOW DO YOU INTEND TO COOK THIS MONSTER?
Ah WELL, IT TAKES A MONSTER TO COOK A MONSTER.
SO, WE'VE HIRED GOD-GRILLA, THE WORLD'S MOST POWERFUL BARBIE!
IT CAN COOK A THOUSAND REGULATION LENGTH SNAGS AT ONCE.
THREE CHEFS WILL BE COOKING CONSTANTLY AT GREAT PERSONAL RISK...
...IN FRONT OF WHAT I BELIEVE IS TERMED A TWO-METER WALL OF SOLID FLAME.

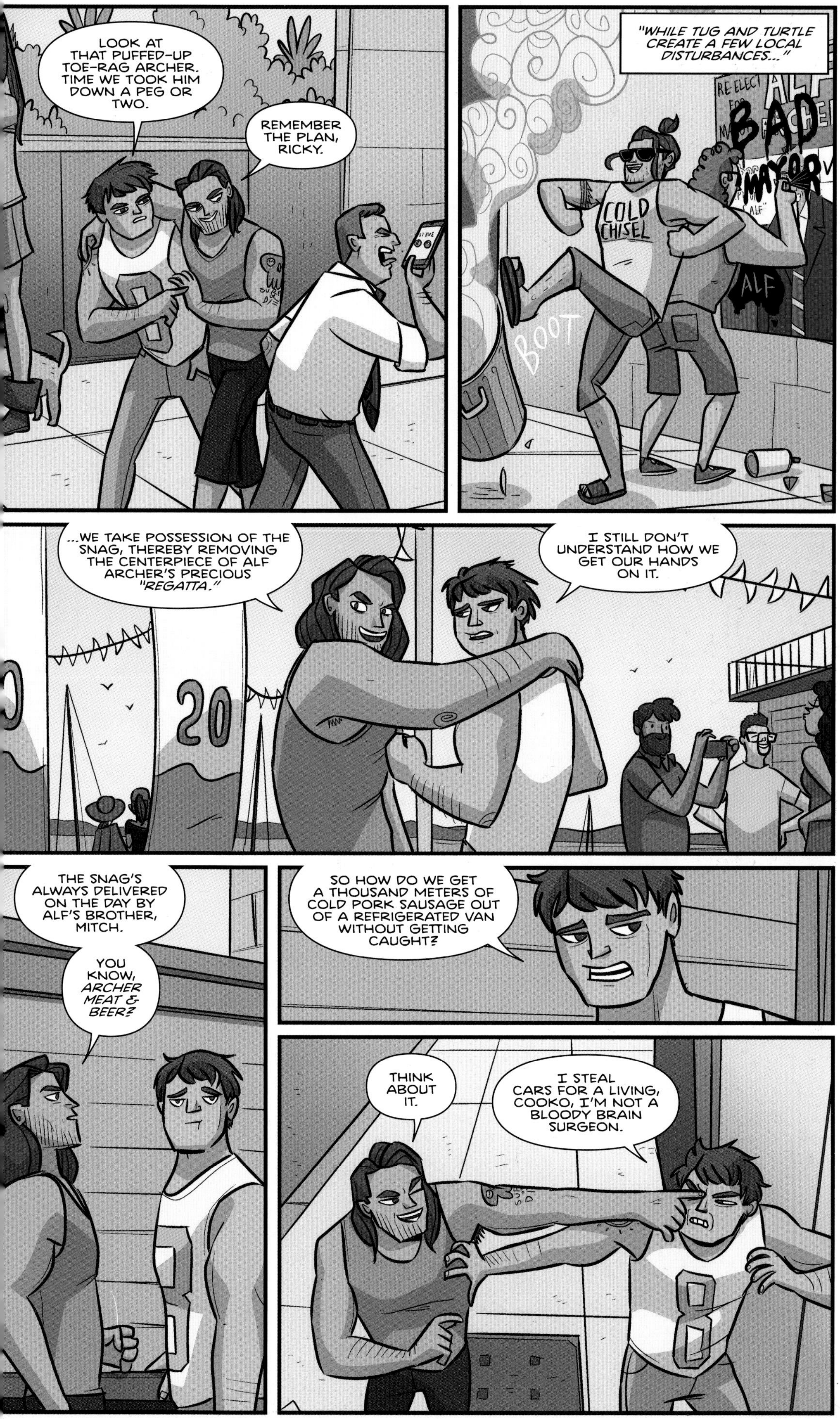
LOOK AT THAT PUFFED-UP TOE-RAG ARCHER. TIME WE TOOK HIM DOWN A PEG OR TWO.
REMEMBER THE PLAN, RICKY.
"WHILE TUG AND TURTLE CREATE A FEW LOCAL DISTURBANCES..."
BAD MAYOR
ALF
BOOT
COLD CHISEL
...WE TAKE POSSESSION OF THE SNAG, THEREBY REMOVING THE CENTERPIECE OF ALF ARCHER'S PRECIOUS "REGATTA."
I STILL DON'T UNDERSTAND HOW WE GET OUR HANDS ON IT.
20
THE SNAG'S ALWAYS DELIVERED ON THE DAY BY ALF'S BROTHER, MITCH.
YOU KNOW, ARCHER MEAT & BEER?
SO HOW DO WE GET A THOUSAND METERS OF COLD PORK SAUSAGE OUT OF A REFRIGERATED VAN WITHOUT GETTING CAUGHT?
THINK ABOUT IT.
I STEAL CARS FOR A LIVING, COOKO, I'M NOT A BLOODY BRAIN SURGEON.

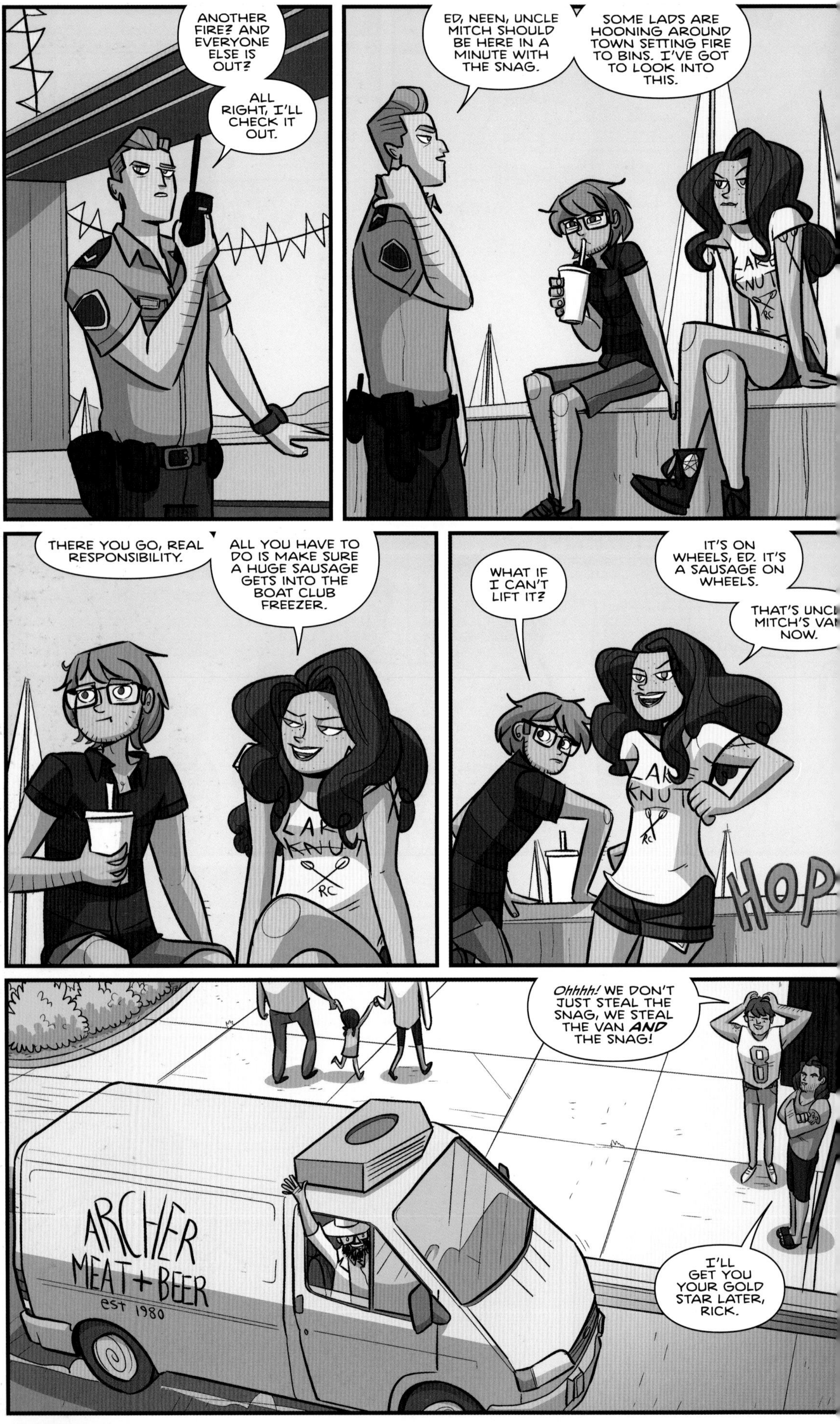
ANOTHER FIRE? AND EVERYONE ELSE IS OUT?
ALL RIGHT, I'LL CHECK IT OUT.
ED, NEEN, UNCLE MITCH SHOULD BE HERE IN A MINUTE WITH THE SNAG.
SOME LADS ARE HOONING AROUND TOWN SETTING FIRE TO BINS. I'VE GOT TO LOOK INTO THIS.
THERE YOU GO, REAL RESPONSIBILITY.
ALL YOU HAVE TO DO IS MAKE SURE A HUGE SAUSAGE GETS INTO THE BOAT CLUB FREEZER.
WHAT IF I CAN'T LIFT IT?
IT'S ON WHEELS, ED. IT'S A SAUSAGE ON WHEELS.
HOP
Ohhhh! WE DON'T JUST STEAL THE SNAG, WE STEAL THE VAN ***AND*** THE SNAG!
ARCHER MEAT + BEER est 1980
I'LL GET YOU YOUR GOLD STAR LATER, RICK.

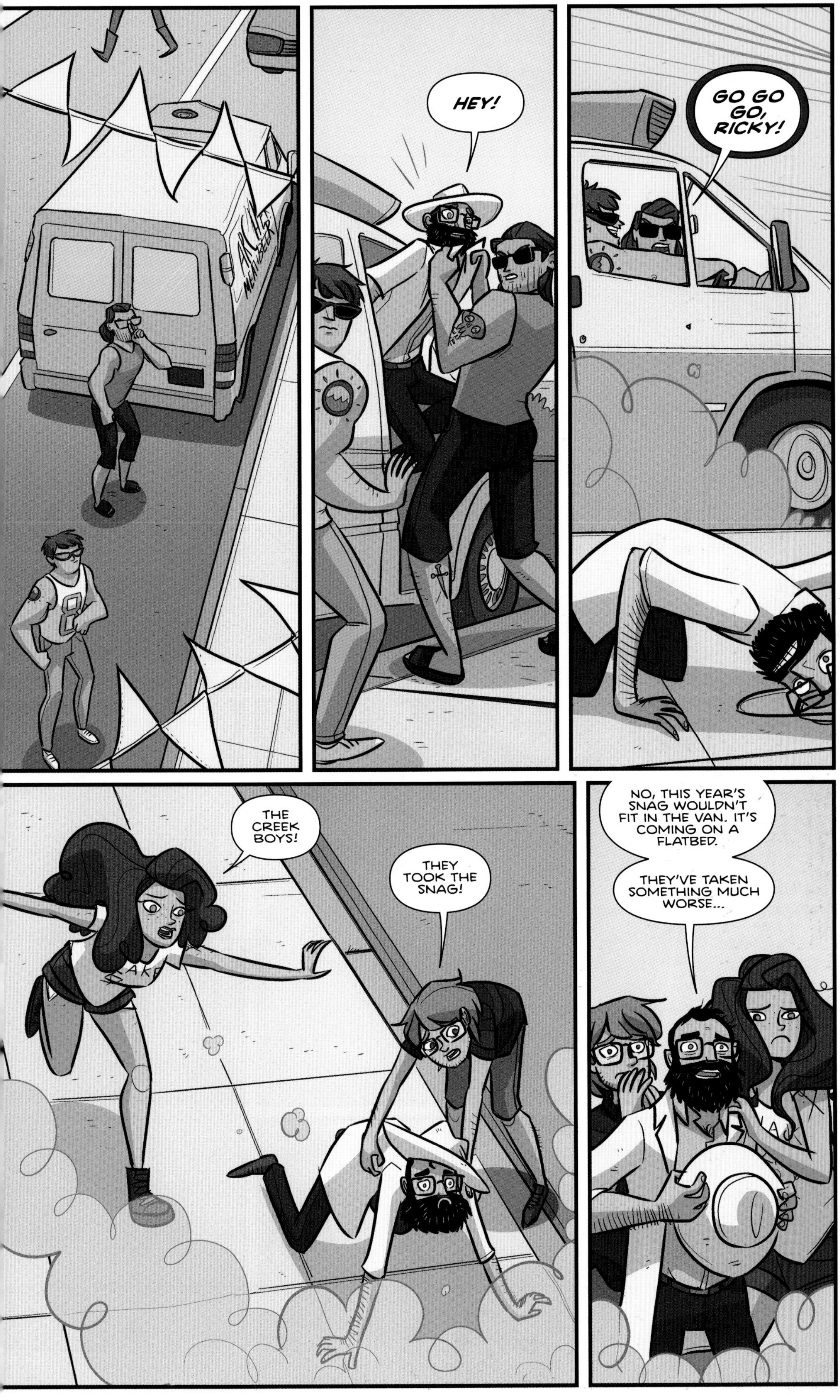
HEY!
GO GO GO, RICKY!
THE CREEK BOYS!
THEY TOOK THE SNAG!
NO, THIS YEAR'S SNAG WOULDN'T FIT IN THE VAN. IT'S COMING ON A FLATBED.
THEY'VE TAKEN SOMETHING MUCH WORSE...

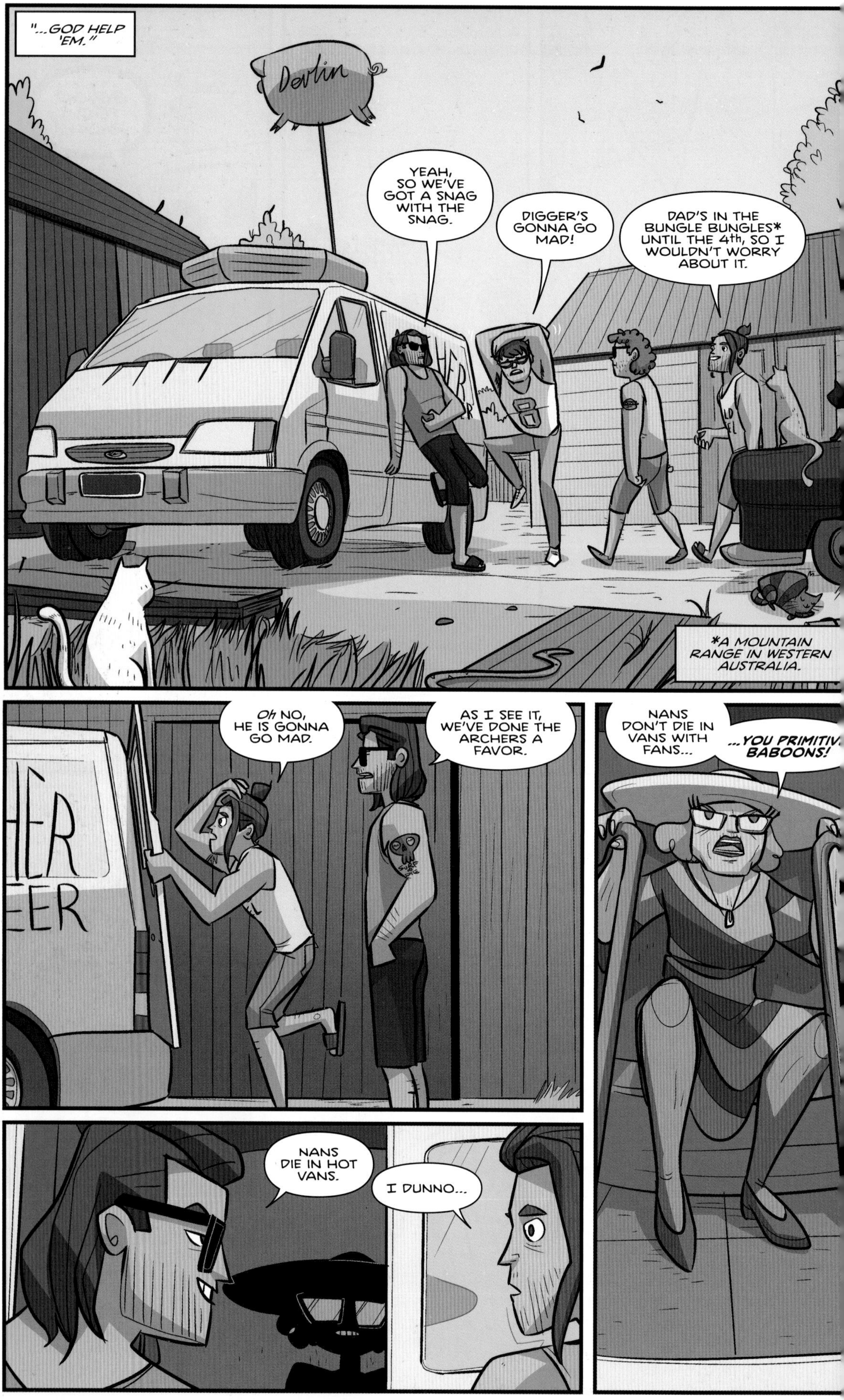
"...GOD HELP 'EM."
Devlin
YEAH, SO WE'VE GOT A SNAG WITH THE SNAG.
DIGGER'S GONNA GO MAD!
DAD'S IN THE BUNGLE BUNGLES* UNTIL THE 4th, SO I WOULDN'T WORRY ABOUT IT.
*A MOUNTAIN RANGE IN WESTERN AUSTRALIA.
Oh NO, HE IS GONNA GO MAD.
AS I SEE IT, WE'VE DONE THE ARCHERS A FAVOR.
NANS DIE IN HOT VANS.
I DUNNO...
NANS DON'T DIE IN VANS WITH FANS...
...YOU PRIMITIV BABOONS!

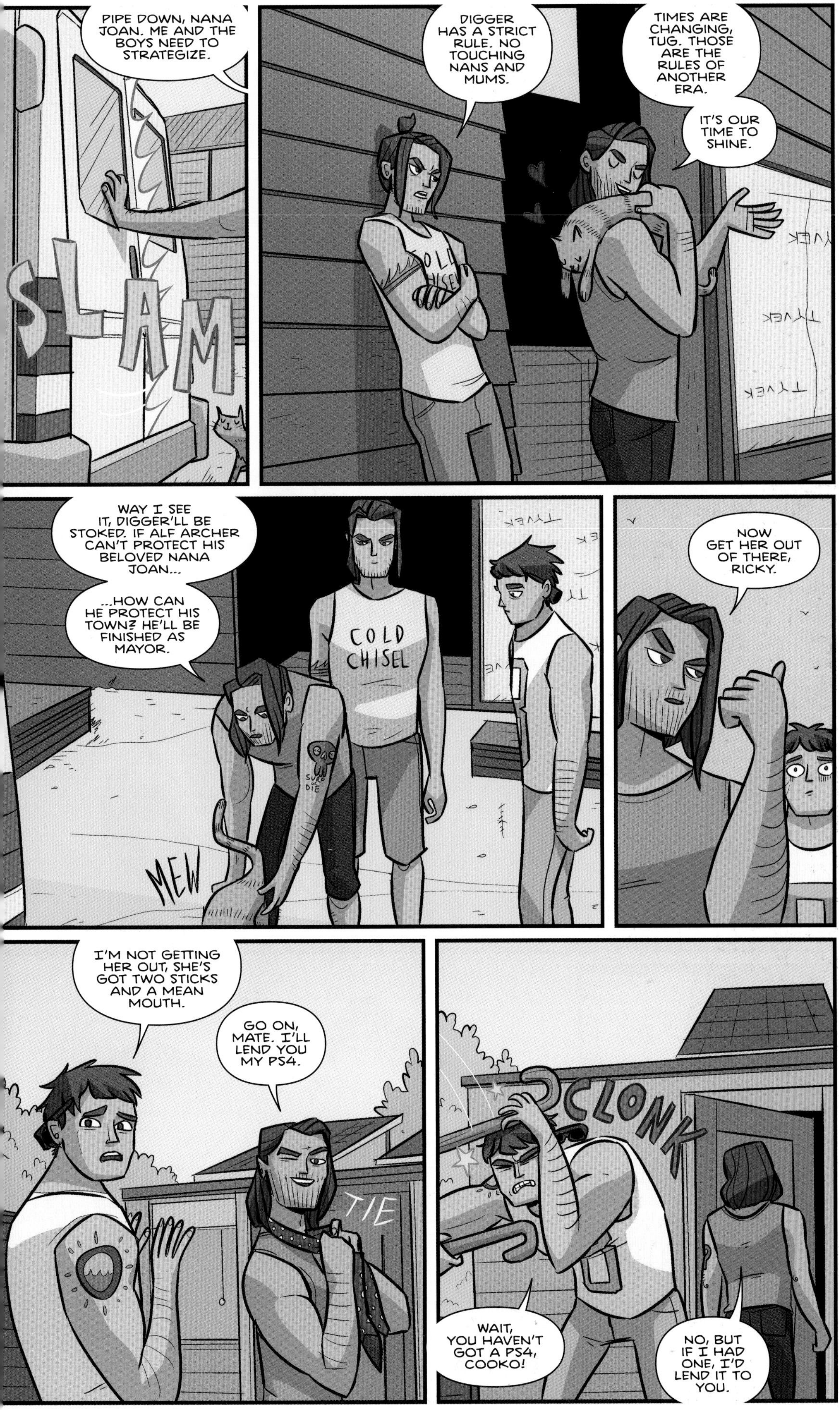
PIPE DOWN, NANA JOAN. ME AND THE BOYS NEED TO STRATEGIZE.
SLAM
DIGGER HAS A STRICT RULE. NO TOUCHING NANS AND MUMS.
TIMES ARE CHANGING, TUG. THOSE ARE THE RULES OF ANOTHER ERA.
IT'S OUR TIME TO SHINE.
COLD CHISEL
TYVEK
WAY I SEE IT, DIGGER'LL BE STOKED. IF ALF ARCHER CAN'T PROTECT HIS BELOVED NANA JOAN...
...HOW CAN HE PROTECT HIS TOWN? HE'LL BE FINISHED AS MAYOR.
COLD CHISEL
SURF OR DIE
MEW
NOW GET HER OUT OF THERE, RICKY.
I'M NOT GETTING HER OUT, SHE'S GOT TWO STICKS AND A MEAN MOUTH.
GO ON, MATE. I'LL LEND YOU MY PS4.
TIE
CLONK
WAIT, YOU HAVEN'T GOT A PS4, COOKO!
NO, BUT IF I HAD ONE, I'D LEND IT TO YOU.

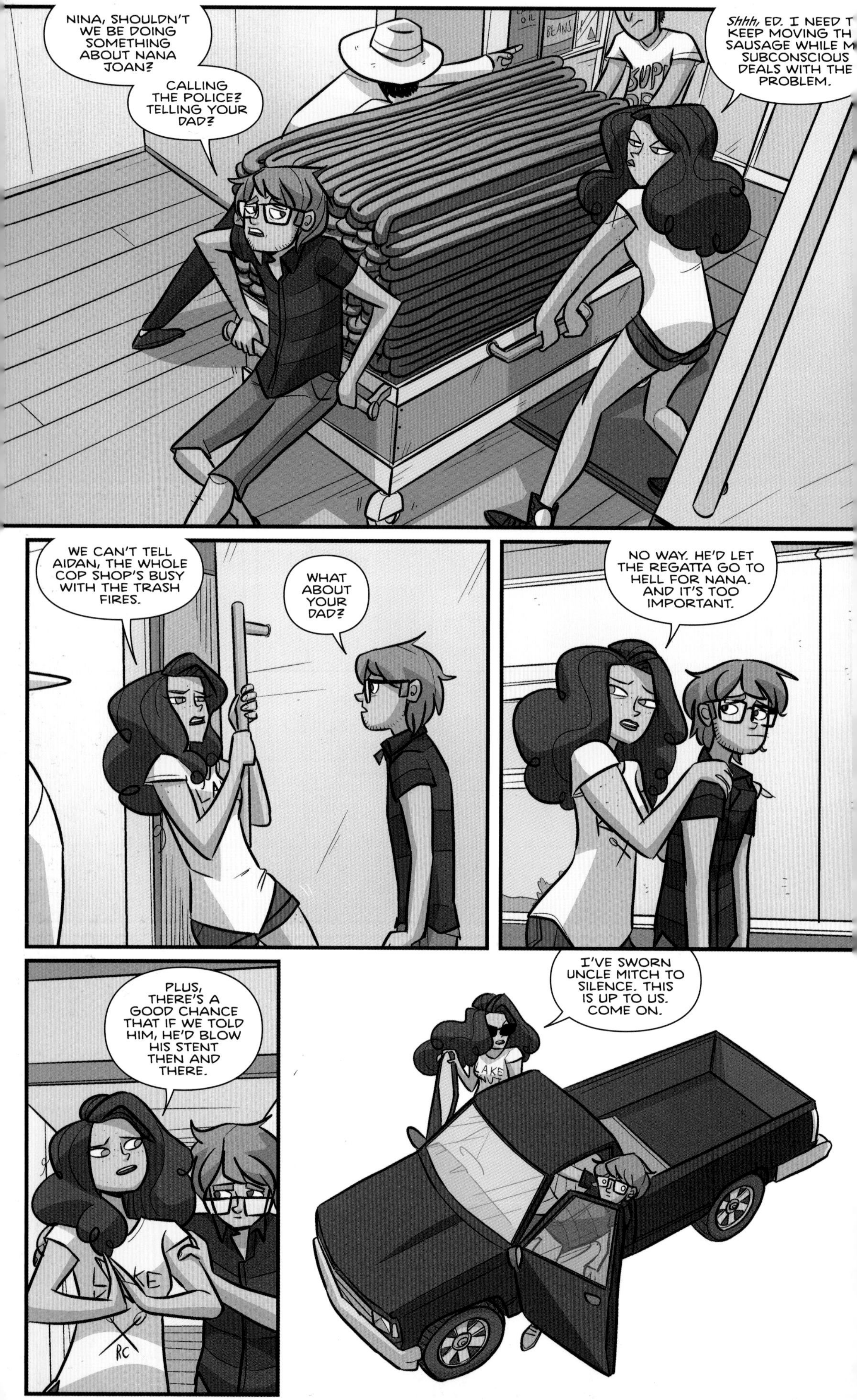

NINA, SHOULDN'T WE BE DOING SOMETHING ABOUT NANA JOAN?
CALLING THE POLICE? TELLING YOUR DAD?
Shhh, ED. I NEED T KEEP MOVING TH SAUSAGE WHILE M SUBCONSCIOUS DEALS WITH THE PROBLEM.
OIL
BEANS
WE CAN'T TELL AIDAN, THE WHOLE COP SHOP'S BUSY WITH THE TRASH FIRES.
WHAT ABOUT YOUR DAD?
NO WAY. HE'D LET THE REGATTA GO TO HELL FOR NANA. AND IT'S TOO IMPORTANT.
PLUS, THERE'S A GOOD CHANCE THAT IF WE TOLD HIM, HE'D BLOW HIS STENT THEN AND THERE.
I'VE SWORN UNCLE MITCH TO SILENCE. THIS IS UP TO US. COME ON.
LAKE NUT

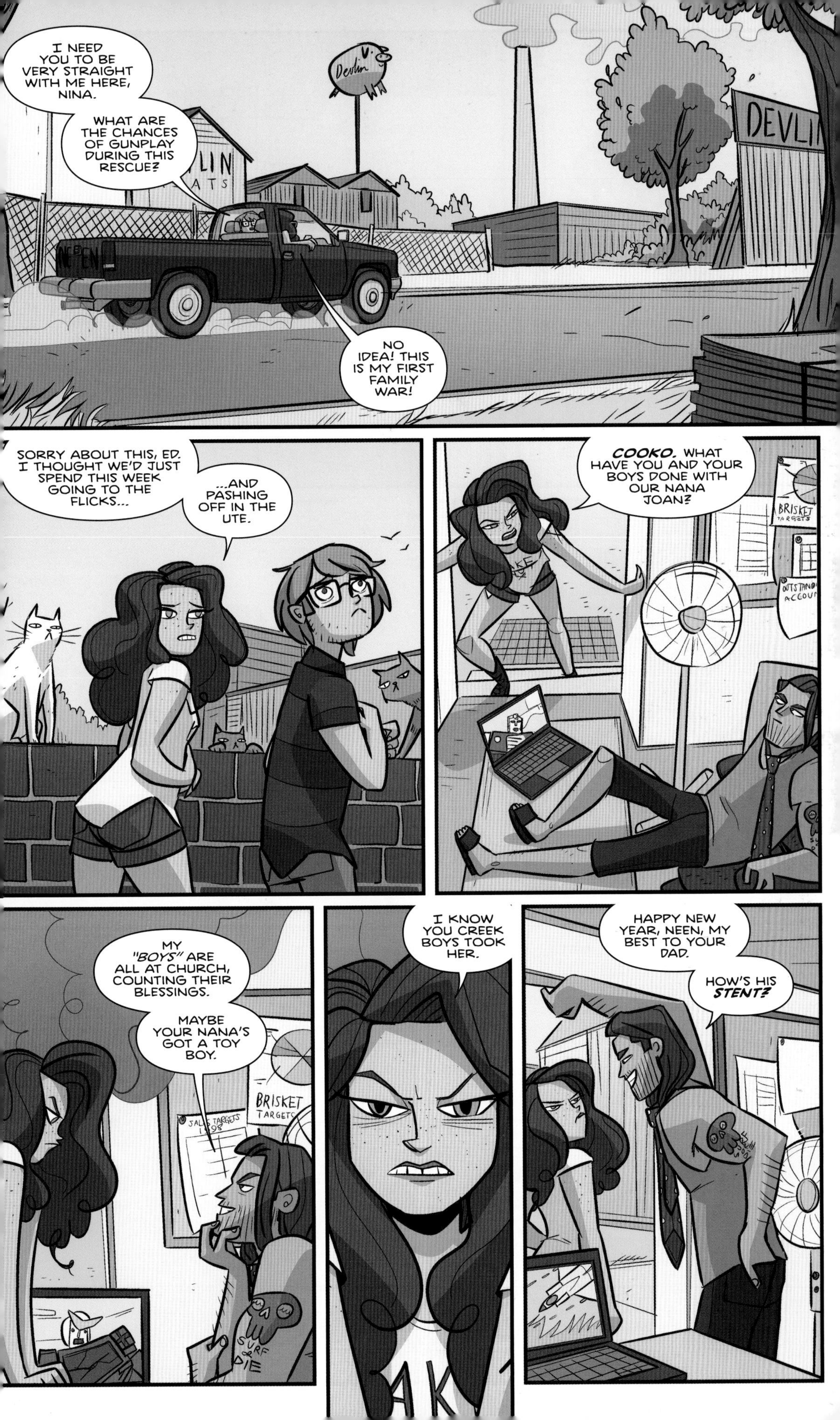
I NEED YOU TO BE VERY STRAIGHT WITH ME HERE, NINA.
WHAT ARE THE CHANCES OF GUNPLAY DURING THIS RESCUE?
NO IDEA! THIS IS MY FIRST FAMILY WAR!
SORRY ABOUT THIS, ED. I THOUGHT WE'D JUST SPEND THIS WEEK GOING TO THE FLICKS...
...AND PASHING OFF IN THE UTE.
COOKO. WHAT HAVE YOU AND YOUR BOYS DONE WITH OUR NANA JOAN?
BRISKET TARGETS
MY "BOYS" ARE ALL AT CHURCH, COUNTING THEIR BLESSINGS.
MAYBE YOUR NANA'S GOT A TOY BOY.
BRISKET TARGETS
SURF OR DIE
I KNOW YOU CREEK BOYS TOOK HER.
HAPPY NEW YEAR, NEEN, MY BEST TO YOUR DAD.
HOW'S HIS *STENT?*

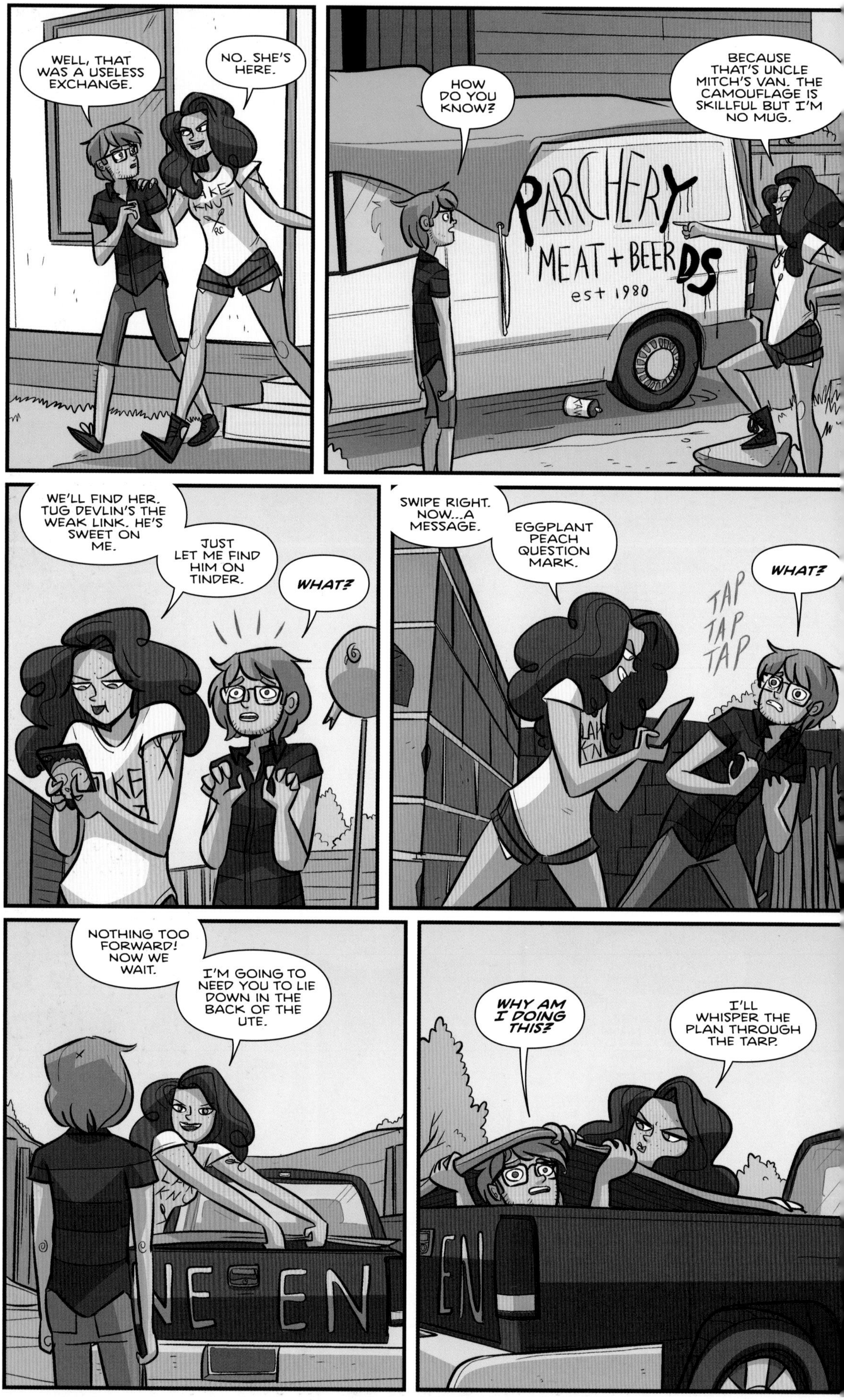

WELL, THAT WAS A USELESS EXCHANGE.
NO. SHE'S HERE.
HOW DO YOU KNOW?
BECAUSE THAT'S UNCLE MITCH'S VAN. THE CAMOUFLAGE IS SKILLFUL BUT I'M NO MUG.
PARCHERY
MEAT + BEERDS
est 1980
WE'LL FIND HER. TUG DEVLIN'S THE WEAK LINK. HE'S SWEET ON ME.
JUST LET ME FIND HIM ON TINDER.
WHAT?
SWIPE RIGHT. NOW...A MESSAGE.
EGGPLANT PEACH QUESTION MARK.
TAP TAP TAP
WHAT?
NOTHING TOO FORWARD! NOW WE WAIT.
I'M GOING TO NEED YOU TO LIE DOWN IN THE BACK OF THE UTE.
WHY AM I DOING THIS?
I'LL WHISPER THE PLAN THROUGH THE TARP.

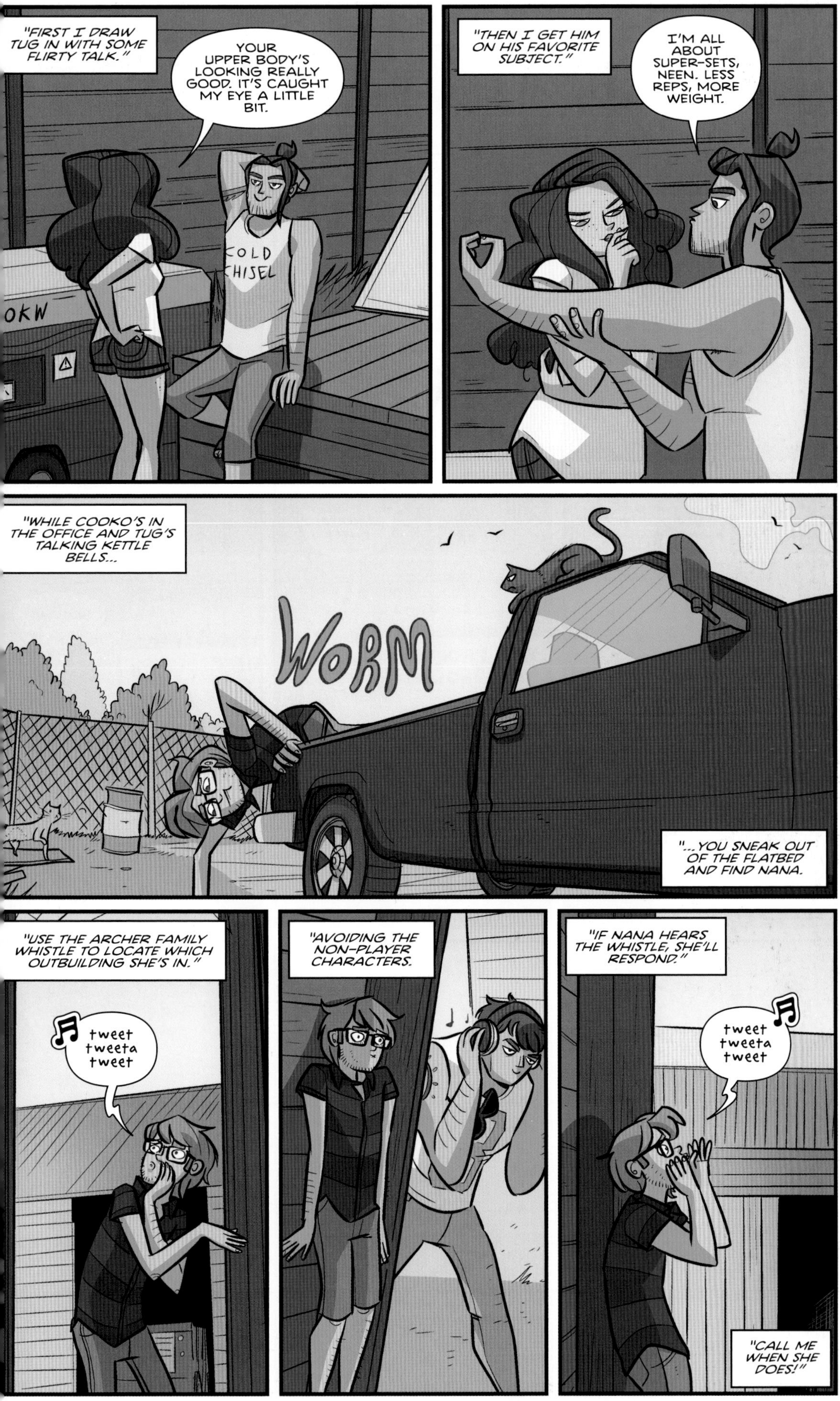
"FIRST I DRAW TUG IN WITH SOME FLIRTY TALK."
YOUR UPPER BODY'S LOOKING REALLY GOOD. IT'S CAUGHT MY EYE A LITTLE BIT.
COLD CHISEL
OKW
"THEN I GET HIM ON HIS FAVORITE SUBJECT."
I'M ALL ABOUT SUPER-SETS, NEEN. LESS REPS, MORE WEIGHT.
"WHILE COOKO'S IN THE OFFICE AND TUG'S TALKING KETTLE BELLS...
WORM
"...YOU SNEAK OUT OF THE FLATBED AND FIND NANA.
"USE THE ARCHER FAMILY WHISTLE TO LOCATE WHICH OUTBUILDING SHE'S IN."
tweet tweeta tweet
"AVOIDING THE NON-PLAYER CHARACTERS.
"IF NANA HEARS THE WHISTLE, SHE'LL RESPOND."
tweet tweeta tweet
"CALL ME WHEN SHE DOES!"

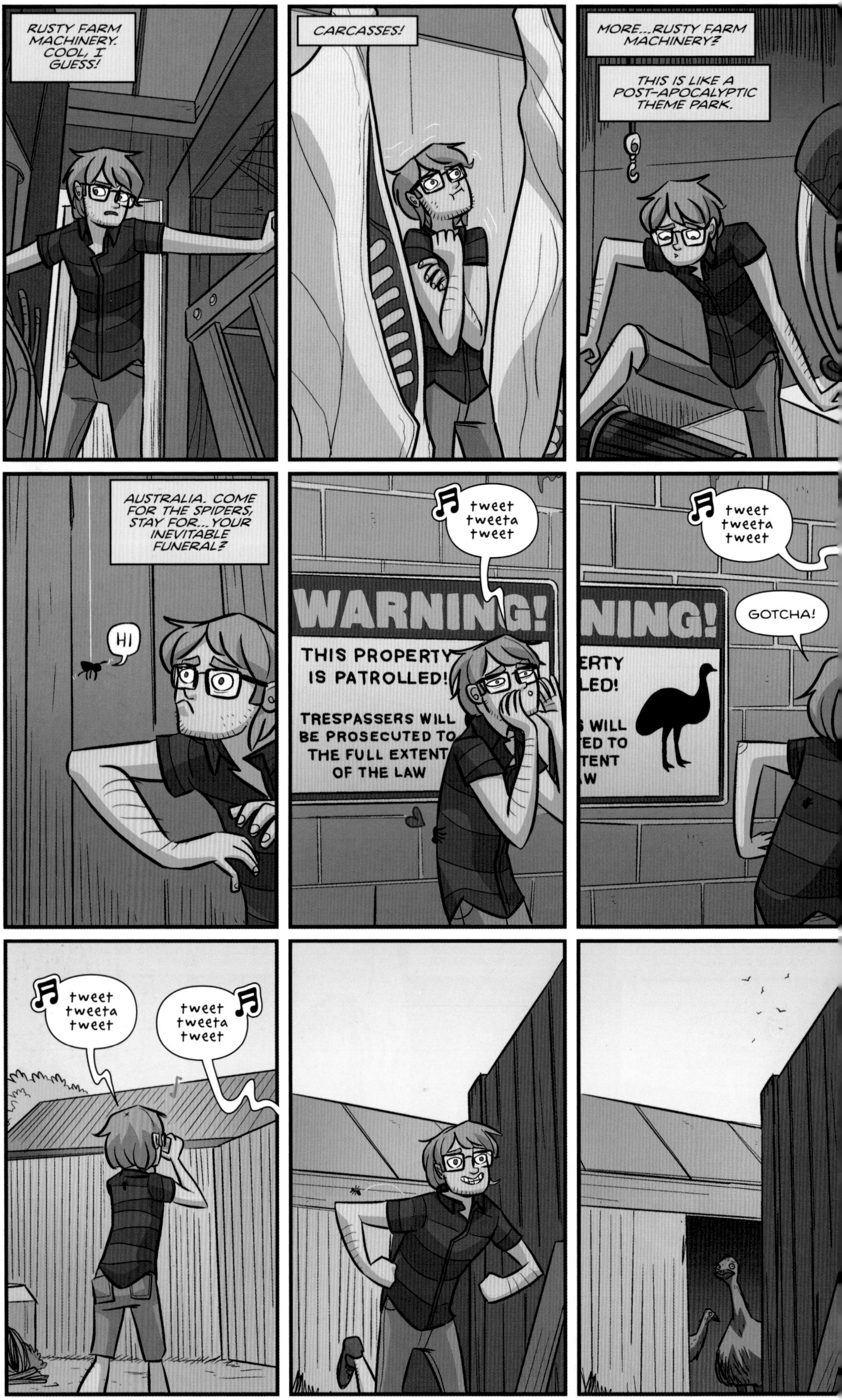
RUSTY FARM MACHINERY. COOL, I GUESS!
CARCASSES!
MORE...RUSTY FARM MACHINERY?
THIS IS LIKE A POST-APOCALYPTIC THEME PARK.
AUSTRALIA. COME FOR THE SPIDERS, STAY FOR...YOUR INEVITABLE FUNERAL?
HI
tweet tweeta tweet
WARNING!
THIS PROPERTY IS PATROLLED!
TRESPASSERS WILL BE PROSECUTED TO THE FULL EXTENT OF THE LAW
tweet tweeta tweet
GOTCHA!
tweet tweeta tweet
tweet tweeta tweet

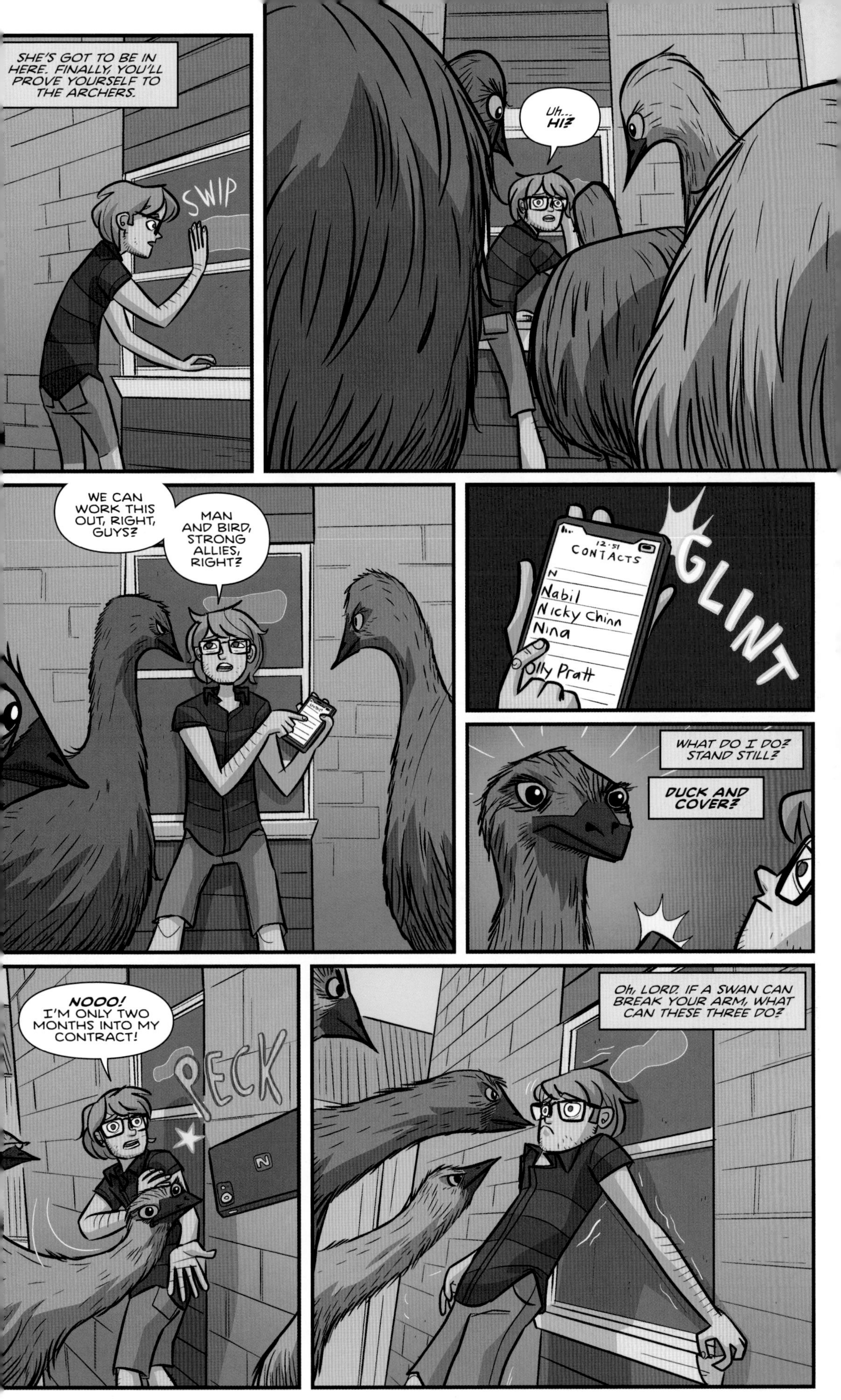
SHE'S GOT TO BE IN HERE. FINALLY, YOU'LL PROVE YOURSELF TO THE ARCHERS.
SWIP
Uh... HI?
WE CAN WORK THIS OUT, RIGHT, GUYS?
MAN AND BIRD, STRONG ALLIES, RIGHT?
12:51
CONTACTS
N
Nabil
Nicky Chinn
Nina
Olly Pratt
GLINT
WHAT DO I DO? STAND STILL?
DUCK AND COVER?
NOOO! I'M ONLY TWO MONTHS INTO MY CONTRACT!
PECK
Oh, LORD. IF A SWAN CAN BREAK YOUR ARM, WHAT CAN THESE THREE DO?

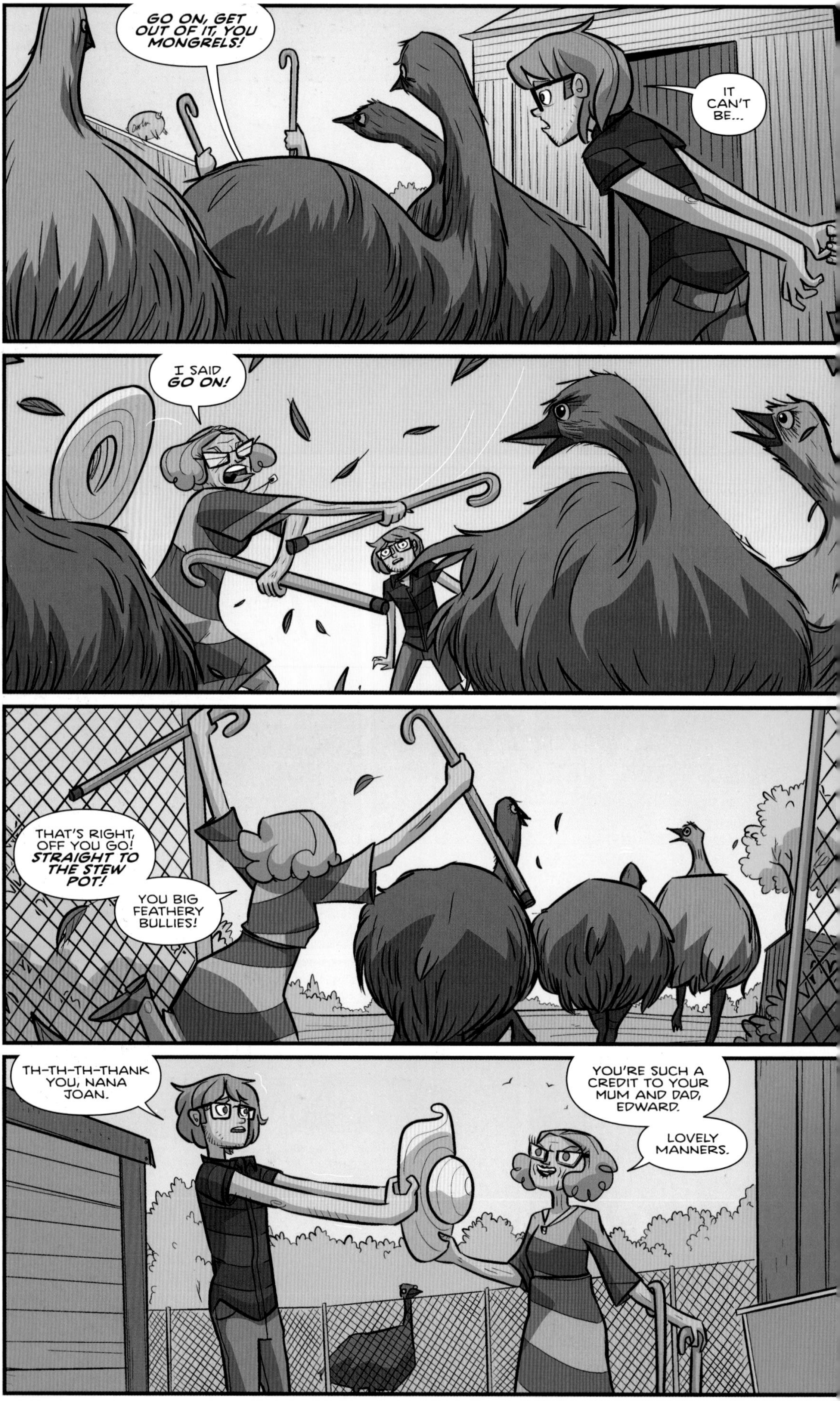
GO ON, GET OUT OF IT, YOU MONGRELS!
IT CAN'T BE...
I SAID GO ON!
THAT'S RIGHT, OFF YOU GO! STRAIGHT TO THE STEW POT!
YOU BIG FEATHERY BULLIES!
TH-TH-TH-THANK YOU, NANA JOAN.
YOU'RE SUCH A CREDIT TO YOUR MUM AND DAD, EDWARD.
LOVELY MANNERS.

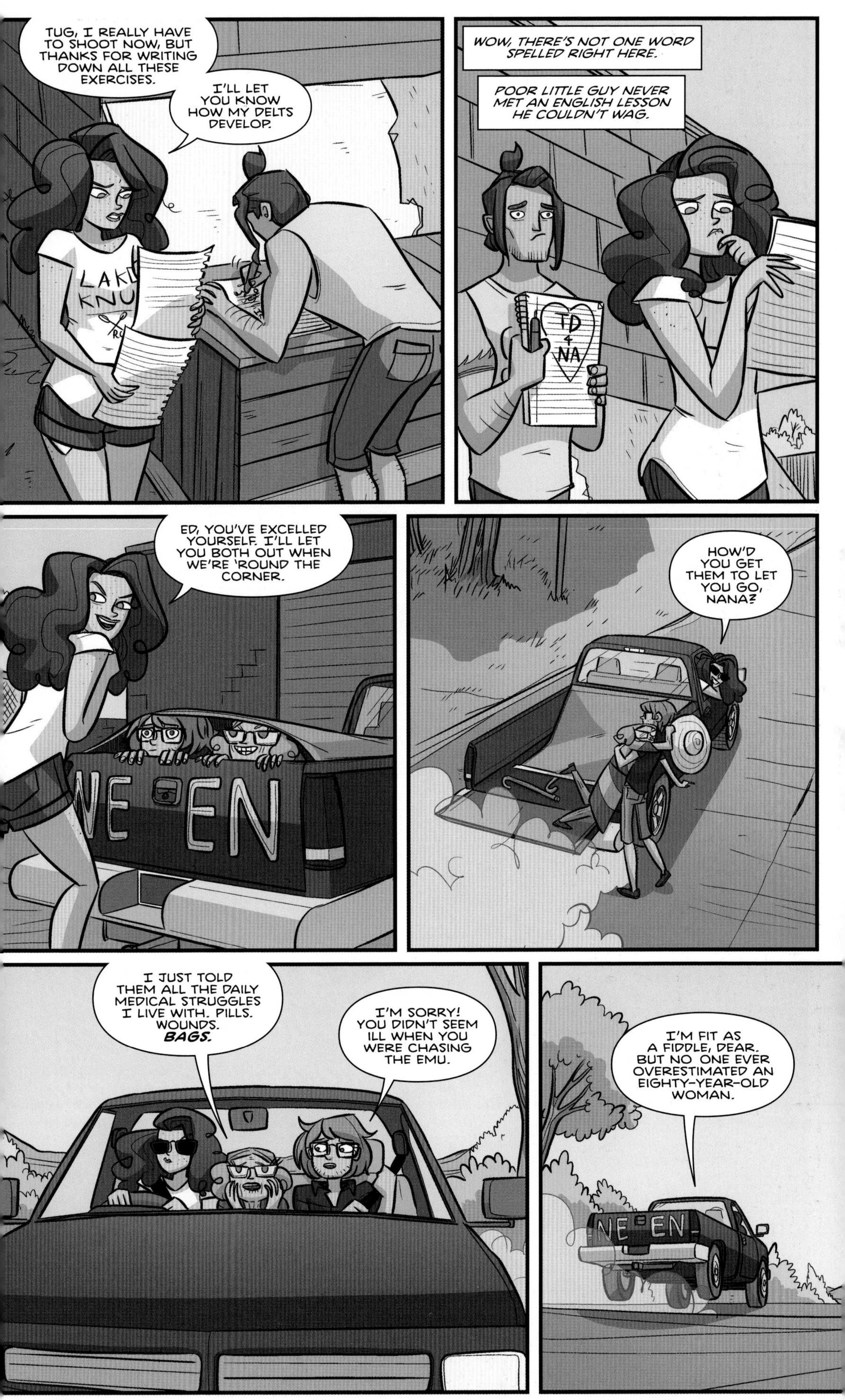

TUG, I REALLY HAVE TO SHOOT NOW, BUT THANKS FOR WRITING DOWN ALL THESE EXERCISES.
I'LL LET YOU KNOW HOW MY DELTS DEVELOP.
WOW, THERE'S NOT ONE WORD SPELLED RIGHT HERE.
POOR LITTLE GUY NEVER MET AN ENGLISH LESSON HE COULDN'T WAG.
TD 4 NA
ED, YOU'VE EXCELLED YOURSELF. I'LL LET YOU BOTH OUT WHEN WE'RE 'ROUND THE CORNER.
NE EN
HOW'D YOU GET THEM TO LET YOU GO, NANA?
I JUST TOLD THEM ALL THE DAILY MEDICAL STRUGGLES I LIVE WITH. PILLS. WOUNDS. ***BAGS.***
I'M SORRY! YOU DIDN'T SEEM ILL WHEN YOU WERE CHASING THE EMU.
I'M FIT AS A FIDDLE, DEAR. BUT NO ONE EVER OVERESTIMATED AN EIGHTY-YEAR-OLD WOMAN.
NE EN

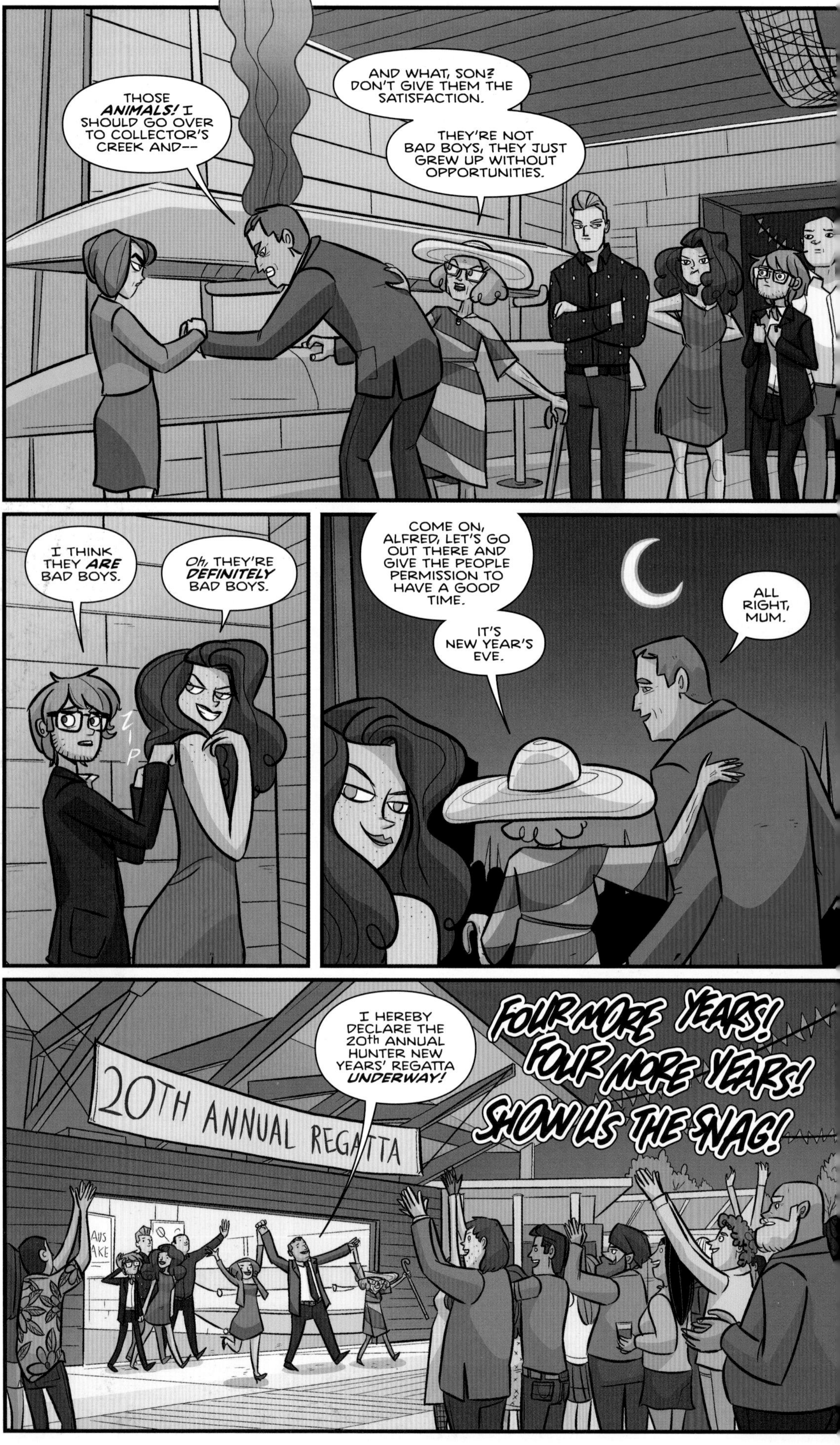
THOSE ANIMALS! I SHOULD GO OVER TO COLLECTOR'S CREEK AND--
AND WHAT, SON? DON'T GIVE THEM THE SATISFACTION.
THEY'RE NOT BAD BOYS, THEY JUST GREW UP WITHOUT OPPORTUNITIES.
I THINK THEY ARE BAD BOYS.
Oh, THEY'RE DEFINITELY BAD BOYS.
ZIP
COME ON, ALFRED, LET'S GO OUT THERE AND GIVE THE PEOPLE PERMISSION TO HAVE A GOOD TIME.
IT'S NEW YEAR'S EVE.
ALL RIGHT, MUM.
I HEREBY DECLARE THE 20th ANNUAL HUNTER NEW YEARS' REGATTA UNDERWAY!
20TH ANNUAL REGATTA
FOUR MORE YEARS! FOUR MORE YEARS! SHOW US THE SNAG!

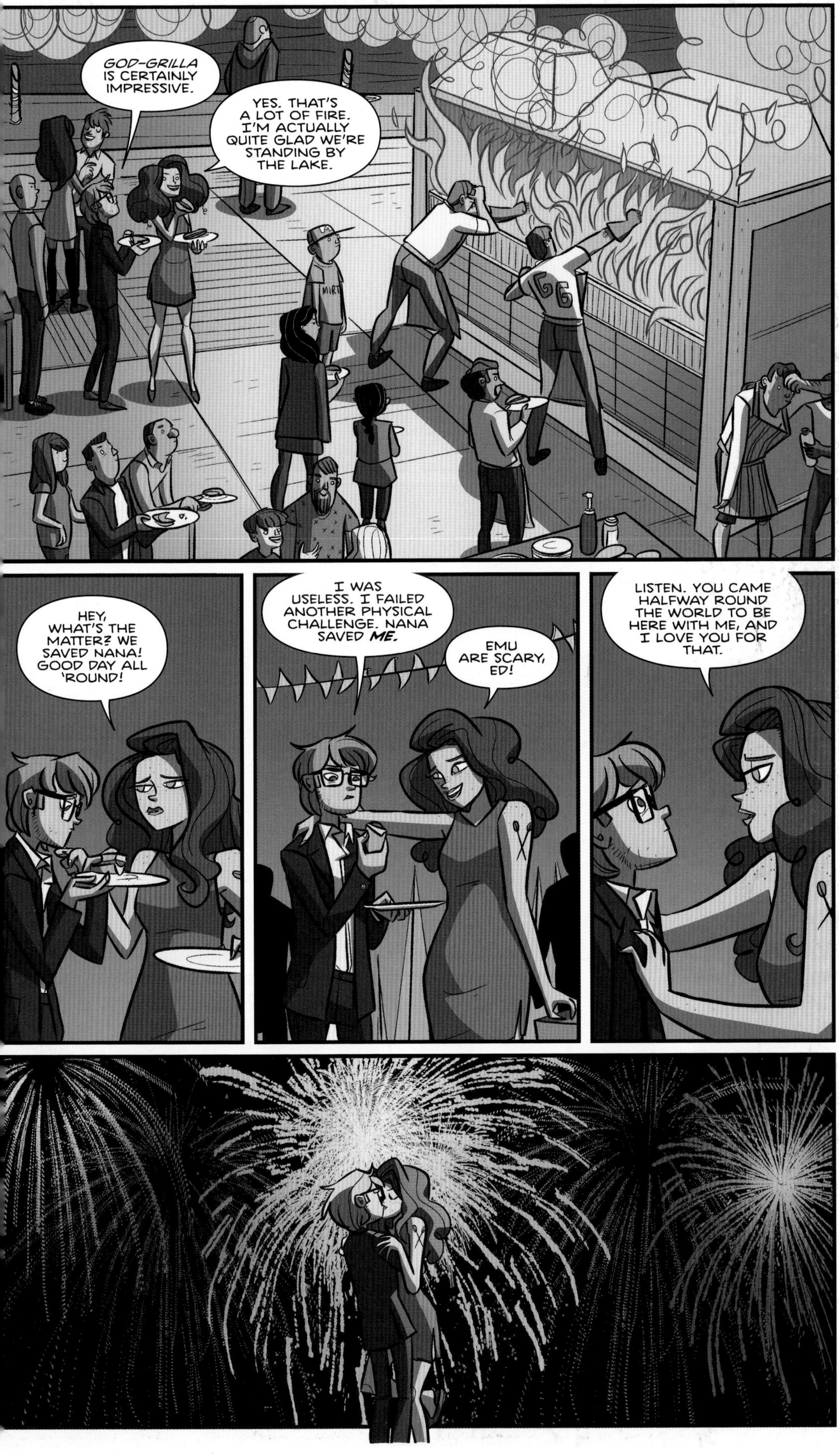
GOD-GRILLA IS CERTAINLY IMPRESSIVE.
YES. THAT'S A LOT OF FIRE. I'M ACTUALLY QUITE GLAD WE'RE STANDING BY THE LAKE.
HEY, WHAT'S THE MATTER? WE SAVED NANA! GOOD DAY ALL 'ROUND!
I WAS USELESS. I FAILED ANOTHER PHYSICAL CHALLENGE. NANA SAVED ME.
EMU ARE SCARY, ED!
LISTEN. YOU CAME HALFWAY ROUND THE WORLD TO BE HERE WITH ME, AND I LOVE YOU FOR THAT.

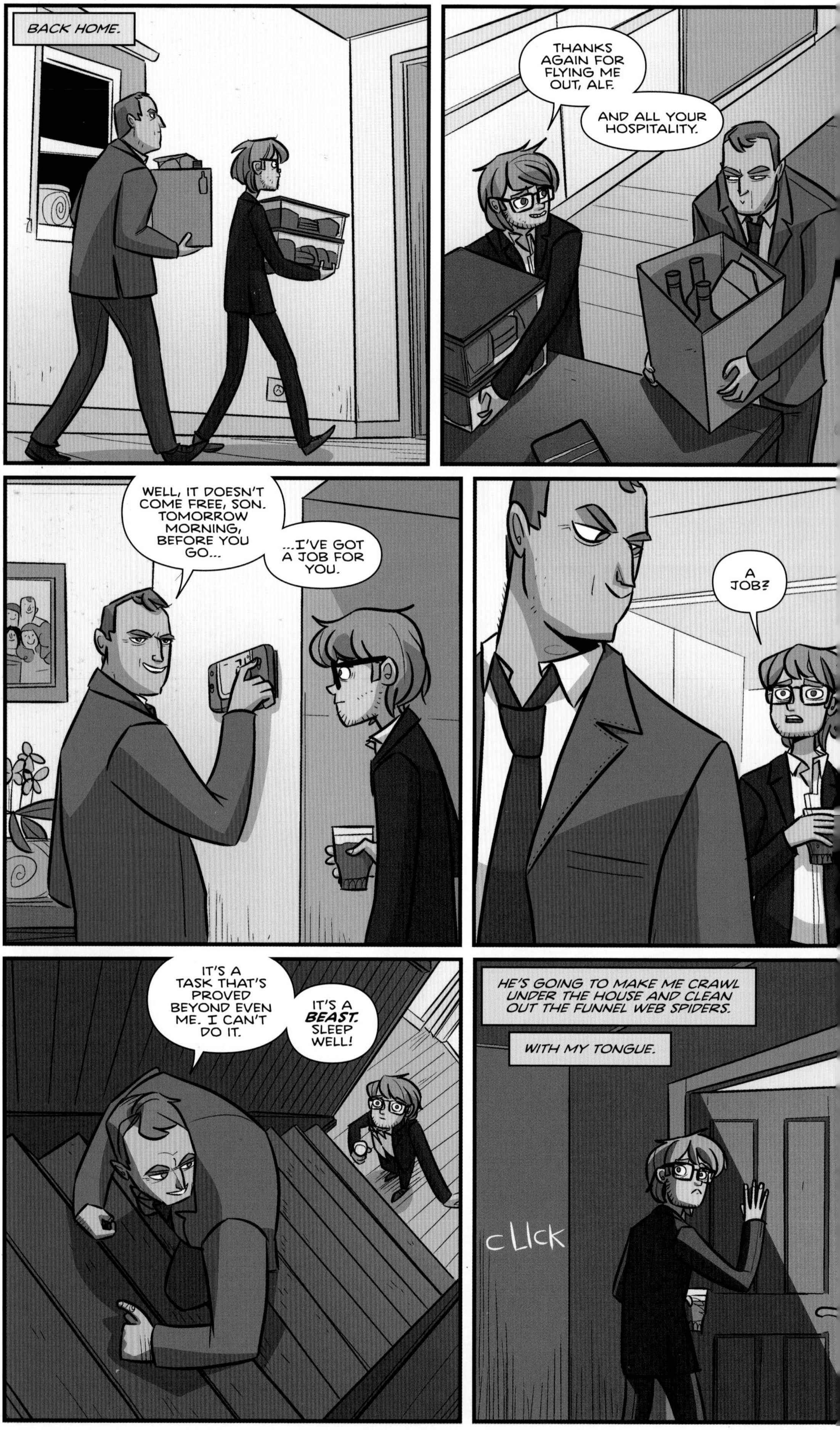
BACK HOME.
THANKS AGAIN FOR FLYING ME OUT, ALF.
AND ALL YOUR HOSPITALITY.
WELL, IT DOESN'T COME FREE, SON. TOMORROW MORNING, BEFORE YOU GO...
...I'VE GOT A JOB FOR YOU.
A JOB?
IT'S A TASK THAT'S PROVED BEYOND EVEN ME. I CAN'T DO IT.
IT'S A **BEAST.** SLEEP WELL!
HE'S GOING TO MAKE ME CRAWL UNDER THE HOUSE AND CLEAN OUT THE FUNNEL WEB SPIDERS.
WITH MY TONGUE.
CLICK

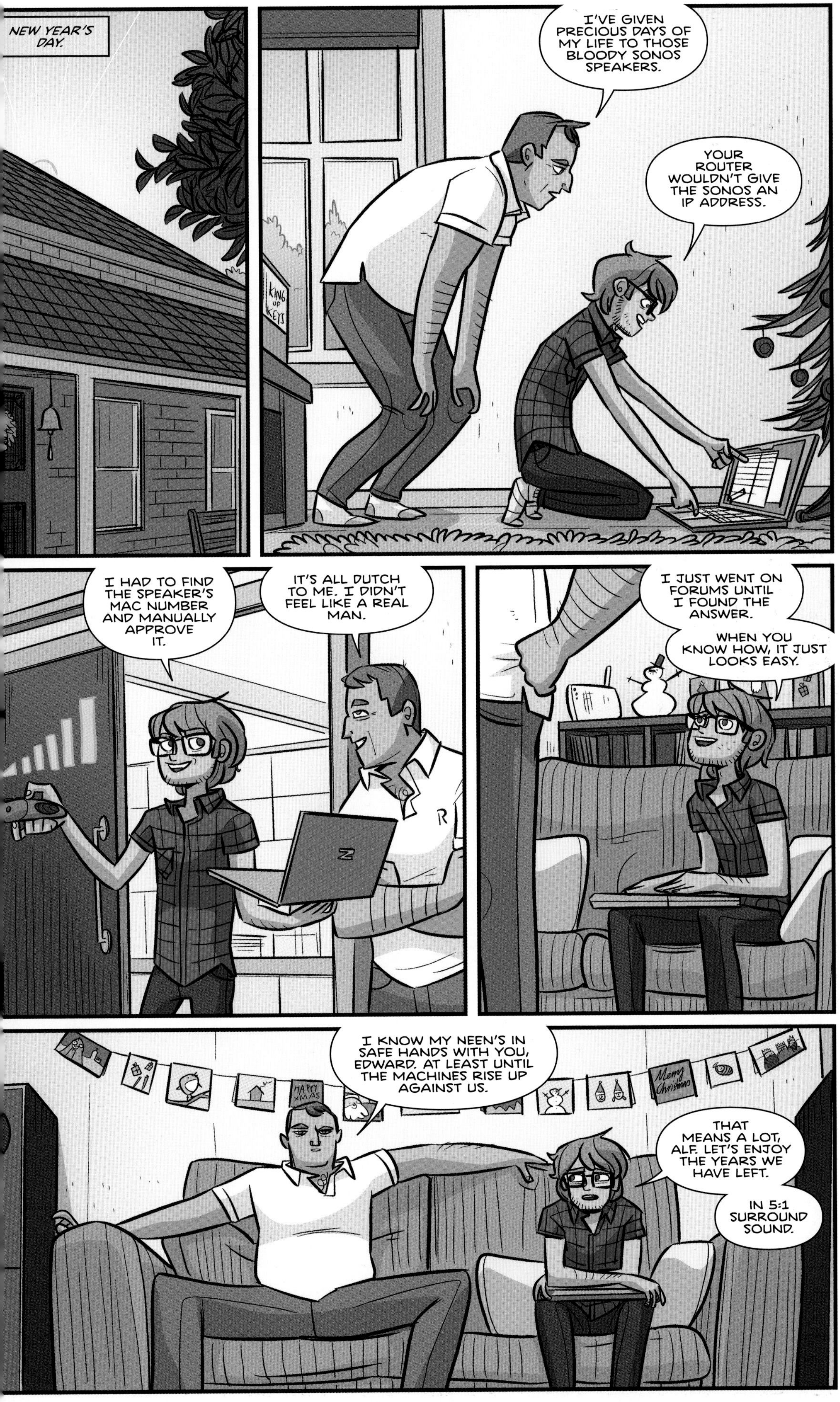
NEW YEAR'S DAY.
I'VE GIVEN PRECIOUS DAYS OF MY LIFE TO THOSE BLOODY SONOS SPEAKERS.
YOUR ROUTER WOULDN'T GIVE THE SONOS AN IP ADDRESS.
KING OF KEYS
I HAD TO FIND THE SPEAKER'S MAC NUMBER AND MANUALLY APPROVE IT.
IT'S ALL DUTCH TO ME. I DIDN'T FEEL LIKE A REAL MAN.
I JUST WENT ON FORUMS UNTIL I FOUND THE ANSWER.
WHEN YOU KNOW HOW, IT JUST LOOKS EASY.
I KNOW MY NEEN'S IN SAFE HANDS WITH YOU, EDWARD. AT LEAST UNTIL THE MACHINES RISE UP AGAINST US.
HAPPY XMAS
Merry Christmas
THAT MEANS A LOT, ALF. LET'S ENJOY THE YEARS WE HAVE LEFT.
IN 5:1 SURROUND SOUND.

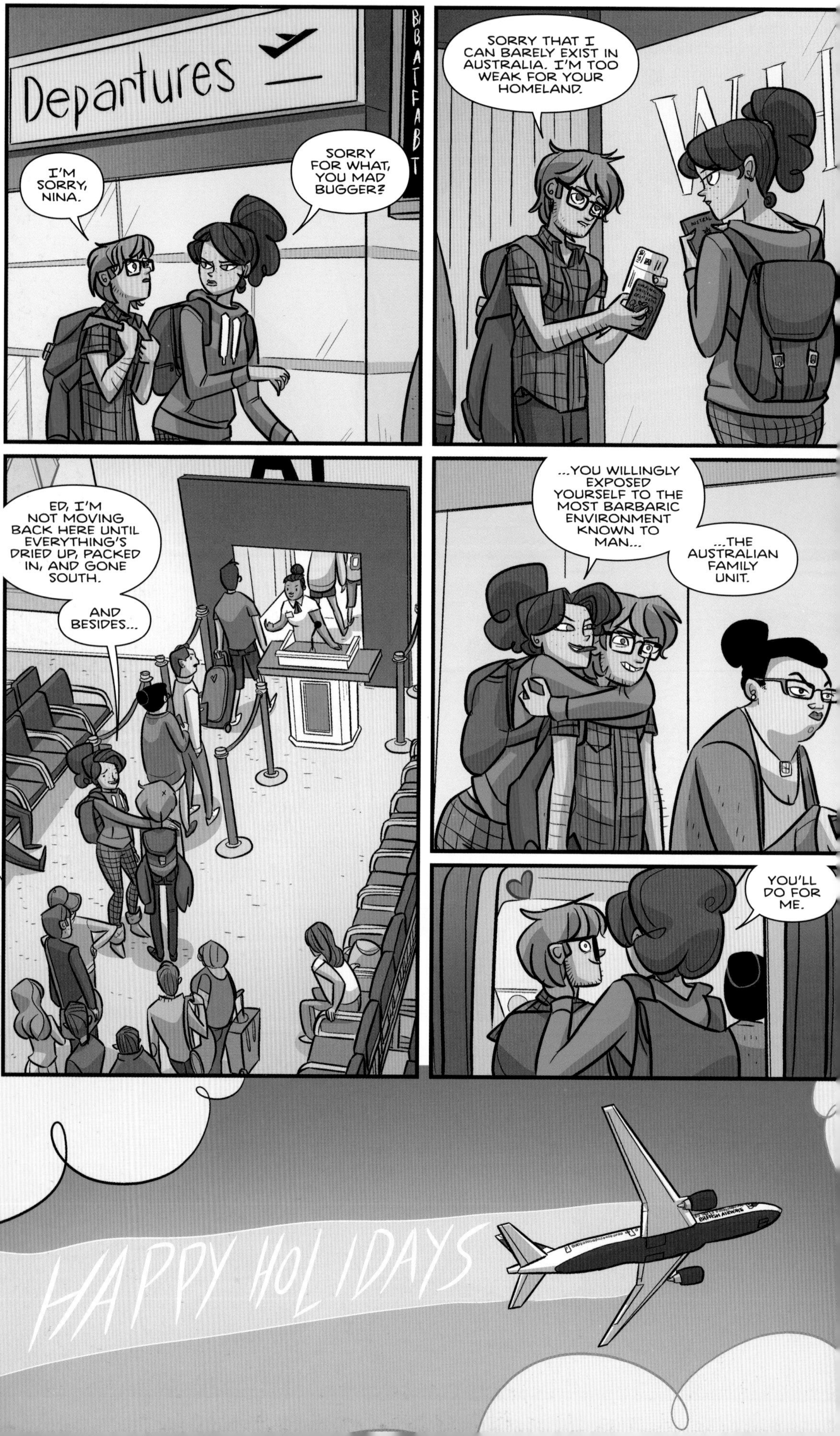
Departures
I'M SORRY, NINA.
SORRY FOR WHAT, YOU MAD BUGGER?
SORRY THAT I CAN BARELY EXIST IN AUSTRALIA. I'M TOO WEAK FOR YOUR HOMELAND.
ED, I'M NOT MOVING BACK HERE UNTIL EVERYTHING'S DRIED UP, PACKED IN, AND GONE SOUTH.
AND BESIDES...
...YOU WILLINGLY EXPOSED YOURSELF TO THE MOST BARBARIC ENVIRONMENT KNOWN TO MAN...
...THE AUSTRALIAN FAMILY UNIT.
YOU'LL DO FOR ME.
HAPPY HOLIDAYS
BRITISH AIRWAYS

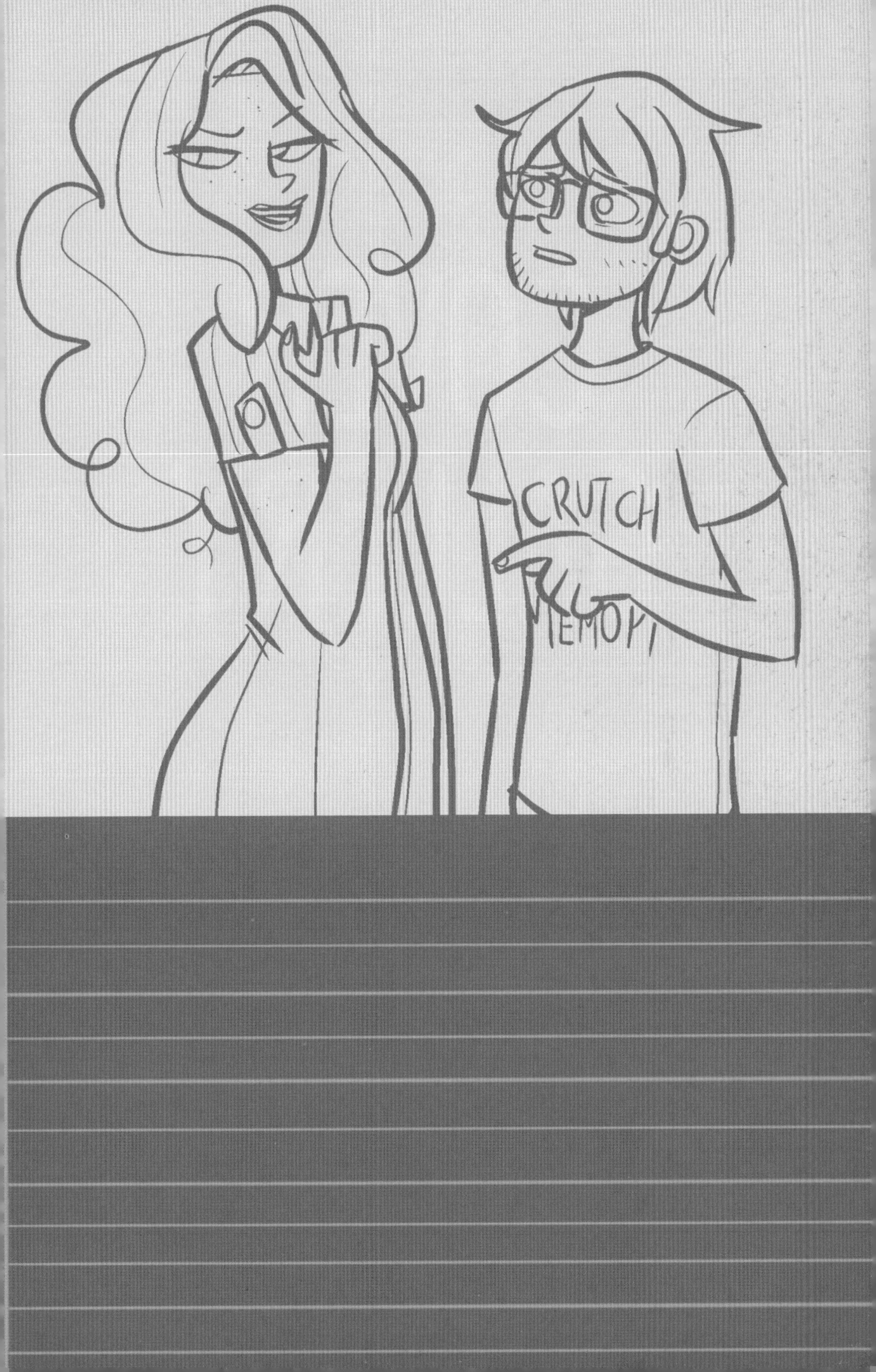
CRUTCH

COVER GALLERY

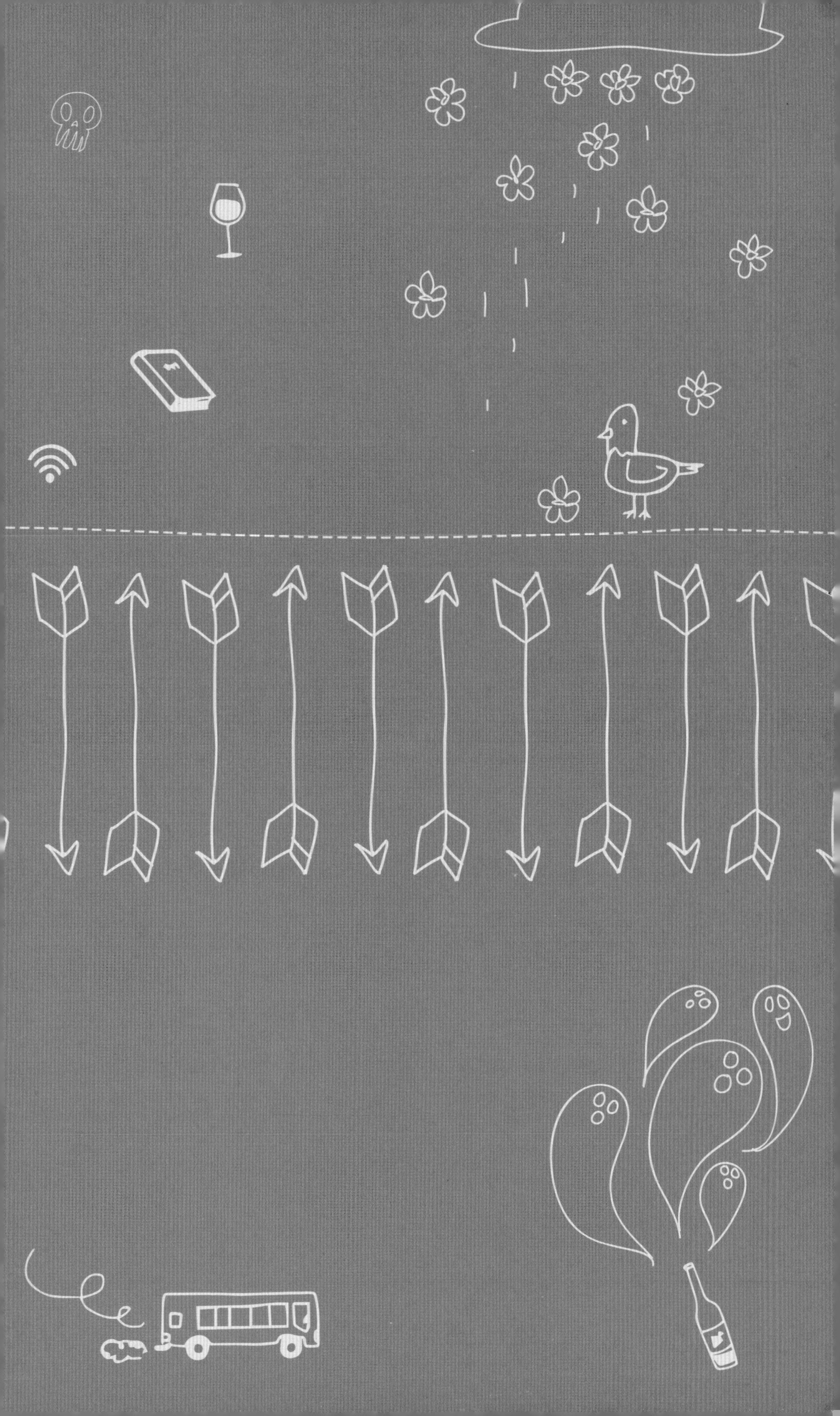

ISSUE #41 COVER

MAX SARIN

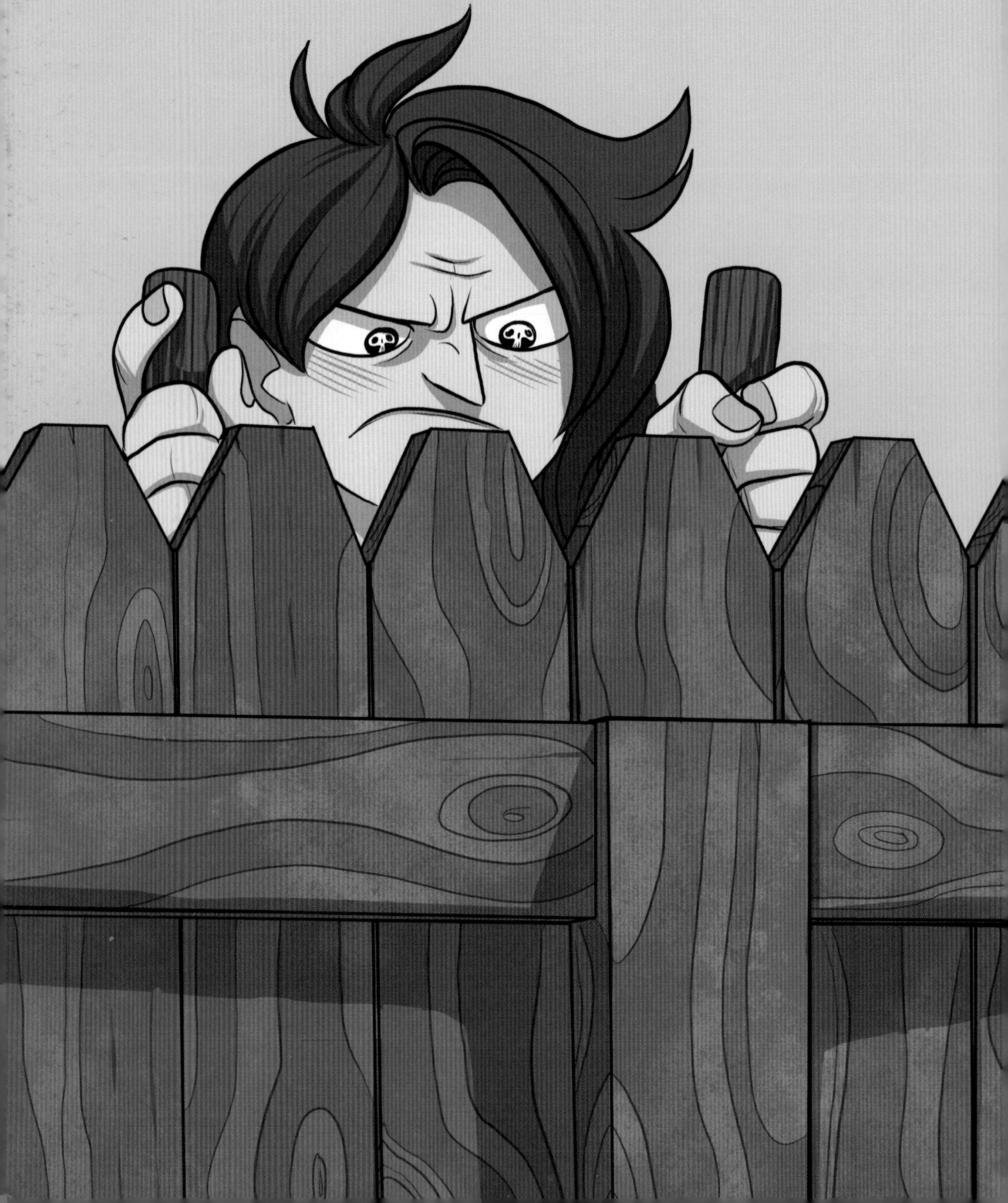

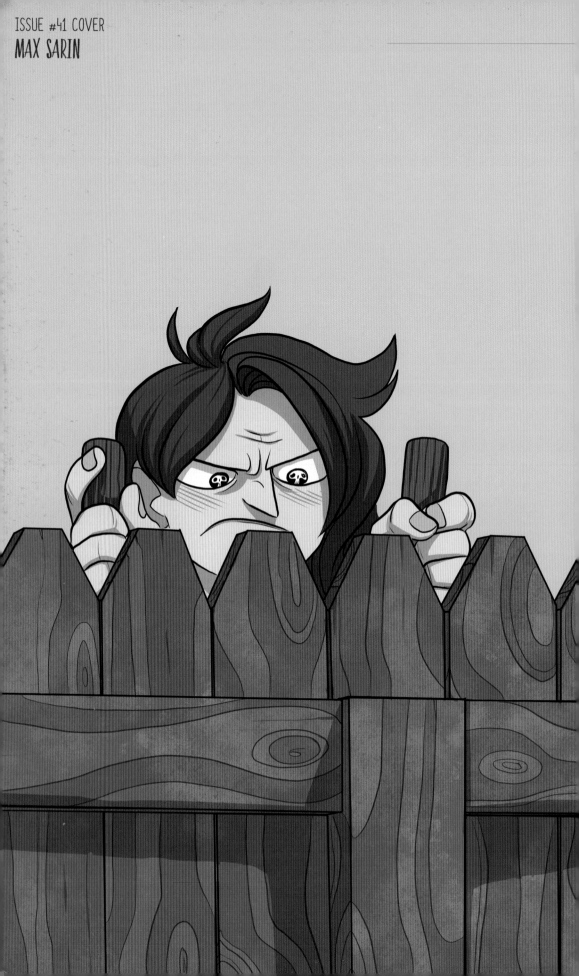

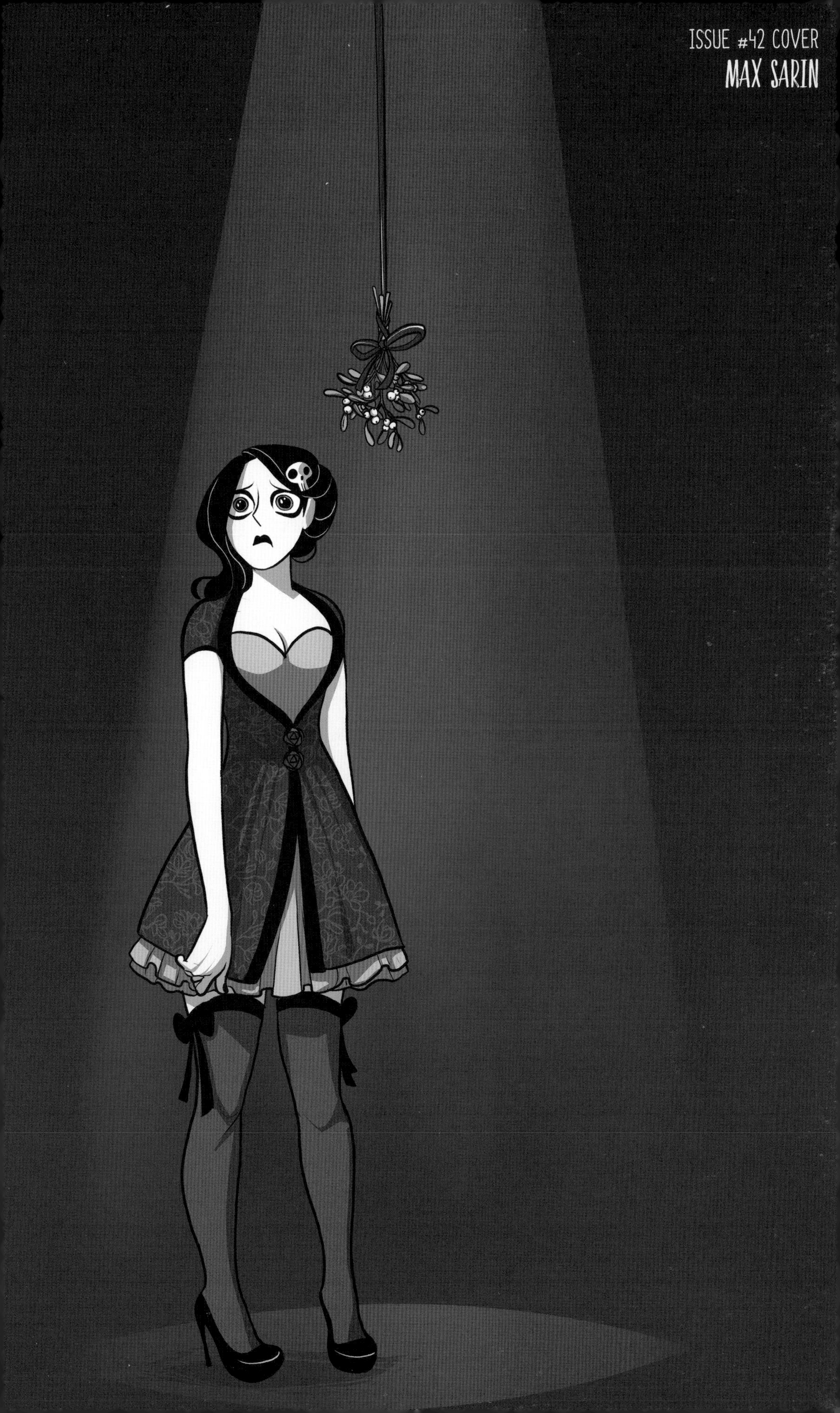

ISSUE #42 COVER
MAX SARIN

ISSUE #43 COVER

MAX SARIN

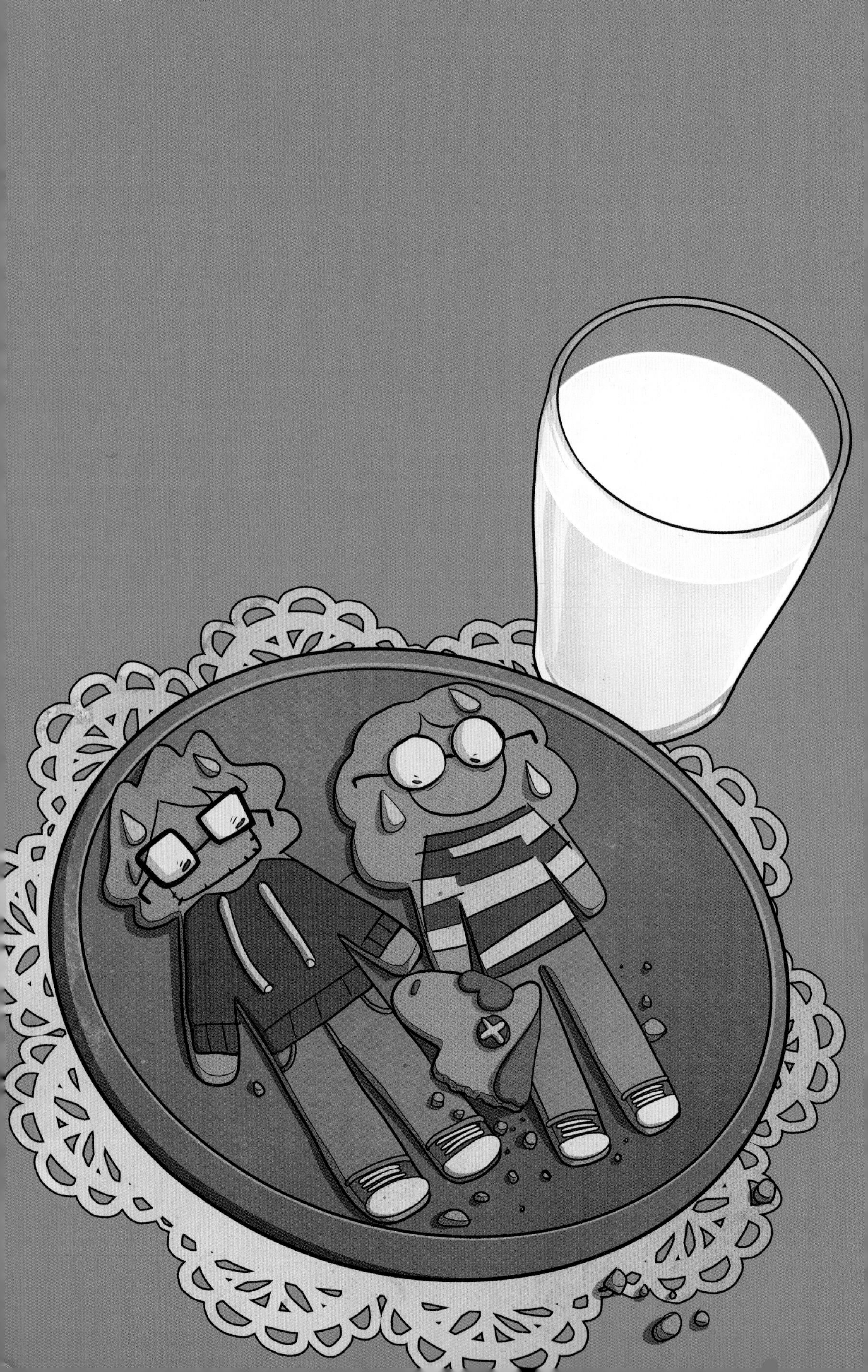

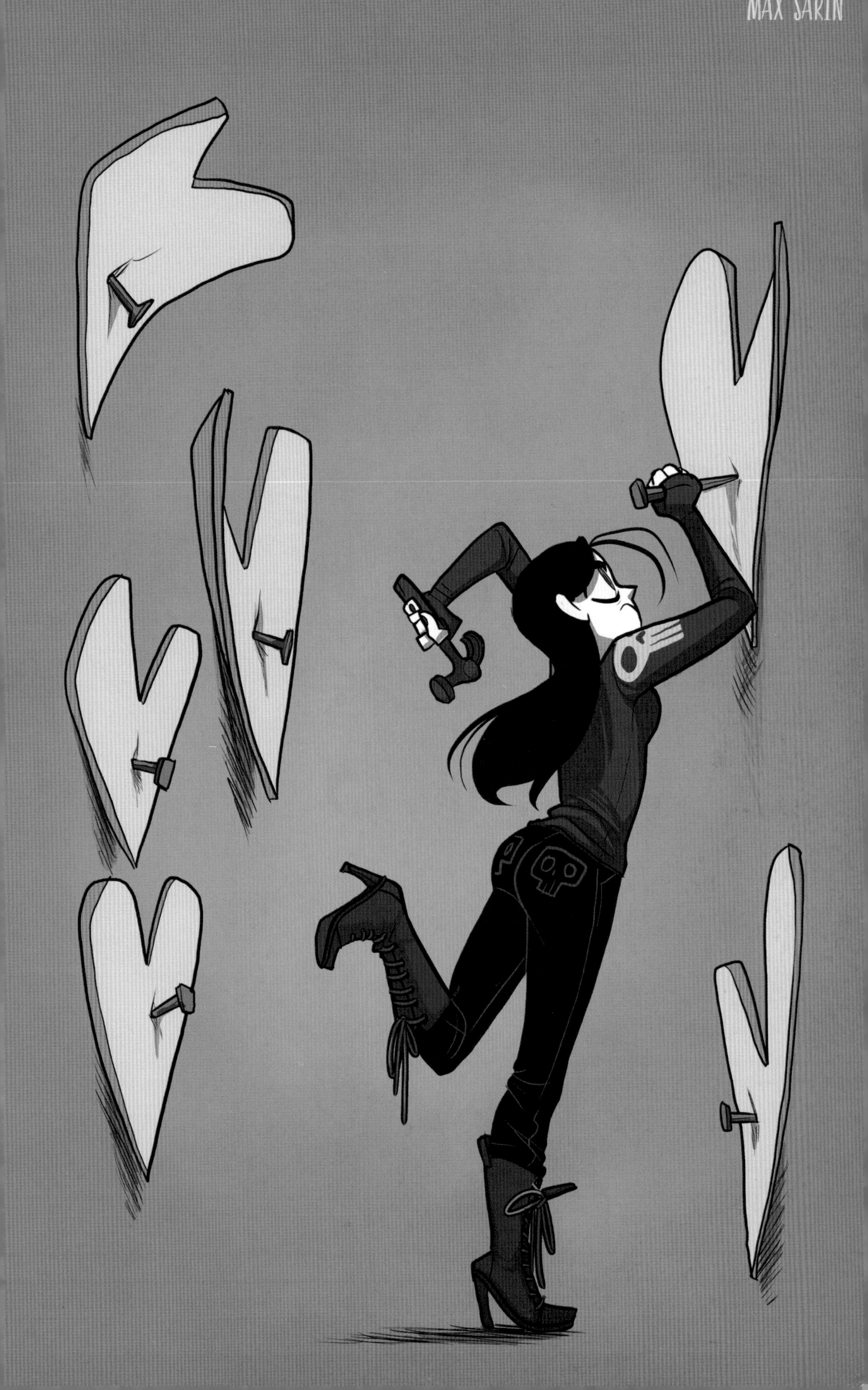

ISSUE #44 COVER
MAX SARIN

WHERE WOMEN GLOW AND MEN PLUNDER COVER

JOHN ALLISON

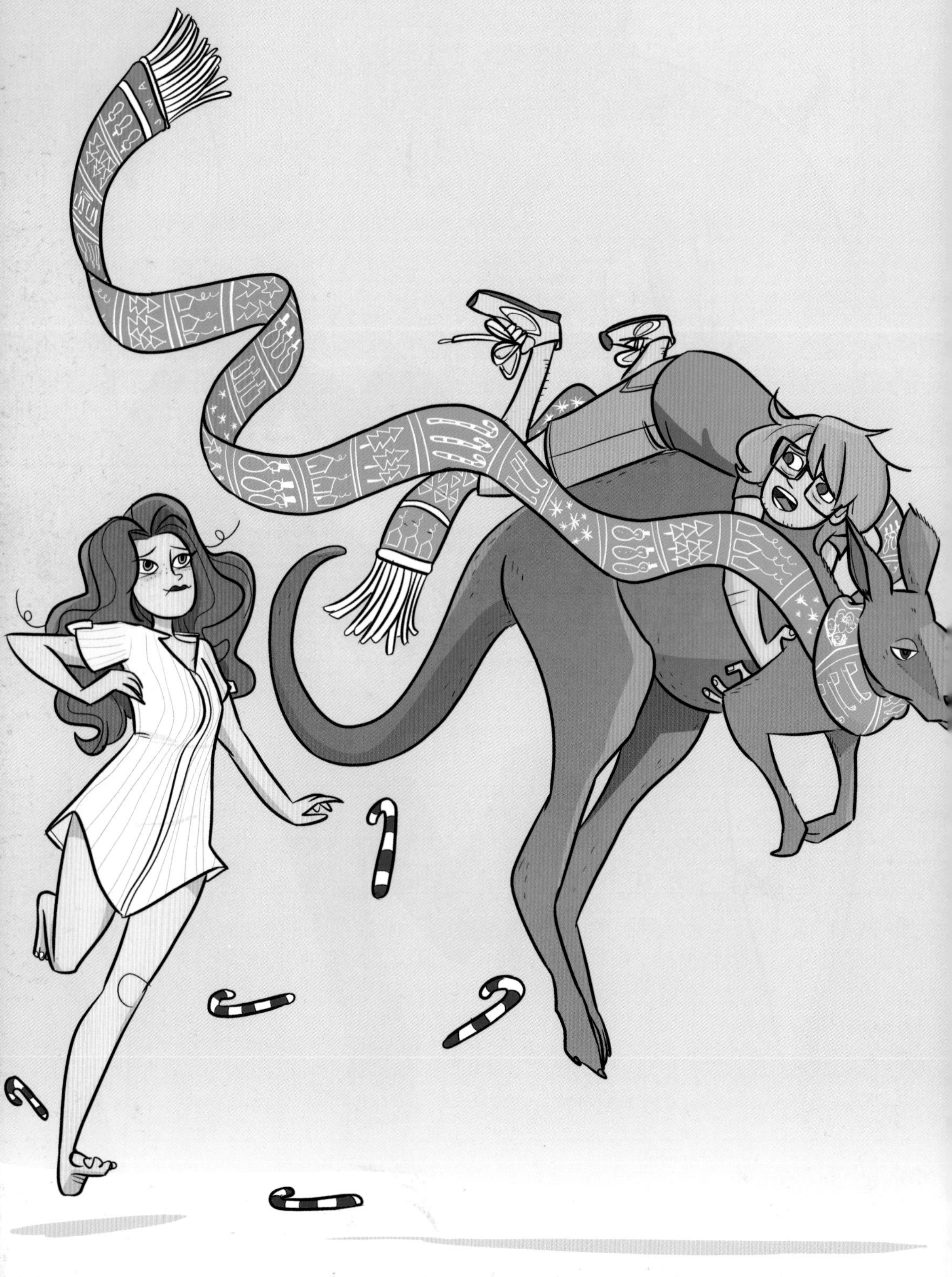

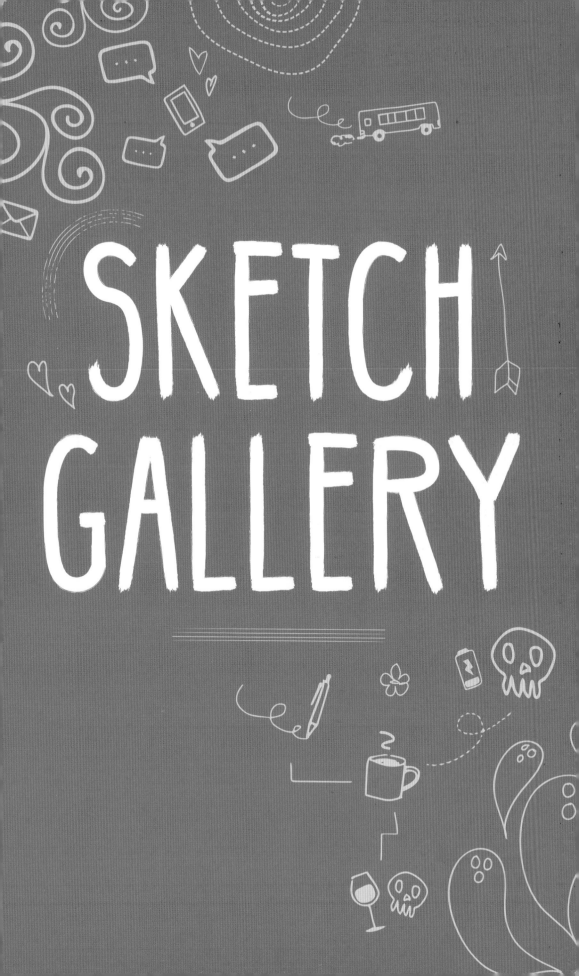

SKETCH GALLERY

SKETCHES AND DESIGNS BY JOHN ALLISON

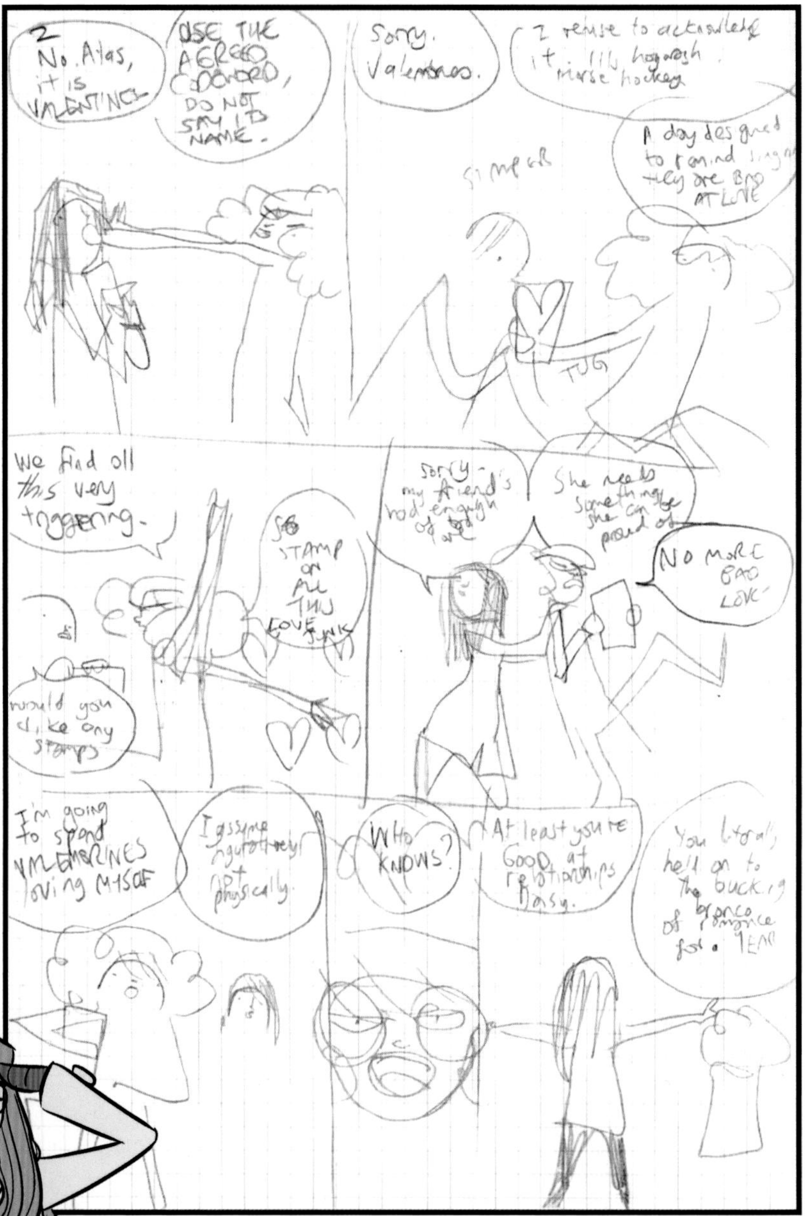
No. Alas, it is VALENTINES.
Sorry. Valentines.
A day designed to remind singles they are BAD AT LOVE
TUG
We find all this very triggering.
SO STAMP ON ALL THIS LOVE JUNK
Would you like any stamps
NO MORE BAD LOVE
I'm going to spend VALENTINES loving MYSELF
WHO KNOWS?
At least you're Good at relationships Daisy.
You literally held on to the bucking bronco of romance for a YEAR

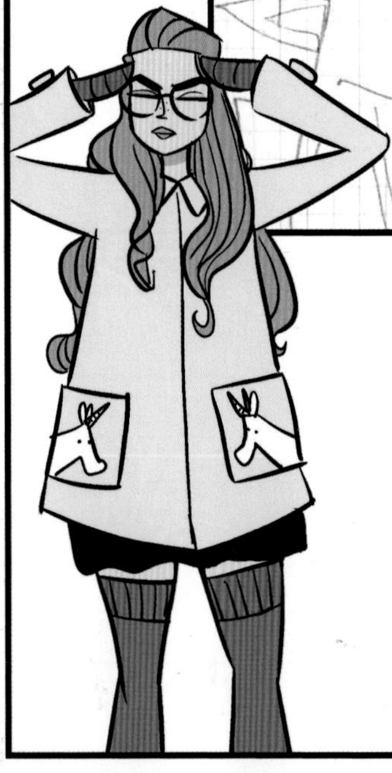

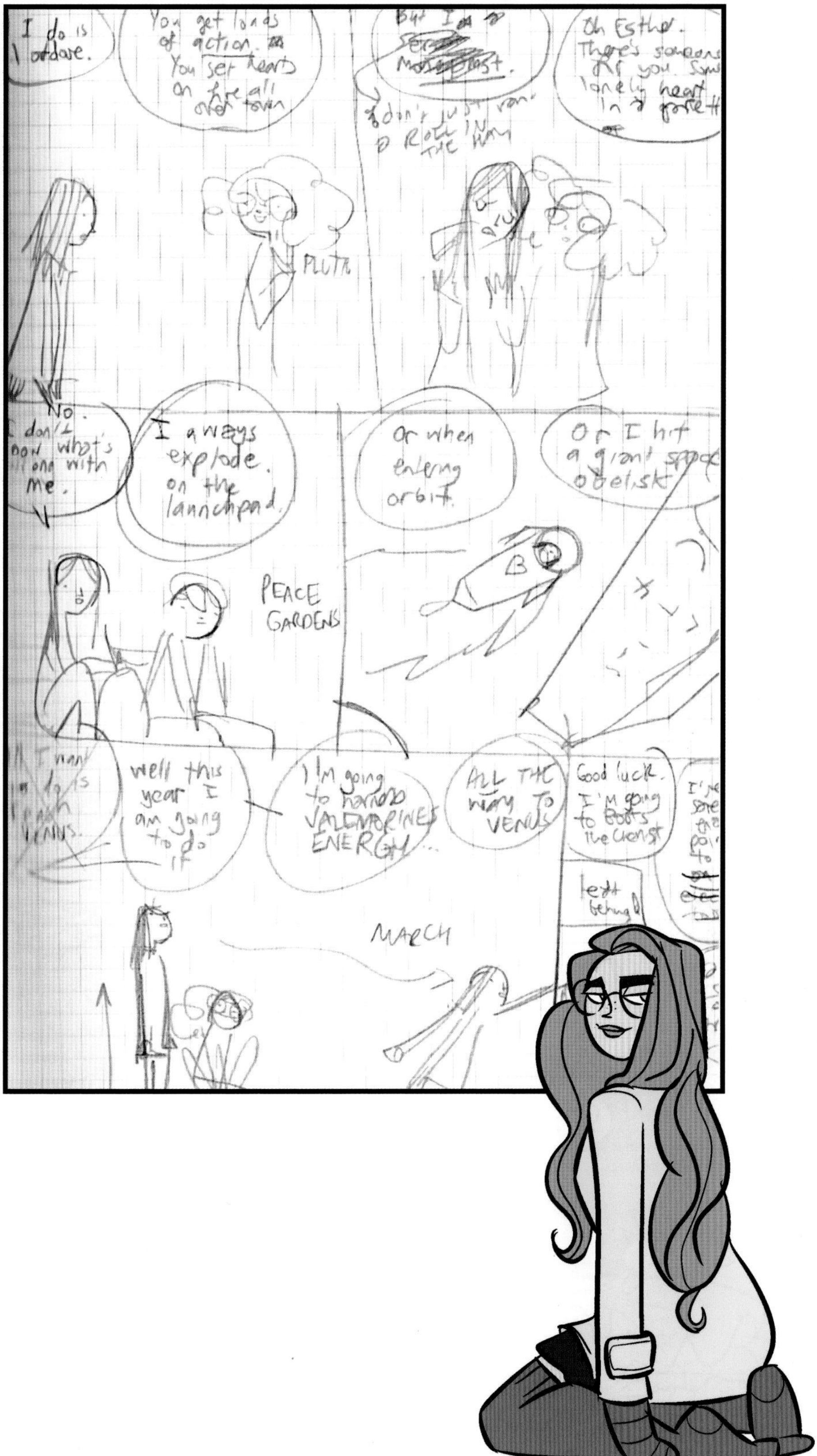

You get loads of action. You set hearts on fire all over town
Oh Esther. There's someone for you.
PLUTO
I always explode on the launchpad.
Or when entering orbit.
Or I hit a giant space obelisk
PEACE GARDENS
well this year I am going to do it
I'M going to harness VALENTINE'S ENERGY...
ALL THE way TO VENUS
Good luck. I'M going to Boots the Chemist
left behind
MARCH

SKETCHES AND DESIGNS BY MAX SARIN

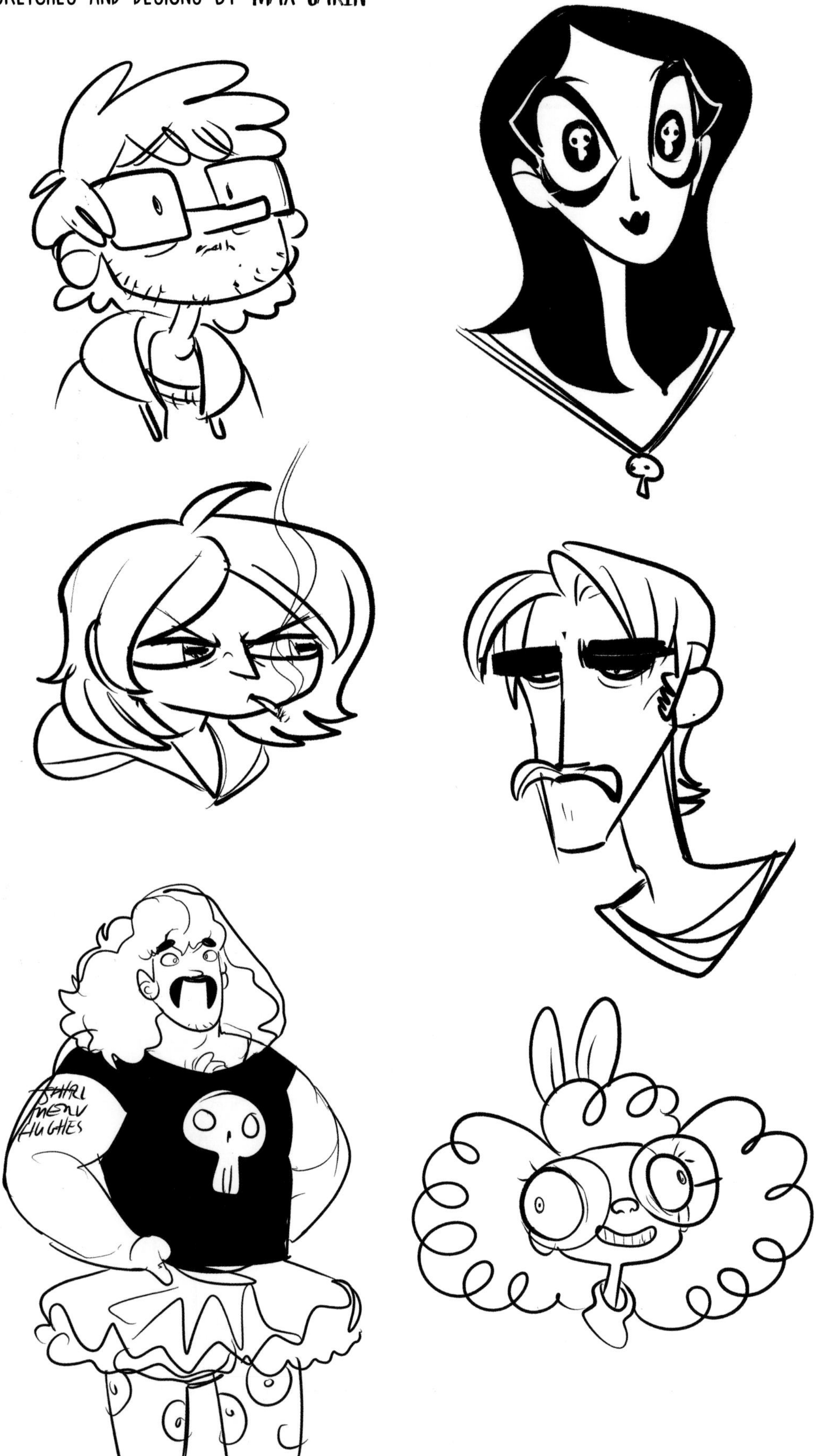

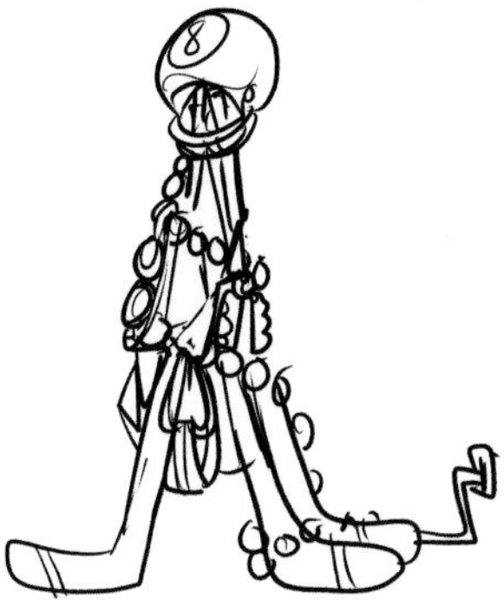

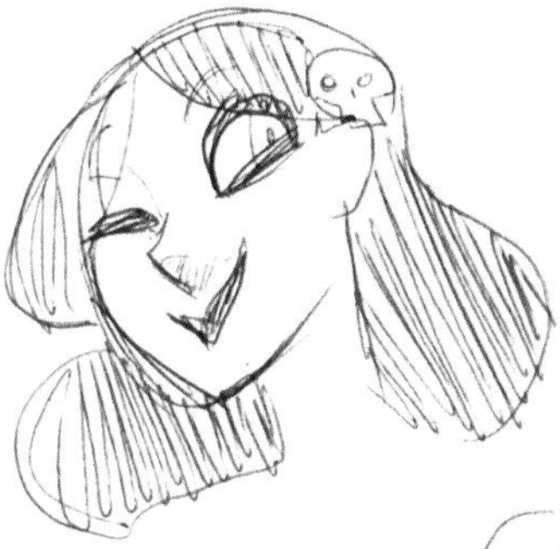

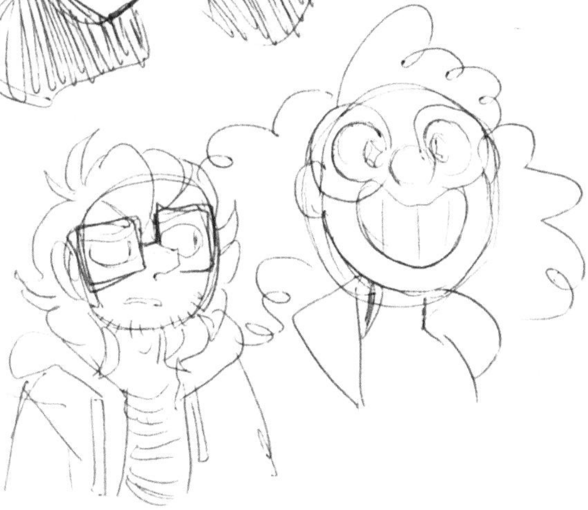

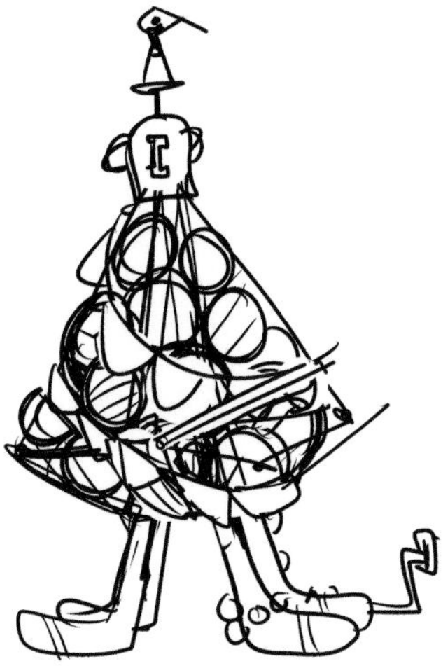

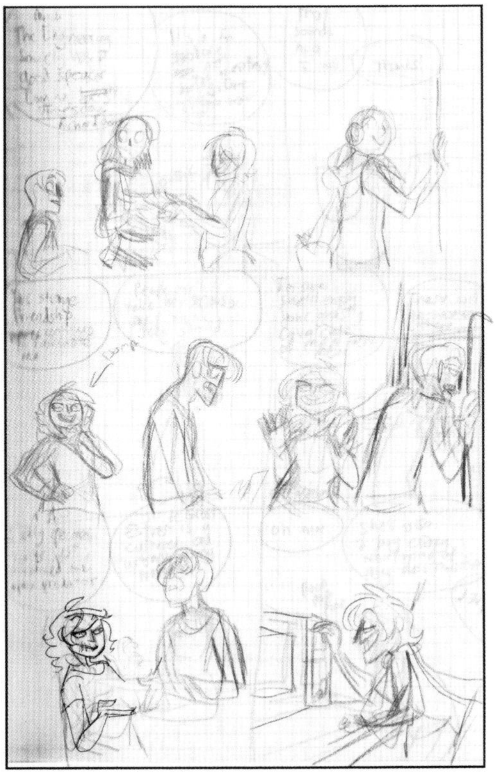

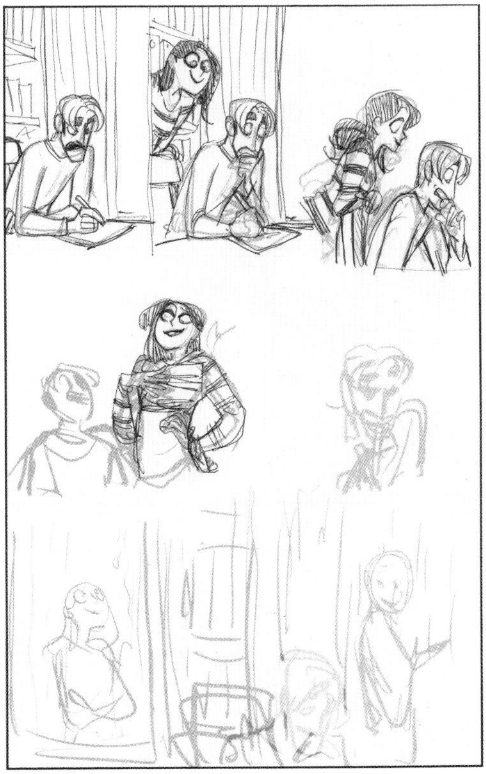

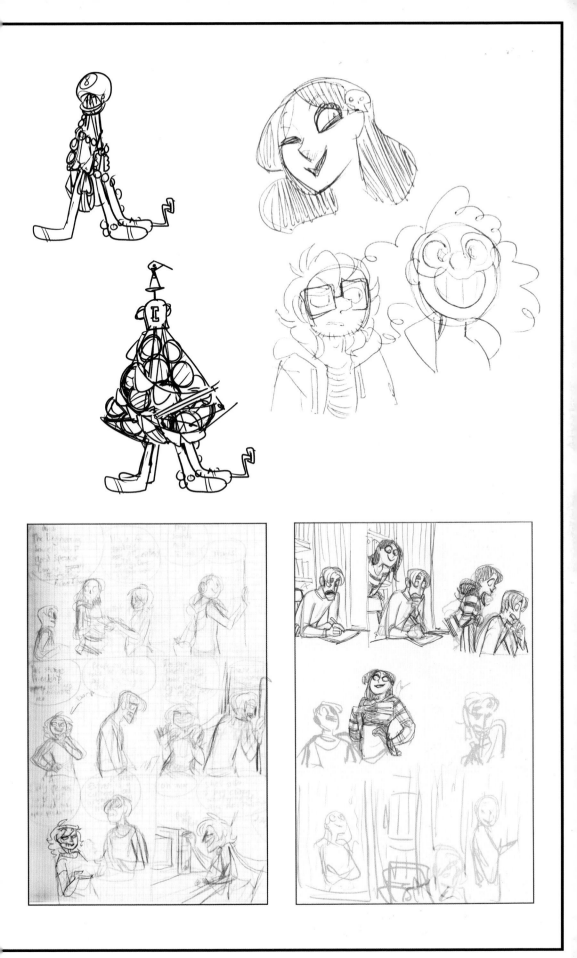

PENCILS BY JOHN ALLISON

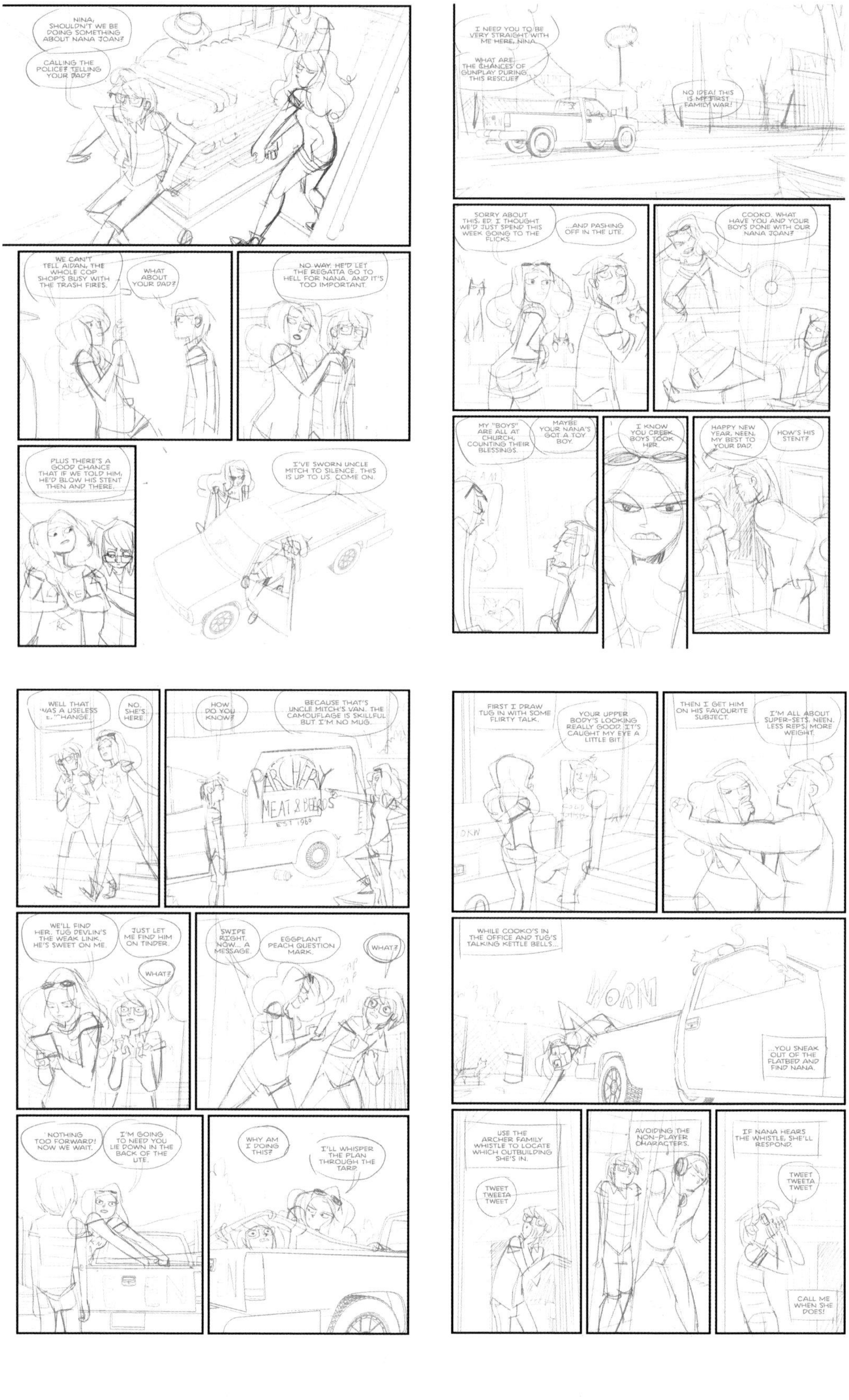

NINA, SHOULDN'T WE BE DOING SOMETHING ABOUT NANA JOAN?
CALLING THE POLICE? TELLING YOUR DAD?
WE CAN'T TELL AIDAN, THE WHOLE COP SHOP'S BUSY WITH THE TRASH FIRES.
WHAT ABOUT YOUR DAD?
NO WAY. HE'D LET THE REGATTA GO TO HELL FOR NANA, AND IT'S TOO IMPORTANT.
PLUS THERE'S A GOOD CHANCE THAT IF WE TOLD HIM, HE'D BLOW HIS STENT THEN AND THERE.
I'VE SWORN UNCLE MITCH TO SILENCE. THIS IS UP TO US. COME ON.
I NEED YOU TO BE VERY STRAIGHT WITH ME HERE, NINA.
WHAT ARE THE CHANCES OF GUNPLAY DURING THIS RESCUE?
NO IDEA! THIS IS MY FIRST FAMILY WAR!
SORRY ABOUT THIS, ED. I THOUGHT WE'D JUST SPEND THIS WEEK GOING TO THE FLICKS...
...AND PASHING OFF IN THE UTE.
COOKO. WHAT HAVE YOU AND YOUR BOYS DONE WITH OUR NANA JOAN?
MY "BOYS" ARE ALL AT CHURCH, COUNTING THEIR BLESSINGS.
MAYBE YOUR NANA'S GOT A TOY BOY.
I KNOW YOU CREEK BOYS TOOK HER.
HAPPY NEW YEAR, NEEN. MY BEST TO YOUR DAD.
HOW'S HIS STENT?
WELL THAT WAS A USELESS EXCHANGE.
NO. SHE'S HERE.
HOW DO YOU KNOW?
BECAUSE THAT'S UNCLE MITCH'S VAN. THE CAMOUFLAGE IS SKILLFUL BUT I'M NO MUG.
WE'LL FIND HER. TUG DEVLIN'S THE WEAK LINK. HE'S SWEET ON ME.
JUST LET ME FIND HIM ON TINDER.
WHAT?
SWIPE RIGHT. NOW... A MESSAGE.
EGGPLANT PEACH QUESTION MARK.
WHAT?
TAP TAP TAP
NOTHING TOO FORWARD! NOW WE WAIT.
I'M GOING TO NEED YOU LIE DOWN IN THE BACK OF THE UTE.
WHY AM I DOING THIS?
I'LL WHISPER THE PLAN THROUGH THE TARP.
FIRST I DRAW TUG IN WITH SOME FLIRTY TALK.
YOUR UPPER BODY'S LOOKING REALLY GOOD. IT'S CAUGHT MY EYE A LITTLE BIT.
THEN I GET HIM ON HIS FAVOURITE SUBJECT.
I'M ALL ABOUT SUPER-SETS, NEEN. LESS REPS, MORE WEIGHT.
WHILE COOKO'S IN THE OFFICE AND TUG'S TALKING KETTLE BELLS...
WORM
...YOU SNEAK OUT OF THE FLATBED AND FIND NANA.
USE THE ARCHER FAMILY WHISTLE TO LOCATE WHICH OUTBUILDING SHE'S IN.
TWEET TWEETA TWEET
AVOIDING THE NON-PLAYER CHARACTERS.
IF NANA HEARS THE WHISTLE, SHE'LL RESPOND.
TWEET TWEETA TWEET
CALL ME WHEN SHE DOES!

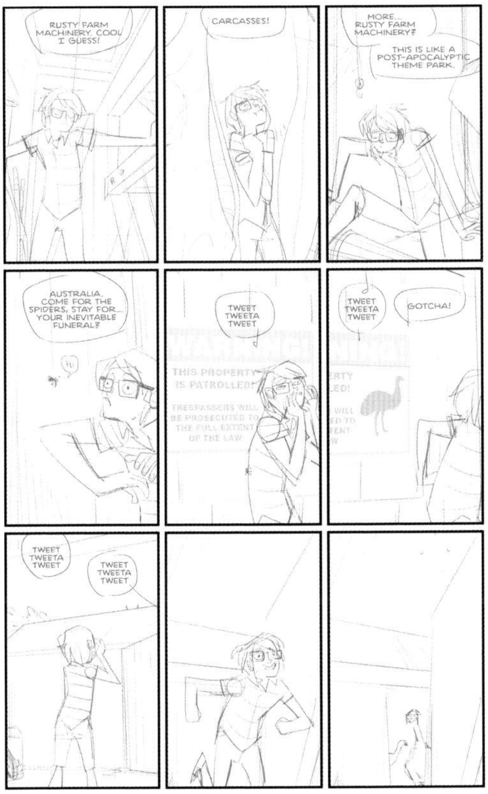
RUSTY FARM MACHINERY. COOL I GUESS!
CARCASSES!
MORE... RUSTY FARM MACHINERY?
THIS IS LIKE A POST-APOCALYPTIC THEME PARK.
AUSTRALIA. COME FOR THE SPIDERS, STAY FOR... YOUR INEVITABLE FUNERAL?
THIS PROPERTY IS PATROLLED!
TRESPASSERS WILL BE PROSECUTED TO THE FULL EXTENT OF THE LAW
TWEET TWEETA TWEET
TWEET TWEETA TWEET
GOTCHA!
TWEET TWEETA TWEET
TWEET TWEETA TWEET

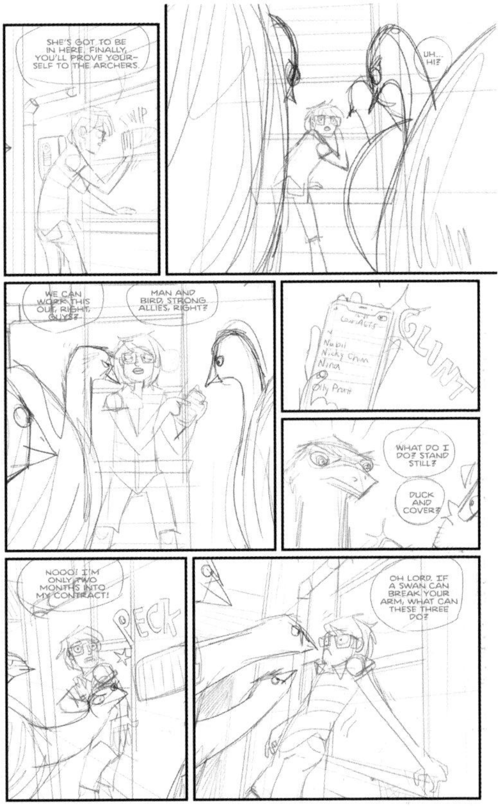
SHE'S GOT TO BE IN HERE. FINALLY, YOU'LL PROVE YOURSELF TO THE ARCHERS.
UH... HI?
WE CAN WORK THIS OUT, RIGHT, GUYS?
MAN AND BIRD, STRONG ALLIES, RIGHT?
GLINT
WHAT DO I DO? STAND STILL?
DUCK AND COVER?
NOOO! I'M ONLY TWO MONTHS INTO MY CONTRACT!
PECK
OH LORD. IF A SWAN CAN BREAK YOUR ARM, WHAT CAN THESE THREE DO?

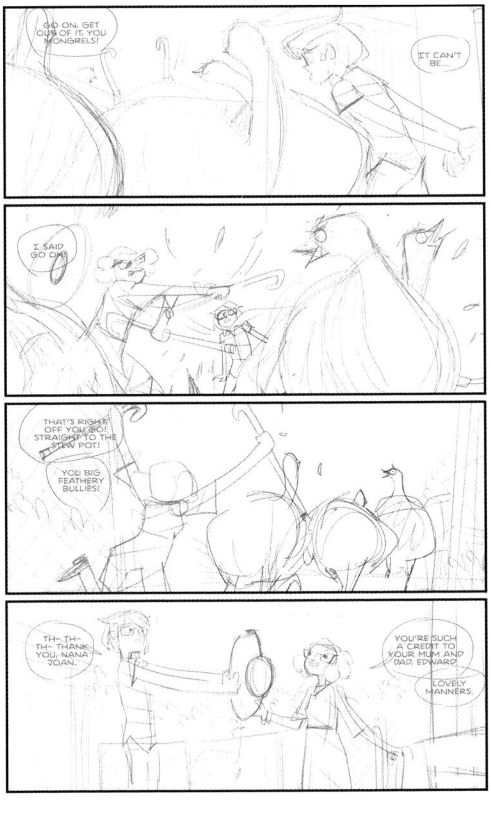
GO ON, GET OUT OF IT, YOU MONGRELS!
IT CAN'T BE...
I SAID GO ON!
THAT'S RIGHT, OFF YOU GO! STRAIGHT TO THE STEW POT!
YOU BIG FEATHERY BULLIES!
TH- TH- TH- THANK YOU, NANA JOAN.
YOU'RE SUCH A CREDIT TO YOUR MUM AND DAD, EDWARD.
LOVELY MANNERS.

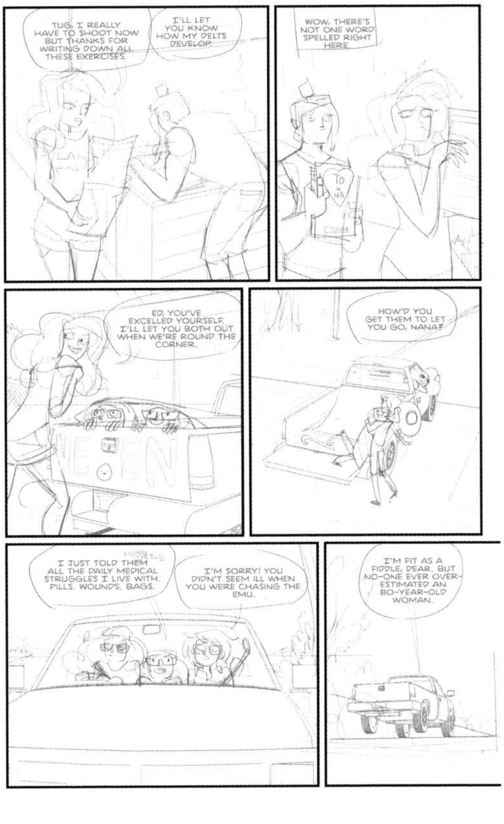
TUG, I REALLY HAVE TO SHOOT NOW BUT THANKS FOR WRITING DOWN ALL THESE EXERCISES.
I'LL LET YOU KNOW HOW MY DELTS DEVELOP.
WOW, THERE'S NOT ONE WORD SPELLED RIGHT HERE.
ED, YOU'VE EXCELLED YOURSELF. I'LL LET YOU BOTH OUT WHEN WE'RE ROUND THE CORNER.
HOW'D YOU GET THEM TO LET YOU GO, NANA?
I JUST TOLD THEM ALL THE DAILY MEDICAL STRUGGLES I LIVE WITH. PILLS. WOUNDS. BAGS.
I'M SORRY! YOU DIDN'T SEEM ILL WHEN YOU WERE CHASING THE EMU.
I'M FIT AS A FIDDLE, DEAR. BUT NO-ONE EVER OVERESTIMATED AN 80-YEAR-OLD WOMAN.

PENCILS BY MAX SARIN

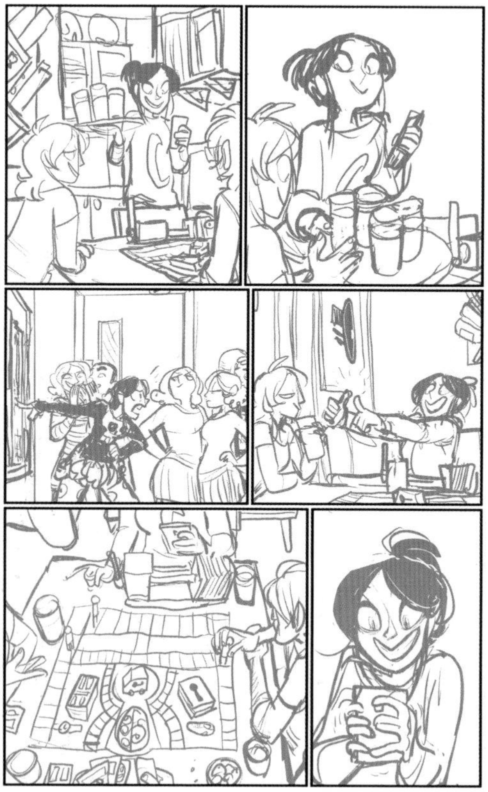

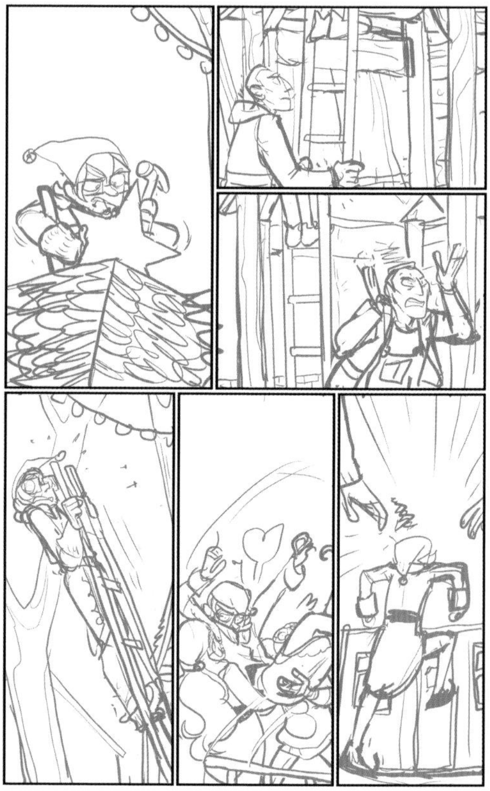

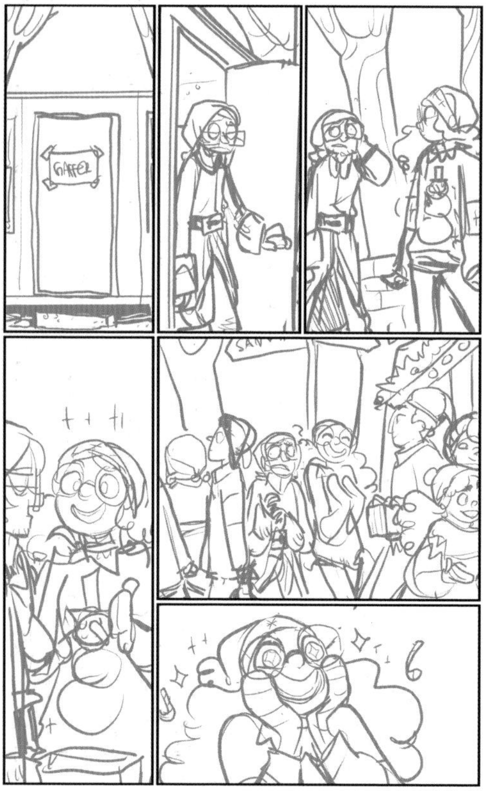
GAFFER

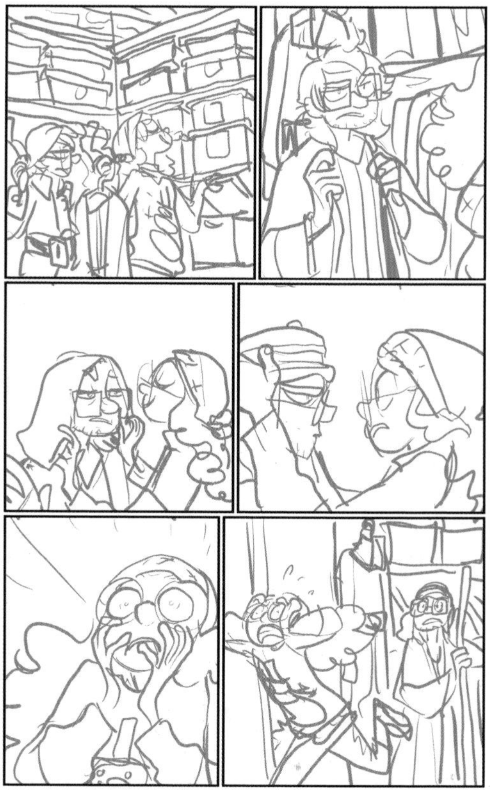

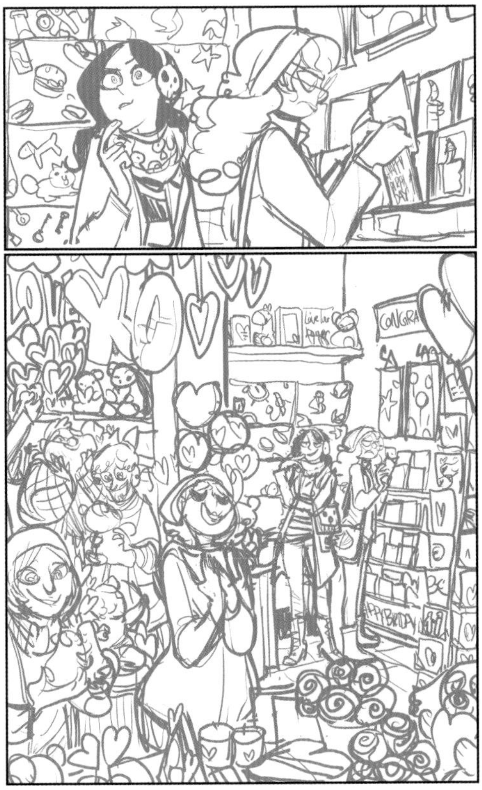
XO
CONGRA
APPY BIRTHDAY

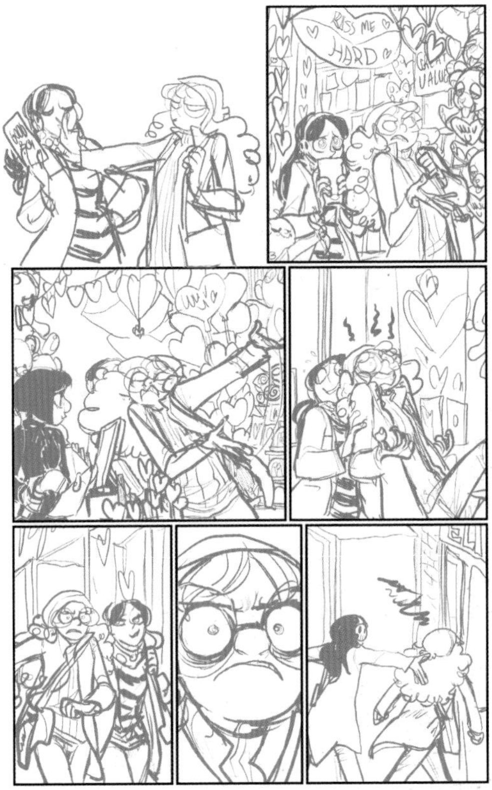
KISS ME
HARD

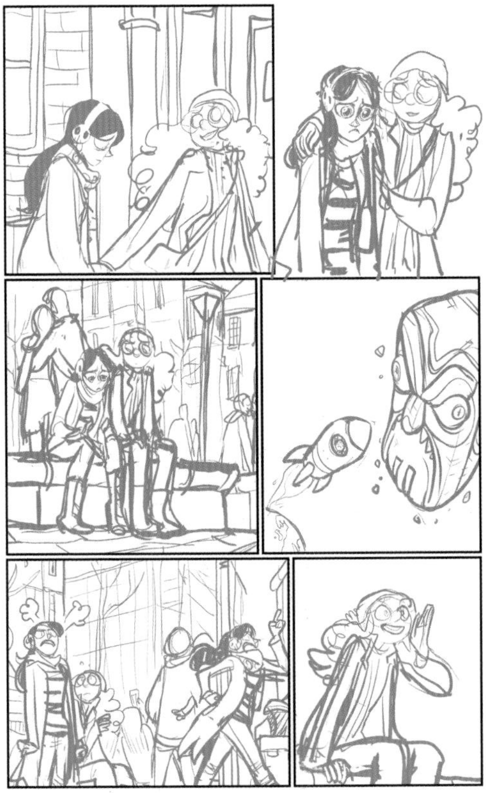

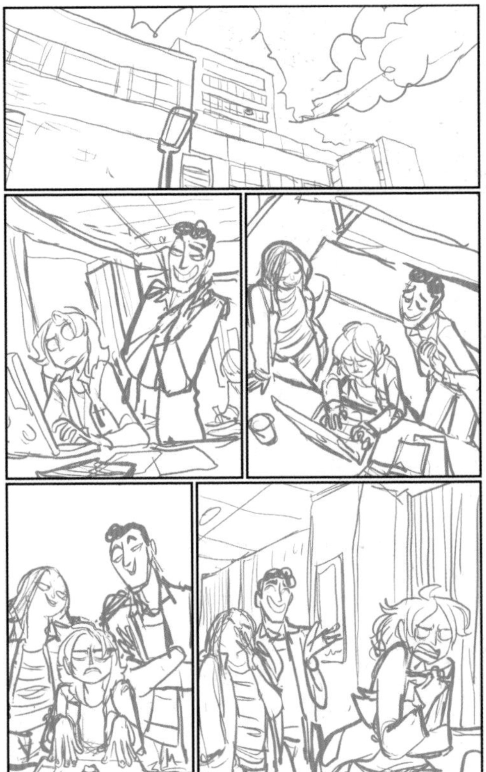

DISCOVER
ALL THE HITS

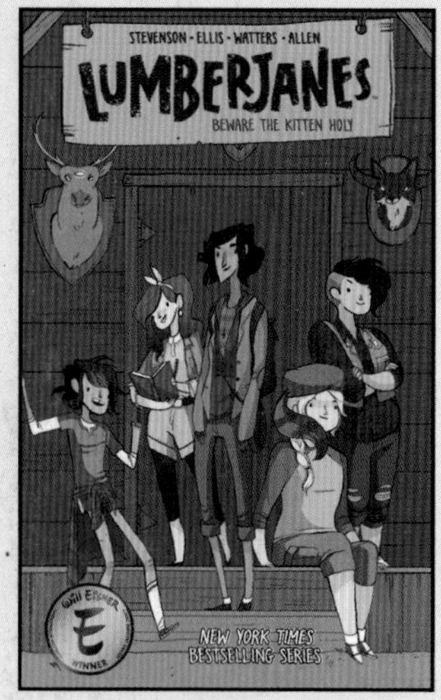
STEVENSON • ELLIS • WATTERS • ALLEN
LUMBERJANES
BEWARE THE KITTEN HOLY
NEW YORK TIMES BESTSELLING SERIES

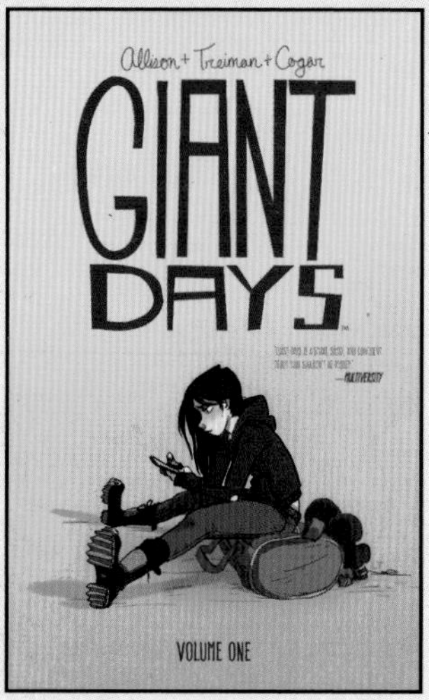
Allison + Treiman + Cogar
GIANT DAYS
VOLUME ONE

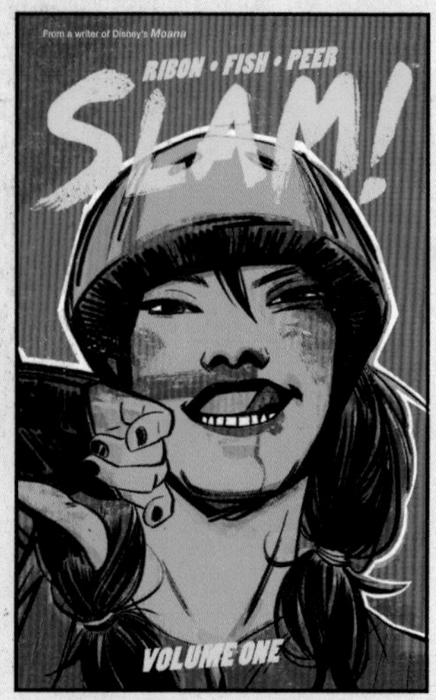
From a writer of Disney's Moana
RIBON • FISH • PEER
SLAM!
VOLUME ONE

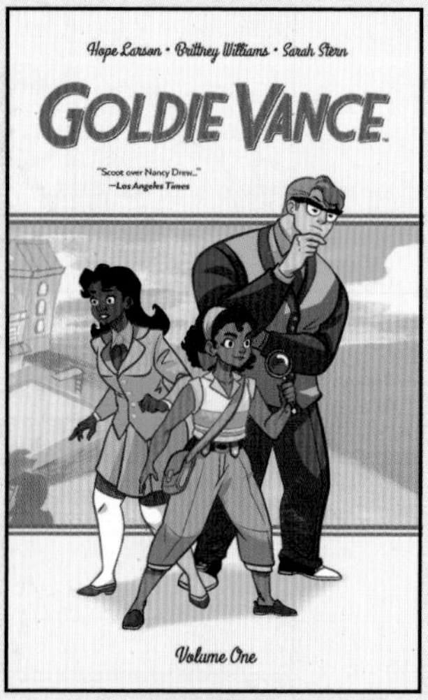
Hope Larson • Brittney Williams • Sarah Stern
GOLDIE VANCE
"Scoot over Nancy Drew..." —Los Angeles Times
Volume One

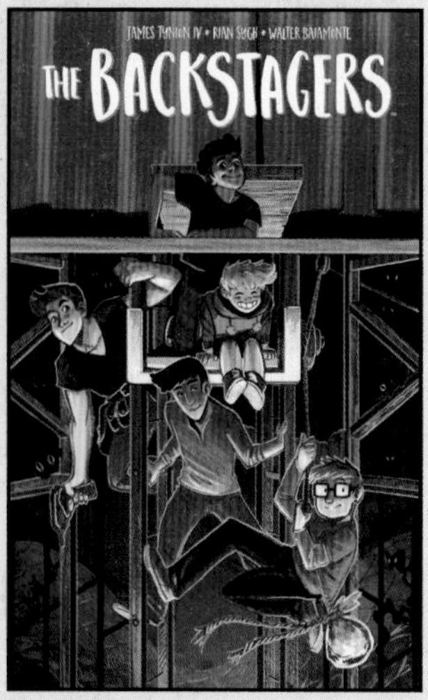
JAMES TYNION IV • RIAN SYGH • WALTER BAIAMONTE
THE BACKSTAGERS

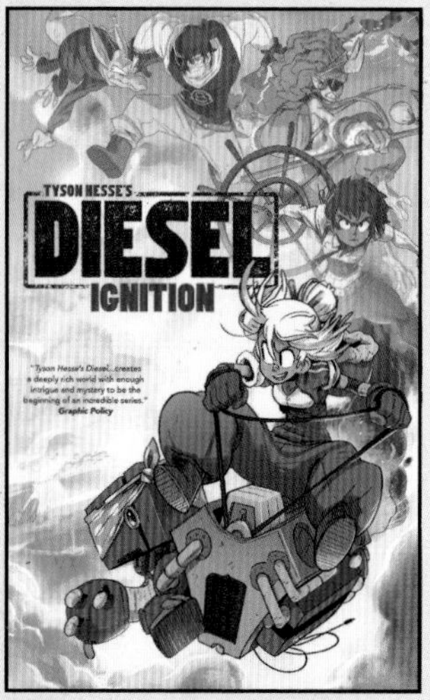
TYSON HESSE'S
DIESEL
IGNITION

BOOM! BOX

AVAILABLE AT YOUR LOCAL COMICS SHOP AND BOOKSTORE

To find a comics shop in your area, visit www.comicshoplocator.com

WWW.**BOOM-STUDIOS**.COM

Lumberjanes
Noelle Stevenson, Shannon Watters, Grace Ellis, Brooklyn Allen, and Others
Volume 1: Beware the Kitten Holy
ISBN: 978-1-60886-687-8 | $14.99 US
Volume 2: Friendship to the Max
ISBN: 978-1-60886-737-0 | $14.99 US
Volume 3: A Terrible Plan
ISBN: 978-1-60886-803-2 | $14.99 US
Volume 4: Out of Time
ISBN: 978-1-60886-860-5 | $14.99 US
Volume 5: Band Together
ISBN: 978-1-60886-919-0 | $14.99 US

Giant Days
John Allison, Lissa Treiman, Max Sarin
Volume 1
ISBN: 978-1-60886-789-9 | $9.99 US
Volume 2
ISBN: 978-1-60886-804-9 | $14.99 US
Volume 3
ISBN: 978-1-60886-851-3 | $14.99 US

Jonesy
Sam Humphries, Caitlin Rose Boyle
Volume 1
ISBN: 978-1-60886-883-4 | $9.99 US
Volume 2
ISBN: 978-1-60886-999-2 | $14.99 US

Slam!
Pamela Ribon, Veronica Fish, Brittany Peer
Volume 1
ISBN: 978-1-68415-004-5 | $14.99 US

Goldie Vance
Hope Larson, Brittney Williams
Volume 1
ISBN: 978-1-60886-898-8 | $9.99 US
Volume 2
ISBN: 978-1-60886-974-9 | $14.99 US

The Backstagers
James Tynion IV, Rian Sygh
Volume 1
ISBN: 978-1-60886-993-0 | $14.99 US

Tyson Hesse's Diesel: Ignition
Tyson Hesse
ISBN: 978-1-60886-907-7 | $14.99 US

Coady & The Creepies
Liz Prince, Amanda Kirk, Hannah Fisher
ISBN: 978-1-68415-029-8 | $14.99 US